Reluctantly, Kaylee met the Indian's gaze. Something passed between them, something she didn't recognize. Something that made her heart skip a beat. He had the most amazing eyes she had ever seen, deep and black and mysterious. She had the feeling that he knew exactly what she was thinking.

Rising, she crossed the room to the other cot and curled up on the mattress, her back toward him. But she could still feel him watching her. She kept her gun close at hand.

Blue Hawk listened to the girl's breathing, knew the moment when sleep claimed her. She was a mystery to him. He knew just by looking at her that she was afraid of him. Why, then, had she saved his life? He had seen the hatred in the white men's eyes. But the girl was different. He had never met anyone like her, never seen anyone like her, with her long golden hair and sky blue eyes. Never, except in his vision . . .

LAKOTA
LOVE SONG

Madeline Baker

A SIGNET BOOK

SIGNET
Published by New American Library, a division of
Penguin Putnam Inc., 375 Hudson Street,
New York, New York 10014, U.S.A.
Penguin Books Ltd, 80 Strand,
London WC2R 0RL, England
Penguin Books Australia Ltd, Ringwood,
Victoria, Australia
Penguin Books Canada Ltd, 10 Alcorn Avenue,
Toronto, Ontario, Canada M4V 3B2
Penguin Books (N.Z.) Ltd, 182–190 Wairau Road,
Auckland 10, New Zealand

Penguin Books Ltd, Registered Offices:
Harmondsworth, Middlesex, England

First published by Signet, an imprint of New American Library,
a division of Penguin Putnam Inc.

First Printing, January 2002
10 9 8 7 6 5 4 3 2 1

For

William, Julie, John, Debra, David, and Maricela
Ashley, Amanda, Wade, and Willow
Roxanne and Pam
McKayla and Luke
Bill
Mary, Nancy, Linda, and Bronwyn
Marian, Hilda, Helen, Vicki, and Lucy

I love you guys!

Lakota Love Song

I have seen the wind
dance upon the water
followed the rain into its mystery . . .
seen the shadow of the Great Spirit
in the rising sun

As I hold you in the song of life
the heat of my glance
collects upon your skin
allowing me to become the moisture
that covers you

As the song of my love dissolves
into the depths of your soul
we fly into the wind
two halves now and forever
made whole

—M. Dearmond

Prologue

He lay on his back and stared, unblinking, at the mid-night sky. Pain engulfed him, radiating from the bullet wounds in his side, shoulder, and arm. He could feel the blood oozing from his body, falling drop by drop onto the sun-bleached prairie grass beneath him, watering the earth like warm summer rain.

It was an effort to breathe, to think. He focused on the twinkling stars scattered across the sky. Soon, his spirit would leave his body to travel Wanagi Tacaka, the spirit path, which led to Wanagi Yatu, the Place of Souls. He would find rest there, water to ease his nagging thirst, endless herds of buffalo to hunt.

The thought should have filled him with peace, but instead he felt a cold and bitter anger toward the white man who had betrayed him. The need for vengeance rose strong within him. He was a warrior in his prime, a leader of his people. There were battles he had yet to fight.

His hands clenched at his sides as shards of pain stabbed through him. He felt himself weakening, felt his spirit trying to free itself from the tortured shell of his flesh.

"No." The word left his mind as a shout, only to emerge from his throat as a hoarse whisper that was lost in the prairie wind. "No . . ."

Lost in a haze of pain, he prayed to Wakan Tanka

for strength, for courage. He drifted in and out of consciousness, lost track of time.

Wakan Tanka, help me. His vision blurred, and Mato appeared to him, running across a vast sunlit prairie.

The bear rose on his hind legs and pawed the air, his growl filling Blue Hawk's mind like thunder in the high country. *Make my strength yours.*

Hovering between life and death, he watched in awe as the bear began to shimmer before his eyes. The dark brown fur turned to honey gold. The bear's massive shape transformed itself into the figure of a slender young woman with sky-blue eyes and hair the color of the summer sun.

But it was still Mato's growl echoing in the back of his mind. *Follow the woman. She holds the answer.*

He reached for the bear-woman, but the movement, slight as it was, caused his wounds to blaze afresh, and forced him back down.

And down.

Darkness blacker than the night opened beneath him. Helpless to resist, he felt himself falling, falling, spinning down into the endless black abyss . . .

Chapter 1

Dakota Territory
Spring 1876

Kaylee Matthews glanced over her shoulder as she pounded her heels against her mare's flanks. "Can't catch me!" she hollered.

"That'll be the day!" Randy Harris shouted back.

Kaylee laughed with excitement as Dusty surged ahead, flying over a rotting deadfall, jumping across a narrow section of the shallow river without breaking stride. "Come on, girl," she urged. "We're almost there!"

The fleet-footed bay mare laid her ears back and raced onward, scrambling up the sandy bank and galloping across the meadow to a narrow path that led into the woods.

Kaylee glanced over her shoulder again. Randy was lost from sight around a bend in the trail. This time, she thought, this time he wouldn't find her! It was a game they had played since they were children. In the beginning, Randy had always won, partly because he was older, partly because his father took him hunting and taught him how to track. But, just like a man, Randy had bragged and boasted about what he knew, and, just like a girl, she had teased and taunted him until he taught her everything he had learned.

Kaylee guided Dusty off the path, through a stand

of tall timber. The trees grew so close together, she
had to rein the mare to a walk. She rode for several
minutes until she cleared the trees. Pausing, she glanced
around. She couldn't remember ever having come this
far before. Her stepfather would likely skin her alive
if he found out she had crossed the river. It served as
an unmarked boundary line, with the ranches on one
side and the Indians on the other. No doubt her
mother would be upset when she found out Kaylee
had left her chores unfinished so she could go galli-
vanting with Randy again. Not that her mother didn't
like Randy. It was just that her mother and her stepfather both hoped she would marry Garth Jackson,
who was their neighbor to the south. Jackson owned
the G Slash J ranch, which was the biggest spread in
the territory. Garth was older and more settled, and
Kaylee's mother and stepfather both considered him
to be a better match. But Kaylee wasn't ready to
marry anyone—not now, perhaps never!

Glancing around, she spotted some tall grass and
wild berry bushes a ways off in the distance. It was
the only cover in the immediate area, and while it was
not the kind of hiding place she would have preferred,
it would have to do.

The ground between the timber and the tall grass
was hard and barren, too hard to hold a print, she
hoped. In the cover of the berry bushes, she dismounted and pulled Dusty's head down and to the
side, forcing the mare to lie down on her side. Kaylee
lay across Dusty's neck to keep her from scrambling
to her feet, then put one hand over the mare's nostrils
so she couldn't call out to Randy's horse and give
their hiding place away.

Grinning with triumph, Kaylee peered through the
grass. Randy was just breaking through the trees. He
paused at the edge, his gaze sweeping the area.

Kaylee knew he couldn't see her from there and

debated whether she should stay hidden until he gave up, and then follow him back home, or jump up now and surprise him.

She was still trying to decide when she heard what sounded suspiciously like a groan behind her. Brow furrowed, heart pounding, Kaylee glanced slowly over her shoulder. She saw nothing, and she blew out a sigh of relief. Then she heard it again. Definitely a groan.

Sliding off Dusty's neck, Kaylee crawled around a pile of rocks located a little to her left. The mare immediately scrambled to her feet.

The groan came again, and then Kaylee saw him— an Indian sprawled in the grass.

She stared at him uncertainly. It had been drummed into her head that Indians were the enemy. Her first instinct was to run, even though she could see that she was in no immediate danger, at least not from him. He had been shot several times. Flies were crawling over the bullet wounds in his side, arm, and shoulder. She shooed them away, all the while glancing around in case there were other Indians lurking about.

"Found you!" Randy crowed. Brush crackled as he urged his mount in beside Dusty. The mare tossed her head restlessly, disturbed by the scent of blood. "Why didn't you keep your horse down? I never would have seen you if you'd just kept Dusty down the way I showed you."

Kaylee scrambled to her feet as Randy rode up beside her.

"What made you cross the river? Old Shaun will have a fit if he finds out. Have you forgotten this is Indian . . . ?" Randy's voice trailed off when he saw the wounded man. "What the hell! Is he dead?"

"No, not yet."

"Damn!" Dismounting, Randy dropped his horse's reins to the ground and drew his six-gun.

"What are you going to do?" Kaylee exclaimed.

"Hell, Kay, he's an Injun! What do you think I'm gonna do? They've been stealing our cattle, and yours, too. That's probably why he's here."

"Oh, for goodness' sakes, Randy, put that thing away and help me get him on the back of my horse."

Randy stared at her. "What? Why?"

"He's hurt. We can't leave him out here. He'll die."

Randy shrugged. "One less Injun. One less thief."

She glared at him. He sounded just like her stepfather. "Are you going to help me or not?"

"Kaylee, this isn't a wounded fawn. You can't take it home."

She looked up at him. "Please, Randy? For me?"

Randy shook his head. "Don't look at me like that, Kaylee Marie. It won't do you any good. And there's no sense in me taking him home, anyway. My pa would shoot him on sight, same as yours."

The thought gave Kaylee pause. Like most of the men in the valley, her stepfather had no love for the Indians. Thieves and beggars, he called them. In the last month, the Double R had lost more than a hundred head of cattle. Her stepfather was certain the Indians were stealing them.

"Well, I can't just leave him out here to die," Kaylee said. She removed her kerchief and wrapped it around his arm to stanch the bleeding. Too bad she wasn't wearing a skirt and petticoats, she thought. A ruffle off one of her petticoats would have worked perfectly.

"Randy, give me your shirt."

"What?"

"You heard me. I need something to bind up his wounds."

Randy shook his head. "I'm not letting you ruin my shirt for no stinkin' Injun." He wrinkled his nose. "He smells like he's already been dead a week!"

Kaylee rocked back on her heels, one hand fisted

on her hip. "Well, I can't very well use *my* shirt. And he can't help how he smells. Who knows how long he's been lying out here?"

With a huff of irritation, Randy took off his shirt and tossed it to her. He grimaced when she ripped it in two, using one half to bind the wound in the Indian's shoulder and the other half to wrap around the wound in his side.

"All right, you bandaged him up good." Randy glanced around, all too aware that they were on the wrong side of the river. "Now let's get out of here."

"I'm not leaving him," she said stubbornly. "I can't, and I won't."

"I don't know what else you can do, Kay."

"Me, either. Can't you think of something?" She looked up at him. "Please, Randy?" she asked sweetly.

"Well," he said thoughtfully, "there's no one staying in that old line shack up on Cedar Ridge. You could take him there."

"Of course!" she exclaimed. "Why didn't I think of that? Come on, help me get him on my horse."

Randy did a lot of muttering and complaining on the ride up to the line shack, but Kaylee was glad to have him along. There was no way she could have lifted the Indian by herself. He lay facedown over Dusty's withers, with Kaylee holding him in place so he didn't slide off. His skin was fever-hot beneath her fingertips. She had never seen an Indian up close before. She couldn't seem to stop looking at him, couldn't help noticing the dark copper color of his skin, the width of his shoulders, the length of his legs. He wore nothing but a breechclout made of what looked like deerskin and a pair of moccasins. His hair was long and black, glossy as a raven's wing.

Her stepfather hated Indians. Shaun Randall claimed the West wouldn't be a fit place to live until every last Sioux and Cheyenne had been shipped off to a reservation or, better yet, killed. Kaylee knew her mother didn't feel that way, but Emma Matthews Randall never argued with her husband. Shaun was a big man with a quick temper, and Kaylee had quickly learned to tiptoe around him. As a child, she had been afraid of him; as an adult, she wondered why her mother had ever married him.

When they reached the line shack, Kaylee slid from Dusty's back and hurried to open the door.

Randy swore softly as he slung the unconscious Indian over his shoulder and carried him inside, dropping him none too gently on one of the bunks.

"You'll have to tie him up," Randy said. "I'll find some rope."

"Tie him up!" Kaylee protested. "Why? He's hurt. Bleeding," she added. "Look." The cloth wrapped around his middle was red with his blood.

"He's probably gonna die anyway," Randy said. "We should have just left him for the coyotes."

"Randy Harris, that's a terrible thing to say!" She looked up at him, then down at the Indian. Randy was as long and lean and lanky as a year-old colt; the Indian was broad-shouldered and well muscled. Randy smelled of hay and well-oiled saddle leather; the Indian smelled of sage and woodsmoke and sweat.

"Well, it's true."

"How can you even think such a thing? He's a human being, too."

"Better not let your stepfather hear you talking like that," Randy muttered. "Not if you know what's good for you. Anyway, you'd best keep him tied up for your own protection. They're sneaky, them Injuns."

Kaylee made a sound of disgust as she pulled her shirttail out of her trousers. Her mother didn't like her wearing pants, but riding in a skirt just wasn't practical. Using the knife she carried in her pocket, she cut off a strip of material and slipped it under the bandage over the wound in his side, wondering how she would explain her torn shirt to her mother.

"Maybe the Indians are hungry," she said. "Maybe that's why they steal our cattle. Maybe if we hadn't killed off the buffalo and scared all the game away, they wouldn't have to steal."

"This is our land," Randy retorted.

"It was their land first," Kaylee said, suddenly wondering why she was arguing with Randy. She had never had any strong opinions about the Indians one way or another. Why was she defending them now?

Muttering under his breath about the stubborn foolishness of women, Randy grabbed the Indian's left wrist and tied it to the bed frame with a length of piggin string he'd found in a box on the floor. He secured the Indian's right wrist as well, then stood back, his arms folded over his chest, while Kaylee drew a dusty blanket over the Indian.

"I'll have to come back later and replace those bandages," she said, wiping her bloody hands on a grimy rag she had found in a bucket in the corner. "Mama's got some carbolic and some powders the doc left when she had a fever."

"I tell you, you're wasting your time."

Kaylee scowled at him. "Well, it's my time to waste."

"Reckon so," Randy said.

"You'll come back with me, won't you?"

He didn't want to. She knew that, just as she knew he wouldn't let her come out here at night alone.

Randy nodded. "But there's gonna be hell to pay if your stepfather finds out about this. Come on, we'd best be getting back. It'll be dark soon."

With a nod, Kaylee followed him toward the door. She paused once to look back, wondering if the Indian would still be alive the next time she saw him.

*   *   *

Blue Hawk woke slowly, aware of little more than the pain that throbbed through him. He opened his eyes, blinked several times. It took him a few moments to realize that he was inside one of the white men's dwellings, though he had no memory of how he had gotten there.

He tried to sit up. His wrists were tightly bound to the frame of the cot. Ignoring the pain that lanced through him with every movement, he spent several minutes trying to get free, then fell back on the hard, narrow cot, breathing heavily. A glance out the window showed that it was night. Was it the same night Mato had come to him, he wondered, or another?

Someone had brought him here and bound up his wounds. But who? And why?

He closed his eyes, his mind searching for answers where there were none.

His wounds throbbed. He had been a fool to trust the white men, but he had been desperate. Back on the reservation, his people were starving, waiting for promised government supplies that seldom came. Even when the supplies did come, there would be moldy flour, spoiled beef, and moth-eaten blankets. Wagon loads of decent supplies intended for his tribe were sold by corrupt government agents to other white men for personal profit.

The old ones among his people had turned their backs on life. Sunk in bitter despair, they refused to eat what little food they had so that the children might live. His warriors, once proud hunters and fighters, were hungry and without hope. The men would have gone hunting, but they weren't allowed to have any weapons except a few old bows. They had only a few scrawny ponies now, whereas they had once had hundreds. The buffalo, once as plentiful as the stars in the sky, were now few in number, having been slaughtered by the white man. Hunting was hard, for the surviving game had been spooked by the careless rifle fire of the *wasichu*.

The warriors hated life on the reservation, and yearned for their freedom. They had taken their families and left, finding refuge in the hills, preferring to die as free men rather than exist in misery on the white man's charity and lies.

Theirs was a small band. Their chiefs were dead, killed in battle. With no one else to lead them, the role had fallen to Blue Hawk. He was determined that they should have rifles. So he had gone alone to the white man's town, leading a string of stolen Crow ponies for trade. Clad in clothes he had stolen from some white woman's wash line along the way, he had gone into one of the saloons. He sat quietly out of the way and watched and listened until he heard talk of men with rifles to trade. Then he sought them out, promising to trade them horses for the guns his warriors needed for hunting. He should have known the *wasichu* could not be trusted. When had the White Eyes ever kept a promise, a treaty? The Grandfather in Washington had promised that the Paha Sapa would belong to the Lakota so long as the grass grew, but that promise had been broken when Yellow Hair discovered gold in the pine-covered mountain country of the sacred Black Hills. Thousands of miners had swarmed into the Hills, scaring off the game, raping the land and the rivers in search of the yellow iron.

Now the betrayal had come again. His honorably stolen horses had been stolen by the whites, and he had been left for dead in a pool of his own blood.

He opened his eyes and stared out the window. He had to get out of here, had to get back to his people. They were waiting for him, trusting him, and he had let them down. He groaned low in his throat, discouraged by his failure. His people were waiting for him to return, and he was—where?

He went suddenly still when he heard sounds outside the cabin. Heavy footsteps, a white man's booted heels. And a lighter tread that he could not immediately place. Voices that seemed faintly familiar.

There was a rush of cool air as someone opened the door, and he saw two figures silhouetted in the doorway.

He closed his eyes and waited.

"Randy," Kaylee said, "light the lamp. I can't see a thing."

There was the sudden smell of sulfur as Randy struck a match, and then the room filled with light.

Randy set the lamp on an overturned crate. "Is he still alive?"

"Yes." Kaylee breathed a sigh of relief, though why she was so concerned about the Indian's survival, she couldn't say. Perhaps it was just a feeling of responsibility because she had found him. Or maybe it was the same instinct that made her carry home the small birds and animals she sometimes found, some deep inner need to comfort anything that was hurting. Or maybe it was just heredity. Her mother was a natural-born healer.

She studied the Indian's profile as she laid out the bandages and medicine she had brought from home. It was a very masculine face, starkly handsome with high cheekbones, a strong jaw, a straight nose. His brow was damp with perspiration. She drew back the blanket so she could check his wounds, her gaze moving over him in frank feminine appreciation. Such a broad chest, tapering to narrow hips and long, long legs.

Randy took up a position near the hearth and ostentatiously loosened his big Colt in its holster.

With an impatient shake of her head, Kaylee turned back to the task at hand. The Indian seemed to be unconscious. Surely no threat in his present condition,

she thought. Lifting the lid on the basket she had
brought from home, she rummaged around inside until
she found what she wanted.

The wound in his side was the worst. After removing the blood-soaked bandage, she poured water from
a canteen into a bowl, added a small amount of carbolic acid, and washed the wound and the surrounding
area as carefully as she could. Patting it dry, she made
a compress, soaked it with carbolic, and placed it over
the wound. She tied it securely in place with a length
of clean cloth.

She frowned when she saw fresh bloodstains on the
bandage around his shoulder. Had he been thrashing
around in his sleep?

"Randy, untie him."

"Why?"

"I need to examine his arm and shoulder."

With an irritated sigh, Randy loosed the Indian's
wrists, then stood hip-shot near the foot of the bed,
one hand resting on his gun butt.

Kaylee shook her head. "Honestly, Randy, what do
you think he's going to do? Jump up and scalp us?
He's lucky to be alive."

"I'm not taking any chances. I've never met a redskin yet that you could trust." He jerked his chin in
the Indian's direction. "You just fix him up. Don't
worry about me."

"Just how many 'redskins' have you met?" Kaylee
asked, growing more exasperated by the minute.

"Never mind." A dull flush crept up his neck and
into his cheeks.

Randy had wanted to join the Army to fight Indians, but his father was in poor health and his mother
had begged him not to go. Knowing that his mother
needed his help to run the ranch, he had stayed home.

"Just do what you have to do," he said gruffly, "and
let's get out of here."

Well, that was good advice, Kaylee realized. If she got caught sneaking into the house at this time of night, she would have a lot of explaining to do.

Removing the bandage from the Indian's shoulder, she tossed the bloody cloth into the bucket.

"That used to be one of my favorite shirts," Randy muttered.

"I'm sorry, Randy, truly. I'll make you a new one."

"Forget it," he said with a lopsided grin. "I've seen your needlework. I can do better myself."

She made a face at him, then smiled and turned her attention back to her patient, glad to see Randy's good mood had been restored. She treated the wound in the Indian's shoulder the same way she had treated the injury to his side, glad that she wasn't squeamish about the sight of blood, the way her stepfather was. She had often wondered why her mother had agreed to marry Shaun Randall. He was a big brute of a man, so unlike Kaylee's father. What had Emma seen in Shaun to convince her to marry him, to leave their pretty little house and their friends in the East and move to the untamed frontier?

Not that Kaylee didn't like the West. She loved its vastness, its endless blue sky that seemed so much bigger and bluer than the sky in the East. She loved the prairie, the hills, the horses, the cattle, the ranch itself. She had taken readily to life on the frontier. She was more at home in a shirt and a pair of pants than in frilly dresses and petticoats, preferred riding roundup with cowhands to sewing and cooking. She helped with the branding and the calving and loved it all. But she had never developed any love for her stepfather. He was a hard man, one who had wanted a son to carry on his name. Three times her mother had endured the pains of childbirth. Three times Emma had borne sons. Three times the infants had been stillborn. Now her parents slept in separate rooms.

When she finished bandaging the wound in the Indian's shoulder, she removed her kerchief from the wound in his right arm. It was the least serious of his injuries, but, wary of infection, she treated it as carefully as she had his other wounds, then wrapped it in a strip of clean cloth.

She thrust the thoughts of her mother and stepfather to the back of her mind as she poured water from the canteen into a tin cup and stirred in one of her mother's headache powders. Sitting on the edge of the cot, she lifted the Indian's head, held the cup to his lips, and dribbled some of the liquid into his mouth. She was pleased when he swallowed it.

Slowly, his eyelids fluttered open. Dark eyes, filled with pain and distrust.

He stared at her for a long moment.

Then he drank again, thirstily. When it was empty, she refilled it. "Drink it slowly," she cautioned, wondering if he could understand her words.

Perhaps not, because he drained the cup, sighed, and closed his eyes.

She lowered his head to the pillow and wiped the perspiration from his brow with a cloth. She let out a shriek when his hand closed tightly over her wrist.

"Turn her loose!" Randy's gun was in his hand, hammer rocked back to full cock. "Turn her loose or I'll put a hole through you that even she won't be able to fix."

Kaylee stared at the Indian's face, her heart pounding, her insides fluttering wildly as if a million hummingbirds were beating their wings inside her chest. The Indian's grip was like iron, every muscle in his arm taut and clearly defined.

"We're trying to help you." She spoke slowly and distinctly, still wondering if he even understood what she was saying.

"Turn her loose!" Randy repeated curtly. "Now!"

The Indian's gaze held Randy's, his eyes filled with implacable hatred. Then, slowly, he released Kaylee's arm.

She stood up and moved away from the cot, rubbing her wrist.

"Tie him back up, Kay."

She didn't want to get near the Indian again, but she did as Randy said. She could see the wisdom of tying the Indian up now. Like a wild animal, he struck out at what he didn't understand. Still, she wished it wasn't necessary.

The Indian watched her intently as she tied his hand to the cot. There was no hatred in his eyes when he looked at her, no censure of any kind, only a quiet understanding that disturbed her on a level she couldn't comprehend.

Randy checked the ropes when she was through. "Let's go."

"Wait. I brought him something to eat."

"Dammit, Kay, he'd as soon cut your throat as look at you. Don't you know that? They can't be trusted, none of them. They're nothing but savages."

"Go on home, if you want. I'm not leaving until he's had something to eat."

"Damn stubborn woman," Randy muttered. "I'll wait for you outside." He stopped at the door, turned, and shook his finger at her. "Mark my words, Kaylee Marie. No good will come of this day. No damn good at all." He sent a last withering glance at the Indian, then left the shack.

Lifting another canteen from the basket, Kaylee poured some broth into a cup. She hesitated a moment, afraid to get too close to the Indian even though his hands were again securely tied. He met her look with fathomless black eyes, his expression closed to her. She wondered what he was thinking. He wasn't afraid. Not of Randy, and certainly not of her. She was sure of that.

"It's beef broth," she said. "Do you want some? You must be hungry."

He didn't answer, just continued to stare at her. She had the feeling that even if he were starving to death, he wouldn't admit it. Even if he couldn't understand her words, he must know that she was trying to help him.

With a sigh, she eased herself gingerly onto the very edge of the cot and silently offered him the cup. He stared at her for another long moment, then lifted his head and took a swallow, and then another, and another.

She refilled the cup twice before he sank back and closed his eyes.

She studied him carefully, her gaze lingering on his face. His lashes were short and stubby and thick. He was a handsome man. Even as the thought crossed her mind, she knew it was wrong to think so. He was the enemy. As soon as he was strong enough to travel, she would turn him loose, and he would be gone from her life.

The thought saddened her more than it should have.

Chapter 2

Randy was unusually silent on the ride back to the ranch, and for that she was grateful. She wasn't in the mood to be scolded or teased, and that seemed to be all he did lately.

But it wasn't Randy who filled her thoughts as they rode through the quiet night. It was the Indian, the look of hate and distrust in his deep, dark eyes when he stared at Randy, the softening in his expression when he looked at her, an intensely masculine expression that had caused an odd fluttery feeling in the pit of her stomach.

She glanced over at Randy. "Did you say something?"

"You're home."

She looked down the road at the big white ranch house with its high-peaked roof and wide verandah. "Thanks for going with me."

He shook his head. "You're making a big mistake, you know, keeping that redskin alive."

"I don't think so."

"Well, we'll see, won't we?"

She nodded. "I guess so. Good night, Randy."

"Good night."

Kaylee watched him ride away. Then, dismounting, she led Dusty toward the barn, taking the long way around in case Shaun was sitting out on the porch, as he often did late at night. She unsaddled Dusty and turned her loose in the corral, then crept around to the back of the house, shinnied up the tree, and climbed into her bedroom window.

As soon as she climbed over the sill, light filled the room. Knowing she was well and truly caught, Kaylee turned to find her mother sitting in the old wooden rocking chair beside the bed.

"Where have you been, Kaylee Marie?" Emma asked. She blew out the match and put the chimney on the lamp sitting on the table beside her.

Her mother was a pretty woman, a little on the plump side, with smooth, clear skin and dark-brown hair. Kaylee had inherited her father's blond hair and her mother's blue eyes.

Kaylee took a deep breath. She had never lied to her mother before, and she didn't like doing it now, so she told her a part of the truth. "I was out with Randy."

"At this time of night?" Emma lifted one brow, then frowned. "Oh, Kaylee," she said anxiously. "You haven't—You didn't let him—?"

It took her a minute to realize what her mother was asking. "Of course not!" she exclaimed. She sat down on the edge of the bed. "Ma, how could you think such a thing?"

"Why else would you be sneaking out of the house in the middle of the night? Oh, Kaylee, don't . . ."

"Oh, Ma, stop worrying, it's nothing like that. I don't love Randy."

"He'd make you a good husband, Kaylee, better than Garth in some ways, even though Shaun is set upon joining our ranch with Garth's. You know that."

"Garth!" Kaylee stood abruptly and began to pace the floor. "He's old enough to be my father!"

"He's a good man, Kaylee. They both are. And there aren't that many choices, you know. Not out here."

"I don't care. I don't want to marry either one of them."

"A woman has to marry someone, Kaylee. A woman's life is defined by her husband, her children."

"Well, I'm not going to marry a man I don't love."

The words *the way you did* hung unspoken in the air between them.

Kaylee knelt at her mother's side, one hand resting on her mother's arm. "Why did you marry Shaun?"

"You needed a father."

"That's why you married him? For me?"

"Not entirely. Life is hard for a woman alone, especially a woman with a young child." Emma sighed heavily. "How can I make you understand how it was? I was recently widowed, with no money. I worked at whatever I could find, Kay. I took in laundry and ironing, but there was never enough money. And then I met Shaun. He was rich and single and . . . can you understand?"

"Did you ever love him?"

Emma's gaze slid away from hers. "Not the way I loved your father," she said quietly, and then she covered Kaylee's hand with her own. "Shaun is set on your marrying Garth. I know he's older than you are, but he's a good man, Kaylee. He'll take care of you and whatever children you may have."

"But I want more than that," Kaylee said earnestly. "I want a man who loves me, who can't live without me. And I want to feel the same way about him."

Emma stroked her daughter's cheek. "You're so young. You don't know what the world is like. You don't know how unforgiving it can be. Love is wonderful, but it can't put a roof over your head, or food in your children's mouths."

"Ma—"

"Think about what I've said, Kaylee. Your father was a wonderful man, but he was a dreamer, always talking about tomorrow when he should have been worrying about today. He was always so certain things would get better, but they never did. I loved him with all my heart, but love is hard to sustain when you're hungry all the time, when you have no place to call home, when you hear your baby crying because she's hungry and cold."

Kaylee stared up at her mother. She had always wondered why Emma married Shaun. Now she knew.

Emma rose slowly to her feet and kissed Kaylee on the cheek. "Good night, dear. Think about what I said."

Kaylee nodded. "I will," she promised, but in her heart she couldn't help feeling that her mother had been wrong to sacrifice love for a home and security.

Blue Hawk shifted uncomfortably on the cot, the pain of his wounds momentarily overshadowed by a raging thirst and the need to relieve himself. He tugged against his bonds until the skin on his wrists was raw. It was a new day; warm sunlight filtered through the window and the chinks in the logs. He had to get away, had to get back to his people.

His thoughts turned to the white girl. He had recognized her immediately as the woman he had seen in his vision. Who was she? Why had she brought him here? He had seen other white women—they had looked at him with disdain and distrust. Not so the girl with the sky-blue eyes. She had looked at him the way a woman looks at a man. Her touch had been gentle, her voice soft and compelling. He had felt the attraction that had flowed between them. Had she felt it, too?

"Kay-lee." He said her name aloud. It fell softly on his ears, like the morning birdsong that had brought him out of his fevered dreams.

Follow the woman. She holds the answer.

What did it mean? The answer to what? And even
as the thoughts crossed his mind, he heard the sound
of hoofbeats, and in moments she was there, a large
basket on her arm. He was surprised to see that she
had come alone this time.

She stopped just inside the door, looking somewhat
uncertain, and then she approached the cot. Putting
the basket on the floor beside her, she leaned over
him and put one hand on his brow.

"You've still got a fever," she remarked. Lifting the
lid of the basket, she withdrew a canteen, a cup, and
a small packet. She filled the cup with water, added
the powder, and held the cup to his lips.

He shook his head.

"You've got to drink this." She held the cup to his
lips again. "It will bring the fever down."

He shook his head again.

"Do you understand what I'm saying? I'm trying to
help you. Now drink it!"

He shook his head yet again. "I understand. No."

"Oh!" she exclaimed, exasperated. "You drank it
last night. Why not today?"

"Because I do not want to—to—" He broke off,
unable to find the word he was looking for. Instead,
he jerked against the ropes that bound his wrists to
the cot's frame.

"Turn me loose."

She backed up a step, her eyes widening.

Knowing that his anger would only frighten her more,
Blue Hawk took a deep, calming breath. "Turn me
loose. I will not hurt you. I just want to go outside."

"I don't believe you."

He stared up at her. "If you are so afraid of me,
why did you bring me here?"

"Because you were hurt. I couldn't just leave you
out there to die."

He thought of the white men who had stolen his

horses, then shot him and left him for dead. "You could have. Others did." He shifted on the bed, his discomfort growing. "I need to go outside." He spoke the words through clenched teeth. "Now."

She suddenly understood his urgency. Embarrassment washed over her cheeks in a flood of red.

"Now," he repeated.

Flustered, she stared at him. Untied one hand. Hesitated a moment, and then freed the other.

As soon as his hands were free, Kaylee reached into the basket and withdrew a shiny nickel-plated .41-caliber Colt Lightning, a gun Shaun declared was better suited to a woman's hand. A shaft of sunlight glinted on the barrel as she tracked the Indian rising from the bed.

He spared the weapon hardly a glance as he stood up and moved none too steadily toward the door. Stepping outside, he took a deep breath, wondering only briefly if she would follow him.

He glanced over his shoulder, but there was no sign of the girl. He sighed with relief as he emptied his bladder. Then, summoning what little strength he possessed, he took up her horse's reins and pulled himself into the saddle.

He had to get back to his people. Now.

Kaylee looked at the gun in her hand, wondering if she could have used it if he attacked her. He could hardly stand up. She doubted he was capable of doing her any harm. Still, she remembered how he had grabbed her arm the first night, the strength in his grip. Unconscious, he had seemed harmless, but now . . . She frowned. She didn't really believe the Indian would hurt her, not when she was trying to help him. But her mother always said it was better to be safe now than sorry later, and with that in mind, she put the gun within easy reach.

She poured a cup of broth, thinking he would be hungry when he returned. She laid out clean bandages and salve, wondering if Randy would keep her secret. If he let it slip that she was hiding an Indian up here, all hell would break loose. Their neighbors all felt the same as Shaun did where Indians were concerned. No doubt Garth and the other ranchers would storm the cabin and string him up without a second thought.

She tapped her foot, wondering how she would tie him up again if he refused to let her, and then thought how silly that was. Of course he wouldn't let her. She hadn't wanted to tie him up in the first place.

She ran a hand through her hair. He was certainly taking a long time doing his business out there.

Too long.

She walked to the door and looked outside. The Indian was nowhere in sight. And neither was Dusty.

He had stolen her horse! And done it so quietly she hadn't even heard them go.

She shook her head angrily, unable to believe the nerve of the man. She had saved his life, and he had repaid her by stealing her horse!

She had worked herself into a fine rage when she saw Dusty trotting toward her, head lifted high and to one side to avoid stepping on the reins.

"Easy, girl." Closing the door behind her, Kaylee walked toward the mare, one hand outstretched. "Easy, girl, easy now."

The mare tossed her head and danced sideways. There was a smear of blood on her neck and down her side. No doubt it was the smell of it that was making her so skittish.

"Easy now," Kaylee said. Catching hold of the reins, she stroked the mare's neck. "Where is he, Dusty?" she wondered aloud. "You didn't throw him, did you?"

She looked past the horse, wondering why she

should care what happened to a horse thief. But she couldn't help remembering how weak he had been, how badly he was hurt.

She pulled a handkerchief from her skirt pocket and scrubbed the blood from Dusty's coat. The Indian was bleeding again, and even though he had stolen her horse, she knew she couldn't just leave him out there.

With an aggrieved sigh, she retrieved her Colt from the shack, slipped it into the waistband of her riding skirt, and swung up into the saddle. Reining the mare around, she followed the tracks, wondering what there was about the Indian that caused her to worry so.

He hadn't gotten far. She found him about half a mile later, lying facedown in the dirt, the bandages around his middle and shoulder stained red with fresh blood.

She shook her head, muttering, "Darn fool" as she dismounted. She hesitated a moment before rolling him over, fearing that he might be dead.

At her touch, his eyelids fluttered open. She stepped back and drew the Colt, not quite pointing it at him. For a moment they stared at each other, her gaze filled with wariness and pity, his with pain and self-disgust.

"Well," Kaylee said, sitting back on her heels. "That was a dumb thing to do. You're bleeding again."

He didn't say anything, but he didn't have to. The expression on his face said it all.

"You'll have to stand up," Kaylee said, gesturing with the barrel of the Colt. "I can't lift you."

He nodded. She watched him take a deep breath, could almost see him gathering his strength. She offered him her free hand when he started to get up. He looked at it. Ignored it. And stood up.

Kaylee blew out a breath, wondering at his stubbornness. Or maybe it was pride.

Whatever it was, it had taken its toll. He was pale, his breathing shallow. Swaying unsteadily, he grabbed the stirrup.

"Why are you being so foolish?" Kaylee asked. "Here, let me help you."

He turned to glare at her, his dark eyes filled with disdain. "I do not need the help of a white woman."

"Fine." She took a step back, her arms folded across her breasts, gun barrel pointed skyward. "But don't expect me to pick you up if you fall flat on your face. And don't try to ride off again. I do know how to use this thing."

He turned his back to her. One hand clutching the pommel, the other braced on the cantle, he put his foot in the stirrup and pulled himself into the saddle. She had to admire his tenacity even though she thought he was acting like a spoiled child.

She looked up at him, her head cocked to one side. "Do you mind if I ride, too?" she asked, handing him the reins. "Or do you expect me to walk three paces behind?"

She couldn't be sure, but she thought she saw his lips twitch in what might have been a smile. He didn't say anything, just took his foot out of the stirrup so she could climb up behind him.

It was uncomfortable, sitting behind the cantle with the Colt tucked in the waistband of her skirt, but her saddle was too small to hold both of them. When she was settled, he clucked to the mare.

Kaylee rested her hands lightly on his waist for balance. She could feel the heat radiating from his skin even before she touched him. His fever was growing worse. She had a terrible feeling that he was going to die.

Chapter 3

The Indian was barely conscious when they reached the cabin. Kaylee backed over Dusty's rump, then hurried around to help him dismount. He didn't argue this time. Sliding her arm around his waist, she helped him inside. He was staggering by the time they reached the cot, unconscious before his head hit the pillow.

She spent the next thirty minutes treating his wounds, silently berating him for undoing all her good work. The wound in his side had opened again because of his exertions, but the carbolic seemed to be keeping infection at bay. He needed a doctor, she thought. At the very least, he needed someone who knew more about doctoring than she did. Someone like her mother. Emma's father had been a doctor back in New York City, and Emma had been his assistant before she got married.

When she had done all she could for him, Kaylee covered him with the blanket. She stood beside the cot, watching him, wondering why she felt so drawn to him. What was there about him that intrigued her so? She lost track of the time as she stood there, watching the shallow rise and fall of his chest. Unable to help herself, she smoothed the hair back from his forehead. Such a strong, masculine face. She studied him a moment more and then, afraid he might try to leave again when he woke up, she tied his hands to the bed frame.

It was for his own good, she told herself. Not because she was afraid he would leave and she would never see him again.

She covered him with a quilt and then, with a last look, she left the shack.

Shaun Randall frowned when his stepdaughter came to the dinner table, late for the second night in a row. "Where have you been, Kaylee Marie?"

"Out riding."

"You've been spending a lot of time in the saddle lately."

Kaylee held her stepfather's gaze. He was a tall, handsome man, with thick black hair going gray at the temples and hard brown eyes. "My chores were done."

He grunted softly. "Be on time for dinner in the future."

"Yes, sir." Kaylee glanced at her mother, then looked down at her plate, remembering happier days.

When she was a child, mealtimes had been a time of conversation and laughter. Gaylord Matthews had been a cheerful man, imbued with an outrageous sense of humor, a man given to telling tall tales at the dinner table. The good times she and her mother had known at meals had died with her father, though. Shaun Randall was a stern man who did not waste time indulging in idle chatter with his womenfolk.

Shaun finished his dinner, tossed his napkin on his plate, bestowed a cool kiss on his wife's cheek, and left the dining room. Kaylee knew he would spend the rest of the evening in his study, going over the ranch accounts.

"Where were you, Kay?" her mother asked quietly.

She looked up to find her mother watching her, a speculative look in her eyes. "Out riding, like I said." Her chin lifted stubbornly.

"You've never lied to me before, Kaylee Marie," her mother said, as quietly as before. "Don't start now."

Kaylee felt herself wilt under that calm regard. "I need your help, Mama."

Concern clouded Emma's eyes. "Are you in trouble?"

"No, Mama, no! Nothing like that." She leaned across the table. "Could you come with me? Now?" she asked urgently.

"Come where?"

"I can't tell you."

"Kaylee."

She knew that tone, but she pressed onward. "And you have to promise you won't say anything to Shaun."

Emma studied her daughter for what seemed like an eternity. She folded her napkin precisely and placed it on the table beside her plate before she spoke. "Kaylee Marie, what's wrong? What have you done now?"

"I haven't done anything. Well, not exactly. Will you come? And promise you won't tell Shaun?"

Her decision made, Emma stood up. "I promise."

Her mother made no effort to hide her shock as she looked down at the Indian tied to the cot. No doubt Emma had entertained a dozen possibilities as to what awaited her when they reached their destination, but Kaylee was pretty sure that tending a wounded Indian had not been one of them.

But Emma reacted like the surgeon's daughter she was, cutting away the soiled cloth that held her daughter's dressings in place and gently lifting the edges of the compress, which was glued to the Indian's skin with his own blood. After she assessed the damage, she glanced at Kay. "Where did he come from?"

"I found him across the river."

"Kaylee Marie! What in the name of heaven were you doing across the river?"

"Hiding from Randy. We were playing hide-and-seek. Is he going to be all right?"

Emma turned her attention back to the man on the bed and finished peeling the bandage away from his side.

"You did well with the carbolic, Kay, but this wound needs to be stitched closed. Heat some water for me."

Warmed by her mother's praise, Kaylee laid kindling in the old woodstove, fanned it until it was burning steadily, added a few larger pieces of wood, then took the blackened kettle outside. Her stomach knotted at the thought of what her mother was about to do.

She primed the old pump, rinsed out the kettle, and filled it. It was a warm, clear night. Millions of stars twinkled high overhead, tiny pinpoints of light shining like dewdrops against an indigo sky. Crickets played an evening serenade, accompanied by the croaking of frogs. An owl swept past on silent wings.

She had stalled long enough. With a sigh, she returned to the cabin and put the kettle on to heat.

Emma was seated on one of the cabin's rickety chairs beside the bunk, calmly threading the slender silver needle she always carried with her. As far as Kaylee knew, her mother had never been this close to an Indian before, but you'd never have known it by looking at her. She seemed as calm and serene as always.

The Indian was awake, his body tense as his gaze shuttled back and forth between her mother's face and the needle.

Emma looked up at Kaylee and smiled faintly. "Nothing to do now but wait for the water to boil."

If the ensuing wait seemed long to Kaylee, she could only imagine how it must seem to the Indian. But he showed no emotion save for the perspiration that covered his face and chest.

When the water was boiling, Emma wet another cloth, waited for it to cool a moment, then carefully swabbed the wound. Next, she dipped the needle and thread in the boiling water, then hitched her chair closer to the bunk.

"Bring that light over here, will you, dear?"

Kaylee picked up the lantern and held it where her mother directed. She didn't mind the sight of blood. She could castrate bulls with the best of them, but the thought of taking stitches in a man's skin made her break out in a cold sweat.

Kaylee held the lamp in both hands in an effort to keep it steady. She bit down on her lower lip as her mother slipped the shiny silver needle through the Indian's sweat-sheened flesh. She knew she couldn't watch.

When she looked away, her gaze met the Indian's. His jaw was rigid, his entire body tense, as her mother took another stitch in his side. How did he endure the pain? She knew she would be screaming, crying, thrashing about, but he just lay there, unmoving, his breath coming in shallow gasps, his fists tightly clenched.

She risked a glance at his side and had to choke back the bile that rose in her throat as she watched her mother take one last tiny stitch, neatly closing the wound.

Kaylee looked back at the Indian's face. He was staring at her, his jaw rigid, his lips almost white with pain. She had an overpowering urge to brush the hair back from his brow, run her fingers over his cheek, and assure him that everything would be all right.

His eyes narrowed and his expression softened, almost as if he could read her thoughts.

"There," Emma said, wiping the blood from the area around the wound. "We'll redress the others, and that should do it."

"Will he be all right?"

"I don't know, Kay, but I've done all I can. The rest is up to him. And to God. Is there any hot water left?"

"A little."

"I'll brew him a cup of willow-bark tea, and then we'd better get home."

"Is it safe to leave him?"

"Whether it is or not, we can't spend the night here. You know that."

Kaylee nodded. Even though her parents no longer shared a room, she knew there were nights when Shaun couldn't sleep. When that happened, no matter what the hour, he sought his wife's company.

"I could stay with him," Kaylee suggested.

"No."

"But he has a fever. What if it gets worse?"

"And what will I tell Shaun if you miss breakfast? And what about church?"

Kaylee shrugged. "Tell him I got up early and went out to check the north pasture with Rudy and Chad," she said, thinking fast. "I was going to do that anyway."

"I don't like it, Kaylee. And what difference will it make if you come home with me now, or first thing in the morning? I wish there was somebody else we could trust with this."

Kaylee was heartened by the "we." It meant her mother was on her side, that she too was concerned for the Indian's life.

"There is," Kaylee said. "Randy helped me bring the Indian here. He promised not to tell anyone."

Emma's expression brightened. "Randy's not much for going to church. I don't imagine it will grieve him to miss another meeting, so this is what I'll do. I'll stop by the Harris place on my way home and ask him to come out here. If I know Randy, he'll be here just as soon as he can." She glanced at the Indian. "You're not to untie him for any reason. I know you have your gun, but have you considered whether you would really use it? To take a human life?"

Kaylee looked at the Indian uncertainly, knowing he was following their conversation. She met his gaze unflinchingly. "I saved his life. So it's mine to take if he gives me any trouble." She fancied she saw a glimmer of admiration in the obsidian eyes.

"All right," Emma said at last. "Just keep your gun handy. And remember that Randy will be along soon."

"Don't worry, Mama, I'm not like the Thomas sisters. I can take care of myself." She patted the Colt in her skirt pocket for reassurance. "He's just one sick Indian, not a whole tribe."

"This is no time for jokes, Kaylee Marie," Emma said sharply. "And if you were as flighty as Charlene and Geraldine, I'd never let you out of the house alone. Now you let that tea steep for a few more minutes, and if his fever gets worse, you come home and get me."

"Do we have to keep him tied up? He looks so uncomfortable. I hate to cause him any more pain."

"I know he's uncomfortable, Kay, but there's no sense taking any chances. Either you promise me you'll keep him tied up and keep that little Colt close to hand, or you're coming home with me now."

Kaylee knew when to quit. "All right, Mama," she said solemnly. "I promise."

Emma glanced at the Indian and shook her head. "I think I liked it better when all you brought home were birds with broken wings."

Kaylee smiled again as she walked her mother to the door and gave her a hug good-bye. Then, with a sigh, she closed the door.

She was aware of the Indian's gaze on her back as she went to the stove and poured the tea into a tin mug. She stirred it, reminding herself that he was tied up, that he was weak and injured, that there was nothing to be afraid of.

He watched her walk toward him, his eyes betraying none of his thoughts, his face impassive.

"You need to drink this." Slipping one arm under his shoulders, she lifted his head so he could drink.

He drank the tea slowly, watching her the whole time.

When the cup was empty, she drew the covers over him and moved away from the bed. Needing to be busy, she rinsed out the cup, then went outside and gathered some more wood. She dropped the bloody rags in a bucket of water to soak and then, with nothing else to do, sat down in the rickety chair beside the fireplace.

To keep from staring at the Indian, she took a visual inventory of the shack's sparse furnishings: two cots, one on either side of the room. The cast-iron stove, a rickety table, and two chairs, including the one she was sitting on. A shelf made out of two wooden crates was nailed to the wall. One door. One window.

From the corner of her eye, she saw the Indian shift his weight on the bed. He must be terribly uncomfortable, she thought. Lying there with his wrists tied to the frame of the cot didn't allow him much movement. But that was good. It would keep him from tossing and turning and maybe reopening his wounds. Still, she was tempted to turn him loose, but she was getting sleepy and knew she would never be able to close her eyes if she released him.

Reluctantly, she met his gaze. Something passed between them, something she didn't recognize. Something that made her heart skip a beat and her insides go all soft and mushy. He had the most amazing eyes she had ever seen, deep and black and mysterious. She had the feeling that he knew exactly what she was thinking.

Rising, she crossed the room to the other cot and

curled up on the mattress, her back toward him. It
didn't help. She could still feel him watching her, but
there was nothing she could do about that. She kept
her gun close at hand, remembering when she had
fallen asleep clutching her favorite doll. Back east. A
lifetime ago.

Blue Hawk listened to the girl's breathing, knew the
moment when sleep claimed her. She was a mystery
to him. He knew just by looking at her that she was
afraid of him. Why, then, had she saved his life,
brought him here? He knew there was no love lost
between her people and his. There had been too many
battles between his people and the White Eyes. Too
many deaths. Too much blood shed. He had seen the
hatred in the boy's eyes, heard it in his voice. But the
girl was different. She hadn't looked at him and seen
Indian. She had just seen someone who was hurt and
in need of care.

He had never met anyone like her, never seen anyone like her, with her long golden hair and sky-blue
eyes. Never, except in his vision . . .

He closed his eyes as pain twitched through his
wounded shoulder. He needed to get away from here,
needed to get back to his people. His grandmother
was old and alone, her grief still fresh over the loss
of his parents and his grandfather. But he was tired,
so tired. Weak from the blood he had lost. And he
hurt. Everywhere.

Tomorrow, he thought. Tomorrow he would find a
way to escape.

Tomorrow . . .

Chapter 4

Kaylee stifled a yawn as she took a last look at her reflection in the mirror, making sure her bonnet was on straight. She hadn't gotten much sleep in the last two days, what with doing her chores and riding back and forth to the shack whenever she could sneak away to look after the Indian. But today was Sunday. Church day. No chores, no excuses. And no chance to ride out to the line shack until late this afternoon, if she could get away then.

She tilted her head to one side, wondering what Garth would say about her new dress. It was a dark blue print, with short, puffy sleeves trimmed in white lace. She thought it was very pretty, very feminine, and quite different from her usual attire. She would have liked to hear what Randy would have to say, but Randy was up at the line shack, keeping an eye on the Indian.

She frowned, wishing she could think of some way to get out of going to church. She had tried pretending to be sick, but her mother had quickly seen through that. Emma let her daughter ride with the men. She let Kaylee rope and brand and help with the castrating. She pretended to turn a deaf ear when Kaylee sometimes let go with a curse word. She even let her wear pants, which was considered quite scandalous in some parts of the country. But on one thing Emma was unbending: She insisted that Kaylee attend church every Sunday, rain or shine, winter or summer.

"Kaylee Marie!"

Her stepfather's voice shook the walls like thunder.

"Coming." She left her room and hurried along the hallway and down the stairs.

Shaun was standing in the doorway, waiting for her. He looked quite prosperous in a dark brown pin-striped suit, neatly pressed white linen shirt, brown cravat, and brown boots polished to a high shine. He held a tan Stetson in his hand.

His gaze swept over her, cool and impatient. "Your mother's in the carriage, waiting."

With a nod, Kaylee squeezed past Shaun and hurried down the porch steps. Lifting her skirts, she climbed into the rear seat.

"Kay, you know how he hates waiting."

"I'm sorry, Mama." She glanced at Shaun, who was walking toward them. "Do I have to go to church? I need to take care of that—" She lowered her voice. "That problem."

Shaun took his place beside his wife, his gaze flicking from Kaylee's face to Emma's. "What problem?"

"It's a female ailment, Shaun," Emma said, smiling up at her husband. "Nothing you nccd to concern yourself about."

Shaun grunted. Taking up the reins, he released the brake and clucked to the team.

Kaylee sat back, surprised beyond words that her mother had told a lie. And on a Sunday, too!

The Eagle Springs church was a large square building made of wood and stone, topped by a large wooden cross. Judging by the number of carriages and saddle horses hitched in the shade, they were among the last to arrive.

Shaun lifted Emma from the carriage, then offered

Kaylee his hand, his annoyance at being late evident in his expression.

Kaylee followed her parents into the church. The service hadn't started yet. Emmaline Gregory was coaxing a hymn out of the old organ. Garth Jackson was already there, of course. Garth made a point of being early to services. He was sitting in the front pew, which he shared with Kaylee's family.

Shaun and Emma paused to let Kaylee enter the pew first. She didn't want to sit next to Garth, but she didn't dare make a scene. He rose and smiled down at Kaylee, offering her his hand.

"Thank you, Mr. Jackson," she whispered, "but I really don't need any help."

Something flickered in his eyes, but then he smiled, though it seemed forced. "Lovely dress," he whispered back. "Accentuates the blue of your eyes perfectly."

She murmured her thanks and turned her attention to the reverend, though she was aware that Garth was watching her. He was a tall, slender man with dark-brown hair and light gray eyes. His first wife had died in childbirth some five years earlier; the child had died a few days later. He had observed far more than the customary year of mourning but for the past six months he had been courting Kaylee. The fact that she made it plain she did not love him had not deterred him in the least. He viewed the potential marriage as beneficial to both families, and so did Shaun.

Kaylee disliked Garth as much as Shaun admired him. There was something about Garth. She couldn't quite put her finger on it, but he made her uneasy. She had the feeling that the face he showed to the world wasn't his real face, that there was more to the man than met the eye. She was certain he was hiding something, though she couldn't imagine what it might be.

She thought about Randy, who was missing the Sunday socializing in town to help her do something he disapproved of. Randy wanted to marry her, too. If she had to choose, she would probably choose Randy. He didn't have a spread of his own yet, and he would probably never be as rich as Garth Jackson, but Randy was closer to her own age, someone she could laugh with and talk to. Being with Garth was like being with Shaun.

She paid little attention to Garth or the service, her thoughts centered on the Indian awaiting her care in the line shack. She wondered who had shot him and why, and where he came from, and if he had a family waiting for him, worrying about him.

She hadn't been up to the line shack since last night. Would Randy really look after the Indian? No doubt her patient was hungry and thirsty and in need of going outside again. Would Randy see to his needs? Well, there was no help for it. She would just have to wait.

She shifted on the hard wooden bench as the Reverend Joshua Hillman droned on and on. His sermons were as dry as old saddle leather, his voice a monotone as he preached against the evils of coveting what belonged to thy neighbor, including thy neighbor's wife. She saw her mother and Shaun exchange glances and guessed there was some serious coveting going on in Eagle Springs.

After an interminable time, the reverend's sermon rolled to a solemn conclusion. He reminded the congregation of the box social the following Saturday night, urged them to be generous when contributing to the school fund, and sought their prayers in behalf of Fred and Paula Blevin's daughter, Nancy Ann, who was seriously ill with a fever.

After a lengthy prayer, the final amen was said and the congregation filed out of the church. Outside,

Emma went to exchange recipes and gossip with a group of her friends, while Shaun went to discuss ranching and cattle prices with his.

Kaylee paced in the shade, her thoughts on the Indian and Randy, until Garth Jackson intercepted her.

"I thought the reverend preached a mighty fine sermon today," Garth remarked, tipping his hat.

Stifling the urge to say what she really thought, Kaylee smiled agreeably and waited for him to leave.

"May I say again what a becoming dress that is," he said. "Will you be wearing it to the church social next Saturday?"

"Perhaps."

"I was wondering if I might have the honor of escorting you to the dance?"

"I'm sorry," she replied, "but I'm going with Mr. Harris." Randy hadn't asked her yet, but she knew he would.

Garth's brow furrowed. "With that boy? I see. I don't suppose you'd consider changing your mind?"

"No, Mr. Jackson, I'm sorry, but I couldn't do that. A promise is a promise."

Garth nodded. A faint flush stained his cheeks. "Perhaps you'll save a dance for me."

"Yes," she said, feeling forced into it. "Of course."

"I'll see you Saturday, then."

Kaylee smiled politely. "I'll look forward to it."

He touched his forefinger to his hat brim, then stalked away, anger evident in every line of his body. Garth was not a man who was accustomed to taking no for an answer. Now she just had to remember to tell Randy that he had already asked her to the social. He hadn't, of course. He would just assume they would go together, like he always did. Randy had a way of taking things for granted that was infuriating sometimes. She was never sure if he really meant the things he said to her. He kidded her a lot about being in love with her and getting married, but he had never said it like he meant it.

She watched Garth swing up on his big gray thoroughbred and spur the horse unnecessarily. Probably wishing he was spurring Randy. An idea that had occurred to Kaylee more than once.

Shadows lengthened across the floor of the line shack. Blue Hawk stirred restlessly on the narrow cot. His wounds ached. His wrists were sore where the ropes cut into the skin. He was hungry again. He was thirsty again. His bladder was full. Again.

The boy who had replaced the girl as his jailer sat on a chair against the far wall. The boy had offered him water and allowed him to relieve himself. Would the *wasichu* allow him outside again so soon?

Blue Hawk groaned softly. He would not ask; he would wait. He wondered where the girl with the sky-blue eyes had gone, but, trusting his vision, he was certain she would return.

Knowing it was useless, he tugged covertly on the ropes that bound him, wincing as the rough hemp abraded his skin. He had to get out of here.

"Getting antsy again, huh?"

Blue Hawk glanced at the boy. Perhaps he had underestimated him. The *wasichu* was young, but he was no fool. "I need to go outside."

"Well, ain't you just full of it," the boy muttered, his expression cold and unfriendly. "Why the hell don't you die? Sure would save us all a heap of trouble." He let the chair drop down on all four legs, stood, and walked toward the bunk.

Blue Hawk remained silent, his body tensing as the boy approached.

"Kaylee asked me to look after you, and I said I

would. Promised her, I did." He grunted softly. "Just remember what I told you. One wrong move, and you're dead. Savvy?"

At Blue Hawk's nod, the *wasichu* untied his left hand, then drew his gun and moved out of reach.

"You can untie your other hand," the boy said, gesturing with his gun. "Just remember what I said."

Moving carefully so as not to alarm the boy, Blue Hawk sat up and untied the rope around his right wrist. He sat there for several minutes, taking slow, shallow breaths while he waited for the worst of the pain to pass, and then he stood up, his gaze on the *wasichu*'s face.

The *wasichu* jerked his chin toward the door. "Let's go."

Blue Hawk left the shack and walked a few feet away. Turning his back to the boy, he considered making a break for it.

The sound of approaching hoofbeats drew his attention. Glancing over his shoulder, he saw the girl with the sky-blue eyes ride into the clearing. She jerked back on the reins when she saw him. Her lathered pony stopped so quickly it almost sat down on its haunches.

"Whoa, Kaylee!" the boy exclaimed. "Where's the fire?"

"I was worried. Is he okay? What are you doing?" She slid out of the saddle and hurried toward the boy.

"Just doing what the boss lady ordered," the boy replied with an exaggerated drawl. "Lookin' after your Injun. And better'n you're looking after Dusty, I'd say." He ran a critical eye over the lathered mare. "That's no way to treat a good horse, Kay. Shaun would skin you alive if he was here."

They seemed to have forgotten his existence for a moment. Seeing what might be his only chance to escape, Blue Hawk picked up a large rock and padded up behind the boy.

The girl let out a startled gasp when he brought the rock down on top of the boy's high-crowned hat. The boy grunted and collapsed.

Ignoring the pain in his side, Blue Hawk bent down to retrieve the gun the boy had dropped.

When he straightened, Kaylee was holding her own gun in two trembling hands, her face drained of color. "You killed him!"

"No." Blue Hawk aimed the long muzzle of the Colt at the boy's head. "The boy lives. If you do not wish me to kill him, you will do as I say."

"Put the gun down." Her gaze darted to the boy's still form, then rested on him again. "I mean it! You sneaky, low-down bastard! To think I saved your life!"

Blue Hawk saw the fear in her eyes—and the determination. Worse, he saw loathing there, heard it in her tone. He did not understand. A warrior defeated an enemy any way he could, especially if that warrior was wounded and far from home. But he knew he was diminished in her eyes. The thought saddened him.

Follow the woman. Mato's words echoed in the back of his mind. He stared at the girl. She possessed Mato's courage; she was strong enough to be gentle but fierce when defending her own.

"I must return to my own people," he said. "And you must go with me. There is no other way."

She chewed on her lower lip. "Put your gun down." She glanced at the boy again. "Are you sure he's not dead?"

Blue Hawk nodded.

"I'll make a bargain with you," she said. "You put your gun down and help me look after Randy, and I'll help you get back to your people. You shouldn't travel alone, not in your condition."

He considered her proposition for a long moment and again heard Mato's voice.

Follow the woman.

"I have your word?" he asked, wondering, as he did so, if her word was any better than that of the *wasichu* who had stolen his horses and left him for dead.

"Yes, I promise."

With a nod, he lowered the gun. "It shall be as you say."

Kaylee was relieved to see that the thick crown of Randy's hat had cushioned the blow. His breathing was deep and regular, despite the ugly knot on the back of his head. He would most likely have a heck of a headache when he woke up.

She looked at the Indian. "Can you help me get him inside?"

It was easier said than done. Randy was completely limp, and the Indian was weak. But between them they finally managed to get Randy inside and settled as comfortably as possible on one of the bunks.

Kaylee was tending the lump on Randy's head when she noticed the Indian standing beside the cot. He was tying Randy's wrist to the bed with the same rope that had bound him.

"No!" she said curtly.

"Yes. He must not alert the others too soon. We will not be able to travel fast."

"I won't have it!"

"I have traded a life for a life," he replied, securing Randy's other wrist to the frame of the cot. "It will not hurt him to be bound until your mother comes looking for you. We must go now. Did you bring food?"

"There's a basket behind my saddle. I brought some water, too." She glanced back at Randy, her expression worried. "What if nobody comes?"

But the Indian was already out the door. Before

he could return, she fumbled with the knot on Randy's right wrist, loosening it just enough, she hoped. A shadow fell across the doorway. She moved quickly away from the bed as the Indian stepped into view.

"Woman, let us go." He did not wait for her answer, but turned and went outside again.

With a last glance at Randy, Kaylee moved toward the door, her stomach fluttering, more with excitement than fear. And why was that? She had no time to examine her feelings closely.

When she got outside, the Indian was already mounted on Randy's horse, a tall, handsome dun with wide, intelligent eyes. She noted with some irritation that there was a lead line attached to Dusty's bridle.

Her gaze fell on Randy's gun, tucked into the Indian's breechclout.

He noticed her glance. "I will keep the gun," he said. "You will keep yours. They might be needed."

When she was mounted, he led out north, toward a distant line of mountains.

"I can handle my own horse," she said, suddenly frightened again.

"I know," came his laconic response.

They rode in silence for a while, Dusty trailing behind Randy's gelding. Kaylee had plenty of time to study the long line of the Indian's bare back as he swayed in the saddle, his muscles rippling beneath his copper-colored skin. That fluttery feeling returned to the pit of her stomach.

They crossed the river into Indian territory. Dark clouds gathered overhead, presaging a summer storm. The slant of the afternoon sun took on a different, ominous cast.

Indian territory. She had practically grown up on stories of massacres and bloodletting. What was she doing here? Why had she made such a ridiculous promise? Her mother would be frantic when Randy told her what had happened.

Her gaze was drawn to the Indian again. Shaun said the Indians were nothing but godless savages who killed for the sheer love of it. She had seen a glimpse of that savage mask on the Indian's face when he attacked Randy and scrambled for his gun. And again when he had threatened to shoot him in cold blood. She had reacted to the Indian's fierceness as she reacted to Shaun's unreasonableness: by negotiating. And it had worked. Or seemed to have worked. At least Randy was still alive, and as safe and comfortable as possible. Her only alternative would have been to shoot the Indian.

Could she have done it?

She searched her heart and knew she could have fired when the Indian was crouched like a big cat over Randy's unconscious body. Could she shoot him now, with that broad back so disdainfully turned to her? Her fingers caressed the butt of her Colt. They hadn't gone so far that she couldn't find her way back to the line shack. What if Randy was more seriously hurt than she thought? How long would it be before her mother came looking for her? She chewed on her lower lip. With every passing mile the decision to act was being taken out of her hands.

A brisk wind, surprisingly cold, sprang up to stir the dust. Kaylee shivered. The Indian, she noticed, seemed as impervious to the cold as he was to everything else, sitting squarely in the center of the unfamiliar saddle, moving steadily toward the mountains. Even soiled, the bandage swathed around his middle was startlingly white against the dark bronze of his skin. His hair was as black as the thunderclouds overhead and fell thick and straight to his waist.

The first flash of lightning made her flinch; a sharp crack of thunder jerked her attention from the man to the storm. Another flash of lightning split the skies, unleashing a torrent of rain. In seconds, she was soaked to the skin.

The Indian rode stolidly northward, water cascading down his back, plastering his hair to his shoulders and back. He glanced back once. He was in pain. She could see it in his eyes, in the set of his mouth. He must be operating on sheer willpower, she thought, or mule-headed stubbornness.

She was hunched over in an effort to keep warm, blinking rapidly to keep the rain out of her eyes, when, without warning, he toppled off his horse, twitched once, and lay still.

Chapter 5

Randy's horse shied away from the fallen Indian. Kaylee thought the dun was going to bolt, but the horse was a well-trained cow pony. Ground-reined, he stopped a few feet away, tail turned to the buffeting of the wind.

Kaylee stared at the Indian, the cold and rain momentarily forgotten. Her first thought was to turn around and head for home. She was anxious to make sure Randy was all right. Even the thought of facing her stepfather's anger, should he learn the whole truth of what had happened, didn't dampen her spirits. Shaun could yell at her until he was blue in the face, or lock her in her room for a year for missing dinner again. She didn't care. She was going to go home where she belonged, and she was going to stay there. She had done her last good deed, and if she never saw an Indian again, it would be too soon!

The promise she had made the Indian gave her pause, but she told herself it had been made under duress and was therefore invalid. Leaning forward, she scooped up the lead line. Clucking to Dusty, she rode around the Indian and took up the dun's reins.

She was going home. She wondered if Randy had managed to free himself, and if so, if he had decided to ride out the storm in the shack or strike out for home on foot.

She hadn't gone more than half a mile or so when

her conscience began to bother her. Tempting as it was, she couldn't just ride off and leave the Indian lying there in the rain and the mud. He was hurt, might be dying. But that wasn't the only reason. She couldn't forget the way he had looked at her, or the way that look had made her feel, all soft and fluttery inside. No one else had ever made her feel that way.

With a sigh of resignation, she reined Dusty to a halt. How could she live with herself if she went off and left him lying back there? She had saved his life once and now, right or wrong, she felt responsible for him. She couldn't just abandon him.

Chiding herself for being a softhearted fool, she turned around and headed back the way she'd come, though she hadn't the faintest idea of what she could do for him out here. They would probably both die of pneumonia if they didn't get out of this downpour soon, she mused, and it would serve her right.

She found him where she had left him, sprawled facedown in the mud.

Swinging her leg over Dusty's withers, Kaylee slid to the ground. She stood there a moment, watching, relieved that the Indian was still breathing. He groaned softly when she bent down and rolled him over.

"Now what?" she wondered aloud.

His eyelids fluttered open and he stared up at her. "Why did you not run away?"

"Beats the heck out of me. We'll probably both drown."

The faintest of smiles flitted across his face. She marveled that he could find anything to smile about while lying helpless on his back in a cloudburst.

"There." He lifted one hand and pointed to a tall hill in the distance. "Cave."

She led Randy's gelding over to the Indian. Offering him her hands, she pulled him to his feet. He leaned against the gelding's shoulder and she could almost see him fighting back the pain, gathering his strength. He grabbed hold of the saddle horn and put his foot into the stirrup as Kaylee gave him a boost.

"Thought the big brave Indian didn't need a white woman's help," she muttered, remembering how he had disdained her help only days ago.

The Indian picked up the reins. When he was settled in the saddle, Kaylee caught up Dusty's reins and swung onto the mare's back. "Are you ready?"

The Indian's gaze moved over her face, his eyes filled with an expression she couldn't read, and then he turned the gelding toward the hill.

Kaylee felt as if the storm was trying to pound them into the prairie. The grass lay flat against the ground. Sizzling flashes of lightning lit up the sky, and the thunder came in one long drumroll after another. Dusty danced sideways as a tumbleweed skittered past, blown by the gusting wind.

It seemed to take forever to reach the cave, which was located at the base of the hill. Dismounting, she tethered the horses to a clump of brush. Then she retrieved the basket from behind her saddle and watched the Indian dismount. As soon as his feet hit the ground, she moved up beside him, one arm sliding around his waist to steady him. He looked down at her and heat flowed between them, sizzling like the lightning arcing across the skies. It was most disconcerting. And pleasurable.

The cave was just tall enough for her to stand erect. The Indian had to bend over to keep from hitting his head. As they moved deeper into the cavern, it grew higher and wider. And darker. But at least it was dry and protected them from the wind.

The Indian was staggering by the time they reached the rear of the cave.

"Over there," he said. "Look."

Kaylee dropped the basket on the ground, and then glanced from side to side. "Over where?"

He put one hand on her shoulder, turned her around, and gave a little push. "There."

She stumbled forward, gasping with alarm when her foot hit something furry. At first she thought it was an animal of some kind, but when it didn't make any noise and didn't move, she bent down and discovered that it was a large bundle wrapped in a buffalo hide.

"What is this?" she asked, fumbling with the thong that held the hide in place.

"Food. Flint. Clothes."

"And a rifle," Kaylee muttered as her hand closed around the stock. She put it aside and searched for the flint. "We need wood."

"Against the wall."

Crawling forward on her hands and knees, she found a pile of wood, and after a great deal of trial and error she managed to get a small fire going. Turning back to the bundle, she found a buckskin shirt, a pair of leggings, a trade blanket made of wool, a hide pouch that held what looked like beef jerky, and some other substance that she didn't recognize. Was it edible, too? she wondered. There was also a canteen of water. The words "7th U.S." were stamped on the side. She glanced at the Indian over her shoulder, wondering if he had killed the former owner.

She picked up the shirt and leggings and thrust them at the Indian. "Here, put these on."

He took the leggings from her hand. "Keep the shirt," he said. "You need to get out of your wet clothes as well."

"You need it more than I do."

"Do not argue with me, woman," he said.

He was right. She was so cold her teeth were chattering. "Turn your back." She didn't wait to see if he did or not. Turning her back to him, she peeled off the shirtwaist and divided skirt she had changed into after church, removed her boots and stockings, and slipped the shirt over her head. It was huge. And warm.

When she was dressed, she turned around to see how the Indian was doing. He had managed to pull on the leggings but had left his clout on. It was then that she realized that the leggings were not trousers, as she had first thought, but two separate pieces. She picked up the blanket and draped it around his shoulders, then sat down close to the fire, which had quickly heated this part of the cave.

The Indian was staring into the flames. The bandages around his arm, shoulder, and middle were soaking wet. They needed to be changed, but she had nothing with which to replace them.

"Are you all right?" she asked.

"In there," he said, gesturing at the pouch. "Food."

"I brought food," she said, not certain what his idea of food might be. But the bread and meat and pound cake she had brought wrapped in a napkin were waterlogged.

Closing the lid of the basket, she picked up the pouch and pulled out several hunks of dried meat. "Our beef?" she asked.

He took a piece from her hand and shrugged.

They ate in silence for a few minutes. Kaylee glanced around the cave. There was a narrow ledge cut high into the wall. A draft coming from behind her made her wonder if there was another entrance. She would have to go outside and tend to the horses when the rain let up.

Uncapping the canteen, Kaylee took a drink, then offered it to the Indian. Closing his eyes, he took a long drink, paused, and took another. It was the fever, she thought. Fevers always made a body thirsty. Kaylee placed her Colt on the ground within easy reach but not too close to the fire.

She glanced toward the cave entrance. The way it was raining, water was the least of their problems. The Indian was shivering in spite of the fire and the blanket.

Picking up the heavy buffalo robe, she draped it over his shoulders.

He looked up. When his gaze met hers, heat flashed between them that had nothing to do with the campfire. It blazed between them, urgent and unfamiliar, hotter than the lightning that sizzled outside. A vivid flush spread over her cheeks.

"Why did you not leave when you had the chance?" he asked.

"I did, but I came back."

"Why?"

"Because I promised to help you get home." It was only part of the truth, but it was the only answer she was prepared to give. "What's your name?" she asked, sitting down beside him.

"Blue Hawk."

It was kind of pretty, she thought, yet strong and masculine. And it suited him, with his hawklike nose and dark, piercing eyes.

"And you are Kay-lee?"

"Yes."

"What is its meaning?"

"I don't know if it has any meaning. I was named for my grandmother. Who shot you?"

Anger glittered in the depths of his eyes. *"Wasichu."*

"Wa-she-choo? What's that?"

"White men."

"Why did they shoot you?"

"Because they are white men," he said, his voice thick with contempt. "They promised me guns in exchange for horses, but they shot me and left me for dead and took the horses."

"Why did you want guns?"

"My people need them."

"To make war against us?" Kaylee asked, but it wasn't really a question.

"No. For hunting. To defend our old ones, our women, our young." A shadow passed over his face. "Our warriors are few in number now. Our old ones are hungry. Our little ones cry."

"Why don't you go stay on the reservation? There's food and shelter there."

His eyes smoldered with barely suppressed fury. "Have you ever been on a reservation?"

"Of course not," she replied, confused by his anger. "What's that got to do with anything?"

"Until you have, you cannot understand. The *wasichu* in charge have no care but for themselves. The beef they give us is spoiled, the flour infested, the blankets worthless."

"You've lived on a reservation?"

He nodded, his expression grim. "The White Eyes would not allow us to have weapons, so we could not hunt. The rations that were promised almost never came. When they did, they were late and there was never enough. The old ones gave what food they had to the children, choosing death for themselves so that our little ones could survive." His eyes turned cold and hard. "The white man has stolen our land, but it was not enough. He wanted to steal the pride of our young men, the dignity of our ancient ones. He would make us beggars."

"I'm so sorry," Kaylee said, and even though she meant it, she knew the words sounded trite. "You speak English very well. Do all of your people speak English?"

"No, but I wanted to learn so that I would know

what the *wasichu* were saying. So that I would know if the words of our chiefs were being interpreted correctly when we sat in council with the White Eyes."

"Where did you learn to speak our language?"

"My friend Shappa captured a white man who spoke our language. He was going to give the *wasichu* to his wife to be her slave. When I learned that the *wasichu* spoke Lakota, I told him that I would ask Shappa for his freedom if he would teach me to speak your language." Blue Hawk grinned faintly. "He was very agreeable."

"And a very good teacher. What happened to him?"

"Kirk-land stayed with us for a year, and then he went back to his own people. His freedom cost me a fine horse and a buffalo robe."

Kaylee placed her hand on his brow. He was hot, so hot. "You should get some sleep now."

With a nod, he spread the buffalo robe on the floor of the cave. "Come, lie beside me."

"No."

He handed her the blanket. Pulling one edge of the robe over him, he indicated the remaining expanse. "Wrap yourself in the blanket and come lie beside me. We will share the blankets and the warmth."

There was a time for modesty and a time for common sense. She knelt on the robe. He nodded encouragement, then rolled, very carefully, onto his uninjured side, putting his back toward her. Still, it was with a great deal of trepidation that she stretched out beside him. She covered them with the blanket, then pulled her side of the robe up over her until she was cocooned in fur. The fever burned through the Indian, warming her like heat radiating from a stove.

She was exhausted, drained, and yet, lying there beside him, she felt safe.

Coals shifted in the dying fire.

It was rather cozy, lying there warm and dry while the storm raged outside.

She fell asleep listening to the rain.

Chapter 6

"Indian? What Indian?" Shaun Randall drummed his fingertips on the desktop while he waited for Randy to answer. The boy looked all done in, his face pale beneath his tan. The clock in the parlor chimed the hour.

"Some buck Kaylee found across the river," Randy replied wearily.

Shaun's eyes narrowed. "When was she across the river?"

"A couple days ago, sir."

"Go on."

Randy shifted from one foot to another. It had been a long walk through a cold rain to get here. His head throbbed from where that thievin' redskin had hit him. Randy grimaced. Snuck up behind him the minute his back was turned. When he regained consciousness, his first thought had been for Kaylee, and he had come straight to the Double R in hopes that she was here. Mrs. Randall had given him a change of clothes, clucking over him like a mother hen. She asked him if he had seen Kaylee while she tended the goose egg on the back of his head, and he hadn't had the courage to tell her what had happened. Instead, he'd made up some story about losing his horse.

And now he stood in front of Shaun Randall's desk, feeling like a kid being reprimanded by the schoolmaster.

"Get on with it," Shaun said brusquely.

"Well, sir, she found this Injun a few days back. He'd been shot. I was all for putting him out of his misery then and there, but Kaylee wouldn't hear of it. She insisted that we take him to that abandoned line shack up on Cedar Ridge."

Shaun placed his hands flat on the desktop and leaned forward. "Why didn't you stop her?"

"I tried, Mr. Randall. Believe me, I tried." He lifted one shoulder and let it fall. "You know Kaylee."

Shaun snorted in derision. "You gonna stand there and tell me you couldn't stop one skinny girl? Go on."

"I was looking after him today so she could go to church. She rode in this afternoon to bring some food. And . . ." Color suffused his face and neck. "The Indian hit me from behind." He lifted a hand to the back of his head. "Damn, feels like my head's broke."

"Ought to be your neck," Shaun said grimly. "Where is Kaylee?"

"I don't know. When I came to, they were both gone. I came here, hoping to find her."

"Well, she's not here, you damn fool." Shaun rounded his desk. "Get out of my way! Emma! Emma, where the hell are you?"

"I'm here." She glanced briefly at Randy as she entered the room. "What's wrong, Shaun?"

"Your daughter's been kidnapped by a damned savage, that's what's wrong!"

"Kidnapped!" Emma shook her head in denial, one hand pressed to her breast.

"Yes, kidnapped!"

Emma turned to face Randy. "Why didn't you tell me?"

Randy shifted uncomfortably. "I'm sorry, Mrs. Randall, but—"

Emma shook her head in disbelief. "How could it have happened? He was badly hurt."

"And just how would you be knowing that?" Shaun asked, his voice deceptively calm.

"Kaylee asked me to take a look at him. He'd been shot."

"And you didn't think it was important enough to tell me?" Shaun asked, his voice rising. "You didn't think I needed to know there was a damned redskin on my land? Being doctored by my womenfolk? Dammit, woman!" He was shouting now. "Why the hell didn't you tell me?"

Emma stared up at her husband, mute. There was no reasoning with him when he was this angry, and she didn't try. Worse, she had nothing to say in the face of Randy's devastating news. She could only stand there, assailed by guilt. She would never forgive herself if anything had happened to Kaylee. She should have told Shaun about the Indian, promise or no promise, but Shaun would probably have gone up to the shack and shot him and then punished Kaylee. But at least Kaylee would be here, at home, where she belonged. *Oh, Lord,* she prayed, *please let my daughter be alive.*

Shaun jabbed a finger in Randy's chest. "Get the hell out of here, and don't come back. Ever!"

Randy didn't argue; he just turned and left the room.

"Stupid!" Shaun roared. He paced the floor. "How could she have been so stupid? And you—" He slammed his fist down on the desk, scattering the papers on it.

Emma remained silent, her hands clasped, head slightly bowed, until Shaun's temper ran its course. Only then did she speak. "You'll go after her?"

"Damn right. But he's got a good head start. And trackin' a redskin is never easy. If we're lucky, we'll get up there before the rain washes their tracks out."

"Shaun . . ." Emma pressed her lips together, fighting the urge to cry.

"Don't worry," Shaun said gruffly. His anger seemed to have turned away from her, toward the Indian. "We'll find her, head start or not, and when we do, that dirty redskin will be sorry he was ever born."

Chapter 7

Blue Hawk was still asleep when Kaylee woke the next morning. She lay there for a long time, listening to his even breathing. There was something intimate about the feel of his back pressed against hers, even through two layers of cloth. His fever had broken during the night, so heat no longer radiated from his body.

She couldn't remember the last time she had slept with someone beside her. Probably when bad dreams had driven her to her mother's bed after her father died. Thinking of her father brought a smile to her face. If only he could see her now!

She sat up, groaning softly, her whole body stiff from sleeping on the hard ground. Her stomach growled loudly, and she closed her eyes for a moment, visions of scrambled eggs and bacon, and buttermilk pancakes swimming in butter and syrup running through her mind. Extricating herself from the robe, she draped the blanket over him and tucked it in. He sighed heavily, but didn't awake.

She stood, pleased to see that the rain had finally stopped.

She reached for her skirt, but the heavy serge was still damp. Draping it over her arm, she picked up her shirt, stockings, and boots, grabbed a hunk of jerky, and headed for the entrance of the cave.

Dusty whinnied when she stepped outside.

Randy's dun stood hip-shot, tail swishing. After spreading her clothing across a bush to dry, Kaylee took up the reins to both horses and led them away from the cave to a patch of grass. While they were grazing, she removed Dusty's saddle, and then the dun's, and spread the saddle blankets on the ground to dry.

It was a beautiful day, bright and clear and already warm. The pines gave off a strong resinous aroma, the earth smelled clean and fresh. With the horses taken care of, she moved away to relieve herself. Noticing a creek a short distance away, she rinsed her hands and face and arms, then stretched out on her belly, drinking from her cupped hands. They would be missing her at home by now. Her mother would be frantic. If Randy hadn't managed to free himself, his people would be looking for him, too.

She was on her way to get the horses when half-a-dozen warriors rode into view.

Kaylee ducked behind a low bush, her heart pounding like thunder. Had they seen her? Oh, Lord, what was she going to do now? She had seen what Indians did to white people. One of their cowhands had been killed and scalped. It had not been a pretty sight.

Bent low, she hurried back toward the cave entrance, praying that they wouldn't notice her.

She glanced over her shoulder, her heart pounding. They were riding straight toward her, six nearly naked copper-skinned warriors with paint-streaked faces and feathers tied in their long black hair. One wore the horns of a buffalo on his head. The earth beneath her feet vibrated as the riders drew closer. She wasn't going to make it.

"Heciyani!"

One of the warriors shouted as he lifted his lance and pointed in her direction.

They had seen her.

Overcome by a sense of panic, she began to run. It was stupid, foolish, hopeless, but she was beyond rational thought. She had never been afraid of Blue Hawk, not like this.

She heard a whoop behind her, the sound of the Indians riding in pursuit. She knew she would never get away, knew she couldn't hope to outrun their horses, but she kept going, running until her sides ached and black spots danced before her eyes. She knew they could have caught her long ago, and then she realized they were just playing with her, the way a cat plays with a mouse. And still she ran, until exhaustion was stronger than her fear, until her legs gave out.

Just when she was about to fall, a long brown arm reached down, curled around her waist, and lifted her off her feet. A high-pitched cry of victory rang out as the warrior deposited her, none too gently, across his horse's withers.

She was trying to wriggle out of his grasp when a gunshot ripped through the air. The warrior released her abruptly, and she fell to the ground, rolling quickly to one side to avoid the horse's hooves.

By the time she gained her feet, the warriors had their mounts under control and sat facing the cave mouth.

Blue Hawk stood there, propped against the side of the cave. He held the old Army Springfield that had been part of the cache of supplies in the cave. A thick curl of dark gray powder smoke hung above his head.

His voice rasped out, harsh and commanding, in his native tongue.

The warriors slid off their ponies, weapons clutched in their hands. They rushed toward Blue Hawk. To Kaylee's dismay, she saw that he was swaying, about to collapse. He let the heavy rifle fall to the ground as the warriors approached him. Certain that they were going to do him harm, she cursed herself for leaving her gun inside the cave.

Then the warriors were on Blue Hawk—but they were not attacking.

They dropped their lances and bows and clustered around him, holding him up, muttering rapidly in what she guessed was Lakota. She saw him gesture weakly in her direction, and one of the warriors broke away from the group and trotted toward her.

Kaylee clenched her fists, wondering if she should make a run for it, or scratch his eyes out.

"Kay-lee." Blue Hawk's voice was weak but distinct. "He will not harm you. These are my people."

She eyed the lean young Indian standing before her skeptically. He gestured impatiently, indicating that she should follow him.

"Kay-lee."

They were lifting him, carrying him back into the cave. The young Indian gestured again. She nodded and followed them inside.

A familiar voice. The scent of sage and sweet grass. The touch of a cool hand, gentle on his brow. Blue Hawk opened his eyes to see his grandmother looking down at him, her expression one of love and concern. She was a tiny old woman, with long gray braids and knowing black eyes. Life had left its mark upon her face.

"Blue Hawk."

"Hau, unci," he said. Hello, Grandmother.

"Hou ke che wa?" She placed a gnarled hand on his brow. "You have been wandering in the land of spirits." She cocked her head to one side. "Did you see your grandfather there?"

"No, *unci.*"

He was surprised, and pleased, to see her out of

bed. Since his grandfather's death two moons ago, Wichapi had been withdrawn, seeking solace in sleep. He had feared for her health, feared she would will herself to die. Except for his cousin Chapa, his grandmother was all that remained of his family.

She grunted softly. "Shappa found you. I knew he would."

"And the woman? Is she well?"

"*Ai.* She is well. She is young and strong, and only a little frightened. She will make a fine slave."

"No, *unci.*" Blue Hawk struggled to sit up. "She saved my life. If it were not for her, I would be with Grandfather now."

Wichapi placed a gnarled hand on his shoulder and gently pushed him back down. "You must rest, Blue Hawk."

"No, *unci.* I must go to the woman."

"You must rest and regain your strength, *cinksi.*" She looked at him thoughtfully. "Who is this white woman who causes you such concern?"

"She is the woman of my vision." And he knew suddenly why Kaylee had been sent to him. She was the answer he had been looking for. He would trade her back to her family for the guns and supplies his people needed so desperately.

He lay back and closed his eyes, troubled by the thought of parting with her. He remembered the feel of her body beside his. Even when he was exhausted and wracked with fever, it had felt right for her to be there, beside him.

But the needs of his people had to come first.

Kaylee paced the floor of the tipi. The warriors who had rigged the travois for Blue Hawk had treated her with deference but no nonsense. They had let her change into her own clothes after searching the garments. One of the Indians had taken her Colt. They had waited while she saddled Dusty, allowed her to check Blue Hawk's wounds after he was secured to the travois. He had assured her that she was in no danger.

When they reached the small village hidden in a pocket of lodgepole pines near a good-sized creek, the whole village had come out to welcome their leader. Over her protests, she had been deposited here. She had been offered a bowl of something that looked like stew and a cup of water.

That had been yesterday. Today, she was still being treated politely, but unceremoniously. Like a prisoner. She wondered where Blue Hawk was. Stooping, she pushed aside the hide flap at the tipi entrance.

A wiry boy, probably in his early teens, sat cross-legged facing her, a bow and quiver of arrows on the ground beside him. He motioned for her to go back inside.

"No," she said, and stepped out.

He rose lithely, bringing his weapon with him, but she saw the gleam of uncertainty in his dark eyes. She turned and strode purposefully toward the creek with him trailing uncertainly in her wake.

She glanced around, studying the tipis, noting that some were larger than others. Many of the lodgeskins were painted with stick figures and horses, which she guessed represented battle scenes; others were decorated with garish suns and moons. The tops of the tipis were blackened from the smoke of countless fires.

It seemed everyone in the camp was busy. She saw women kneeling on the ground, scraping hides with what looked like pieces of bone. Others were cutting meat into thin strips. Some were sewing with odd-looking needles and thread. One was nursing a baby; another was holding a sleeping child in her arms. She saw only a few men, and most of them were older. One man was wrapping a piece of hide around a bow, another was making arrows, another repairing what looked like a halter. She saw only a few children. The older ones regarded her through dark, suspicious eyes, but the younger ones smiled shyly. Several elderly men and women dozed in the sun. A few boys were shooting arrows at a target, and a little girl played with a doll.

She noticed that all the women wore dresses and leggings. Many of the dresses were decorated with bead and quillwork on the yoke. The men wore breechclouts and moccasins. Some wore leggings that reached from ankle to thigh and were tied to a belt. Some of the more elderly men wore loose-fitting shirts with fringed sleeves.

Smoke wafted through the tops of some of the tipis and from outside cookfires. Some distance away, she saw a small herd of horses grazing.

All in all, it was a tranquil scene—except that the people were too thin, the children too quiet.

Two women who were kneeling beside a tipi next to the one where she had spent the night looked up as she walked by. The boy spoke to them, his tone excited.

Her head held high, Kaylee walked past them as if she hadn't a care in the world.

She gasped as rough hands grabbed her from behind. Twisting away, she was surprised to see it was one of the women.

"Get away from me!" Kaylee exclaimed.

The other woman rose to her feet.

Alarmed, Kaylee turned and ran. It was the wrong thing to do. The women and the boy gave chase, and the boy caught her easily. He grabbed her from behind and they both tumbled to the ground. The two women were on her in a minute. The three of them struggled, oblivious to the gathering crowd, until a male voice called out.

The Indian women released her immediately.

Scrambling to her feet, Kaylee turned toward the familiar voice.

Blue Hawk stood a short distance away. "Where do you think you are going?"

"Shouldn't you be in bed?"

He looked at her, one brow arched. It was, she thought, a silly thing to say. What he did was none of her business. Her gaze moved over him. Except for the bandages on his wounds, he looked quite fit.

"Kuwa." He held out his hand.

Kaylee shook her head. "No. I said I would help you get back to your people, and I did. Now I'm going home."

"No."

"Yes." She stared at him, her heart pounding. She couldn't stay here. She wouldn't. He frightened her in ways she did not understand.

He took a step toward her, and she backed up.

"It is decided," he said. "You will stay here, for now."

"Go away. Leave me alone."

"Kay-lee, you saved my life. I will not hurt you."

"Please, just let me go home."

"I cannot. Not yet."

"Why?"

"Your people have many cattle roaming the land that once belonged to my people. The *wasichu* count their wealth in cattle as we once counted our wealth in horses."

She frowned at him. "What has that got to do with me?"

"My people need guns and ammunition."

"I still don't understand."

"I will trade you back to your family in exchange for guns."

"Trade me?" She didn't know whether to laugh or cry.

He nodded, though she thought he looked uncertain. "What if my family won't trade?"

His eyes glittered. "They will not refuse. They will not leave you here, alone among"—his lip curled into a sneer—"among savages."

"What am I supposed to do until then?"

Blue Hawk gazed at her. She was young and beautiful, spirited and brave. Had she been a Lakota maiden, he would have raided a ranch and offered stolen ponies to her father. "You will stay here."

"But I don't want to stay here. I want to go home."

A slow smile curved his lips as he added "stubborn" to her other qualities. Again he held out his hand. "Come, let us go back."

"If I have to stay here, I want to take a bath. And wash my clothes."

"You can bathe in the river."

She looked doubtful. "I don't have any soap. Or anything to dry with."

"We have soap. You can dry in the sun. And my cousin Chapa will give you something to wear until your clothes are clean again."

Kaylee blew out a sigh, and then nodded, the thought of being clean too tempting to resist.

She followed him back through the camp. He spoke briefly to the two women she had struggled with earlier. The taller of the two went into her lodge. She returned a few minutes later and handed Blue Hawk a small bundle of what looked like clothing. Blue Hawk nodded his thanks, then gestured for Kaylee to follow him.

They walked down a narrow, winding path that led along the river, then branched off to a small, quiet sunlit pool secluded from view.

Blue Hawk thrust the bundle into her arms. "I will wait for you here."

With a nod, she started walking toward the pool, only to be stopped by his voice.

"Do not try to run away, Kay-lee."

"I won't."

"I have your word?"

"Yes, for now."

He regarded her thoughtfully for a moment, then turned and walked a short distance away.

She watched him sit down, his back to the pool. She couldn't help noticing that it was a very nice back, broad and long, the muscles well defined beneath the smooth copper-colored skin. She had the strangest urge to go to him, to run her hand over his sun-warmed flesh.

Chiding herself for her foolishness, she tested the water with her toe. Warmed by the sun, it was not as cold as the river. She opened the bundle, which turned out to be a deerskin dress wrapped around a pair of leggings, moccasins, and a chunk of what she guessed was soap.

She looked at the pool, at the moccasins, and then at Blue Hawk. His back was still turned. In his weakened condition, he probably couldn't move very fast. She had overheard the cowhands talking about the Sioux and the Cheyenne, saying that they were all thieves and robbers, godless savages who burned and plundered, stealing horses and cattle, killing white women and children.

She wondered if Blue Hawk had ever stolen Double R cattle, if he had attacked any of the neighboring ranches, killed women and children and taken their scalps. Her breath felt trapped in her throat as she recalled every horrible, bloody tale she had ever heard, tales of women who were tortured and raped or who were forced to become slaves, begging for food and shelter. Was that what was in store for her? Had all his talk about trading her to Shaun been a tall tale?

The thought spurred her to action. She wasn't going

to wait around and find out. Sitting on a boulder beside the stream, she pulled off her riding boots and stepped into the moccasins, which were a surprisingly good fit. The fact that she had given him her word was of no importance now. She had to get away from here, had to get back home where she belonged, before it was too late.

Fear put wings on her feet. She ran along the riverbank, her mind empty of every thought except escape. She had to get away from here, away from him, now. Who knew if she would ever get another chance?

She ran and ran, not daring to look back, ran until her sides ached. She shrieked when a muscular arm wrapped around her waist and jerked her to a halt.

"Let me go! Let me go!" Arms and legs flailing, she struggled to free herself from his grasp, but his arm was like iron around her waist. Breathless, she went limp. As soon as he relaxed his hold a little, she drove her elbow back, into his wounded side.

He gasped with pain, but he didn't release her. Panting heavily, he swung her up into his arms and carried her back to the pool. Without hesitation, he dumped her, fully clothed, into the water.

She landed on her backside, hard.

He stood bent over, his hands resting on his knees, his breathing ragged. He looked unusually pale. In spite of her fear and outrage, she felt a sharp pang of alarm flood through her. It was her fault that he was hurting.

"Do not run away again, Kay-lee," he warned in a hard voice.

"I hate you!"

"You are behaving like a foolish child. Why did you run?"

"Because I want to go home!"

"You gave me your word you would not."

"You're keeping me here against my will," she retorted sharply.

"What are you afraid of, Kay-lee? I have told you I will not hurt you. You have nothing to fear from me or my people."

"I don't believe you. I've heard what Indians do to white women!"

"What do we do?" he asked, his voice taut.

"You know." She wrapped her arms around her body, feeling suddenly vulnerable and more than a little foolish sitting on her rump in the water, fully clothed.

He straightened, his eyes narrowed. "Tell me, Kay-lee. What do we do?"

"Kill them. Scalp them." She felt a rush of heat climb into her cheeks. "Rape them."

"Have I hurt you in any way, Kay-lee?"

"No."

"And I will not. I cannot deny that my people have killed yours, just as yours have killed mine. But you have nothing to fear from me. No one will harm you while you are here, under my protection." Bending down, he grabbed the soap and tossed it to her. "Wash yourself."

She watched him walk a few feet away and turn his back. She felt suddenly foolish for running away. He had treated her kindly, done nothing to inspire her fear. If she'd managed to elude him, what would she have done? She had no idea where home was, couldn't hope to survive on the prairie alone, on foot. If she decided to try again, she would wait until she could get to Dusty. The mare would show her fleet heels to the scrawny Indian ponies. And ranch horses could always find their way home, to where the oats waited.

Filled with new hope, she stripped out of her newly sodden riding outfit, scrubbed it hastily with the soap, wrung each piece out and spread it on rocks around the pool. She squeezed the water from the moccasins as best she could and placed them in the sun. Then, keeping one eye on Blue Hawk's back, she washed herself. The soap didn't make much lather, but she scrubbed until her skin glowed, and then she washed her hair, twice.

She felt much better when she stepped out of the water. Blue Hawk was sitting as before, with his back to her. Feeling terribly self-conscious, she stood in a patch of sunshine and let the heat dry her skin. Her hair was still damp when she picked up the buckskin dress. She turned it back and forth to determine which was the front, then slipped it over her head. It was a plain, loose-fitting garment, made of what she thought might be doeskin. It felt almost like velvet against her bare skin.

She pulled on the leggings and stamped her feet into her riding boots again. Even though she was fully clothed by Lakota standards, she felt almost naked without her chemise, drawers, and stockings. The boots at least felt familiar.

How did she look in this strange apparel? Grasping the trunk of a sapling, she leaned out over the pool, studying her reflection. Abruptly she was seeing a double reflection. Blue Hawk was beside her.

She didn't quite jump out of her skin. "How do you do that?" she asked irritably.

"Do what?"

"Move like that. One minute you're sitting over there, and the next you're here. I never even saw you move. I didn't hear you come up."

He grinned at her. "Our enemies never hear us."

"Is that what I am?" she asked, turning away from the pool. "The enemy?"

The grin faded from his face. "No, Kay-lee," he said quietly. "You are not the enemy."

The intensity of his gaze brought a rush of color to her cheeks. "Stop that."

"What?"

"Stop looking at me that way."

"What way?"

"Like that! The way a man looks at a woman when he—" She pressed her hands to her burning cheeks. "Just stop it."

"I am a man," he replied, his voice suddenly low and husky. "And you are a woman."

"I'm sure I don't know what you mean!"

He took a step toward her.

Her heart began to beat faster. She licked lips gone suddenly dry as he lifted one hand and reached toward her, felt a sharp sense of disappointment when he merely plucked a small leaf from her hair.

He looked at it a moment, then let the leaf fall to the ground. And then his gaze met hers again. "Tell me you do not feel it, Kay-lee," he said, his voice thick. "Tell me your heart does not pound like a buffalo stampede whenever I am near."

Heat flowed between them, hotter than the sun shining on her back.

He took another step toward her. He was close, so close she had to tilt her head back to meet his eyes. She wanted to run away, but she refused to let him think she was afraid of him. And she wasn't afraid of him, she realized. But she was terribly afraid of the way he made her feel.

She lowered her gaze to his shoulders and chest. It was a very nice chest, well muscled and smooth save for a faint white scar over each breast. His shoulders were broad, and she was overcome once again with the urge to touch him, to rest her hands on those broad shoulders, to feel the warmth of his skin, to run her fingertips down his arms, to curl her hands around his biceps . . .

She looked up to find him watching her, a knowing look on his face.

"Tell me again that you do not know what I mean," he said.

She didn't answer. Lifting her chin defiantly, she swept past him.

She came to an abrupt halt as his hand gripped her arm. "This way, Kay-lee," he said, and pointed her in the right direction.

His laughter made her cheeks burn all the hotter. He chuckled all the way back to camp. When she veered off toward the lodge in which she had been held, he stopped her.

"Come," he said.

"Where?"

"To my lodge."

Kaylee shook her head, certain her face must be as red as the sunset. "No."

"You will be safe there." He grinned at her. "My grandmother will protect you."

"You live with your grandmother?"

He nodded. "Come."

Thinking that a grandmother would probably make an excellent chaperone, Kaylee fell into step beside him.

"You are a stranger to our ways," he said. "While you are with us, there are things you must know."

"What things?" she asked suspiciously.

"The lodge belongs to my grandmother. Her place is to the left of the fire. Mine is to the right. You may sit anywhere else. You must not walk between Unci and the fire. It is considered impolite to do so."

"Is *Unci* her name?"

"No. Her name is Wichapi. *Unci* means 'grandmother.'"

She followed him across the camp and into one of the larger tipis. It was dim inside and smelled of smoke and sage.

She paused just inside the entrance. The floor was covered with furs. A small fire burned in a pit in the middle of the floor. Two objects that she guessed were backrests were placed on either side of the fire. On the far side of the fire pit there was a small raised mound of earth, and beyond that, several bags and bundles. A woman with long gray braids was asleep under a blanket to her left. Even in repose, she looked careworn.

To the right was another pile of bedding. Some cooking utensils were stacked just inside the door, and a couple of hide pouches hung from the lodgepoles. Lining the tipi was a cloth of some kind, painted with scenes that depicted warriors hunting and fighting.

Blue Hawk gestured at one of the backrests. "Sit."

She did so, crossing her legs beneath her. "Is your grandmother ill?" she asked quietly.

He nodded and tapped his chest. "She is sad in here. She mourns for my parents and her husband."

"What happened to them?"

His expression turned hard. "They were killed by *wasichu* soldiers."

"I'm sorry."

"Are you?"

"Of course!"

He looked skeptical. "Your people will not rest until we are all dead or on reservations."

She didn't know what to say to that. Conversation at the ranch often concerned the Indians. They were savages, her stepfather said, a menace that must be dealt with firmly, destroyed if necessary.

"When will I be able to go home?"

"I have sent two of my men with a message for your father."

"My stepfather."

He frowned. "Stepfather?"

"My mother's second husband."

"Ah. If he agrees, we will meet with him when he has the guns."

Of course Shaun would agree, Kaylee thought. How could he refuse?

Chapter 8

Emma stood on the porch, squinting into the late-morning sun, her hands worrying her apron as she watched Shaun and three of the men ride into the yard. They had ridden out yesterday morning to search for Kaylee. Her heart sank at the dejected slope of their shoulders.

Shaun swung off his horse. He tossed the reins to one of the men, watched as they moved off toward the corral. Heaving a sigh, he climbed the stairs to the porch. The look in his eyes said it all.

Emma sagged as the strength seemed to go out of her legs. Shaun's arm around her waist was all that kept her upright.

"Still nothing?" she asked.

"We found some tracks that had been made after the storm died down," Shaun said. "Two shod horses. One set of prints belonged to Dusty—I put those shoes on her myself. We found some unshod pony tracks, too. One was dragging a travois. I left the rest of the men camped on the trail. We're going to need more men and some fresh horses."

"Oh, Shaun . . ."

"No sense crying until we know if there's something to cry about," he said, not unkindly. "Go on now," he added briskly. "Tell Roscoe to pack enough grub to last a dozen men four or five days. And tell him to load it on a packhorse. A chuck wagon will only slow us down."

Emma nodded, relieved to have something to do, but she couldn't put the Indian's image out of her mind, couldn't help wondering if she had given aid to a man who had repaid her kindness by killing Kaylee and leaving her body for the wolves and coyotes.

By midday half a dozen Double R cowhands were mounted and ready to ride. Shaun had sent word to Garth Jackson, who had shown up with another half-dozen men and enough rifles and handguns to start a war.

Emma stood beside Shaun. "Please find her."

"Don't worry," Shaun said. "We'll—" He broke off as two of the Double R cowhands who had been out checking cattle on the east range rode up leading an Indian pony. "What the hell?"

Emma's eyes widened when she saw that the pony Grady was leading carried a dead brave tied to its back.

For a moment she thought, hoped, it was the Indian who had stolen her daughter. But as they came closer, she could see that the dead warrior was not nearly the size of the man she had tended.

"Caught him riding through the herd," Grady said. "There were two of 'em. The other redskin got away."

"Damned Injuns," Shaun muttered. "This part of the country won't be safe until they're all dead. Why the hell did you bring him here?"

Grady shrugged. "Thought we'd dump him in the ravine that runs behind the south pasture and then turn his horse loose. Me and Rocky didn't think it would be a good idea to leave the body lying out there on our range where his kin might find him and decide to retaliate. You know?"

Shaun grunted. "I guess you're right. You two go take care of it." His eyes narrowed thoughtfully. "Hang on to that pony. Those two might have been looking for the redskin who kidnapped Kaylee. Could be that pony might lead us to them."

Jackson nodded. "Good idea."

"There's one other thing," Rocky said, looking uneasy.

"Shut up!" Grady said sharply.

Shaun's gaze cut from Grady to Rocky. "Go on, spit it out."

"Well"—Rocky shifted in his saddle—"I'm not sure, but I think—that is, I'm pretty sure—the other redskin had a white cloth tied to the tip of his lance."

"What the hell difference does that make?" Shaun asked brusquely. "They were trespassing on Double R land. Probably looking to steal some more of our cattle."

"What if it was a flag of truce?" Emma asked. She grabbed her husband's arm. "What if they were coming to tell us about Kaylee? Now we'll never know!"

"Calm down, woman!" Shaun said gruffly. "You don't know that."

"Why else would they be coming here with a white flag?"

"If they had Kaylee, they would have brought her. They probably . . ."

Emma looked up at her husband, the color draining from her face. "What?" Her fingers dug into his arm. "What, Shaun?"

"Go on into the house, Emma. Make yourself a cup of tea and let me take care of this."

She stared at him, her eyes dark pools of pain. "He wouldn't," she said, her voice a choked whisper. "We saved his life. Oh, my poor Kay . . ."

Shaun wrapped his arm around his wife's shoulders, afraid she might faint. "Grady, you and Rocky go dump that body, and then tell Noah I want a couple of the hands to stay close to the house till I get back."

"Right, boss."

"I'm right sorry about your daughter," Rocky told

Emma. He glanced briefly at Shaun, then turned and rode after Grady.

"Not as sorry as those damned redskins will be when we find them," Garth said.

Shaun patted his wife's arm, then swung into the saddle. "Don't worry, Emma. We'll find her."

Emma nodded, but deep in her heart she was afraid it was already too late.

Chapter 9

Kaylee sat in the shadows, trying to be inconspicuous. She had never been surrounded by so many people, men and women who not only looked and dressed different but spoke a diffcrent language as well. As near as she could tell, there were about thirty adults in Blue Hawk's band, mostly elderly men and women, and perhaps a dozen children.

Earlier that evening, Blue Hawk had introduced Kaylee to his grandmother, Wichapi. Later, Kaylee had watched Wichapi drop heated stones into some sort of animal paunch filled with water. The old woman had added chunks of meat and wild vegetables. Kaylee had stared at the meat suspiciously, recalling that Shaun had once told her that Indians ate their dogs and horses.

While waiting for the meat to cook, Wichapi had brushed the tangles out of Kaylee's hair. Kaylee had tried to refuse the offer, but the old woman had insisted. Kaylee had no idea what the brush was made of, but it had served the purpose and now her hair fell in soft waves down her back and over her shoulders.

The meal was served in bowls made of wood and eaten with spoons made of deer horn. When Kaylee asked Blue Hawk what kind of meat it was, he grinned at her and said beef. She knew by the gleam in his eye that it was Randall beef. Somehow, that made her feel better.

And now she sat in the shadows, fighting a wave of homesickness, while three old men beat on a drum and a dozen warriors danced. She thought it strange that only the men danced. As far as she could tell, there was no rhyme or reason to the steps. Each man moved in his own way, as if lost in his own world. She found it fascinating to watch. Later the women did dance, their steps much more subdued than those of the men.

The Lakota were a handsome people. The young women were, for the most part, tall and willowy, with delicate figures, long blue-black hair, dark eyes, and dusky skin.

Blue Hawk's grandmother sat beside her. Kaylee had been surprised by the old woman's kindness to her. After all, she was a white woman, the enemy, yet Wichapi treated her kindly. When Wichapi had brushed her hair, it reminded Kaylee of how much she missed being home. Sometimes, before bed, Emma would brush Kaylee's hair. It was a private, quiet time, an opportunity for Kaylee to share her hopes and dreams with her mother.

Blue Hawk sat on the opposite side of the circle with the other men. He seemed to be feeling remarkably well for one so recently wounded. The men he had sent to parley with Shaun should be back soon, and then this whole nightmare would be over.

That thought had no sooner crossed her mind than she heard a distant shout, the drumming of hoofbeats. Several warriors sprang to their feet, and there was a high-pitched wail.

Overcome by a sudden sense of foreboding, Kaylee looked across the circle at Blue Hawk.

Blue Hawk rose slowly to his feet. He glanced at Kaylee, then joined a group of men gathering around the warrior who had just ridden into camp.

Hands clasped, she listened to the swell of angry

voices, wished she could shut out the heart-wrenching wail that pierced the air.

She stood up when Blue Hawk approached her, his face grave.

"What is it?" she asked anxiously. "What's wrong?"

"One of the warriors I sent to your people has returned."

She felt a sudden coldness in the pit of her stomach. "One of them?"

"The other was killed."

She stared at Blue Hawk. His eyes were dark with anger, his jaw clenched. She felt a rush of guilt. His people had treated her kindly; hers had killed one of his warriors. Would they take revenge on her for what her people had done? "What happens now?"

"We will leave this place in the morning."

Fear turned to panic at the thought of going further from home. "Leave? Why? For where?"

"We will go north and join with the people of Crazy Horse."

"Crazy Horse!" It was a name well known in the territory. She had heard of horrible atrocities committed by Crazy Horse and his warriors. She had been only seven years old when a war party led by Crazy Horse had massacred Captain William Fetterman and his troops near Fort Phil Kearny. The incident had been written up in the local newspaper, and her stepfather had talked of nothing else for days. She could still remember Shaun calling Fetterman a damn fool for letting the Indians lure him into a trap.

Blue Hawk nodded. "He is the leader of the Oglala Bad Face band. We will spend the summer with his people in the Paha Sapa. Many bands will join together there to celebrate the Sun Dance."

"But I need to go home!"

"So do my people, but it is not to be. We will leave tomorrow at dawn."

*   *   *

He was as good as his word. Wichapi woke Kaylee
from a sound sleep while it was still dark outside.
Yawning, she stumbled outside and stood there, shivering, while the Lakota dismantled their camp. She
watched in amazement as the women took the tipis
down in a matter of minutes. Young boys rounded up
the horses. In less than an hour they were riding north.
Blue Hawk rode ahead of her, Wichapi to her left.

Kaylee glanced over her shoulder. The Indians
stretched out behind her in a long line. The warriors
were all mounted; most carried bows and arrows, a
few carried lances. The older women and small children rode double, the young women and older children walked. A herd of perhaps two dozen horses,
mostly mares and yearlings, came last, followed by two
warriors. Kaylee patted Dusty's neck, glad that Blue
Hawk had let her keep the mare. At the moment
Dusty was her only link to home. She wondered how
she would ever get back home now. Surely they were
looking for her, but they would never find her—not
now.

Tears blurred her eyes at the thought of never
seeing her mother again. They were more than mother
and daughter. Emma was her best friend, her confi-
dante. And Randy they had played together, grown
up together. Randy had been the first boy she danced
with, the first boy she kissed. Had he made it home
all right? Was he healing from his injury? Would he
ever forgive her for getting him involved in this mess?

Thoughts of escape rose in her mind. Somehow she
had to get away, had to find her way back home.

They rode for several hours. It was pretty country.
Kaylee concentrated on the scenery in an effort to
take her mind off her predicament. The prairie was
covered with tall grass that waved gently in the mild
summer breeze. There were mountains in the distance,

thick with pines that were such a dark green they looked almost black. Once she spied a trio of deer resting in a copse of trees; later she saw an eagle soaring high overhead. Now and then they crossed a stream, and when they did, the Indians paused to let their horses drink.

It was late afternoon when they stopped to rest the horses. Kaylee dismounted with a low groan, grateful for a chance to stretch her back and legs. She rode often at home, but not for hours and hours at a time.

She led Dusty down to the stream, idly patting the mare's shoulder while she drank her fill.

The Indian women unpacked food and passed it to their families. The children ate quickly, then began to play, the boys chasing each other, the girls playing with dolls made of buckskin. The warriors stood in small groups, talking. She noticed that several of them remained mounted, apparently keeping watch for enemies.

Wichapi handed her a strip of dried meat and an odd-looking patty. Seeing her frown, the older woman pointed at the patty and said, *"Wakapapi wasna,"* as if that explained everything.

Kaylee stared at it, wondering what it was. Just then, Blue Hawk came by to see how she was doing.

"What is this?" she asked, holding up the patty.

"Wakapapi wasna. Pemmican. It is made from pounded meat and chokecherries and fat."

Kaylee grimaced. It sounded awful.

"Taste it," he said.

Kaylee took a small bite. It was surprisingly good, and she ate it all, then licked her fingers.

"Here," Blue Hawk said and handed her his own patty.

"Don't you want it?" Kaylee asked.

"There is more."

"Thank you. I'm sorry about what happened to your friend."

"I should have gone myself." A muscle worked in his jaw. "It is my fault he is dead. My fault my people have no guns."

"You can't blame yourself for what . . . for what my stepfather did."

"I was a fool once to think the *wasichu* would honor his word when he promised me guns for horses. A fool twice to think they would honor a flag of truce. *Wasichu* have no honor."

"That's not true," she replied, stung that he held her people in such low esteem.

He looked at her, his expression harsh, and when he spoke, his voice was filled with anger. "The *wasichu* chief promised my people that the Paha Sapa would be ours so long as the grass was green and the sky was blue, so long as water flowed in the rivers. Do the sacred mountains still belong to the Lakota? No! The *wasichu* diggers came and found gold in our mountains, and now they say that our people must leave their land. They say we must live on reservations on the white man's charity. They have fouled the rivers looking for yellow iron. They kill the buffalo for their tongues and hides and leave the meat to rot in the sun. They would see us all dead as well."

It was an impassioned speech, and the truth of it could not be denied. Even worse, she had heard that the government gave free ammunition to buffalo hunters, because the more animals they killed, the fewer the tribes would have available to them. Perhaps Blue Hawk's low opinion was justified.

She had often heard Shaun and the other ranchers talking about the "Indian problem," but it had never affected her, not until now. Shaun had complained of losing cattle from time to time. Other ranches, deeper into Indian territory, had been attacked. Homes had been destroyed, people had been killed. But the fighting had never touched anyone she knew, never af-

fected her personally. Now, because she had saved
Blue Hawk's life, she was suddenly in the midst of it,
surrounded by people who were the enemy.

She glanced at the men and women around her.
They wore clothing made of animal skins, painted
their faces and bodies, wore feathers in their hair. But
they did not act like the savages Shaun proclaimed
them to be. It was easy to see that the women loved
their children. The men cared for their families. The
mothers sang lullabies to their babies. The children
were well behaved. She heard them laugh; oddly, she
could not recall hearing any of them cry.

She looked at the land around her, acres and acres
of prairie, with the mountains in the distance, and
wondered why there was no room for the Indians.

It was a question that repeated itself several times
that day as the hours passed and they rode on and on
across the vast land. Her back and shoulders ached.
Her legs grew weary, the skin chafed by the saddle.
Sweat pooled between her breasts.

Finally, when she was beginning to think they were
going to ride until nightfall, Blue Hawk signaled for
a halt. Kaylee slid wearily off Dusty's back. Blue
Hawk came for her horse, assuring her that he would
be back soon.

A new camp was set up in a remarkably short time.
Everyone had something to do. Everyone but her. She
stood to one side, a stranger, ill at ease, while fires
were started, horses looked after, babies fed.

It was amazing, she thought, how quickly and effi-
ciently the women worked, making a section of prairie
seem like home in no time at all. Some of the women set
up their tipis; others spread their bedrolls on the ground.

They ate pemmican and jerky for dinner, and the
camp settled down for the night.

Small groups gathered here and there, talking and
laughing.

Overcome by a wave of homesickness, Kaylee sat on the blanket Wichapi had given her, apart from the others

A short time later Blue Hawk came to sit beside her.

"You are sad, Kay-lee."

She nodded, afraid that if she tried to talk she would start crying.

"It is a hard thing, to be far from home, among strangers."

She nodded again. She had never been away from home before, never been cut off from her loved ones. Never realized what a sheltered life she had led, until now.

"Come," he said, "walk with me."

She looked up at him, touched by the gentleness in his voice. When he offered her his hand, it seemed like the most natural thing in the world to take it. He drew her effortlessly to her feet. The warmth in his hand flowed up her arm and straight to her heart. Hand in hand, they walked away from the camp.

Blue Hawk looked up at the sky, which was clear save for a few slow-drifting clouds.

"It was on a night like this when my friend Otaktay and I raided the Crow camp. I told my father where we were going, but not my mother, for I did not wish to worry her. Before we entered the camp we put on Crow clothing that we had gotten from earlier battles. That way we could look like our enemies."

"Why are they your enemies?"

"It has always been so."

"Oh. Go on."

"I waited until a Crow man went out through the tipis to relieve himself. Then I went into the camp that way, so that anyone who was awake and saw me would think it was the same person returning and not be suspicious.

"It was summer and the tipis were close together. Many horses wandered within the camp circle. The best horses were picketed near the tipi entrances.

"When one enters an enemy camp, one must walk boldly, as if he belongs there, and this I did." She heard the smile in his voice. "When someone spoke to me, I nodded and walked on, as if I had business elsewhere, and in this way I walked through the whole camp, looking at the best horses. I remembered a buckskin I had seen when the Crow attacked our camp the summer before, and that was the horse I sought. When I found him, I left the camp.

"I met Otaktay and told him where the good horses were, where the largest herd was located. Then I took off my Crow clothing and put on my own. We waited until the camp was asleep, and then we snuck in. I took the buckskin I had picked out earlier, and Otaktay took a fine black, and then we stampeded the largest herd, driving them before us through the camp."

Blue Hawk grinned with the memory.

"Why did you steal their horses?"

He looked at her with surprise. "Because it is a good thing, to steal horses from the enemy."

Kaylee shook her head. "Stealing is wrong."

"It is wrong for Lakota to steal from Lakota. It is not wrong to steal from your enemy."

She stopped walking. "You shouldn't steal people, either."

He stopped and turned to face her. The darkness seemed to close in around them, cocooning them in a space and time all their own. She was acutely aware of him, of the tension that hummed between them whenever he was near. Without conscious thought, she placed her hand on his arm. He was all that was familiar in this alien place.

"Kay-lee."

She gazed into his eyes and didn't know what to say, wasn't sure what it was she felt whenever he was close to her. But he knew. She could hear his voice in her mind. *Tell me you do not feel it, Kay-lee,* it said. *Tell me your heart does not pound like a buffalo stampede whenever I am near.*

It was pounding now, pounding so hard, so loud, she was sure he could hear it. She wanted him, she thought, wanted him to hold her, to make love to her. Shocked by the turn of her thoughts, she jerked her hand from his arm, and immediately regretted it.

Desire flowed between them when he took a step toward her, closing the distance between them. His hand brushed her arm, moved up to cup her cheek, as if he felt the need to touch her in return. She stared up at him, warmth spreading through her. They stood that way for what seemed like a long time, with his hand lightly framing her face, and then he lowered it and moved away.

"Come," he said, his voice strangely thick. "You must rest. We will be leaving early in the morning."

With a nod, she followed him back to camp.

But sleep that night was a long time coming.

Chapter 10

Shaun sat near one of the campfires the men had lit at dusk, his shoulders hunched beneath a sheepskin jacket. He grunted his thanks when one of the men handed him a cup of coffee.

What if Emma had been right? What if those two redskins had been coming to dicker a trade for his stepdaughter? Such things had happened before. He spent a quiet moment cursing Tom Grady for shooting one of the redskins and for letting the other one escape. But the shooting was his responsibility; after all, Grady had been acting on Shaun's orders, had done exactly what Shaun would have done in his place—shoot first and ask questions later.

But in this case . . . Shaun shook his head. What if Emma had been right? What if, unlikely as it seemed, the Injuns had been bringing word of Kaylee?

He blew out a sigh. Kaylee had been a gangly child when he married Emma, a constant reminder that Emma had loved another man before she came to him. He had hoped he would come to love the child as much as he loved the mother, but Kaylee had been distant, distrustful. He had put in long hours running the ranch back then, even longer than he did now, and he hadn't had the time or the patience to try and win her over. And then, suddenly, it was too late. Kaylee was no longer a child, but a young woman. He knew it grieved Emma that he wasn't a real father to Kaylee, that his stepdaughter avoided him whenever possible. And now this. Would Emma believe he had done his best to find her daughter?

He swore under his breath. He loved Emma, and yet it seemed he had brought her nothing but unhappiness. Nothing but hard work and three miscarriages. And now this.

He glanced up as Garth Jackson came to squat beside him.

"You look like a whipped cur," Jackson said gruffly.

"Yeah, well, I feel like one, too," Shaun retorted. "I've been thinking about what we might find when we catch them Injuns."

Jackson sobered. "If they've ruined Kaylee, I'll see every last one of them in hell."

"What about if they've just killed her?" Shaun asked bitterly.

Jackson eyed him narrowly. "You're distraught. I'll overlook that."

Shaun stared into the flames again. He couldn't go home without Kaylee, or solid proof of what had happened to her. He couldn't face Emma and tell her that he had failed. Couldn't leave her to wonder if her daughter was dead or alive.

Shaun had always believed you paid the consequences for your own actions. His headstrong stepdaughter had defied all reason by taking in a wounded savage. By his own harsh code, she was paying the price for her foolishness now. But Emma lived by a different, gentler code. Shaun muttered an oath. He had let Emma down so often in the past, he couldn't do it again, couldn't go back and see the hurt in her eyes. She wouldn't blame him. Oh, no, never that. She would assure him that she knew he had done his best, and then she would comfort him.

If Kaylee was alive, whether injured or "ruined," as

Jackson had so delicately put it, Shaun was going to get her home to Emma. No matter the cost.

This time he wasn't going to let his wife down.

He had to make this right. Dammit, whatever the cost, he had to make it right.

Chapter 11

They had been riding for hours and hours. The countryside was still beautiful, but Kaylee's appreciation of it was dimmed by the fact that her legs ached, her back hurt, her shoulders were sore. And she was tired, so tired.

Not surprising, since she'd had so much trouble getting to sleep the night before. Last night she had told herself it was the unfamiliar surroundings that made sleeping difficult. After all, she was accustomed to sleeping on a soft mattress beneath clean sheets, not lying on the ground wrapped up in furs. But now, in the light of day, she knew that hadn't been the only thing keeping her awake. It had been thoughts of Blue Hawk lying only a few feet away that had kept her awake far into the night. She kept remembering the look in his dark eyes. The sound of his voice. The feel of his skin beneath her fingertips. The touch of his hand on her cheek. The way the very atmosphere between them seemed charged, like the air before a storm. The way her heart pounded at the mere sight of him.

This afternoon she found herself constantly looking for him. She never tired of watching him. He rode tall and straight astride a big spotted horse. Clad in only a clout and moccasins, an eagle feather tied in his long black hair, a single jagged stripe of red paint on his cheek, Blue Hawk looked every inch the savage her stepfather would claim he was, and yet she knew he was not a savage. She had seen the tenderness with which Blue Hawk treated his grandmother, the way the children clustered around him, their huge dark eyes shining with affection and admiration. He was a man who was respected by his people, a man they looked to for wisdom and advice.

Wichapi rode beside her, and Kaylee was grateful for that because Blue Hawk dropped back every now and then to make sure the old woman was all right. At least Kaylee told herself that was his reason for riding with them from time to time, even though she knew, deep in her heart, that he was checking on her, too. She felt a surge of excitement in the depths of her belly, a warmth in the region of her heart, whenever she saw him riding toward her.

Thinking about him, about the new feelings awakening deep inside her, left her feeling confused and a little on edge.

It was early afternoon when they stopped to rest the horses. Kaylee slid wearily to the ground, surprised that her legs didn't bend like wet reeds. Blue Hawk rode up a moment later to help his grandmother dismount.

The old woman smiled at him, then hobbled over to sit in the shade of a nearby cottonwood.

"Is she all right?" Kaylee asked. "Is there anything I can do for her?"

Blue Hawk shook his head. "She is stronger than she looks," he said, his gaze on his grandmother. He tapped his chest with his forefinger. "Strong in here."

Taking up the reins of Wichapi's horse and his own, Blue Hawk led them to the stream to drink. Kaylee followed him, leading Dusty.

"How soon will we get to wherever we're going?" Kaylee asked.

He shrugged. "As long as it takes."

She groaned softly. What kind of answer was that? And when they got there, then what?

She stood beside Blue Hawk while the horses drank. For a moment she pretended she belonged there, at his side, that she was an Indian girl. The doeskin dress and moccasins were comfortable, though she felt strange, vulnerable somehow, without her chemise, petticoats, and stockings.

Berry bushes grew wild on the other side of the stream. Several of the women and children waded across and began to pick the fruit. The children laughed, the juice running down their chins as they ate the berries. Smiling at the antics of their children, the women gathered the fruit into leather pouches.

One little girl with thick black braids wandered away from the others toward a distant bush. Kaylee grinned as she watched the girl pluck two handfuls of dark red berries and stuff them into her mouth. Juice oozed from the corners of her mouth and dripped down her chin. The girl licked her lips and hastily picked more berries, eating them as fast as she could pick them.

Kaylee laughed at the girl's antics, and then gasped in horror as a large bear suddenly rose up from behind the clump of bushes. Its snout was stained red. At first Kaylee thought it was blood, but then she realized it was only berry juice. She froze in terror for herself, and the child.

True to her upbringing, the child stood very still, making no sound that might startle the bear or trigger an attack. Kaylee was awestruck at such discipline in one so young. She also noticed that no cry of warning had been needed. At first sight of the bear, everyone had gone still and quiet.

Blue Hawk thrust the horses' reins into Kaylee's hand. "Stay here," he muttered curtly.

He waded across the stream without any weapon save the knife sheathed at his belt. Several other warriors started to follow him, nocking arrows, raising lances, but Blue Hawk waved them back.

He made his way toward the little girl with unhurried, deliberate strides. He slowly picked the child up and thrust her behind him into the arms of her mother. The child's mother remained motionless, as if a nearly naked man was all the bulwark she and her child needed against the bear.

For a timeless moment, the bear stood on its hind legs, nostrils sniffing the wind, lips curled back to reveal sharp yellow teeth dripping pink saliva, its small eyes focused on the man who confronted it.

Kaylee, too, had eyes only for Blue Hawk.

None of the Indians spoke or moved. This confrontation was between Blue Hawk and the bear.

Kaylee feared that lances and buffalo bows would have little effect on the beast if it decided to attack them. She stared at the sharp teeth and long, curved claws that could so easily rip into soft flesh. She doubted if even the old Army Springfield held by Mato'zi would be able to bring the beast down.

A movement to her left caught her eye, and she saw that several warriors had inched toward the edge of the stream, their weapons drawn.

Kaylee bit down on her lower lip, her hands clenched at her sides. Blue Hawk was a tall man, lean and well muscled, yet he appeared small and defenseless beside the bear's bulk; the knife sheathed at his side looked like a harmless child's toy when compared to the bear's curved claws.

Across the creek a horse whinnied nervously, and one of the dogs whined. A second dog barked a challenge. The bear let out a growl, its massive jaws snapping at the air.

Blue Hawk took a slow step forward, his stance confident but not threatening. *"Hau, mato sunkahu."* Hello, brother bear.

The bear lowered its massive head and sniffed.

"Heyab iya yo, sunkahu mita," Blue Hawk said, his voice low and calm. *"Letan keyab eyaya yo."* Go away, my brother. Get out of here.

The bear shook its head. Pink saliva sprayed from its mouth.

The warriors waited on the bank, weapons at the ready. Sweat glistened on their bodies. Every muscle was taut, every sense focused on the scene playing out across the river.

Blue Hawk took another step forward. *"Heyab iya yo, sunkahu mita. Henala."* Go away, my brother. I have spoken.

With a bellow that seemed to shake the very ground, the bear swiped at Blue Hawk, its claws coming perilously close to his face.

Blue Hawk didn't flinch.

The bear regarded him for several long moments, and then, with a disdainful glance at the other puny humans before it, dropped regally and majestically to all fours, turned, and lumbered away.

Relief rushed out of Kaylee in a long sigh. Never in all her life had she seen such a show of courage as that displayed by Blue Hawk.

Some of the women quickly scooped up their children and hurried back across the stream. Others picked as many berries as their bags would hold and then they, too, waded back across the stream.

Blue Hawk was the last to cross.

Kaylee shook her head as he walked up to her. "Are you crazy?" she exclaimed. "You could have been killed! That bear could have ripped you to shreds."

"Mato is my brother," he said calmly.

"Your brother? What does that mean?"

"Come," Blue Hawk said. "We cannot talk of it here."

He turned the horses over to a boy standing nearby, and then, as was becoming his habit, he took her hand and they walked away from the others until they came to a shady place. Blue Hawk sat down, and Kaylee sat beside him.

"I tell you this, though it is *wakan*," he began. "Sacred to me. I tell you so that you may understand."

Wrapped in layers of anticipation, Kaylee nodded, aware that something rare was happening between them but not knowing exactly what it was.

"It is the custom among my people for young men to seek a vision," he began, and his voice took on a storytelling rhythm. "So it was, in the summer of my sixteenth year, that I sought a vision to guide me. I cleansed myself in the sweat lodge, and then I left our village and went to Mato Paha to be alone. Three days I lingered there. I did not eat or sleep, but prayed to Wakan Tanka, begging for a vision. Morning and evening, I offered sage and tobacco to the four winds, to Wakan Tanka, to Mother Earth."

He paused, his gaze fixed on the horizon, remembering. "It was dawn, the morning of the third day, when Mato appeared to me. He said he had been watching me for many years. Because I did not run at his coming, because I did not show my fear, he said he would be my spirit guide. He promised that I should have long life, that I should always have his strength and cunning. 'Your enemies will fall before you,' he said, 'and my spirit shall guard you in battle so long as you walk the Life Path of the People, so long as you do not shed Mato's blood.'"

Kaylee wanted to interrupt, to tell him he was crazy, that men and bears couldn't speak to each other, but she knew by the sound of his voice and the look in his eyes that, as impossible as it was for her to comprehend, he believed every word.

"You do not believe me?"

"It goes against everything I have been taught, but, yes, I do believe you," she said, and wondered if maybe she was crazy, too.

"Hecheto welo," he said, smiling at her. "It is good."

"Yes." She smiled back at him, pleased that he wanted her to understand, warmed by the knowledge that he trusted her enough to share a part of his life that he considered sacred.

He stood up and offered her his hand. "Come," he said, "It is time to go."

A short time later the Indians were mounted and riding again.

Long after they had left the stream behind, Kaylee found herself glancing over her shoulder, half expecting to see the bear come charging after them. She looked at the countryside with new respect, even fear. At the ranch, the most vicious thing she had ever faced was a first-time mother cow protecting her calf. She had heard the cry of coyotes and wolves, even seen them from a distance. But nothing had ever been quite as terrifying as seeing that bear rise up from the bushes, its snout and teeth stained red with berry juice.

Apparently her companions harbored no such fears. They continued on with their journey as though nothing untoward had happened. Shaun said the Indians were godless savages, incapable of any human emotion or affection. But she had seen firsthand that Shaun was sadly mistaken. And now she had seen something that nothing in her schooling or her religion had prepared her for, something magical, mystical.

Since being with the Lakota, she had watched the women care for their children as tenderly as her own mother had cared for her. She had seen old men and women sitting on the ground surrounded by little ones. When she asked Blue Hawk what they were doing, he told her that the ancient ones were telling the children the stories and legends of the People.

She wondered if there would be a new story now, a new legend, to be told around the campfires, of how Mato the Bear had been disturbed by a small child while feasting, and how his brother, Blue Hawk, had spoken to him and sent him away.

But for now the incident was too fresh in her mind, too frightening, for her to see it as some kind of Indian fairy tale. She cast her thoughts back to one of the stories Blue Hawk had told her, about a wolf and a raccoon and a dull brown bird.

She tried to remember it now to pass the time. How had it gone? If she recalled correctly, a squirrel had passed a coyote and made an insulting remark. The coyote got angry and chased the squirrel. The squirrel scrambled up a tree and crawled out on a limb overhanging a river. When the coyote saw the squirrel's reflection, he jumped into the water and almost drowned. Wet and weary, the coyote climbed out of the water and fell asleep on the grass. While he was sleeping, the squirrel covered the coyote's eyes with mud.

When the coyote awoke, he couldn't see. Scared and blind, he began to cry. A small brown bird stopped to ask the coyote what was wrong. The coyote told the bird what happened and asked if he would help. The bird said he would, if the coyote could make him beautiful. The coyote told the bird he knew of a place where the bird could find some blue paint.

The bird thought he would like to be blue instead of brown, and so he pecked the mud from the coyote's eyes. The coyote took him to a place where there was a pool of blue paint, and the bird dipped himself in the paint until he was no longer a dull brown bird but had become a lovely shade of blue.

It was a sweet story, Kaylee mused. Maybe someday she would tell it to her own children.

The thought had no sooner crossed her mind than Blue Hawk rode up beside her. His gaze met hers, strong and direct, and it went through her like a bolt of lightning. She had a sudden mental image of herself standing beside Blue Hawk, a baby with straight black hair and tawny skin cradled in her arms. Heat rose in her cheeks, heat that had nothing to do with the sun that burned her skin but everything to do with the way Blue Hawk was looking at her.

They rode until late afternoon and then made camp beside a narrow, winding river bordered by a thick stand of timber. Kaylee helped Wichapi set up her lodge, then walked downriver to gather wood for a fire. She saw several young girls moving through the timber, talking and laughing as they worked, at ease with each other as only good friends or longtime companions can be. Kaylee felt a rush of homesickness as she watched them. Their camaraderie only served to emphasize that she didn't belong here, would never belong here.

She moved away from the others, walking deeper into the trees, pausing from time to time to pick up sticks for kindling, as well as a few larger pieces of wood. She wondered what her mother was doing, if Emma had told Shaun about Blue Hawk, if the ranch hands were still looking for her or if they had given up. She thought about Randy. Every time she saw his gelding being ridden by one of Blue Hawk's people she felt a fresh pang of guilt for leaving him back at the line shack, unconscious and alone. Had he made it home okay? She was certain she had loosened the rope on one hand enough for him to get free.

She thought briefly of the twins, Charlene and Geraldine Thomas. They lived on a neighboring ranch. They were both rather prim and proper and had nothing in common with Kaylee other than the fact that

they were all female. The Thomas sisters enjoyed nee-
dlepoint and baking and making preserves, while
Kaylee preferred riding with the cowboys, rounding
up strays, and skinny-dipping in the creek.

She heaved a sigh, wondering if she would ever find
a place where she belonged. Shaun was forever telling
Emma it was time to take her in hand, to teach her
some womanly skills, but Kaylee didn't want to spend
her time cooped up in the house, learning to cook and
mend and do fancy embroidery. She wasn't interested
in the latest fashions, didn't care about learning to
play the piano. She liked to be outside, to feel the sun
on her face and the wind in her hair.

She had been walking for some time when she realized she could no longer hear the laughter of the other
girls. Stopping near a hollow log, she glanced over her
shoulder. No one was in sight, nothing but trees as far
as she could see. How had she walked so far? And
which way was the camp?

She cocked her head, listening, but she heard nothing, only the sound of her own breathing, the soft
soughing of the wind through the leaves, and the chit-
tering of a squirrel on a branch above her head.

Remembering Blue Hawk's story, Kaylee grinned
at the furry red critter. "Are you insulting me, Mr.
Squirrel?"

The squirrel reared up on its hind legs and chattered
at her some more.

Kaylee laughed. "I'm not a coyote, so hush, unless
you can tell me how to get back to the camp."

A prickle ran down Kaylee's back as she heard a
howl in the distance. The squirrel stared at her
through shiny black eyes. Then, with a flick of its
bushy tail, it disappeared into a hole in the tree
trunk.

Kaylee shivered. She was lost. Night was falling.
And there were animals in the woods. An image of

the bear, its teeth stained with berry juice, flashed across her mind.

"Blue Hawk," she whispered. "Blue Hawk, where am I? Where are you?"

Her only answer was the distant howl of a wolf.

Chapter 12

Blue Hawk nodded reassuringly as he spoke to an elderly woman. Yes, he told her, they would soon reach the land of their brothers, the Oglala Bad Face band. Crazy Horse and his people would take them in. There was nothing to worry about. His scouts had assured him there were no *wasichu* in the area, no enemy Crow lurking about. They would camp here for a day so the old ones could rest.

He sent two of the men out to hunt for game, picked three others to keep watch, and sent two boys to guard the horses.

He helped Mato'zi find his mother, promised young Tete'kesa he could go on the next hunt, picked Kinma up when she fell, and wiped away her tears.

And all the while he looked for Kaylee, his eyes searching for the bright gold of her hair. It wasn't until his grandmother told him the evening meal would soon be ready that he began to worry. It would be dark soon. He went from campfire to campfire, asking after her. It was Tatoka's daughter, Skoso'ta, who said she remembered seeing the *wasicun winyan* gathering wood.

"You did not stay with her?" Blue Hawk asked.

Skoso'ta shook her head. "She seemed to want to be alone, so we let her be. I am sorry, Blue Hawk, if we did wrong."

He shook his head. "You did nothing wrong, Skoso'ta. *Pilamaya.*"

He walked through the rest of the camp, certain that he would not find her there but needing to make sure, his heart growing heavier with each passing minute.

When he had circled the camp, he struck out for the stand of timber that grew along this side of the river, his gaze searching the ground for sign. Kaylee had taken to wearing moccasins all the time now. He followed her tracks until the carpet of pine needles grew too thick to hold a print and the darkness made spotting any disturbance of the needles difficult.

It grew darker as he moved deeper into the forest. He paused intermittently to listen, but heard nothing save the restless sighing of the wind and the soft scurrying sounds of night creatures emerging from their holes.

He thought of calling her name, but quickly dismissed the idea. A hunter did not draw unnecessary attention to himself or his prey. Had she run away again? Would she be foolish enough to strike out on her own, on foot, after dark? Every Lakota child knew there were dangers on the prairie at night. But Kaylee was not Lakota.

He moved through the trees quietly, patiently, exercising all his considerable tracking skills, listening for that extra sense he was beginning to feel when it came to her, as if he could know which way she had gone if he paid close attention.

He paused when he found a place where a branch had been pulled clear. A single strand of golden hair told him she had passed this way. She was still gathering wood for his fire. He moved on and found another place where the pine needles had been disturbed.

It was almost completely dark under the trees now.

He moved silently, berating himself for striking out on his own. He should have asked some of the warriors to help him in his search, could not believe he had acted so rashly. He had no excuse except that the white woman had bewitched him. From the first moment he had seen her, he had thought of little else. Mato had told him to follow the woman—and now it seemed it was his fate to do so. It mattered not that she was the enemy, that her ways were not his ways. He had touched her and felt the pull between them, felt his spirit speak to hers, felt hers respond. Had the attraction that flowed so sweet and strong between them frightened her away?

He hunkered down on his heels to consider this thing. Had he frightened her away? He had thought her different from other white women, had been so certain that when she looked at him she saw a man, not an Indian. Had he spoken too soon? He knew that learning to live with his people, learning the Lakota customs and language, would not be easy for Kaylee. He knew there would be those among his people who would never accept her, who would always hate and mistrust her because of her white skin, just as her people would never accept him.

But none of that mattered. She was his, and he meant to keep her. Just when he had reached that decision eluded him. Perhaps it had been that first moment when he had looked up and seen her bending over him, her sky-blue eyes filled with compassion. Perhaps it had been her gentle touch that won his heart, or the fact that she had put the safety of a stranger above her own when she tended him. She had won his respect when she pointed her gun at him and insisted that he look after the injured boy before she agreed to help him return to his people. Perhaps, too, it was stronger than all those things, their connection as mysterious and mystical as his was to Mato.

But reasons didn't matter. She was his. Rocking on his heels, eyes closed, he gathered his power around him and waited, his whole being focused on Kaylee.

"Help me, Wakan Tanka."

Quiet settled around him, a stillness from within and without. Her image rose in his mind. He remembered the touch of her skin beneath his hand, the softness, the scent of it. He concentrated on her scent. Calling on the power of the bear that resided deep within him, he moved his head from side to side in imitation of Mato, sniffing the air.

And it came to him on the evening breeze, Kaylee's scent, and in the back of his mind he heard her voice, calling his name. *Blue Hawk. Blue Hawk, where are you?*

Opening his eyes, he sprang up and began to run.

It was almost full dark when Kaylee stopped walking and admitted she was hopelessly, thoroughly, completely lost. She told herself there was nothing to be afraid of. She had spent the night outdoors before, on roundups. Never alone, of course, but she was a big girl.

As she looked for a suitable place to spend the night, she told herself that there was nothing to be afraid of, that there was nothing in the dark that wasn't there during the day, even though she knew that was a lie.

She told herself Blue Hawk would find her, but she was having trouble believing that, too. If he was going to find her, wouldn't he have done so by now?

Suddenly weary, she dropped the firewood she'd gathered and sank down beside a tree, wishing she could start a fire, but she didn't have flint and steel, let alone kitchen matches. Closing her eyes, she rested the back of her head against the trunk. *Blue Hawk. Blue Hawk, where are you? Please, find me. I don't want to spend the night out here, alone, in the dark.*

She would just rest for a while, she thought. Just a few minutes, and then she would be on her way again.

If she was lucky, she would soon find her way back to the village.

She was thinking how nice it would be to snuggle up inside a nice soft, furry robe when she realized she was no longer alone. Fearful of what she might see, she opened her eyes.

The snake was coiled by her foot. She stared at it in horrified fascination, at the distinctive triangular-shaped head, at the long black tongue that darted in and out, in and out, testing the air.

Afraid to move, afraid to breathe, Kaylee sat there, frozen in place, her gaze locked on the snake.

A cold sweat broke out across Kaylee's brow, but she dared not wipe it away, dared not move. She had heard more than one cowboy talk about waking up out on the prairie and finding a rattlesnake curled up in the warmth of his blankets. Was that what this snake was doing? Seeking a warm place to spend the night?

She felt suddenly faint as the snake's head disappeared beneath the hem of her tunic. She couldn't faint, not now. The movement would surely make the snake strike. She had heard stories of men who had died after being bitten by a rattlesnake. It was a slow, horrible way to die.

And then, incredibly, it seemed as though she could hear Blue Hawk's voice calling her name, though the forest remained ominously silent. Could it be? Had she imagined it? She longed to cry out, to let him know where she was, to beg him to hurry, but she was afraid to move, dared not make a sound.

Here! She closed her eyes, her spirit calling to him. *I'm here. Hurry!*

The snake moved again, its head sliding a little further under her tunic. She clenched her hands as every primal instinct urged her to flee.

Blue Hawk, hurry. Please, please, hurry.

Was it her imagination, or did she hear someone moving toward her? Opening her eyes, she glanced from side to side without moving her head, went weak with relief when she saw Blue Hawk striding toward her.

"Kay-lee?" he called softly.

She stared at him, not daring to answer. Very slowly, she lowered her head.

Blue Hawk paused, wondering why she didn't answer. Was she hurt? In danger? He surveyed his surroundings. Seeing nothing to alarm him, he walked toward her once again. And then he heard it. The unmistakable warning rattle of *sinte hla.*

He stopped, his gaze searching for the snake. And then he saw it, coiled beside Kaylee's right ankle. The head was out of sight beneath the hem of her tunic.

"Kay-lee, do not move. No matter what happens, do not move."

She stared at him, her eyes wide and afraid, her face pale, damp with perspiration.

"Do you understand?"

She nodded once, her gaze never leaving his face.

Blue Hawk took a deep breath, touched by her trust in him. He wiped his palms dry on his clout. "Do not move," he warned again.

He didn't wait for her to answer. Lunging forward, he grabbed the snake by the tail with his left hand and gave a sharp tug.

The snake's head whipped around, striking at Blue Hawk.

In a heartbeat, Blue Hawk released the snake's tail with his left hand, grabbed the snake by the back of the head with his right hand, and hurled the rattler into the trees.

With a cry, Kaylee scrambled to her feet and fell into Blue Hawk's arms.

He held her tight, feeling her shudder as sobs of relief wracked her body. "Kay-lee, are you all right?"

She nodded.

"You are sure? *Sinte hla* did not strike?"

"N-no."

His hand stroked her hair. "You were very brave."

"I was very scared." She drew a long, shuddering breath.

He held her away from him a little, his gaze moving over her as if to reassure himself that she was all right. "Why did you run away?"

"I didn't. I wasn't. I was gathering wood." She pointed at the pile beside the tree. "I guess I wasn't paying attention to where I was going and I got lost. How did you find me?"

"I heard your spirit call to me."

She looked up at him, her eyes wide.

"You doubt me? Did your spirit not call out to me? Did you not ask me to find you, so that you would not have to spend the night out here alone?"

She nodded. "I—I heard your voice, too! In my mind, but—" Words failed her. She shivered. "How is that possible?"

"It is the magic between us." He lifted her hand and placed it over his heart. "From this day on, my heart will beat only for you."

She blinked at him, touched by his words, by the depth of emotion in his voice, the intensity in his eyes.

"Kay-lee." There was a reverence in his voice as he spoke her name, and then he drew her into his arms.

She rested her head against his shoulder, overcome by a sense of peace, of belonging. It felt so good to be in his arms. More than that, it felt right. His hand stroked her hair, slid down her back to draw her closer.

She looked up at him, her body quivering, her heart pounding. She wanted him, she thought, wanted him to hold her, to kiss her.

He gazed down at her, a knowing look in his eyes.

His arms tightened around her as he lowered his head and kissed her, ever so gently.

For all its gentleness, the kiss burned through Kaylee like a flame, and she clung to him, her hands loving the warmth of his skin, her body moving closer, closer, burning hotter, brighter.

It was wrong, she thought, wrong to kiss him like this, to feel like this. He was an Indian. He was supposed to be her enemy, but her heart refused to think of him in that way. She had been drawn to him from the first. She couldn't explain it, and now, with his arms tight around her and his mouth on hers, she needed no explanation. Right or wrong, she was where she belonged.

Blue Hawk felt the change in her, felt her hesitation melt away as she kissed him back.

He caressed her gently. Her skin was soft and warm. He cupped her breast, heard her gasp of surprise, and then she leaned into him, seeking his touch.

He could have taken her then, but she had no family to watch over her, no male cousins or brothers to protect her, no mother to guard her virtue. And as much as he desired her, he did not wish to shame her.

He kissed her again, then let her go.

Kaylee stared up at him, her eyes filled with desire. "Blue Hawk?"

"Come," he said, "let us go back."

"Do we have to?"

"You have no one to protect your honor, *chante mita,* so I shall do it for you."

She smiled at him, touched by his words, by his innate sense of decency. "So, you're going to protect me from you?"

He nodded, his expression solemn.

Kaylee ran her fingertips over his chest. He was beautiful, she thought, with his smooth copper-hued skin and midnight black hair.

Rising on tiptoe, she kissed him again. "What if I don't want to be protected?"

"Do not tempt me, Kay-lee."

"You find me tempting?" She looked up at him, felt her femininity stir to life. She had flirted with Randy from time to time, but this was different. With Randy, it had all been in fun, innocent, harmless. But not now.

Blue Hawk nodded. His dark eyes burned into hers, filled with desire.

She ran her hands over his shoulders. Such broad shoulders. She slid her hand down his right arm, her fingers kneading his biceps. She smiled as the muscle flexed. Hard as the proverbial rock, she thought.

"Kay-lee."

She heard the longing in his voice, the unspoken warning. Blue Hawk was not a boy like Randy, to tease and toy with, but a man, a warrior.

She took a step back. "I'm sorry."

"When I take you to my bed, you will be my woman," Blue Hawk said. "My wife."

"Wife!" she exclaimed softly.

He nodded.

"That's not possible."

"Why?" He frowned at her. "Have you a husband already?"

"No."

"You are promised to another?"

"No."

"Then you do not wish to be my woman?"

"Oh, but I do!" she said, and knew in that moment that it was true. Her mother had known her father only a handful of days before they were married, and Emma had never regretted her decision. *Love has nothing to do with how long two people have known each other,* she had once told Kaylee, *and everything to do with the feelings of your heart.*

"What will your grandmother say when you tell her?" Kaylee asked.

"She will not approve."

"Neither will my mother and my stepfather," she said, but when he looked at her the way he was looking at her now, what did it matter?

He put his finger beneath her chin. Tilting her head up a little, he kissed her. It was all the reassurance she needed.

Bending down, he picked up the wood she had gathered and tucked it under his left arm. "Come," he said, taking her hand in his. "Unci will be worrying."

It was full dark when they reached the outskirts of the camp. Kaylee looked at the lodges, at the women fixing dinner for their families. In spite of what she had said, she began to have doubts. What if his grandmother rejected her? What if his people refused to accept her? She didn't want to spend the rest of her life as an outcast. If his people would not accept her, and hers would not accept him, where would they live?

Blue Hawk stopped at the edge of the trees and placed the wood in her arms.

"Gathering wood is women's work," he explained.

"I guess I have a lot to learn."

"And I will teach you." He caressed her cheek. "Next time you leave camp, you will let me know."

"I will," she said fervently. "Believe me, I will."

Chapter 13

"We'll hit them just before dawn," Jackson said. He took a drink from his flask and then offered the flask to Shaun. The two of them were huddled around a small fire, neither ready to turn in. The other men slept nearby. "It's a small camp. Lenny said they've only got three sentries. We'll take them out, then attack."

Shaun took a drink, grimacing as the whiskey seared down his throat. It had seemed to take forever to close the gap on the redskins. Some of the men questioned Garth's slow pursuit, but Shaun knew it was to keep from raising a suspicious cloud of dust that might alert the Indians to their presence.

He glanced at the men sleeping nearby. There was more tossing and turning among his own men than usual. He suspected some of them were awake, worrying about what the dawn would bring. He had a couple of Civil War vets on the payroll and a couple of men who had fought Indians before. They were sleeping soundly.

So were Jackson's hard-bitten riders. Only a few of Jackson's men seemed like ordinary cowboys; the others seemed more familiar with weapons than cattle. One of the men who had ridden point today had worn a pair of ivory-handled Colts on cross-draw holsters.

Shaun grunted softly. "Are you sure this is a good idea? What if they kill Kaylee when we attack? Hell, we don't even know for sure that she's with this bunch."

Jackson shook his head. "They won't risk killing a hostage with us right there," he said confidently. "Don't worry, we'll find her. She'll be easy to spot with that blond hair."

Shaun had his doubts that it would be as easy as Jackson seemed to think, but he didn't have any better ideas. Jackson seemed to think the Indians were headed for some kind of tribal gathering. If that was true, Shaun and his men had to strike now, while they outnumbered the warriors and before they got any deeper into Sioux territory.

It had to work, Shaun thought bleakly. He remembered the look in Emma's eyes when he rode away. He couldn't go home without Kaylee. Emma had already lost three babies. He was terribly afraid that it would kill her if she lost Kaylee, too.

Chapter 14

Kaylee woke to the harsh rattle of rapid-fire rifles. Something thwapped through the hide walls of the lodge. Gunfire! The realization brought her fully awake. She heard the frantic cries of frightened women, a baby's sobbing, the scream of a man in pain.

She bolted upright, her heart pounding. Were they being attacked? "Blue Hawk . . ."

He was kneeling at the doorway of the lodge, an arrow nocked to his bow. "Stay inside with Unci, Kaylee."

"You're not going out there!" she exclaimed.

"I must." He drew back the bowstring and released the arrow in one smooth motion, grabbed another arrow from the quiver over his shoulder, and then he was gone.

Scrambling to her feet, she hurried to the entrance of the tipi and looked out.

It was like a scene from a nightmare. Everywhere she looked, she saw women running, some dragging their children behind them or clutching infants to their breasts. Men armed with bows and lances or old rifles fought to protect their escape. The earth shook as riders burst into the camp. She had thought the attackers were soldiers, but now she saw they were cowboys. A torch arched through the air and the lodge across the way burst into flame, scattering sparks and bits of burning hide.

Wichapi was speaking to her, tugging on her arm.

There was a dull thud against the back of the lodge. Kaylee screamed as Blue Hawk's tipi caught fire. Grabbing the old woman by the arm, she ducked outside and began to run away from the camp, away from the nightmare that was all too real. A nightmare that grew suddenly worse as Blue Hawk's grandmother tripped and fell, pulling Kaylee to the ground with her.

"Get up!" Kaylee cried. Rolling over, she tugged on the older woman's arm. She glanced around, relieved to see that they were in the clear, at least for the moment. She tugged on Wichapi's arm again. "Hurry . . ."

Her voice trailed off when she saw the blood oozing from a neat round hole in the middle of the old woman's back.

"Oh, no!" Kaylee shook her head in disbelief as she lurched to her feet. "No!" Blinded by her tears, fearing for her own life, she turned and ran for the cover of the trees.

It was a bloody battle. The women and children ran for whatever cover they could find while the warriors fought the intruders. Though outnumbered, the Indians fought fiercely, the knowledge that they were fighting to protect their families giving them strength and courage.

Shaun rode through the village, looking for a blond-haired girl clad in a white shirtwaist and a divided skirt. One of Jackson's men loosed a wild Rebel yell as the riders set another lodge on fire.

Shaun saw a man older than himself pull a young cowboy off his horse and try to knife him, but before he could drive the blade home, the cowboy pulled his Colt and fired, slamming the Indian backward.

Garth Jackson rode beside him, a crazed look in his eyes as he shot at anything that moved. Women, chil-

dren, men with gray in their hair, it made no difference to Jackson.

The battle, one-sided as it was, was over in a matter
of minutes. The Indians were poorly armed, their tenacity and bravery pitiful weapons against Winchester
repeating rifles. Two of Jackson's men had been
wounded; one of the Double R riders was badly hurt,
two others had lesser injuries.

When the fighting stopped, Shaun dismounted.
Leading his horse, he walked through the camp. He
peered into every tipi that was still standing, looking
for some sign that Kaylee had been there. From time
to time, he heard gunshots in the distance as cowboys
chased down the survivors.

Around him, a handful of cowhands were looting
the camp, taking robes and whatever else caught their
fancy, rounding up the Indian ponies that hadn't run
off.

He found a teenage boy sprawled in the dirt at the
far end of the village. The Indian was bleeding badly
from a wound in his chest. Hardly aware of what he
was doing, Shaun drew his pistol and aimed it at the
boy. *One less redskin to steal my cattle,* he thought, *one
less dirty Injun.* His finger curled around the trigger.

And then the boy looked up at him. There was no
fear in the boy's eyes, only pain and resignation as he
began to sing his death song.

Shaun glanced around the camp, suddenly sickened
by the carnage he saw in the light of the rising sun.
Not all the Indian casualties were warriors. There
were women lying among the dead, and children not
yet old enough to walk. The scent of blood and death
hung heavy in the air. Smoke from a burning lodge
stung his nostrils.

He looked down at the wounded boy again, overcome by a sense of remorse and self-loathing. This
was no savage. It was just a boy a few years younger

than Kaylee. Shame that he had been involved in such a cowardly attack engulfed him. What was he doing here? He had always considered himself a decent, God-fearing man, and in spite of his outspoken hatred of the Indians, he had never condoned murdering innocent women and children. But that's what had been done here. Murder. They had attacked these people without provocation, with no real proof that Kaylee was even here.

He was holstering his pistol when Jackson came striding up, a tight grin on his face. "Hell of a fight," he said.

"Did you find Kaylee?"

Jackson shook his head. "I didn't see her, but she was here." He held up a pair of battered hand-tooled riding boots. "Recognize these?"

Shaun swore. He'd bought those boots two years ago, for Kaylee's birthday. "None of the men I've asked so far has seen her. They snuck her out of here somehow. Let's go ask the others. Maybe one of them saw something."

"I'm thinking we'd best go back. Our horses are played out, and we're about out of grub." Jackson looked out over the prairie. "And we're getting hip-deep in Injun country. We've got five wounded men. Much as I hate to quit, I think we'd best go back and let the Army take over."

Shaun swore. He didn't want to give up, but Jackson was right. They didn't have enough men to go on, and if the redskins they had attacked decided to come back with reinforcements, they would be in serious trouble. But how the hell was he going to face Emma?

"You ready to go?" Jackson asked.

Shaun nodded. "As soon as I take care of this kid." He would bind the kid's wounds, leave the boy his canteen, and hope he could find his way to another village somewhere. He brightened a little.

Maybe the kid could tell them where the Indians had gone.

"I'll do it for ya," Jackson said, and before Shaun could stop him, he braced his Winchester on his hip and shot the boy through the head, killing him instantly.

"You damn fool!" Shaun exclaimed. "Why the hell did you do that?"

"What are you talking about? I took care of him."

Shaun stared at Jackson. He had known the man for years, yet he felt as though he were seeing him for the first time. All the ranchers talked about the Indians, about how the West wouldn't be safe until the Sioux and Cheyenne were all dead or on reservations, but to shoot a wounded boy in cold blood . . .

With a shake of his head, Shaun turned and walked away, knowing he would never forget the resigned look in that boy's eyes as he watched the barrel of Jackson's rifle sight in on him. Knew that if he lived to be a hundred, he would never be able to wash that boy's innocent blood from his soul.

Chapter 15

Kaylee ran until she couldn't run anymore, ran until her legs were weak and her lungs were on fire, ran until she stumbled over a tree branch and fell into a shallow hole. Like a wounded animal, she covered herself with leaves and lay still, waiting for the hunters to find her, to shoot her down the way they had killed Blue Hawk's grandmother. She trembled uncontrollably, pressed her hand over her mouth to stifle her sobs, knowing that the carnage she had seen would forever haunt her dreams. Why, she thought, why had those men attacked them? And where was Blue Hawk?

Don't let him be dead. Please don't let him be dead. Blue Hawk, Blue Hawk, can you hear me?

She repeated the thought over and over, hoping he would hear her as he had once before, repeated it until exhaustion claimed her.

Blue Hawk watched impassively as the *wasichu*'s life slowly bled out of him. His arrow had gone almost all the way through the cowboy's chest. A second cowboy was on his knees, hunched over, dying quickly.

Hearing the shouts of other *wasichu* approaching, Blue Hawk melted into the underbrush.

Three riders came into view. Leaping from their saddles, they hurried to their comrades. Blue Hawk waited. The sounds of battle were fading from his camp. Those of his people who had been able to get away would be in hiding. His bitterness almost choked him.

The *wasichu* got the two injured men onto their horses and rode back the way they had come. His jaw tightened when he heard a single rifle shot ring out from the direction of his camp. As if he were there to watch, he knew the *wasichu* were killing the wounded.

Patient as a wolf on the hunt, he waited, his thoughts on his people, on his grandmother, and on Kaylee.

He approached the camp cautiously. It lay quiet in the early-morning sunshine. There should have been the happy sound of women talking, children laughing; instead, there was the silence of death and the stench of fear and bloodshed.

His jaws clenched, he made his way through what was left of the camp. He paused at each body, checking to see if by some miracle others had survived the attack. The rage and grief in his heart grew with each body he found.

Kaylee. Where was Kaylee? Had the White Eyes taken her? He threw back his head, a cry of primal rage bursting from his throat. He had seen the *wasichu* who had betrayed him and left him for dead among the marauders, had been following him, knife raised to strike, when someone had attacked him from behind.

He paused. Had he brought this destruction upon his people? Had the *wasichu* been hunting for Kaylee? Was that why they had attacked the camp? If that was so, then he was to blame for what had happened here.

He dropped to his knees when he came to the body of his grandmother. Taking the knife from the sheath at her back, he slashed his arms. Head thrown back, he sang her death song, the pain from the cuts in his arms nothing compared to the pain of her loss. Wichapi. She had comforted him when his parents died, cared for him when he was sick, made Kaylee welcome in her lodge.

"Wichapi . . ." He whispered her name one last time.

Sick at heart, he wrapped her frail body in a blanket and then carried her to a tree at the edge of the woods. He placed her body in the fork of the tree, then covered the ground surrounding the trunk with rocks and brambles to discourage predators.

He stood there for a long time, his bloodied arms raised over his head in silent supplication, begging Wakan Tanka to give her a safe journey to Wanagi Yatu.

"*Hecheto aloe,*" he murmured. It is finished.

It was nearing noon when Kaylee found him there. She had crept through the camp in shock, fearing that each body she came to might be his. Finding his grandmother's body gone had confused her, but then she saw Blue Hawk's familiar form outlined against the tree.

She cried his name as she ran toward him.

He turned slowly. "Kay-lee."

She collapsed in his arms. He was alive, thank God. Tears of relief spilled down her cheeks.

He glanced around. "Are you alone?"

She nodded, wondering if she would ever forget the horror of what had happened, the awful feeling of being hunted. She had cowered beneath her covering of leaves until the strain of not knowing what was happening, not knowing whether Blue Hawk was alive or dead, had driven her back toward their camp. The memory of the battle, of seeing women and children killed before her eyes, brought a new flood of tears. She sobbed until she was exhausted, until her throat was raw and her eyes burned. And all the while he held her close, comforting her with his presence.

She looked up at the tree behind him, at the small blanket-wrapped bundle lodged in the fork. "I'm sorry, Blue Hawk."

It was her turn to offer comfort now. She held him tight, her heart aching for his loss. She felt his body tremble. A single sob rose in his throat, the hurt so strong it brought tears to her own eyes.

She didn't know how long they stood there before he took a deep breath. "Come," he said, and held out his hand.

Her eyes widened as she saw the streaks of dried blood on his arms. "You've been hurt!" she exclaimed. "What happened? Are you all right?"

"It is nothing," he replied, shrugging it off.

She wanted to question him further, but it was obvious he didn't want to talk about it.

They spent the next few hours wrapping the dead in whatever blankets, robes, and furs they could find. Kaylee was reluctant to help, hesitant to touch the bodies, sickened by the sight of so much blood and death, but she pushed the feeling aside. These were women she had worked with, laughed with, men who had been Blue Hawk's friends. They could not leave their bodies unburied, to be savaged by scavengers. She reminded herself that it could have been her and Blue Hawk lying there. It was easier after that.

Finally the last body had been placed in a tree.

Kaylee pressed a hand to her back. It had been hard work, yet she felt an odd sense of peace and satisfaction knowing that she had helped Blue Hawk lay his loved ones to rest, that the bodies of women and children she had grown fond of would not be savaged by wild animals. Standing there, her back aching, she bowed her head and offered a silent prayer for the souls of the Lakota dead.

They went through the lodges that were still standing, searching for anything they could use. They found only a couple of blankets, one of which was scorched along one corner, a flint, and a waterskin. Everything else had been stolen or destroyed.

Blue Hawk came to stand beside her. "Come. Let us go."

"Are we still going to Crazy Horse's camp?" she asked, but she didn't really care. She just wanted to get away from this place of death and destruction.

"Yes. Any of my people who survived will go there."

With a last look at what was left of the camp, Kaylee started after him. "Why?" she asked after a time. "Why did those men attack us?"

He looked as if he was about to speak. But he did not. Finally he merely shrugged. "The *wasichu* need no reason," he said bitterly.

"That's terrible."

"I recognized one of them," Blue Hawk said.

"You did? Who was it?"

He looked at her, his dark eyes glittering with silent fury. "It was the man who promised me guns in exchange for horses."

"The one who left you for dead?"

Blue Hawk nodded. "Twice he has crossed my path. The next time, I will kill him."

They had no horses, and so they walked, heading north, toward the valley called the Greasy Grass by the Lakota. Kaylee wondered what had happened to Dusty. She'd had the mare for the last six years. She remembered the day Shaun had brought her home. Dusty had been a year-old filly then, too young to ride. Kaylee had spent several hours each day with her, brushing her, handling her feet, teaching her to walk on a lead rope, getting her used to the weight of a blanket and a saddle. Dusty had followed her around like a puppy. When Dusty turned two, the ranch foreman had helped Kaylee break her for riding. Dusty had been her last link to home, and now she was gone.

Kaylee glanced over at Blue Hawk, wondering what he was thinking. They had spent the night well away from the carnage and risen early this morning. It was quiet with just the two of them. She missed the laughter of the children, the camaraderie of the women, the boasting of the young men. So many of them dead! Her mind shied away from the memory. She wondered if she was somehow responsible for the attack, even though she knew it was unlikely. It was more likely that the cowboys' attack had been to avenge an Indian raid on a nearby ranch.

The sun was high in the sky when they stopped to rest beside a shallow stream.

Kaylee lay down on her stomach and buried her face in the cool water. Blue Hawk stretched out beside her.

Kaylee drank slowly. She hadn't had anything to eat since the night before, and she was hungry. The water helped a little, but not much.

She closed her eyes, and her mind filled with images of death and destruction. Sitting up, she glanced at Blue Hawk. He was staring off into the distance, his expression impassive. He had said very little since they left the camp behind. She wanted to touch him, to comfort him and be comforted in return, but there was a gulf between them now and she didn't know how to cross it. She thought back, wondering what she had done to make him angry, but she couldn't think of anything. Was he upset because she had survived and his grandmother had not? Did he blame her for his grandmother's death? Did he think she should have been able to save Wichapi?

He sat up, his gaze meeting hers.

She wanted to ask him what was wrong; instead, she pointed at the long, shallow gashes in his arms. "Won't you tell me what happened?"

"It is the way of my people, to mutilate our flesh when a loved one dies. It is a way to feel pain that is beyond words."

She looked at the two older scars on his chest. "Is that how you got those, too?"

He glanced down, then shook his head. "They are the marks of the Sun Dance."

"Sun Dance? What kind of dance leaves scars?"

"Each year during the Moon of Cherries Ripening the seven council fires of the Lakota nation meet. It is a time to renew acquaintances. It is also the time of the Sun Dance. The Sun Dance is *wakan*. Holy."

"But how did you get scars while dancing?"

"After the time of preparation, skewers are inserted here, and here." He pinched the flesh over his left breast and pantomimed inserting a skewer through the pinched flesh. "After the skewers are inserted, rawhide from the Sun Dance pole is fastened to the skewers, and then the dancer dances around the pole, pulling against the rawhide, until he frees himself."

Kaylee stared at him, repulsed by what he had described. "But why?"

"A man might dance to fulfill a vow in return for a favor granted by the gods, or to seek a vision, or for power."

"What kind of power?"

"Mato is my spirit power."

Kaylee shook her head. "I don't understand."

"When you were lost, I called on Mato's power to find you."

"And a bear told you where I was?"

"You do not believe me?"

She started to say no, but then she remembered how he had talked to the bear they had encountered that day by the berry bushes, how he had told her the very words she had said when she was lost.

"My people believe that Maka, the earth, is alive, that she is the mother of all living things. We believe that the rocks and the mountains and the trees are alive. We are part of the earth, Kay-lee, part of all living creatures. We kill the buffalo and the deer to sustain our life, and when we do, we always give thanks to our four-legged brothers for giving up their lives so that we might live. When we die, our bodies go back to the earth, to nourish the land for those who come after."

"That's very interesting, but what does it have to do with—"

He looked at her, his eyes dark and intense. "When the white man shot me and left me for dead, I saw you."

"Me!"

Blue Hawk nodded. "When I lay there, bleeding, certain that I was going to die, Mato called to me. He told me to be strong. And then . . ."

"And then?" She leaned forward. "Go on."

"Mato was no longer Mato, but a woman with hair like the sun and eyes like the sky. It was you, Kay-lee. I saw you then as clearly as I see you now."

"But—but that's not possible. Is it?"

"It is the truth."

She didn't believe in magic or visions, and yet she couldn't deny that she had felt drawn to him from the first, couldn't forget that she had called out to him when she was lost and he had found her, had told her the very words she had said.

He took her hand, his fingers entwining with her own. "Our hearts and souls are bound together, Kay-lee. Do you not feel it also?"

The touch of his hand bridged the gulf between them, banished whatever doubts she'd had. She felt the bond between them, knew they shared a closeness that was rare. Who was she to deny what he believed in? To talk of these things might help ease the pain of yesterday.

"Tell me more about your people, about what they believe. I know so little."

"We believe there are many powers. Wakan Tanka is the Great Spirit, but there are other, lesser powers. Inyan, the Rock, Skan, ruler of the sky, Wi, the sun, and Maka, the earth. Four is the number of power. There are four directions, four seasons, four winds. There are four kinds of animals—those that fly, those that crawl, those that walk on four legs, and those who walk on two. There are four parts of plants—the root, the stem, the leaves, and the fruit."

It was fascinating, she thought, this belief that everything was alive, that man could draw power from animals. She wasn't sure she believed that, but she did believe in the power of prayer, just as she believed there was only one God, no matter by what name you acknowledged Him.

Blue Hawk glanced up at the sun. "We should go."

"All right."

The plains stretched out ahead of them, gently rolling, endless. Under other circumstances, she would have enjoyed the scenery. Tall grass waved in the gentle breeze. Occasionally they passed a stream flanked by slender trees. The sky was a clear, bright blue ruled by a relentless sun. An eagle soared overhead, drifting on the air currents. Once, they passed a skunk, which stared at them rather imperiously, then lifted its tail and waddled away. Another time, a jackrabbit sprang up in front of Kaylee.

Late in the afternoon they saw a bear. It rose up on its hind legs, pawing the air, then turned and lumbered away.

Kaylee glanced up at Blue Hawk, wondering if it

was a sign of some kind. He didn't say anything, but he changed direction. When they reached the place where the bear had been, they found a tangle of berry bushes heavy with fruit.

With a little cry of delight Kaylee picked a handful. They were ripe and sweet and she ate them quickly, then picked some more, gobbling them down until she was full.

She glanced over at Blue Hawk. He looked at her, smiling faintly as he licked berry juice from his fingers. *"Lila waste,"* he said. "Good."

"Lila waste," she agreed.

She gazed up at him, her stomach all aflutter, as he wiped a drop of juice from her chin and then licked it off his finger.

"Skuya," he said. "Sweet."

She nodded, speechless, as he moved closer to her. Bending down, he licked the corner of her mouth.

"Kay-lee is even sweeter than the berries."

"Ohhhh." Her breath escaped her lips in a sigh. A sigh that was captured by his mouth as he drew her into his arms and kissed her. She leaned into him, her hands sliding over the sun-warmed skin of his back, drifting down his arms to knead the muscles there. She reveled in his nearness, his strength, the touch and the taste of him.

She thought how close to them death had come the day before, and she clung to him, grateful to be alive. He kissed her again and yet again, and she held him tighter, tighter. Afraid to let go, afraid of losing him, she pulled him closer. And still it wasn't close enough.

She wanted him, all of him. It was wrong, she knew it was wrong, but somehow it didn't seem to matter. She had seen how quickly death could come. But he was here now, and she wanted him. Needed him. She ran her hands over his back again, imagining what it would be like to be in his arms without the barrier of her clothing between them, to feel his skin against hers.

She moaned with delight as his arms tightened around her, drawing her body closer to his, until they were pressed intimately together from shoulder to thigh. He kissed her hungrily, his mouth kindling a flame within her. Clinging to each other, they sank down on the grass, arms and legs entwined, bodies yearning toward each other.

"Blue Hawk, Blue Hawk." Her hands moved restlessly over his shoulders and back.

He moaned her name, his hands trembling and eager as they moved over her flesh, learning the curves and contours of her body, fanning the embers of desire into full flame.

"I've never . . ." She licked her lips, feeling suddenly shy and very young.

"Neither have I," he replied, surprising her. "We will find our way together."

They came together in a rush, need and desire blazing between them, their love for each other an affirmation of life in the face of so much death. He took her gently, tenderly, murmuring to her in English and Lakota, whispering that he loved her. A soft cry of mingled pain and pleasure escaped her lips as his body broke the barrier of her maidenhead.

He paused a moment, his mouth swallowing her cry, his kisses soothing her, his voice whispering that he loved her, promising that he would never hurt her again. And then he was moving deep inside her, slowly at first, teasing her, arousing her. She cried his name, cried for something that seemed forever out of reach until, at last, ecstasy washed over her in waves of molten sunshine, warming her from the inside out, leaving her feeling peaceful and complete.

He held her close for a long while, his hand stroking

her hair. Caught up in a maelstrom of emotions, she was almost afraid to look at him. It had happened so fast, she thought, yet it seemed so right.

"Kay-lee?"

She opened her eyes to find him gazing down at her, his dark eyes filled with such love it brought tears to her eyes.

He wiped the tears from her cheeks. "Why do you weep?"

She shook her head, unable to speak past the lump in her throat.

"I did not mean to shame you, Kay-lee."

"No, you didn't! Please don't think that. It was just so . . . so beautiful, and I love you so much."

"We will be married when we reach the camp of Crazy Horse," he said. "The next time I take you, you will be my wife."

She stared at him. She had always thought to be wed in a church, surrounded by her family and friends. She thought of her mother. Emma would be frantic with worry by now, but there was no way for Kaylee to send word to her. It occurred to her that if she married Blue Hawk, she would probably never see her mother or her stepfather again.

"Kay-lee? Something troubles you?"

"I was just thinking of my mother."

"She would not approve of you marrying me?"

"No."

"I will not keep you against your will, Kay-lee. If it is your wish, I will take you home."

She looked up at him and knew she couldn't leave him. "How long until we get to your people?"

"Are you so impatient to be my wife, *wiwasteka mita*?" He smiled down at her, yet she saw the lingering sadness in his eyes, his grief at the loss of his grandmother and friends.

She placed his hand over her heart. "I'm already

your wife, in here," she replied. "What does *wiwaste-ka mita* mean?"

He slid his knuckles over her cheek, very gently. "It means 'my beautiful woman.' "

She felt her insides melt like morning dew beneath the heat of his gaze and knew, in that one crystalline moment, that her fate was irrevocably sealed with his.

Chapter 16

Kaylee woke abruptly, a gasp of surprise rising in her throat when she realized that the hot breath feathering over her face was real and not part of her nightmare. She laughed softly when she recognized the dark form looming over her.

"Dusty! What are you doing here?"

Blue Hawk had lunged to his feet, his knife drawn, at her first wordless cry. Sheathing his blade, he reached for the reins dangling from the mare's bridle.

Kaylee stood up stiffly, her joints aching from sleeping on the ground. "How do you suppose she found me?"

Blue Hawk shrugged. "I do not know, but at least now we will have meat to eat."

Kaylee stared at him aghast, then grabbed the reins from his hand. "You're not eating my horse!"

Blue Hawk's lips twitched, and then he laughed. "Kay-lee, I was only making a joke."

Still caught up in the aftermath of her nightmare, she started to ask him how he could joke at a time like this, then stopped. He was trying to put her at ease the best way he knew how. She punched him lightly on the arm. "Well, it wasn't funny."

"I am sorry."

"You wouldn't really eat her, would you?"

He nodded, his expression solemn now.

"That's awful."

"Meat is meat. Have you ever been hungry, Kaylee?"

"Of course."

"For days at a time?"

"Well, no."

"There have been times when my people ate their dogs and their horses, and when that was gone, they scraped hides and boiled the scrapings to make soup."

Kaylee wanted to believe he was making another joke, but she knew he was serious. She had never been that hungry. Nor had she known horror like the battle of the day before. Once again she realized how sheltered she had been, even though she had grown up on the frontier. At the ranch she had never lacked for food. Shaun had a prodigious appetite, and every day started with a big breakfast of eggs and bacon and fried potatoes, biscuits and gravy, or her mother's melt-in-your-mouth pancakes smothered in butter and syrup. And they always had meat for dinner, usually beef, of course.

She stroked Dusty's neck. She couldn't imagine being hungry enough to eat her horse. The mare was as much a pet as a means of transportation. "What do your people usually eat? In good times?"

Blue Hawk smiled. "When the buffalo come, times are good. Fat cow and hump and tongue. In the summer the women gather berries and cherries and plums, turnips and wild onions. We hunt prairie chickens and gather their eggs. We hunt elk and deer. The boys catch turtles and fish, squirrels and prairie dogs."

"And rabbits," she said, thinking of the one he had trapped for their dinner the night before. "Don't forget rabbits."

His lips twitched again. "And of course there is *wasichu* beef."

"Very funny," she muttered.

He drew her into his arms and she leaned into him,

her body remembering the pleasure they had shared the night before. "How soon will we reach Crazy Horse's camp?"

"Tomorrow night." He kissed her, his lips warm on hers.

When their kiss ended, she rested her head on his chest and closed her eyes. Her dreams had been filled with nightmare images of the day before. She had seen it all again so clearly, heard the cries of the women and children, felt her own fear clogging her throat. So much blood, so much needless death.

"Kay-lee?"

She looked up at him.

"You have not changed your mind?" he asked softly. "About being my wife?"

She shook her head and then frowned. She had heard Shaun say that among the Lakota, a man was permitted to have as many wives as he wished, so long as he could provide for them. He had claimed it was just another example of their godless ways.

"Is it true," she asked, "that Lakota men can take more than one wife?"

He nodded.

"You won't take another wife, will you?"

"No. Unless there are no children," he added teasingly.

"I don't think I could share you."

He looked at her, his expression mischievous. "Women sometimes take another husband."

"They do? I've never heard of such a thing." She knew Mormon men often had more than one wife, but she had never heard of a wife having more than one husband.

"If there are no children, sometimes a woman takes a second husband. Any children that are born belong to the wife and the first husband."

She thought that was very strange, but didn't say so. "Go on."

"It is the woman who owns the lodge and everything in it, except for her husband's personal belongings. It is the woman who rules the lodge. It is the woman who rules over the children. She looks after her daughters until they are wed, and her sons until they reach the age when their voices begin to mature. After that, sons are under the authority of their father. It is at this time that a young man goes to seek his vision. If he receives a vision, he will go to the medicine man, who will interpret it for him. The shaman will paint a design on the boy's chest, and from that day on, the boy will be considered a man and will be treated as such."

"I have so much to learn. Will you teach me to speak your language?"

"Yes."

"What if your people don't like me?"

"Then we will find another place to live." He took her hand in his. "I will do my best to make you happy."

"You already make me happy."

He smiled at her, his eyes dark with desire. "Tomorrow night you will be happier."

Riding double on Dusty, they reached the camp of Crazy Horse just after dusk the following day. The village, located on the banks of a wide river, was far bigger than Kaylee had expected. She could see a large herd of horses grazing in the distance, guarded by several teenage boys.

As they drew closer, she saw women bent over cook pots. The smell of sage and cooking meat was strong. Blue-gray plumes rose from the smoke holes of the tipis. She saw young children playing near their mothers, boys playing some kind of game with a hoop and a stick, warriors standing around in groups, talking. Other men appeared to be gambling. There were large wooden racks hung with drying meat. And there were dogs, large and small, everywhere.

Blue Hawk asked the way to the lodge of a warrior known as Matoskah. They found him sitting in front of a large tipi, sharpening an arrowhead. Kaylee remained in the saddle while Blue Hawk and Matoskah exchanged greetings and Blue Hawk rattled off what appeared to be some pointed questions. Then he seemed to relax slightly, and turned to her with a relieved smile. "My people are here. More than I could have hoped."

He helped her down from the horse, tethered Dusty to a picket pin, and they followed Matoskah into his lodge. Matoskah's wife, Sisoka, welcomed them and offered them food.

Kaylee smiled her thanks as Sisoka handed her a large wooden bowl and a spoon made of horn. Sitting down near the back of the lodge, she stared at the bowl's contents, wondering what kind of meat was in the stew. She remembered all the dogs she had seen outside, and recalled also that Blue Hawk had told her the Lakota ate dog and horse meat, so she was somewhat reluctant to eat it.

"What is wrong, Kay-lee?" Blue Hawk asked.

"Nothing, but . . . I don't want to be rude, but what kind of meat is this?"

He smiled his understanding. "Buffalo."

Relieved, she ate quietly, watching the others. Hungry as she was, the lean meat tasted better than Double R beef.

Blue Hawk and Matoskah talked as they ate. Kaylee glanced around the lodge, wishing she could understand what the men were saying. Matoskah seemed very excited, waving his arms, speaking rapidly. Blue Hawk nodded, his expression concerned and then angry.

When the men finished eating, Matoskah lit a long-stemmed pipe. He lifted it over his head and then to the four directions, took a puff, and offered it to Blue Hawk, who took several puffs and passed it back to his friend. They smoked until the tobacco was gone, and then Blue Hawk stood up.

"I must go see to my people. I will return."

"I'll go with you."

"No," he said. "Wait here. I will not be long."

He was back in less time than she could have hoped.

"Come, Kay-lee," he said. "Let us take a walk before we sleep."

She handed her bowl to Sisoka and stood up. Smiling her thanks to her hosts, she followed Blue Hawk out of the lodge. He turned toward the river, nodding to the men he passed.

"Your friends seem very nice," she said.

Blue Hawk smiled. "I have known Matoskah since we were children. When he married Sisoka, he left our camp to live with his bride's family because he had no family left and she wished to be close to her mother."

"What about your people?"

A look of pain crossed his face. "So few left. Still, more than I had hoped. More still may arrive. So far, seven women, four men, nine children."

They walked silently for a time, Kaylee respecting his grief, feeling her own heart heavy at the loss of so many of his people—her people, she added to herself. It seemed right.

She cast about for another topic to lighten his spirit.

"Your friend seemed very excited while you talked. There must have been good news, too."

Blue Hawk grunted softly. "Two moons ago, the White Eyes attacked a small Cheyenne village on the Powder River. Our allies were victorious. When the battle was over, they came here, to join with Crazy Horse. Eight days ago, Crazy Horse and his warriors defeated Three Stars Crook and his army at Goose Creek. Crazy Horse and his people are breaking camp tomorrow. They are moving north to the Greasy Grass, to join Sitting Bull to make war on the White Eyes."

"War?" Kaylee asked. Her heart slammed against her chest.

Blue Hawk nodded. "Do not be afraid."

Not be afraid? Was he serious? She had already seen enough death and destruction to last her a lifetime. "You're not going to fight, are you?"

He squared his shoulders. "I am a warrior."

"But—but I don't want you to."

"I must, Kay-lee."

She wanted to rage at him, to beg him not to go, but she knew in her heart there was no point in arguing with him. He was a warrior, a man of honor. If his people were going to war, then his place was with them. He would not stay behind, safe with the women, and let others fight in his place.

"There is nothing to fear," Blue Hawk said reassuringly. "During the Sun Dance, Sitting Bull offered one hundred pieces of his flesh to Wakan Tanka. He danced all day and night and on into the next day. He danced until he was too weak to stand, and when he could speak again, he told of a vision he had had, a vision of many soldiers without ears falling like grasshoppers out of the sky, with their heads down. He said he saw them falling into camp and heard a voice say, 'I give you these because they have no ears.'"

"What does it mean?"

"Sitting Bull's interpretation is that the *wasichu* will not hear the truth. The vision of soldiers falling head down means they will be defeated."

She looked up at him. "Promise me you'll be careful?"

"I promise I will always come back to you, *wiwasteka.*" He drew her into his arms, his chin resting on the top of her head. "I had thought to make you my wife when we reached here, but there is no time. We will be married when we reach the camp of Sitting Bull." His gaze searched hers. "You do not mind?"

"No. I can wait if you can."

His arms tightened around her. She was here, in his arms where she belonged. And for now, that was enough.

In the morning, the Lakota dismantled their camp and in no time at all the household belongings and lodgeskins were loaded onto travois, and the people were mounted and ready to go. Warriors dressed in their finest clouts and moccasins rode at the head of the column. The women, children, and old ones came next, followed by the horse herd. More warriors rode at the end of the column, guarding their backtrail. And dogs. They were everywhere. Barking, chasing birds and rabbits, nipping at the heels of the horses, and generally making a nuisance of themselves.

Kaylee knew it was a day she would never forget: the women and their brightly colored saddle blankets, the singing of the warriors, the boys racing up and down, the thundering sound made by the horse herd.

She rode near the back of the column to be near Blue Hawk, who rode in the rear guard on a fine pony supplied by his friend. He moved up to ride beside her from time to time. She was glad for his thoughtfulness and for his company, since she had no one else to talk to.

They rode for hours, stopping only to eat and rest the horses.

Kaylee watched the other women as she rode, the women with their children, the mothers nursing their babies. They made her think of her own mother.

Emma must be worried sick by now. Kaylee wished she had some way to let her mother know that she was alive and well and happy, wished she had some way to know if Randy was all right.

She smiled at the way young men rode back and forth alongside the column, playing tricks and showing off for the young unmarried women, who pretended not to notice. They were a lighthearted, happy people, so different from what she had expected.

They made camp when the sun went down. The skies were clear, the weather warm. Kaylee dismounted, and stood near Dusty's head, not knowing where she should go or what she should do. All around her, women were spreading bedrolls, lighting fires, preparing food for their families. The men looked after their horses.

She felt her heart skip a beat when she saw Blue Hawk striding toward her. How handsome he was, and how much she loved him! He smiled as he drew nearer. Taking Dusty's reins from her, he tethered the mare to a picket pin and stripped off the saddle and blanket.

"Come," he said. "Sisoka has prepared food for us."

Later that night, as they were walking through the camp, Blue Hawk pointed Crazy Horse out to her. Clad in a clout and leggings, the chief stood near a fire with a group of his warriors. She had heard stories of Crazy Horse, had imagined him to be bigger than life, so she was surprised to see that he was a slender man of average height. His skin was a paler shade of copper than Blue Hawk's, his hair not a true black but dark brown, with a slight curl to it. Blue Hawk had told her that as a boy Crazy Horse had been called the Light-Haired One. He had sometimes been mistaken for a captive child because of his light skin and curly hair.

"It is said that Crazy Horse had a great vision in which he saw a warrior wearing blue leggings and a white buckskin shirt. He wore no paint and only one feather in his hair. A small brown stone was tied behind his ear. Shadowy enemies rose up before him, but he rode through them unhurt. Sometimes it seemed as though the warrior's own people tried to hold him back, but he fought them off and rode on, while a storm gathered behind him. There was the sound of thunder in the air, and a zigzag of lightning appeared on the man's cheek. And still he rode on, through friends and enemies, while a small hawk hovered above him."

"What does it mean?"

"It is said that the warrior in his dream was Crazy Horse and that he must dress as the warrior in his vision when he goes to battle, that he must always be a leader, in peace and in war, and that if he does these things, no enemy will ever destroy him."

She did not discount what Blue Hawk said. After all, Bible prophets of old had received visions. And her mother's aunt had sometimes had dreams that came true. Who was she to say such things were impossible just because it had never happened to her?

They reached their destination late in the afternoon of the following day. The camp of Sitting Bull was located in the valley along the winding banks of a wide river. There were lodges as far as the eye could see. What must have been thousands of horses grazed along the river flats and the grassy benches to the west.

It was a beautiful place, wild and rugged, a place of rolling hills, bluffs, and deep-cut ravines. Lacy cottonwoods grew along the river's edge. There were groves of wild plum trees and chokecherries and their scent was heavy in the air, mingling with the aroma of cooking meat and the acrid scent of smoke rising from hundreds of cookfires. The sky was a bright, clear blue.

"They are all here," Blue Hawk said, and she heard the pride in his voice as he pointed out the various bands. "The Sans Arc, the Minniconjou, the Santee, the Two Kettles, the Hunkpapa, the Oglalas, the Brules. All the Seven Council Fires of the Lakota. And over there, our allies, the Arapaho and the Cheyenne."

Each band formed its own camp circle, perhaps a mile or a mile and a half in circumference.

"What's that?" Kaylee asked, pointing at a large white tipi that stood apart from the others.

"It is a Hunkpapa warrior lodge. Sitting Bull belongs to the Kit Fox society, and to the Strong Hearts. The Lakota have similar lodges where the young men go. Crazy Horse belongs to the Strong Hearts and to the Tokala, as do I."

"Sort of a club, you mean? Only members can go there?"

Blue Hawk nodded.

"How many Indians do you think are here?" she asked.

Blue Hawk's glance swept over the lodges. "It is difficult to know. Perhaps two thousand men of warrior age."

The number was staggering, and yet oddly reassuring if there was to be a battle. With so many warriors, surely the Indians would win the fight. She felt guilty as soon as the thought crossed her mind. It seemed wrong, somehow, to hope that the Indians would win. The word "traitor" whispered through the back of her mind.

Blue Hawk left her with Sisoka while he went to take care of their horses and to make arrangements for their wedding.

Sisoka showed Kaylee a chunk of meat and a pile

of vegetables and indicated she should cut them up
for stew.

With a nod, Kaylee picked up a bone-handled knife
and began to slice the meat, hoping it was buffalo or
venison. Her thoughts turned toward Blue Hawk as
she worked.

She was going to marry him. It was a big step. Was
she really ready to get married, to marry a man who
was not of her race or religion? She thought of Garth
Jackson. She could never have married him. Then she
thought of Randy. She cared for him deeply. They
had grown up together. He had given her her first
kiss. But he was like a brother to her. She loved him,
but she was not in love with him and never would be.

She dumped the meat into a pot and began to chop
the vegetables. Was she truly in love with Blue Hawk?
It seemed a silly question. She had thought of him
constantly since the day she found him, worried about
him, dreamed of him. Made love to him. As much as
she missed her mother, she didn't want to go back
home if it meant leaving Blue Hawk. As much as she
missed her own bed and her room and her clothes,
she was content to stay here, to live in a hide lodge,
so long as she could be with him.

She watched Sisoka, who was humming softly as she
mended a tear in her husband's shirt. Like all the
Indian women Kaylee had seen, Sisoka seemed perfectly happy, content with her life.

When Kaylee finished chopping the vegetables, she
put them in the pot with the meat. Sisoka handed her
a waterskin, and she added enough water to cover the
ingredients, then stirred it all with a long-handled
spoon.

Sisoka smiled her thanks, then spread her hands
wide, as though to say there was nothing else for
Kaylee to do.

Smiling back, Kaylee stepped out of the lodge and

found a shady spot, where she could sit and watch the activity around her. Warriors strolled through the camp, pausing at one lodge or another. They all seemed to be in good spirits.

Young women, too, moved through the village. Dressed in their best, they laughed and flirted with the young men. Children ran between the lodges, happy and smiling, carefree as only the very young can be. And there were dogs everywhere. Even as she watched, a gray-haired woman grabbed a puppy and clubbed it over the head.

Kaylee swallowed the bile that rose in her throat and hoped she never had to eat dog meat. Or horse meat.

She stood up, excitement fluttering in her stomach when she saw Blue Hawk striding toward her.

"Has there ever been such a gathering!" he exclaimed. "Let the *wasichu* come! We will defeat them." He smiled down at her, his hand cupping her cheek. "But first a marriage, and a feast to celebrate."

"Feast?"

"Sisoka will arrange it. We will be wed tonight, Kay-lee. Those of my people who are here will attend."

She looked down at her dress with a twinge of regret. It wasn't exactly the dress she had always dreamed of being married in, but she wasn't likely to find a gown of antique satin just lying around anywhere. And, after all, what did it matter what she wore? In her heart she was already his wife.

She smiled up at Blue Hawk. "Tonight."

Chapter 17

Kaylee stood inside Sisoka's lodge, unable to believe her eyes, or the softness of the ankle-length doeskin tunic Sisoka had given her to wear. The skin had been bleached until it was the color of pale cream. Long fringe dangled from the sleeves and from the bottom of the skirt. The yoke was decorated with yellow glass beads. Tiny silver bells, tied to some of the fringes, made a sweet tinkling sound whenever she moved.

Sisoka smoothed back a strand of Kaylee's hair, smiled approvingly, then lifted the lodge flap.

Kaylee took a deep breath and stepped outside. She wished fleetingly that her mother could be here, that Wichapi could be here. And then she saw Blue Hawk waiting for her, and every other thought fell away.

Clad in fringed leggings and an elkskin shirt, his long black hair adorned with a single white feather, he looked so handsome, he fair took her breath away. Perhaps two dozen people stood behind him. She recognized some of them as survivors of his band. Having so recently fled a scene of violence and death, they were ready to witness a celebration of life.

Her throat closed with powerful and conflicting emotions as Blue Hawk stepped forward and took her hand in his. His touch dispelled her nervousness, filled her heart with warmth and peace, an assurance that what she was doing was right, that she had been fated for this man and no one else.

Matoskah came forward, leading five horses. He spoke to Kaylee.

"You have no family here to give you away," Blue Hawk said, translating for his friend, "and I have no horses or gifts to offer you, so Matoskah gives you the gifts that I cannot."

Matoskah handed the reins to Kaylee. She smiled her thanks.

Sisoka and two other women came next. One of the women handed Kaylee a small leather pouch and a pair of moccasins, and the second offered her a buffalo robe. Sisoka smiled shyly, then pointed to a lodge set up near her own.

Kaylee looked up at Blue Hawk. "What did she say?"

"She says the lodge was erected by the women of her family. In the way of my people, it now belongs to you."

Kaylee nodded, humbled by the generosity of Blue Hawk's friends. "How do I thank them? I don't know what to say."

"Our word for 'thank you' is *pilamaya*."

Kaylee smiled at the women and at Matoskah. *"Pilamaya. Pilamaya."*

The women smiled and nodded, accepting her thanks.

"Will you be my wife, Kay-lee?" Blue Hawk asked. "Will you agree, in front of my people and my friends, to take me into your lodge as your husband?"

"Yes, I will."

"I will provide for you, and protect you, all the days of my life."

She gazed up into his eyes, and everything else fell away. "And I promise to love you and cherish you and care for you all the days of my life."

"Hecheto aloe," he murmured. It is finished.

"We're married?"

He nodded. "From this day forward, you will be known as my wife, and you will be welcome in the lodges of my people." Taking the reins of the horses from her hand, he passed them to one of the men to look after. "Come," he said. "Sisoka and the women have prepared a feast for us."

She was too excited to eat much. All she could think of was that it was her wedding night. She listened to the laughter around her, smiled at those who smiled at her, but all she could think of was the time when they would be alone, when he would take her in his arms again, when she could hold him close and feel his body pressing on hers.

And then Blue Hawk touched her arm. It was only a light touch, a mere brush of his fingers across her skin, and yet every fiber of her being sprang to life, yearning toward him with such intensity it was like a physical ache.

No words were necessary.

He stood up, held out his hand. She took it, and he drew her to her feet.

She was aware of people watching them and smiling as they walked away from the campfire into the shadows, but she didn't care.

Her heart was pounding louder than the dance drums she could hear in the distance as they made their way to their lodge.

She stepped inside, not knowing what to expect, and immediately felt a surge of appreciation for the kindness of the Lakota women. A cozy fire burned in the center of the floor. Two backrests were positioned on either side of the fire pit. There were a few cook pots beside the door.

But it was the bed of soft robes spread in the back of the lodge that caused a nervous flutter in her stomach. She was suddenly acutely conscious of the man standing behind her. Her husband.

Her breath caught in her throat when she felt his hands curl over her shoulders. Slowly, he turned her to face him.

"Kay-lee. *Mitawicu, tekihila.*"

"What does that mean?"

"My wife, my love."

"How do you say 'husband'?"

"Higna."

"Higna." She spoke the word softly. *"Higna."* Standing on her tiptoes, she kissed him.

His arms went around her, and she clung to him as he deepened the kiss. Heat flowed through her, hotter and brighter than the heat radiating from the fire.

She leaned into him, wanting to be closer. She needed to touch him, and so she slid her hands under his shirt, loving the feel of his heated skin beneath her palms.

He drew back for a moment, reaching for the ties of her tunic. Soon, the garment was pooled at her feet. He removed her leggings, her moccasins.

His gaze moved over her, and she flushed from the soles of her feet to the crown of her head.

"Beautiful," he murmured, his voice husky. "So beautiful."

Somewhat shyly, she tugged on his shirt. In a single deft movement, he yanked it over his head and tossed it aside. His clout, leggings, and moccasins followed.

Kaylee's blush deepened. They had made love once before, but it had been hurried, colored by the horror of the battle and Blue Hawk's grief. She stared at him now, captivated by the sight of him. The light from the fire played over his skin, bathing him in a soft golden glow. His body was long and lean and well muscled, his desire for her obvious in every taut line.

He took her in his arms again, and she felt a thrill

of excitement at the touch of his heated skin against her own. Locked in an embrace, they sank down on the soft furs.

She explored his body, running her hands over his shoulders, down his arms, over his broad back and chest, her kisses falling like rain on his skin, her tongue tasting him from time to time. He was solid and warm, his dark eyes glowing with passion and delight as she poked and tickled and touched and tasted him from head to foot.

And when he could wait no longer, he began an exploration of his own, his hands drifting slowly over her, discovering what made her laugh and what made her gasp with pleasure. She was soft and round, her skin smooth and unblemished, flushed with desire.

Their leisurely exploration gradually grew more urgent as the fires of desire blazed hotter. When they were both quivering with need, when he thought he must possess her or die, his body merged with hers. She arched up to meet him, embracing him as the other half of her heart and soul. Complete at last, she held him close as he began to move within her, each slow thrust adding to the delicious warmth that engulfed her, the growing tension that thrummed through her. Was there ever in all the world any sensation to equal that of being in his arms, feeling his heated skin beneath her fingertips, muscles rippling as his body pleasured hers. She reveled in his touch, in the strength of his arms, holding her as if he would never let her go. His voice moved over her, husky with longing, whispering to her in Lakota and English, telling her how much he loved her, wanted her, needed her. She cried out his name, clutching his shoulders as waves of pleasure washed over her, heard his own cry as the warmth of his release swelled within her, completing her.

With a sigh, he buried his face against her shoulder.

His hair felt like silk as it brushed her skin. She smiled as happiness bubbled up inside her, spilling out in peals of laughter.

Blue Hawk rose up on his elbows, a grin spreading over his face. "Did I not tell you we would find the way?" he said, a touch of masculine arrogance in his voice.

With a smile Kaylee drew his head down and kissed him. And then, feeling suddenly daring, she whispered, "Do you think we can find it again?"

Blue Hawk nodded, his dark eyes smoldering with reawakened desire as her hands moved over him. "I am a Lakota warrior. I will find the path for you, *mitawicu*, if it takes all night."

Kaylee's arms twined around his neck, her tongue exploring the lobe of his ear, the hollow of his throat.

Outside she could hear the beat of a Lakota drum, its rhythm echoing the beating of her own heart as she followed Blue Hawk down the path again, and yet again.

She woke in his arms, a smile on her face. "Good morning, *higna*," she murmured.

"Hinhanni waste, mitawicu."

Kaylee trailed her fingers over his arm. "What did you just say? I understood *mitawicu* and *waste*. How long do you think it will take before I can speak your language?"

"I said, 'Good morning, my wife.' Do not be impatient, Kay-lee. The words will come to you."

He was right, of course. She knew several words already. Her new life seemed to be moving fast now, every heartbeat carrying her farther from everything she had ever known, everything she was familiar with.

"I love you," she murmured. "Do you love me?"

"Han."

"Han? Means 'yes'?"

Blue Hawk nodded, then brushed his lips across hers. "Come," he said, and rising to his feet, he took her hand and drew her up beside him.

"Where are we going?"

"To bathe."

She grinned. "Good idea."

A short time later, they made their way down to the river. Because of the size of the encampment, it took a while to find a place where they could bathe in privacy, but they finally found a secluded spot in the bend of the river.

Afraid that someone might come along, Kaylee stepped out of her tunic and moccasins and slipped quickly into the water. Turning, she watched Blue Hawk walk toward her. Just looking at him filled her with a glow and brought a smile to her face. The early-morning sunlight caressed his back and shoulders as he waded into the water. And then he was turning, reaching for her, drawing her into his arms, his mouth seeking hers.

It was deliciously arousing, the touch of Blue Hawk's wet skin against hers, the feel of the water swirling around her legs. She leaned into Blue Hawk, her hands moving restlessly up and down his back, her hips pressing against his in blatant invitation.

She drew back a little so she could see his face. "Is it awful of me to want you again?"

"No, Kay-lee. It pleases me. *You* please me, more than I can say."

"Show me," she whispered.

Lifting her into his arms, he carried her out of the water until he found a quiet place screened by a thick stand of brush.

All her senses seemed to come alive as they sank down, arms and legs entwined, his body a welcome weight. The grass was warm against her back. The breeze whispered through the trees. The birds warbled their cheerful reply while the river sang its own song, but none was so sweet as the love song Blue Hawk's body sang to hers.

Later, they bathed again, taking turns washing each other. After dressing, they walked back toward the Lakota camp.

It was a beautiful day, and it seemed everyone was outside enjoying it. Children chased each other through the tall grass. Young women, dressed in their best, strolled through the camp, talking, giggling behind their hands or turkey-feather fans. Old men sat nodding in the sun. Women could be seen sewing, cooking, tanning hides, caring for their children. Little girls played with their dolls; little boys played with small bows and arrows. Young men strutted through the camp. Warriors were gathered in small groups, talking. Others could be seen repairing their weapons or making new ones. On the far side of the river, a horse race was in progress.

"It's like a big party," Kaylee remarked, thinking of the church socials back home.

Blue Hawk nodded. "Yes, but there has never been a gathering like this." And never would be again, he thought. Scouts rode back and forth constantly, bringing news of the white man's approach. "Sitting Bull's vision has drawn the tribes together. Yellow Hair Custer is coming. Together we will meet him. And defeat him."

Kaylee felt a sudden sense of despair. Blood and death again—perhaps worse than what they had already experienced. And Blue Hawk would be in the middle of it.

He seemed to sense her mood swiftly and pointed to a group of children gathered around a warrior with long gray braids. "The old one is telling stories. Come, we will listen." He smiled down at her. "Time enough to worry about the battle when it comes."

They stood behind the children, with Blue Hawk translating for Kaylee.

"The *wasichu* do not know where the center of the earth is," he said, following the story. "That is why they are such a strange people. They build square houses, when all the world is round."

The old man pointed to the lodge behind him. "Our homes are round, for there is strength in a circle. They are cool in summer and warm in winter. The sides roll up to allow summer breezes to pass through. They are easy to move. The *wasichu* live summer and winter in the same house. Wakan Tanka did not intend for man to remain in one place. He knew that man and animal alike need to move so that they might always have fresh water and grass.

"The Power of the World is found in a circle. The nests of birds are round lodges because there is strength in a circle. The four winds circle the earth. The sun, the moon, the earth, and the sky are round. The bodies of plants and animals are round. Everything in nature, save Inyan, the rock, is round."

It was true, Kaylee mused. Why had she never noticed it before? Caught up in the rhythm of the old man's voice overlaid by Blue Hawk's deep tones, she put all thought of the coming battle out of her mind.

"Man's life is a circle," the old one said. "When I was a child, my mother cared for me. When I was a young man, I cared for my children. Now that I am old, my children care for me. From life to death is also a circle. When we are born, Mother Earth nourishes us. When we die, our bodies nourish the earth, so that the next generation might have life."

Blue Hawk tugged on Kaylee's hand and they walked toward their lodge.

"I must go speak with the warriors," Blue Hawk said. "Will you be all right while I am gone?"

"Yes." She felt strangely at peace after listening to the old man's recitation.

"I will not be long."

"Don't worry about me."

He squeezed her hand and started to walk away.

"Blue Hawk?"

He paused and glanced over his shoulder.

"Aren't you going to kiss me good-bye?"

"Not out here. There are too many eyes watching."

"Oh." Unreasonably, perhaps, she felt stung. "Well, see you later, then." She went into their lodge and slapped the hide covering closed. Not as satisfying as slamming a door, but it would have to do.

"Kay-lee."

She hadn't heard him come in, and she whirled around, surprised to see him there. "Did you forget something?" she asked, her voice cool.

"I came to kiss you good-bye. No one is watching in here."

Later that evening, after he returned from his pow-wow, she greeted him as if he had been gone a month. His hands grasped her shoulders, drawing her close as he bent his head and claimed her lips. He made love to her slowly and thoroughly, until they were both sated and breathless.

She sighed now, as she snuggled against Blue Hawk's side, her head pillowed on his shoulder. Her only wish was that she might always be as happy as she was at this moment. She watched him sleep, filled with such an aching tenderness that it brought tears to her eyes. What would she do if something happened to him? How could she let him risk his life in the battle to come? How could she not? What would be, would be. She was beginning to understand the grief women had always felt when their men went away to war.

"Please don't let him die." The prayer rose in her heart. "Please, please." She knew those of her own race would think it blasphemy, perhaps even traitorous, to pray for Blue Hawk's safety, but she didn't care.

She was on the brink of sleep when she heard what sounded like a flute being played, its notes piercingly lovely against the quiet murmur of camp life. It was almost like an answer to her prayer. She felt a strange chill.

Blue Hawk's eyes opened at the sound of the first notes, and he smiled.

"What is that music?" she asked.

"Siyotanka."

"Si—what?"

"It is a courting flute."

"Oh? You never played a flute for me."

"There was no time," he said simply. "And your family was not near, for me to woo you away from them."

"Can you play the si—whatever you call it? Tell me about the flute."

"Our men are very brave in battle," Blue Hawk said.

"I don't want to talk about fighting," she said, putting her fingers to his lips. "I want to know about the flute."

He took her hand in his and kissed it. "Then listen," he said. "Our men are brave in battle, but very shy in the way of love. There is no private place in a crowded lodge or within the camp circle for a warrior to court a woman. It is not always wise to walk away from the village. There is danger in the tall grass, in the forest."

She shuddered, remembering the snake. And the bear.

"So, our young men wait for a chance to see the

girl of their choice early in the morning, when she is on her way to the river to draw water. They meet by accident on the trail, and in that way the girl knows he is interested in her. If the girl is also interested, she will take her time filling her waterskin, giving the young man a few moments to look at her, and perhaps speak to her.

"At night, as now, the young man lets his flute do his courting. Lying in her lodge, a girl will hear the sad lament of the flute. And if her heart is touched, and if his medicine is very strong, she might sneak out of her lodge and meet him somewhere."

"Oh, that's so romantic," Kaylee murmured.

Blue Hawk nodded. "Sometimes, in the spring, the air is filled with flute song."

"Did you ever woo a girl in that way?"

"No."

"But you can play?"

"All warriors can play the *siyotanka*."

"Even though I'm your wife, will you play for me? One day?"

His answer was a smile as he gathered her into his arms.

With a sigh, she closed her eyes.

That night she dreamed that she was a Lakota maiden and that Blue Hawk rose early in the morning to follow her to the river, that he sat outside her lodge late at night and poured out his love and longing in the plaintive notes of a Lakota flute.

That night her dreams were full of peace, not of war.

Chapter 18

Blue Hawk puffed on the pipe and passed it to the warrior on his right. From outside came the carefree sounds of children playing, the laughter of the women, but there was no laughter in here. He glanced at the solemn faces of the men seated in the lodge. Many of the leaders of the tribes were assembled here: Crazy Horse and Big Road of the Oglalas, Sitting Bull and Black Moon from the Hunkpapas, Touch the Clouds and Fast Bull from the Minniconjou, Two Moons and Old Bear from the Cheyenne. He saw Kicking Bear and Bad Heart Bull, and crippled old Black Elk, who was the cousin of Crazy Horse. These were men who were well respected among the tribes. Men with Power.

Two Moons rose to speak. He spoke of the *wasichu*, and how they could not be trusted. He spoke of the treaty made with the Grandfather in Washington, which had promised the Black Hills to the Cheyenne and the Lakota. He spoke of Yellow Hair's invasion of the Black Hills, and the discovery of the yellow iron that made the *wasichu* crazy.

Blue Hawk nodded in agreement. He remembered how the Grandfather had sent a commission to meet with the Lakota, the Arapaho, and the Cheyenne. Ten thousand warriors had attended the meeting on the White River. Sitting Bull had agreed to meet in council with the representatives from Washington, but

Crazy Horse had refused and sent Little Big Man in
his place. Blue Hawk had been among the many warriors who had galloped over the crest in a show of
force. Little Big Man was an Oglala shirt wearer. It
was said that he had threatened to shoot any man who
agreed to sign away the Black Hills, but the chiefs had
needed no threat. The Black Hills were the heart of
the Lakota and the Cheyenne.

Realizing that the Lakota would not sell the sacred
Hills, the commission had sought to negotiate for
mineral rights, but the Lakota and their allies would
not hear of it. The chiefs had demanded that the
Grandfather in Washington honor the treaty they
had signed. But it was not to be. That winter, the
commissioner of Indian Affairs declared that all Lakota people must report to their agency at the end
of January or be considered hostiles. It had been
impossible for the Lakota to meet such an ultima-
tum, even if they had been so inclined. To travel
such a distance in the dead of winter would have
meant the deaths of many Lakota elders and children. Many of the bands were not even notified, as
blizzards and severe cold prevented government cou-
riers from getting through.

During the Moon of Popping Trees, an agency Indian had brought word that the Army was on the
move.

During the Moon of Snowblind Eyes, a band of
Lakota had been attacked.

When Two Moons sat down, Crazy Horse rose to
speak. His voice was filled with fire as he recounted
the fight with Three Stars Crook at the Rosebud. The
warriors had not fought for coups and scalps and
horses, as in days past, he said. They had been united,
charging at the soldiers, breaking their lines, not stopping to count coup or take scalps until the fighting
was over.

Later, when the battle was won, Crazy Horse had sent some of his warriors to follow Three Stars and his men to make sure they were leaving the country. His scouts had brought word that Three Stars was headed for the mountains to hunt the bighorn sheep, and that Three Stars' Crow scouts had gone home. Eight warriors had died in the fight. Fifty-seven White Eyes had been killed or badly wounded in the battle. The Lakota scouts had fired arrows into Crook's night camps to keep the soldiers on edge. Runners had been sent to the agencies to the north and the south, carrying the tale of Three Stars' defeat. It was a good victory, but not the one Sitting Bull had seen in his vision.

Sitting Bull spoke next. He was an orator without equal, a man with a deep and abiding hatred toward those who would not leave his people to live in peace. Once he had believed in peace. Once he had spared the lives of captives. Once he had declared that prisoners must be freed or adopted so that there would be no slaves in his camp. Now he spoke for war without mercy.

Blue Hawk listened and said little. He learned that warriors had been traveling to nearby trading posts, trading furs and blankets for guns and ammunition.

A short time later, a scout came in saying that hunters packing antelope meat had returned from beyond the Greasy Grass.

Yellow Hair was coming.

The line of march of the White Eyes made it clear that Yellow Hair was looking for the camp of Sitting Bull, spoiling for a fight. Excitement blazed through the council, and voices spoke more urgently.

When everything that needed to be said had been said, the warriors passed the pipe around one last time, and the gathering broke up.

Blue Hawk ducked out of the lodge, his warrior

blood running hot in his veins. Yellow Hair was coming. Blue Hawk drew a deep breath, inhaling the familiar scents of sage and smoke. He was eager to fight. For too long he had hidden away in the mountains with his small band. Outnumbered and without adequate weapons, they had avoided battle. But his people had not found peace that way—they had found only hunger and betrayal and death. The Lakota would not be defeated this time. Sitting Bull had promised them a great victory. Blue Hawk would avenge his own dead.

Matoskah called to Blue Hawk as he passed by. *"Hau, kola."* Hello, my friend.

"Hau, kola," Blue Hawk replied.

Matoskah made a broad gesture, encompassing the camp. "I have never seen anything like this before, my brother. It is something we will speak of to our children and our children's children."

Blue Hawk nodded. It was a proud thing, to see the bands all come together. In the evenings everyone enjoyed feasting and dancing and courting.

"Every day more and more people join us," Matoskah said. "Warriors coming from the north say there are many soldiers marching up the Yellowstone. Soon there will be a fight such as we have never seen before."

Blue Hawk nodded. He glanced toward his lodge, wondering if Kaylee was awake. He had made love to her all through the night. He had not awakened her when he left the lodge this morning.

Seeing the direction of Blue Hawk's gaze, Matoskah laughed softly. "I think it is another kind of fighting that you think of now, *kola*," he said, punching Blue Hawk on the arm.

Blue Hawk grinned at his friend and shrugged. "Can you blame me?"

Matoskah gave him a little push. "Go. Pleasure your woman while you can."

"I have always listened to your advice," Blue Hawk said. "I will do my best to do as you say."

The sound of Matoskah's laughter followed him as he walked away.

Kaylee made a soft sound of contentment as Blue Hawk's hands explored her body. Such a nice dream, she thought, and snuggled deeper under the furry robe that covered her.

His hands, so big and strong, were ever so gentle as they caressed her, moving over her breasts, her belly, sliding down, down, to stroke her thighs. She moaned softly, her body writhing with pleasure.

"Kay-lee?"

"Hmm, don't stop," she murmured.

Her hands slid over his shoulders, down his chest. His skin was warm, his body firm, his belly ridged with muscle. She never tired of touching him, of being touched by him. Without conscious thought, she was careful of the healing gunshot wound in his side. Impatient to touch him, she frowned in annoyance when her fingers closed over his clout, frowned because it concealed what she desired. She found the ties, unfastened them, and tossed the annoying garment away.

She felt his breath on her face, heard his low moan as her hands touched his aroused manhood, reveling in the strength she felt there, in the joy she found in arousing him.

She gasped, her eyelids fluttering open as he gently removed her hand and lowered his body over hers, and into hers, melding them together, bringing her out of the delicious dream into the sensual heat of reality.

"Blue Hawk!"

His dark eyes blazed with a desire as overpowering as her own.

She wanted him all the time, she thought, wanted him with a fierce desperation that seemed to grow stronger every day. He looked at her, and she wanted him. He touched her, and she burned for more.

His lips found hers, and his need consumed her the way hungry flames consumed kindling. Caught once more in a feverish desire, lost in a world of swirling sensations, she clung to him, his name a cry on her lips as they reached the pinnacle together and then tumbled down, down, down, into a sea of contentment.

Later, after they had bathed and eaten, they found a shady place near the river and Blue Hawk began to teach her a few words of Lakota.

"Hau," he said. "Hello."

"Hau," she repeated.

"He taku hwo? Who is that?"

"He taku hwo?"

"Han. But when asking questions, women say *he,* men say *hwo."*

"He taku he?"

"Toniktuka hwo? How are you?"

"Toniktuka he?"

Blue Hawk nodded. *"Waste."*

Leaning forward, he kissed her. *"Skuya,"* he murmured. "Sweet." His fingers threaded through her hair, lightly massaged her nape. *"Cocola.* Soft." He drew her into his arms. *"Mitawicu,"* he said, his voice husky. "My wife."

"Yours," she agreed and wrapped her arms around him, everything else forgotten as he pressed her down to the ground.

Two days later, all the bands moved across the river.

An aged warrior stood on the far bank, calling out where the people were to go. The Cheyenne went first, going farthest downriver, followed by the Oglala, the Brule, the Minniconjou, the Santee, the Two Kettles, and the Sans Arc. The Hunkpapa came last, stopping near the mouth of Ash Creek.

By evening the camps were set up, looking as though they had been there for days instead of only a few hours.

That night there was dancing. It was not ceremonial dancing, Blue Hawk told Kaylee, but social dancing for the young people, who moved from camp to camp, singing and dancing around the drums in the light of the campfires. The prettiest girls chose their partners from among the young warriors who had fought bravely on the Rosebud.

Kaylee saw three women dancing apart from the others, their movements graceful as willows bending in the wind. Curious, she nudged Blue Hawk. "Why are those women dancing alone?"

"They are not women."

"Not women." She looked closer. "What do you mean, they're not women?"

Blue Hawk grunted softly. "They are *winktes*."

"What does that mean?"

"A *winkte* is a man who, when he is very young, dreams of being a woman. They dress in women's clothes and work and live as women. They live on the outside of the main circle, always apart. They are regarded as Wakan, both feared and disdained. They make good shamans. It is believed that if a *winkte* is asked to name a child, that child will grow up without sickness and have long life."

Kaylee nodded, fascinated by what she had learned.

As they wandered from camp to camp, Kaylee stayed close to Blue Hawk, wondering if she would ever truly be a part of his world. It was all so alien to her.

At the Cheyenne camp, Chief Comes-in-Sight told how his sister, Buffalo Calf Road, had saved his life.

"My horse was shot out from under me," he said. "The Crows saw that I was helpless and they raced their ponies toward me, certain of taking my scalp, of counting coup. Singing my death song, I turned to face my enemies, when my sister galloped out from behind the rocks. The Crow were coming fast when she reached my side and carried me to safety. From this day on, her name will be sung among the lodges of my people."

Kaylee looked up at Blue Hawk as he translated the story for her. "Your women go to war?" she asked.

"If they wish. Our women are as brave as our men. They participate in the Sun Dance. We have women who wish to fight, just as we have men who do not. To each is given the right to do what she will."

She considered that as they walked back to their own camp. She doubted that she had the courage to go into battle. She had been taught by her mother that women were the bearers and preservers of life.

The dancing and singing went on far into the night. Long after Kaylee and Blue Hawk had retired to their lodge, she could hear the sound of drumming and merrymaking.

Snuggled close to Blue Hawk's side, she drifted off to sleep.

The camps slept late the next morning. Upon waking, Blue Hawk and Kaylee went down to the river to bathe. All up and down the river, men, women, and children were laughing and splashing in the cool water.

Kaylee smiled at the people nearby, pleased when they smiled back at her. It was a start, she thought, and hoped that someday they would think of her as one of them.

Returning to the lodge, she went inside to straighten their sleeping robes and tidy up while Blue Hawk went to visit Matoskah. A little before noon, she went outside, and sat in the shade. An air of lethargy hung over the camp, no doubt brought on by the heat and the fact that most everyone had been up late the night before. Sitting there, she wished she had something to read. Just one book from the dozens back at the ranch. Thoughts of books turned her mind toward her mother and she felt a sudden rush of homesickness. Though she loved Blue Hawk, she couldn't help missing her mother, or the comforts of home. And while their lodge was quite large, it couldn't begin to compare with the house at the ranch.

She looked up as Crazy Horse rode past, headed for the Cheyenne encampment down river. He was a handsome man, held in high esteem not only by the Lakota, but the other tribes as well. His bravery in battle was well known, boasted of by the Oglala warriors. It was said that no white man could kill him.

She glanced around the camp, thinking how peaceful it all was, when she heard a shout. Looking toward the Oglala camp, she saw a great cloud of dust.

She stood up as Blue Hawk came hurrying toward her. "What's happening?"

"Custer is coming!"

"Here? Now?"

Blue Hawk nodded. He could hear criers from the Hunkpapa camp shouting, "The White Eyes are coming! Warriors, get ready to fight! The White Eyes are coming!"

Looking in the direction of the Hunkpapa camp, Blue Hawk saw a great cloud of dust, and riding out of the dust a long line of soldiers, with Ree scouts riding at the head.

Runners went to warn the camps further downriver, while the Oglala warriors rounded up their horses and gathered their weapons. Women ran through the camp, calling for their children. Dogs, excited by the sudden activity, or perhaps sensing the increased tension, began to bark wildly.

Kaylee was clutching Blue Hawk's arm, as if to delay him. She saw a number of women herding their children toward the flats beyond the camp where the tall grass grew. Sisoka came hurrying toward them.

"Go with her," Blue Hawk said. "Stay with her until the fighting is over."

"No. I want to stay with you."

"You must do as I say, Kay-lee." Grasping her arms, he drew her close and kissed her, hard and quick. "Go, Kay-lee."

He watched her until she was out of sight, then he ducked inside their lodge and grabbed his bow. It was a fine, strong bow made of ash wood The bowstring was made from buffalo sinew. Matoskah was renowned for his skill at the making of weapons. Taking the otter-skin quiver of arrows that had also been a gift from his friend, he ran outside and caught up his horse.

Warriors from the other camps were riding toward the sounds of gunfire in the Hunkpapa village where Sitting Bull and his warriors were holding off the soldiers. As Blue Hawk rode up, he saw Gall and Black Moon and Sitting Bull leading a charge straight toward the soldiers. To Blue Hawk's surprise, the soldiers dismounted to fight on foot. The forces came together with a clash and a blast of gunfire, to be obscured in clouds of swirling dust.

Dismounting was a foolish thing for the *wasichu* to do, Blue Hawk thought, but a good thing for the women and children, for it meant the soldiers could not pursue them. He saw several old men herding a group of women and children away from the Hunkpapa camp. The soldiers' tactics were negating the element of surprise they had enjoyed. It was good.

A moment later Crazy Horse came riding up on his yellow pinto, his body painted with hailstones, the lightning streak on his face, the red-tailed hawk that was his medicine on his head. When the warriors saw him coming, they shouted his name, "Tashunke Witke!" over and over again.

"Hoppo!" the Oglala chief cried. "Let us go! It is a good day to die!"

Excitement pumped through Blue Hawk's veins as he followed Crazy Horse. They drove the soldiers back, away from the camp, away from the lodges and the women and children. Gunsmoke and dust lay heavy in the air. Warriors charged the soldiers, counting coup, eager to take scalps and guns. Only a few of the soldiers fought back. The others broke and ran for the river. Those who had dismounted died on their feet, swept down by the fierce riders. Those who stayed in the saddle leaned low over the necks of their horses, trying to dodge the blows of the warriors. There was no crossing here, and they jumped their horses from the banks. Some of the warriors gave chase, others went back to pick off the remaining soldiers and collect their weapons.

A soldier rose up out of the brush. The soldier sighted down the barrel of his rifle, but before he could fire, Blue Hawk's arrow found his heart. With a cry of victory, Blue Hawk leaned over the side of his horse and plucked the rifle from the *wasichu*'s hand. The warrior ahead of him swung his war club, knocking a soldier off his horse.

Blue Hawk reined his horse to a halt as the battle in the Hunkpapa camp slowed. He dismounted, retrieved a cartridge belt from a fallen soldier and slung it over his shoulder. Looking around, he saw that many of the lodges were riddled with bullets. Some had been knocked over, others were on fire. He saw Crazy Horse talking to Sitting Bull. Here and there warriors were stripping the dead soldiers of their clothing and weapons.

A few moments later, a warrior raced by on a lathered horse. "More soldiers are coming!" he shouted. "Follow me!"

Another warrior raised his rifle over his head. "Only

the earth and the mountains live forever! Be brave!
It is a good day to die!"

The shrill notes of war whistles pierced the air, calling the warriors to battle.

They responded immediately. Vaulting onto their
ponies, they raced downriver. Blue Hawk wheeled his
horse around, and then he saw them, a double column
of soldiers riding along the ridge on the far side of
the river across from the lower camps. With a wild
cry, he followed the other warriors.

They would not get there in time, Blue Hawk
thought. The soldiers would reach the river before
they did.

And then, to his surprise, he saw four Cheyenne
warriors cross the river to meet the soldiers. Four
against two hundred. It was a brave thing to do, a
thing so unexpected that the soldiers came to a halt.
The Cheyenne warriors fired their guns as quickly as
they could, and the White Eyes fired back. Five Lakota warriors joined the Cheyenne, nine brave men
holding off the bluecoats until more and more warriors joined them.

And now the fighting was intense. Blue Hawk fired
at one of the soldiers, his blood singing in his veins
as the soldier tumbled from his horse.

Gall and Knife Chief rode into their midst. *"Hoka
hey!"* the chiefs shouted. "It is a good day to die!"

Blue Hawk lifted his voice with those of the other
warriors. "It is a good day to die!"

Shouting the Lakota kill cry, *"Huhn, huhn, huhn,"*
they cut a wide swath through the panicked soldiers.

Relentlessly, the warriors drove the White Eyes
back, away from the village. Caught up in a tide of
warriors, Blue Hawk was swept into another battle,
on a hill away from the river. The White Eyes here
were mounted on gray horses. Soldiers who had lost
their horses fought on foot, some firing so rapidly that

their rifles overheated, making them useless. All
around him the fighting raged on, with red man and
white caught up in the heat of battle, charging each
other on horseback or engaged in fierce hand-to-
hand combat.

Blue Hawk fought his way through, killing several
of the soldiers with the gun he had taken, and he
heard Mato's voice echo in his mind: *Your enemies
will fall before you.* A soldier rose up before him. Blue
Hawk saw the hammer on the soldier's rifle fall, as if
in slow motion. There was no flash. No smoke. Blue
Hawk sighted down the shaft of his arrow. He was
about to let it fly when his horse stumbled and the
arrow, meant for the *wasichu*'s heart, went through
his neck instead. In his mind he again heard Mato's
voice, promising him safety in battle.

He reined his horse around, his heart huge with
war, and rode hard toward a group of soldiers. He
prowled among them, as fierce as Mato himself. Time,
the great circle, seemed to slow as he fought his enemies. The bear snarled within him as he struck them
down one by one. The *wasichu* moved as if caught in
a mire, slow, clumsy, helpless to escape the fury of
the bear.

The rifle he had seized was as well balanced as any
war club, leaping to do his bidding. A revolver flared,
leaving a deep burn along his rib cage. With a wild
cry he fired at the soldier who had wounded him. Another dead *wasichu*. Another coup to avenge Unci's
death.

He followed the Lakota and the Cheyenne as they
moved up the slope. Here were more soldiers on gray
horses, and in the middle was Custer.

The air was thick with smoke. Blue Hawk heard the
screams of wounded horses as they thrashed on the
ground, the shouts of frightened men, the ululating
war cries of the Lakota and the Cheyenne.

Crazy Horse rode up on a fresh horse. He thrust his rifle in the air and cried, "Oglalas, come! Follow me!"

Lifting his own rifle over his head, Blue Hawk galloped after Crazy Horse into the heart of the battle.

Kaylee huddled in the tall grass, watching the battle below her in horror. The sound of gunfire filled the air. Bullets ripped through the lodges. She saw a group of women and children running downriver, followed by several old men and camp dogs. A group of warriors took a stand, making a wall between the fleeing women and the soldiers. A thick haze of dust and smoke lay like a dark shroud over the camp.

A herd of horses ran through the village, and she saw a young man grab for the mane of one of them and leap onto its back. With a whoop he rode off to join the fight.

She pressed her hands to her ears, trying to shut out the sounds of the battle. Where was Blue Hawk? A few women and children stood nearby, huddled together, the children wide-eyed and silent.

She looked up, startled, as a handful of soldiers suddenly appeared from the right.

With a shriek, the women grabbed their children and began to run. Fear pounded through Kaylee as she scrambled to her feet. She screamed as the soldiers began to fire at the women.

The women scattered like hens chased by a fox. Kaylee ran for her life, cried out as her foot caught on a root and she fell to her hands and knees. She heard the sound of hoofbeats behind her. Wrapping her arms around her head, she closed her eyes, sure that she was going to die.

Gunfire roared over her head, and then there was an abrupt silence. Opening her eyes, she saw soldiers lying dead all around her. Sisoka helped her to her feet and smiled. Kaylee smiled in return, but it felt hollow, forced. The warriors who had come to their rescue dismounted and began scalping the soldiers. Some of the women drew their knives and began to mutilate the dead, while others stripped them of their clothing.

Kaylee looked away, gagging. She took a deep breath and closed her eyes, trying not to think of what was happening in other parts of the camp, trying not to picture Blue Hawk out there in the midst of the battle, a knife in one hand and a bloody scalp in the other.

She looked up with a start when someone tugged on her arm. Sisoka stood beside her, motioning for her to follow. Numbly she followed the women and children, many of whom were carrying coats and hats and bayonets taken from the dead soldiers.

The camps along the Little Big Horn were quiet now. All the fighting had moved across the river into the hills beyond.

Heavyhearted, Kaylee made her way to the lodge she shared with Blue Hawk.

She didn't belong here. She would never belong here.

Blue Hawk blew out a deep sigh as he stared at the field of battle. Custer and his men were dead. The Indians who had died at the Washita at the hands of Yellow Hair had been avenged, as had his grandmother, and the men and women of his own band. It had been a good day for his enemies to die. Just as Sitting Bull had foretold.

Reining his horse to a halt on a ridge overlooking the valley, he looked down on the camps below. The women were returning to their lodges. Others were moving toward the battleground to seek their dead or to strike the soldiers who had brought death to their lodges.

Never had he been in a fight like this one. He had seen many acts of bravery. Moving Robe, a Cheyenne woman, had ridden into the thick of the battle carrying the lance of her brother, who had been killed by Three Stars in the fight at the Rosebud. Yellow Nose, a Ute captive, had fought bravely beside his Cheyenne brothers. Blue Hawk had seen one bold Lakota warrior ride right through the midst of Yellow Hair's men.

There had been bravery among the whites, too.

It had been a noisy, bloody battle, and then suddenly it was over. Yellow Hair and all his men lay dead.

Now his thoughts turned to Kaylee.

Touching his heels to his horse, he rode down the hill and across the river, passing several young warriors wearing soldier clothes. One was blowing on a bugle.

He was nearing his lodge when Matoskah rode up beside him.

"Some of the soldiers are dug in up on the bluff, like rats in a hole," Matoskah said with a grin. "Come, we will flush them out."

Blue Hawk shook his head. He had had enough fighting for one day. Now all he wanted was to be with Kaylee.

Chapter 19

Kaylee paced the floor of her lodge, rehearsing what she would tell Blue Hawk. *I'm sorry,* she would say. *We made a mistake. Please take me home.*

It had been a mistake, she thought. She would never belong here. The Lakota believed in many gods; she believed in only one. They believed the rocks and grass and trees were alive. Blue Hawk believed his people could speak to animals. The men took scalps. Would she ever be able to forget the horror of watching the Lakota warriors make their way among the dead soldiers, mutilating the bodies of their enemies, counting coup, taking scalps?

As the minutes passed, she began to wonder what was keeping Blue Hawk. Had he been . . . no! She refused to consider the possibility, yet it remained in the back of her mind.

She was about to go in search of him when he entered the lodge. His hair was windblown, his skin damp with perspiration, splattered with blood, and smeared with the gritty residue of black powder. He smelled strongly of gunsmoke, horse sweat, and the coppery odor of blood.

She hurried toward him and embraced him, relieved that none of the blood seemed to be his, sickened because it meant he had killed others.

"Kay-lee?"

His voice floated over her, through her, tender, gentle. She looked up into his eyes and felt all her doubts and fears melt away. He was here. He loved her. She loved him. Nothing else mattered, nothing but—

She drew away from him, aware of a stickiness along her inner arm. She looked at the blood, then back at him. A long, shallow furrow cut across his ribs, oozing fresh blood where she had touched it.

"You're hurt!"

He glanced down at his side. "It is not serious." He had forgotten all about it in his need to see her, be with her.

Pushing him down on one of the blankets, she wet a strip of cloth and washed the wound, studying it intently. As he had said, it wasn't serious. But it might have been. It had narrowly missed the still-healing gunshot wound she had tended so carefully. She wrapped a strip of cloth around his middle, then gently washed away all evidence of the battle.

Murmuring his name, she sank into his embrace. Peace flowed through her, a sense of contentment, an assurance that she was where she was meant to be.

His hand stroked her hair, and then he leaned back a little so he could see her face. "You were going to leave me." It was not a question.

"How did you know?"

"I felt it while we were apart. I saw it in your eyes when I came in."

She shook her head. "I was having doubts, that's all."

"And now?"

She rested her cheek against his chest. "I'm where I want to be."

Later, after he had put on a clean breechclout, he told her about the battle. The soldiers had fought bravely, he said, his voice filled with respect.

"When their rifles jammed, they fought with their

pistols, and when those were empty, they used their rifles like clubs."

In the end, more than two hundred soldiers had been killed, including Yellow Hair Custer, and Mitch Bouyer, son of a trader the Indians were familiar with. Blue Hawk had heard of only twenty Lakota and Cheyenne dead. Though the fighting was over for the day, there were soldiers dug in on a bluff above the Hunkpapa camp.

"Crazy Horse has placed a night guard around them," Blue Hawk said. "Death lodges have been prepared for our dead."

"So what will happen tomorrow? Will there be more fighting?"

"Crazy Horse and the other chiefs will decide."

His words filled her with uneasiness. She had hoped that when he returned, the fighting would be over and he would be safe. But there could be another battle tomorrow.

"Blue Hawk." She looked up at him, her heart and soul filled with anxiety at the thought of what the morrow might bring.

"Kay-lee, do not worry. Mato promised me a long life."

She held that thought close to her as he drew her into his arms. He kissed her tenderly, as if he was aware of how fragile her emotions were. His need to taste her, to lose himself in her sweetness, aroused him into movement. His hands stroked her back, his fingertips savored the warmth of her breast, coaxing her with gentle urging, asking, not demanding. The rush of heat overwhelmed her, driving her desire into the abyss of want, the sweet ache of need. Unfolding layer by layer, she opened to him. He drew her into his kiss, until there was nothing in all the world but his mouth on hers, his hands sliding over her, under her, arousing her until she quivered with desperate need.

"Now," she whispered and hugged him tighter, moaning with pleasure as his body covered hers.

There was no yesterday, no tomorrow. There was only now, the warmth of his arms, the rhythm of his body moving deep inside, lifting her until she was soaring, flying higher and higher, through rainbows and soul-shattering lightning. Then she was tumbling down, down, through a storm of ecstasy that left her breathless, her body floating, drifting, in a pool of sweet and utter contentment.

The next morning she woke with a sense of dread. Fighting the urge to beg Blue Hawk not to go, she watched him dress for battle, watched him paint his face with jagged streaks of red and yellow, watched him tie an eagle feather into his hair.

He was magnificent to look at, so handsome that her breath caught in her throat.

She forced herself to smile as he came to kiss her, whispered, "Be careful," as he turned and left the lodge.

Blue Hawk rode behind Crazy Horse and Gall as they galloped toward the bluff where the soldiers were dug in. Chiefs and leaders from the other bands and tribes were there. Blue Hawk listened as the head men discussed what to do. Some spoke in favor of making a charge and settling the fight right away. Others spoke against it, saying many warriors would be lost, arguing that their ammunition was used up. Others suggested that they wait. Soon the white men would have to come out for water.

While the head men were still deciding, scouts rode up. A great army was coming upriver, they said. This army had wagon guns and many more soldiers than they had fought the day before.

"Short Bull and his men stayed back there, to slow them," Gall said. "We must hurry and leave, or we must fight."

In the end it was decided that there had been enough fighting. It was time to move on.

The Lakota were somber as they left the valley of the Little Big Horn. There was no singing on this day, no showing off by the young men, as Crazy Horse's people rode upriver toward the Bighorn Mountains, moving fast.

Kaylee tried to look away, but she couldn't seem to take her eyes off the battleground. The Indians had taken their own dead away, but the bodies of the soldiers had been stripped and left where they fell. It was a chilling sight. Some of the bodies had been horribly mutilated, one had been beheaded. The bloated bodies of dead horses littered the field. Cavalry saddles could be seen here and there; bits and pieces of Army uniforms made dark blue splashes against the ground. The lodges of the dead had been left behind. Dogs prowled among the deserted lodges, yapping and snarling.

"What's that?" Kaylee asked. She glanced over her shoulder as the smell of smoke stung her nostrils.

"The warriors are firing the grass."

"Why?"

"So there will be no graze for the horses of the White Eyes."

"Oh."

Blue Hawk was heavyhearted as they left the Greasy Grass behind. Though the battle had been a victory, there had been Indian losses and the people were in mourning. Among the Lakota and Cheyenne dead were many that he knew: Black Cloud, Owns-Red-Horse, Lame White Man, Red Face, Long Road, White Eagle, Black White Man, Two Bears, Standing Elk, Long Robe, Elk Bear, High Horse, Chased-by-Owls. So many names that would not be heard again.

He had heard that the Cheyenne warrior Lame White

Man had been shot by a Lakota who had mistaken him for a Crow scout. An Arapaho named Left Hand was said to have found a wounded Indian and killed him, only to discover later than the Indian had been Lakota. In the heat of battle, when dust and gunsmoke obscured vision and a warrior's blood ran hot in his veins, mistakes such as these were sometimes made. Though tragic, they were understandable, if not forgivable.

Blue Hawk rode back often to check on Kaylee, who rode beside Sisoka. As though aware of his feelings, Kaylee said little, and for that Blue Hawk was grateful.

They rode all that day. That night, they rested, though they did not set up their lodges. At daylight they were on the move again.

The second night after the battle, the Cheyenne staged a victory dance. Some of the Lakota bands joined in. Sitting Bull's Hunkpapas did not. It was a time for mourning, he said, not a time for celebration. Though Blue Hawk did not say so, he agreed with Sitting Bull.

Blue Hawk was not surprised when none of the women took part in the dance. Many of them could barely walk because of the gashes they had inflicted on their legs as a sign of mourning.

They traveled steadily for the next two days before making camp on the banks of Rosebud Creek. It was here that the Lakota and Cheyenne held a scalp dance.

It was, Kaylee thought, both barbaric and beautiful. The warriors, their faces painted black as a symbol of victory, danced in a circle in the center of the camp. Their mothers and sisters joined them, holding poles from which the trophy scalps dangled. The costumes of the men were wide and varied, most often imitating a bird or an animal. They danced with body crouched,

chest up, knees bent, head held high, occasionally
glancing from side to side. The women, dressed in
their finest, sidestepped to the beat of the drum in a
half circle facing the center.

Songs were sung honoring the bravery of the danc-
ers, for scalps taken, for coup counted.

Kaylee watched Blue Hawk. Clad in breechclout
and moccasins, a necklace of bear claws at his throat,
his face painted black, he was both familiar and alien
to her. His steps were quick and sure, his body lithe
as he dipped and swayed. Firelight cast red-gold high-
lights in his hair.

She saw Matoskah dancing nearby, saw Sisoka dancing with the women, four scalps dangling from the
slender pole in her hand.

Knowing her feelings as well as he knew his own,
Blue Hawk had not asked her to take part in the
dance. Though she loved him with all her heart and
soul, she could not take part in a dance that celebrated
the killing of white men, even when those white men
had attacked the camps along the Little Big Horn
without provocation.

When the dance was over, Blue Hawk took her
hand and led her away from the others, and there,
under the cover of night, he made love to her. Their
coupling was wild and sweet, an affirmation of life and
hope in the aftermath of battle and death.

During the next few days, they traveled eastward,
toward the Tongue River, and then farther east to the
Powder. It was here, on the Powder, that the Indians
held a parade.

Kaylee watched with mixed curiosity and amusement as the warriors passed by, two by two, pretending to be American soldiers. They wore the
uniforms of the Seventh Cavalry, except for boots and
trousers, which they apparently didn't care for. One
warrior carried a guidon. Another blew discordant

notes on a badly dented bugle. Another carried a pair of binoculars. Some rode the gray horses that had been captured after the battle.

After the parade, the Indians separated. Sitting Bull and his people headed north toward Canada, while the Cheyenne rode toward the Yellowstone. Crazy Horse's Oglalas headed toward their favorite hunting grounds in the Black Hills. Blue Hawk and his people followed Crazy Horse.

The battle was over. The victory foretold in Sitting Bull's vision had been fulfilled. It was time to move on.

Chapter 20

Shaun Randall sat on the rocker on the front porch and puffed on his pipe as he watched the sun come up over the foothills, wondering, as he often did these days, what he was going to do about Emma. Last week he had sent a couple of his men over to the fort to see if there was any word of Kaylee. When they returned without any news of her whereabouts, Emma had taken to her bed. Randy Harris had gone off half-cocked and joined the cavalry. Damfool kid! Probably get himself killed, Shaun thought. He shook his head. If Randy or Emma had told him about what was going on up at the line shack when they first found that damned redskin, Kaylee wouldn't be missing now.

There was no sense blaming the boy. Emma was just as guilty. No wonder she had taken to her bed. The burden of not knowing if her daughter was dead or alive, combined with her own guilt over what had happened, had finally taken its toll. Dammit, why hadn't they told him what was going on?

It made him sick in his gut when he thought about Kaylee being at the mercy of a bunch of heathen savages. Damned Indians. Nothing but trouble, that was for sure. They forced you into action, and then you wound up feeling bad about some of the actions you took. His conscience still bothered him whenever he thought about that Indian kid Jackson had finished off. Still, if Randy had done the same to that injured warrior who had kidnapped Kaylee, Kaylee would be home, Emma would be up and around, and his stomach wouldn't be twisted in knots.

With a sigh, he looked at the newspaper in his lap. Now this—a slaughter of soldiers by the damn Indians. The headline was almost two weeks old: CUSTER AND 210 MEN WIPED OUT AT THE LITTLE BIG HORN.

It had been a bitter day for the Custer family. Custer's brother, Boston, had also been killed, as had his nephew, Autie Reed. Mark Kellogg, a newspaper correspondent, and Charlie Reynolds, a well-known scout, were among the victims. The article gave a brief description of the battle, then went on to eulogize Custer.

"George Armstrong Custer was born in New Rumley, Ohio. After high school, he enrolled in West Point."

Shaun snorted softly. Custer had gone to West Point, all right—and graduated last in his class. A bunch of half-naked savages had outflanked and outmaneuvered him, and he'd lost his entire command.

"During the Civil War, Custer fought in the First Battle of Bull Run, and served with distinction in the Virginia and Gettysburg campaigns. His aggression in battle resulted in high casualties among his men; however, it also earned him the respect of his superiors."

Well, Shaun reflected, those same superiors ought to respect the hell out of Custer now—he'd lost all his men this time and his hair to boot. He read on.

"In 1866 Custer was appointed Lieutenant-colonel of the Seventh Cavalry."

A step down, Shaun mused, since he'd been a brevet general during the War. Maybe somebody in the War Department knew something after all. The next paragraph seemed to confirm it.

"The next year he campaigned against the Southern Cheyenne. Late in 1867 Custer was court-martialed for being absent from duty during the campaign. He was suspended from duty for one year; however, he was called back to duty by General Phil Sheridan in 1868."

Politics, Shaun figured. There were probably politics in the Army, too, "where he redeemed himself in the battle of the Washita.

"In 1873 Custer was sent to the Northern Plains. The following year he led an expedition into the Black Hills.

"Custer is survived by his wife, Elizabeth."

With a shake of his head, Shaun let the paper fall to the floor. Damned Indians, all they did was cause trouble and misery. To add insult to injury, just when everybody around here thought all the Indians were running from Crook, some damned redskins had come along last week and made off with a hundred head of his cattle and another two hundred of Garth Jackson's. Garth was out with his tough riders, scouring the countryside, looking for sign. Shouldn't be hard to cut a trail—three hundred cattle would cut a wide swath.

Shaun paused at that thought. The Indians didn't usually steal that many head at once. They lived from hand to mouth for the most part, stealing only enough to live on for a while, knowing they could always come back for more. Blasted redskins. They were acting like real rustlers this time.

He let the thought go because it wasn't the cattle that concerned him at the moment. He could afford to lose a hundred head. Hell, he could afford to lose a thousand. But his life wouldn't be worth living if Emma grieved herself to death over her lost daughter.

Rising, he smacked the flat of his hand against the porch rail. Where the hell was Kaylee? And what was he going to do about Emma?

Chapter 21

All during the long journey to the Paha Sapa, the warriors talked of the victory at the Greasy Grass. Blue Hawk knew it was a battle that would be re-fought for years to come, knew that the events of that day would be passed down from father to son for generations.

One of the mysteries of the battle was the fact that the Indians had not been able to identify Custer. An Indian they met from one of the agencies solved it for them. Custer, it seemed, had cut off his long yellow hair before the battle.

The warriors boasted of souvenirs they had taken: tobacco, coffee, gauntlets, guns, hats. Some of the men took McClellan saddles. Others had taken silver dollars, which they used for ornaments on their horses. The paper money meant little to them, and most of it had been torn up or burned. Blue Hawk had seen children playing with some of it, using it to make paper tipis or clothes for dolls, saddle blankets for toy horses made of mud. It was such a waste, Blue Hawk thought. He could have bought food, or ammunition for the guns they had taken from the soldiers, with the *wasichu* paper money, but it was too late now. He had managed to collect a few dollars, which he had hidden away in his belongings to avoid the scorn of other warriors at keeping such useless trophies.

The warriors told tales of individual fights within

the larger battle, of coup counted, of close calls. They spoke of the soldiers. Most had been brave, which was a good thing. A brave enemy made for a better story around the campfire. Some of the *wasichu* were not so brave. There were stories of soldiers who had killed themselves, or who had tried to surrender and were killed for their cowardice. Some of the cowards had provided entertainment.

Matoskah told of two old women he had seen going through the bodies, taking uniform shirts and body parts for trophies. One of the women had peeled the trousers off a *wasichu* and applied her skinning knife to the man's genitals. He had suddenly jumped up. He had only been pretending to be dead. Matoskah said it was very funny, watching the naked white man try to escape through all the women armed with skinning knives. He had not succeeded.

For all the satisfaction over the outcome of the battle, Blue Hawk wondered what the final consequences of the Greasy Grass would be. It was impossible to learn a people's language without learning something of the culture that went with it. Blue Hawk wished with all his heart that the *wasichu* would leave the Lakota and their allies in peace now, as a number of the warriors seemed to believe they would. But Blue Hawk feared that the soldiers would come after them with renewed fury, a new hatred, determined to avenge the deaths of Yellow Hair and his men. He feared that this time they would keep coming until the last of his people were on a reservation or dead. He felt a terrible unease at the certainty of this knowledge, wanted to ignore it, but he greatly feared that the triumph at the Greasy Grass would be the last great victory his people would know.

Though he spent much of his time thinking of the battle and its consequences, thoughts of his woman were uppermost in his mind. In the last few days,

Kaylee had become adept at erecting and dismantling their lodge. She was learning how to cook over an open fire, and how to skin the small game he brought her, though she could not quite conceal her look of distaste. She was learning more and more of his language. She and Sisoka were becoming friends. He praised Kaylee often for her efforts, and ate the meals she prepared without complaint, even though the meat was often overdone. He was proud of her accomplishments, of her efforts to learn all she could about his people.

Returning from watering the horses one evening, he paused to watch her add a bit of seasoning to the pot over the fire. He saw her smile into the flames and knew she knew he was there. He had lost the ability to sneak up on her. She always knew when he was nearby.

She looked up now, with the warm, sweet smile that was for him alone, and hurried toward him.

He swept her into his arms and carried her into their lodge. That night, it was not her fault that the meat was overdone.

Kaylee smoothed the robes they used for sleeping, smiling as she remembered the night past. She never tired of being in Blue Hawk's arms, of hearing him whisper that he loved her. Each day, each night, her love for him grew deeper, stronger.

Sometimes they walked a little ways from the camp so they could be alone. They would find a quiet place, sit side by side, and talk softly while they watched the stars overhead. He told her of his childhood, of his parents, of learning to hunt and track. He told her of the first time he had killed an enemy, his revulsion and his exultation.

She told him of her mother, of the father she hardly remembered, of Shaun, and how she had tried to love him even though she had been afraid of him. She told him about Randy and Garth, of being lonely because she had no close friends except the snooty Thomas sisters.

Inevitably, they ended the night in each other's arms. She would never get enough of him, she thought, never tire of his lips on hers, the touch of his heated flesh against her own. She knew now what that dreamy look in her mother's eyes had been when she spoke of Kaylee's father. It was love, but more than love. It was admiration and respect and desire and so much, much more. She had never seen Emma look at Shaun that way.

Midway to the Paha Sapa, Crazy Horse decided they would rest a day and a night to give the old ones a chance to recover from the march. Kaylee was glad for the respite. Though she had always loved to ride, doing it hour after hour, day after day, was not the same as riding a few hours for pleasure.

The place that Crazy Horse's scouts found was a pleasant one. Tall grass waved under a gentle breeze, and a stand of timber grew along a shallow stream. As soon as she had the lodge erected, Kaylee went down to the streambed to look for driftwood. She was sweaty from the labor of setting up the tipi and thought she might sneak in a quick swim if she could find a deep enough pool.

Some of the women were gathered along the bank, keeping an eye on several children who were playing in the water. Kaylee noted that not only were their lodges already up, but cookfires already were burning down to coals. They made it all seem so effortless! But she was learning.

She had learned much about the Lakota in the last few weeks. Colors had a special significance. Red was the color of Wi, the god of the sun, and of all things the Lakota held sacred; green represented Maka, the earth; yellow was the color for Inyan, the rock. Blue was for the most potent of their gods, Skan, the sky. Black and white represented the nature of mankind— black for anger or grief, white for pleasure. Garments that were colored red proclaimed that the wearer was *wakan*; green told of generosity, yellow of bravery. Few things were painted blue, for blue was the symbolic color of Wakan Tanka and was to be used for things of the spirit only.

There were stories to be told in shapes and figures. A circle meant a camp; it could also mean the sun or the world. Marks across a circle could mean a spider or a whirlwind. The four winds were represented by a square, which could also mean the land of the Lakota. Triangles denoted tipis; triangles standing side by side denoted mountains. A single straight line indicated a trail; an arrow represented a journey, a hunting party, or a war party.

A red handprint painted on a horse's flank was known as a blood mark and meant the rider had killed a man in hand-to-hand combat. Short horizontal lines painted on a horse's nose signified coup. Lakota men held their war horses in high esteem. A red circle painted around a horse's nose was believed to give the animal a sharp sense of smell, a red or white line around the eye added strength to its sight. Lightning streaks running from a horse's rump down the rear leg and from the head down the foreleg meant speed and power. A rectangle meant the warrior had led a war party. Battle scars on a horse were circled with red paint as symbols of honor.

Wisdom and bravery were qualities valued by the Lakota, as was generosity. The boys were taught to use a bow and arrow at an early age. They played ferocious games mimicking war, and it was every boy's ambition to seek a vision and become a warrior. Little girls played with dolls. Older girls helped their mothers with the cooking and cleaning, thereby learning housekeeping skills. Girls were also taught tanning, quilling, and beading, either by their mothers, or by an aunt or an older sister. Older children were expected to care for their younger siblings. All well-brought-up children were taught to be polite, to respect their elders, to knock on the side of a tipi before entering.

Onc thing she thought odd was that there seemed to be no word for "good-bye" in the Lakota language. When they went to visit Matoskah, she had noticed that Blue Hawk never said good-bye. When the visit was over, Blue Hawk simply stood up and they left the lodge.

By the time she returned to her lodge with an armful of sticks, Blue Hawk was there.

"Come," he said.

Kaylee dropped the wood inside the lodge door. "Where are we going?"

"Matoskah and some others are having a horse race."

Kaylee considered making a sarcastic comment to the effect that she would have thought everybody in the camp would have had quite enough of riding for the moment, but she decided against it. Her idea of humor sometimes seemed lost on the Lakota.

"Oh. Sounds like fun," was her only comment.

Blue Hawk vaulted onto the back of his horse, then took hold of Kaylee's forearm and swung her up behind him.

Kaylee wrapped her arms around his waist and he urged his horse away from the camp. They crossed the stream and rode to where a dozen or so men and women were gathered, all talking and laughing.

Blue Hawk drew his horse to a halt a few feet away from the crowd.

"Are you racing?" Kaylee asked.

"Ai." He offered her his hand, and she slid to the ground.

Kaylee patted the neck of Blue Hawk's horse. "How long is the race?"

"We will start there," Blue Hawk said, pointing to a group of mounted men. "We will follow the stream to the first bend, over the deadfall, around the rocks, and back to where we started."

Kaylee looked up at him and smiled. "Good luck."

With a boyish grin, he went to join the other men who were going to race. There were eight in all.

The mounted warriors spread out. Blue Hawk rode a long-legged bay with a crooked blaze and one white stocking. The gelding tossed its head, ears flicking back and forth, as if impatient to run, and perhaps it was, Kaylie thought, after the long march from the Greasy Grass. Matoskah was mounted on a walleyed claybank.

Kaylee smiled at Sisoka and the other women, who smiled in return. They were all chattering excitedly, speaking too fast for her to understand more than a few words. Caught up in the excitement around her, she felt almost as if wars and bloodletting and columns of vengeful cavalry had all been just a nightmare.

She didn't hear a signal, but suddenly the race was on.

For a time, the horses ran neck and neck and then, slowly, Matoskah, Blue Hawk, and a warrior mounted on a flashy piebald stallion pulled away from the others.

Kaylee's heart began to pound with excitement. She shouted, "Go, Blue Hawk, go!" as he drew a little ahead.

He was beautiful to watch, she thought. Leaning low over his mount's neck, his hair blowing behind him, Blue Hawk rode as if he was a part of the horse.

They reached the bend and turned back toward

home. She held her breath as Blue Hawk soared over the deadfall with room to spare. A shout drew her attention from Blue Hawk and she glanced back at the other riders. One of the horses had gone down, but the rider had quickly rolled out of the way, apparently unhurt.

She turned her attention back to Blue Hawk, Matoskah, and the third rider. They disappeared behind the rock, briefly, and when they came into view again Blue Hawk and Matoskah were neck and neck.

"Blue Hawk! Blue Hawk!" She chanted his name as the horses lined out, heading for home.

The other spectators were also shouting, cheering for their favorites. The ground vibrated with the pounding of hooves as the horses drew nearer. Matoskah whipped his horse into the lead, and Kaylee feared the race was lost, but Blue Hawk's bay suddenly regained the lead. Ears back, neck extended, the bay streaked across the finish line. Matoskah and the warrior astride the piebald finished neck and neck. The other riders crossed the line a few moments later. The last warrior returned leading his mount, which was favoring its left foreleg.

Kaylee ran toward Blue Hawk. She threw her arms around him when he dismounted. "Congratulations!"

Blue Hawk grinned down at her. *"Pilamaya, mitawicu."*

The warrior riding the piebald stallion approached them. With a look of resignation, he offered the animal's reins to Blue Hawk.

"Hecheto welo," Blue Hawk said, taking the horse's lead rope.

With a nod, the warrior turned and walked away.

Only then did Kaylee notice that the other Indians were exchanging goods: a beaded choker, a trade blanket, an Army canteen, a deer hide, a skinning knife.

Kaylee ran her hand over the piebald's neck. "He's beautiful."

"*Ai*. If you are agreeable, we will breed the stallion to your mare."

Kaylee ran a knowing eye over the stallion, imagining the foals that would come from such a breeding. "I think that would be wonderful."

"I thought you would be pleased," he said, handing her the reins. "The stallion is for you."

"You mean it?" The Lakota weren't much for public displays of affection, but it was all she could do to keep from throwing her arms around him. Instead, she smiled up at him, hoping he could see the love in her heart reflected in her eyes. "Oh, Blue Hawk, thank you!"

The Black Hills, or the Paha Sapa, as the Lakota called them, was a sacred place to the Indians. Blue Hawk told her that the literal translation was "hills that are black," but the name also held a deeper, more spiritual meaning. The Lakota called the Hills "the heart of everything that is."

They had journeyed through some beautiful country to get there. The Black Hills rose thousands of feet above the Great Plains, a vast oasis of pine-covered mountains. From a distance they did, indeed, look black, because of the proliferation of ponderosa pines that covered the hills.

Within the Black Hills were green valleys and lush meadows, foothills and rugged rock formations, canyons and gulches, open grasslands and deep blue lakes. There were caves, too, Blue Hawk said, sacred to the People. The Lakota revered the land. It was a place of Power, of spiritual and physical renewal. It was here, he told her, that he had come to seek his vision. Their allies, the Cheyenne, the Arapaho, and the Kiowa, also came here to seek visions and purify themselves. The Hills had been given to the Lakota by treaty, Blue Hawk told her, a treaty that had been broken when Yellow Hair discovered gold in them. Soon thousands of miners were pouring into the Hills, following the "Thieves Road," which was what his people called Yellow Hair's trail into their land.

As they went deeper into the Hills, Kaylee saw elk, deer, bighorn sheep, and mountain goats.

Crazy Horse and his people made their camp in a lush meadow cut by a winding stream. In just a short time, the lodges were in place. Kaylee felt a surge of pride as she erected her lodge alongside Sisoka's. She had learned much in the weeks since the battle at the Greasy Grass. She could skin game, though she didn't think she would ever be able to do it without a grimace of distaste. She was learning to speak Lakota. Blue Hawk was teaching her to tell time by observing the movement of the sun and the moon. He was also teaching her how to determine in what direction she was going. Sisoka was teaching her how to cook, how to find the wild fruits and vegetables and seasonings that supplemented the Indian diet of venison and buffalo meat. She was slowly getting acquainted with the other women. She was grateful for their friendship, for their willingness to help her.

It seemed she had always worn an elkskin tunic and moccasins, always carried a knife in a sheath at the small of her back. Always slept in a bed of soft furs. Always loved a tall Lakota brave—Blue Hawk. Her love for him grew deeper with the passing of each day. He was strong yet tender, ever caring for her feelings. Never in all her life had she felt so loved, so cherished.

A week after they reached the Black Hills, they bred the piebald stallion to Kaylee's mare.

Kaylee packed enough food for a couple of days and she and Blue Hawk rode away from the village to a small secluded canyon. Blue Hawk built a fence across the narrow opening, and then they turned the horses loose and, as Emma would have said, let nature take its course.

Dusty was in season, but she was a maiden mare, unsure and perhaps a little frightened. Careful to avoid the quick slash of the mare's hooves, the stallion wooed Dusty, lightly nipping her shoulder, rubbing his head against her flanks, prancing back and forth in front of her, his neck arched, his head and tail high. His organ swelled, dropped.

Dusty fled to the far side of the canyon, and the stallion raced after her. He nipped her on her rump, as if to assert his dominance, and then he reared up on his hind legs and covered the mare. Dusty quivered beneath his assault.

Living on the ranch, Kaylee had seen animals mate before: dogs, cats, pigs, goats, even horses, but never quite like this. At the ranch, the breeding had been controlled, with one of the cowhands standing at the mare's head, and Shaun holding the stallion's lead rope. This was a wild, primal act, with no human interference or direction.

The stallion shuddered as, with a shake of his head, he withdrew.

Dusty stood there a moment; then, with a toss of her head, she trotted off and began to graze. The stallion followed her.

Feeling the weight of Blue Hawk's gaze, Kaylee looked up at him. She had been oddly stirred by the mating of the stallion and the mare. One look into Blue Hawk's eyes told her he, too, had been affected.

He held out his hand and she took it, letting him lead her to a shady patch of grass beneath a pair of scrawny trees. Sitting down beside him, she let nature take its course.

*   *   *

The days passed quickly, and a week later they returned to the main camp.

Life soon settled into a pleasant routine. Kaylee fashioned a new tunic. Sisoka helped her paint the yoke, taught her how to cut a pattern for new moccasins for herself and Blue Hawk. She grew more fluent in the Lakota language, adapted to the Indian's customs. When entering a friend's lodge, women went to the left and men to the right. The women rarely looked directly at the men, or the men at the women. It was considered poor etiquette to look directly into another's eyes. When food was served, the men were always served first.

The Lakota were a very religious people. She learned that Blue Hawk prayed to the Great Spirit each morning.

The birth of a child was cause for celebration within the whole tribe, and was considered the fulfillment of a woman's role. Four days after a baby was born, a herald went through the camp inviting everyone to a feast for the naming of the child. Contrary to the way she had been raised, people did not take gifts to the new mother; among the Lakota, the new father and the child's grandmother gave gifts to friends and to the poor. Caring for the new baby, while primarily the mother's responsibility, was also shared by the mother's sisters and female cousins.

Kaylee took a special interest in how the Lakota reared their offspring since she hoped she would one day have a child of her own. Young children ran virtually naked throughout the summer. She noticed that disobedient children were never spanked. Children were never told to do something, but rather were asked. If a child was doing something wrong, he was asked to stop, and it was explained to him why such behavior was unacceptable. Children were not permitted to cry, and to that end their wants were readily catered to or they were held and cuddled until their crying ceased. Sometimes a grandmother cried with the child. Children were taught to respect their elders. At a very early age, they were allowed to make their own decisions about what to wear, what and when to eat.

As soon as a boy was old enough to straddle a horse, he was given a horse of his own and taught to care for it by his father or another male relative. As boys grew older, they were put in charge of their father's horses. As she had noted before, boys were taught the ways of war from a very young age.

As comfortable as she felt living with the Lakota, there were days when she was overcome with a wave of homesickness, when she wanted nothing more than to see her mother. No doubt Emma and Shaun had given her up for dead by now.

With a sigh, she turned her attention back to the shirt she was making for Blue Hawk. It was too painful to think of home, to know she would never see her mother again.

Chapter 22

Dismounting, Randy patted his horse's neck, glad that the lieutenant had called for a rest stop. The hot August sun beat down unmercifully, taking its toll on man and animal alike.

Randy took a long drink from his canteen, then led his horse down to the stream.

Joining the cavalry had been a spur-of-the-moment decision, made when he got home and found out that Kaylee was missing. He had told her that no good would come from looking after that damned Injun, and he'd been right. She had saved the savage's life, and he had repaid her by kidnapping her. For all Randy knew, she might be dead now. His parents and Emma had tried to talk him out of joining the Army, but old man Randall had said it might make a man of him. Randy swore under his breath. Shaun Randall blamed him for everything that had happened. And deservedly so, Randy thought bitterly. He should have killed that damned redskin when he had the chance. Kaylee might never have forgiven him, but at least she would be safe at home where she belonged.

He glanced at the dusty soldiers watering their own mounts up and down the rivulet of water. Army life wasn't quite what Randy had expected it to be. He had signed up for a three-year term of service, unwilling to commit to five. The pay was thirteen dollars a month. He shook his head. The living conditions were primitive, far worse than those of ranch life. The barracks at the fort were crude, and there was no privacy to speak of. He had never lived in a bunkhouse, since his folks owned their own place. Now he had a cot and a wooden footlocker to call his own, and little else. Cots lined the walls, cast-iron woodstoves at either end of the barracks provided heat, and light was supplied by kerosene lamps suspended from the ceiling beams. Troopers took turns standing fire watch through the night, their rotation assigned by the sergeant; more than one barracks had burned with loss of life over the years. A rack held their weapons.

The men assembled at 6 A.M. for roll call; mess was at 6:30, fatigue call at 7:30, sick call at 8. Recall from fatigue duty came at 9:45, mounted drill at 10 on Mondays, Wednesdays, and Fridays; marching and close-order drill at 10 on Tuesdays and Thursdays; recall from drill at 11. First Sergeants Call was at 11:45 for morning reports. Mess was at noon, drill for target practice at 1. Time spent in target practice was Randy's favorite time of the day. Target practice was often done on horseback, first at a walk, then a trot, then a gallop. Randy was the best shot in his company with either a rifle or a six-gun. Of course, he'd been raised with firearms, unlike some of his fellow troopers.

Afternoon fatigue call was at 2, except for Fridays and Saturdays when the men cleaned the barracks for Sunday inspections. There were any number of fatigue details. Men on fatigue dug ditches, hoed weeds in the company vegetable gardens, did the harvesting and planting. Men on kitchen detail chopped wood, carried water, waited on the men during mess, washed the dishes and set the tables.

Recall from fatigue duty was at 4:15. Stable call was at 4:30. It was another part of the day Randy enjoyed. As a born Westerner he knew that if you looked after your mount, it would look after you. Then came evening mess. None of the meals held a candle to ranch food, but he was adjusting. Five minutes before sundown, the entire garrison was assembled in dress uniform; roll call was at sunset. Last roll call was at 9 p.m., when the soldiers gathered in company formations in front of quarters, and lights-out at 9:30.

The routine varied a little on Sundays, when inspection was at 9, and church was held at 10:15 for those who wished to attend. Not surprisingly, most of the men preferred to go back to the barracks and catch a little more sleep. Remembering his early training, Randy went to church, mainly so he could write his Ma and tell her he'd been to church that week.

Though he was adjusting to the food, it remained his biggest complaint, though some of the soldiers from poorer backgrounds seemed to relish it. Hash, stew, beans, bacon, hardtack, bread, and coffee were the mainstays. Army rations didn't include milk, butter, or eggs, so the men used company funds to buy them when they could. Most of their food was boiled. Of all the things he missed, his mother's cooking topped the list. Heck, even chuck-wagon grub during roundup was better than Army chow. Cowboys would have rebelled against the kind of food the Army expected you to march and fight on.

The men found plenty of things to keep them occupied when they had time off. Footraces were popular, as were weight lifting and baseball. Boxing was also popular; wrestling less so. Of course, anywhere there were horses, there were also horse races. Randy was a skilled rider and could get the most out of the Army mounts, but he still missed the gelding that damned redskin had stolen along with his girl. Kaylee. In her last letter, his ma had mentioned that Kay was still missing and feared dead.

Since he had signed up, Randy had learned there

were almost as many reasons for joining the Army as
there were recruits: factory workers who were tired of
the same routine, farmers who were weary of trying
to wrest a living from the earth, drifters, Civil War
veterans, students who had run away from school, im-
migrants who couldn't find work, down-and-outers
looking for three square meals a day and a place to
call home. One man, an immigrant from Denmark,
had fought in the Prusso-Danish War, then gone on
to enlist in the French army during the Franco-
Prussian War. From there he had gone into the French
Foreign Legion, and he finally ended up in New York.
Unable to find work, he had joined the Army. It was
a familiar life, provided food and shelter, and gave
him a chance to learn the ways and language of his
new country. Some joined because they wanted to see
the West, some because they just wanted to fight.

A lot of men who joined up looking for excitement
were soon disenchanted by the harsh realities of
Army life.

The Army knew all about such regrets; that was
why there were morning reports and so many roll calls
per day. Deserters were anticipated and dealt with
harshly. So far, no one had deserted Randy's troop.

He didn't much like the heavy Springfield single-
shot rifle that was standard issue, compared to his own
pet Winchester standing in the corner at home
awaiting his return. His new boots gave him blisters,
the heavy underwear made him itch, and the McClellan saddle had none of the rocking-chair familiarity of
his own double-girth Texas rig. But he had to admit
that he looked mighty fine in his dress uniform, and
the troop made a fine, brave show on parade.

He had quickly learned that the officers rarely
spoke to the enlisted men, except in the line of duty.
It didn't take long to discover which officers were
decent and fair and which were abusive bullies.

The first sergeant was the link between the officers and the squadron sergeants, and basically was in full charge of the troop under the direction of the captain. Certainly the "first shirt" wielded more power than the callow lieutenant who was the troop's executive officer and ostensibly the second-in-command. The first sergeant had a room to himself. He called the roll three times a day, drew all the rations and clothing, made out the guard details, made certain his men were presentable for Sunday inspection, visited the sick and wounded in the hospital. He made twenty-two dollars a month.

Except in time of war, when promotions came fast, it took a long time to make first sergeant in the cavalry. Randy figured that in his short, three-year term he'd be lucky to make buck sergeant.

"Scouts say we're closing in on some hostiles," the trooper watering his mount next to Randy remarked. "Won't be long now, Harris."

Randy nodded at the trooper. Toby Lincoln had signed up about the same time as Randy. Linc was tall and beanpole-thin, with a shock of wheat-blond hair and gray eyes. They had endured the customary hazing by the old-timers together and had been the butt of numerous dirty tricks.

"About time," Randy said with satisfaction. "A guy can train himself to death."

"Wouldn't put it just that way," Linc grinned. "Overheard the lieutenant and the captain talking a while ago. S'posed to be a Cheyenne village about eight miles ahead." His grin revealed a set of tobacco-stained teeth. "Word is, it's some of the hostiles who did for Custer. We'll see action before nightfall!"

As ready as he was for action, Randy felt his insides clench at the thought.

The call to mount came a few minutes later. Randy quickly dipped his hat in the river and settled it back on his head, still dripping, as he swung into the saddle.

"Why didn't I think of that?" Linc asked as they quickly fell into the two-by-two column of a cavalry unit on the march and moved out.

"Old cowboy trick," Randy replied with a grin. He settled in for the ride, lamenting the fact that none of the cavalry mounts had the gait of a good cow pony. Since the Custer massacre, the Army had been riding with only one purpose in mind, and it wasn't to spare the backsides of its troopers. It was to find Sitting Bull, Crazy Horse, and the other bands that had scattered after the massacre at the Little Big Born and avenge the deaths of Custer and his men.

Since the Custer massacre, Army policy appeared to be that in a combat area an Indian was an Indian regardless of gender or age. Randy knew that most of the soldiers agreed, since the Indians had raped and killed white women and killed and kidnapped white children as well. And kidnapped Kaylee too, Randy thought grimly, his mind refusing to take that thought to its logical conclusion. But the idea of making war against women and children didn't sit well with Randy. Killing an armed warrior was one thing, shooting defenseless women and children was something else.

It was a little after three that afternoon when all hell broke loose. One of the column's Crow scouts came riding hell-for-leather, followed by a howling tide of paint-streaked savages.

For a moment the entire column seemed frozen by their fiendish cries. Randy could only stare, his mind capturing quick images of copper skin daubed with garish streaks of paint, black hair adorned with feathers. Their horses were painted, too, with circles around their eyes and stripes on their legs. Some had red hand prints painted on their flanks. He wondered if there was any significance to the symbols.

Up ahead, the lieutenant was shouting orders, and Randy heard the sergeants begin to relay them down the line. Smoke puffed from the midst of the hostile riders, followed by the bark of a rifle. Behind him in the column, a horse screamed in pain, and a man cursed bitterly.

Then the Indians were splitting into two lines, flowing along both flanks of the column. Randy saw arrows arc, glinting, in the afternoon sunlight. One whizzed dangerously close to his cheek.

What followed was cowboy reflex, honed by hours of practice out on the prairie before he ever saw an Army uniform.

Randy flipped his Army Colt out of the awkward flapped holster, slower than he would have with his old holster, and drilled the savage who had loosed the arrow at him. Up and down the halted column, other soldiers were firing. Randy saw a trooper slump forward and then slide from his saddle, but he couldn't tell who it was. Steadying his mount with his knees, he fired off two quick shots, swearing when he missed.

He sucked in a deep breath, let half of it out, and focused on a brave riding one of those horses with the red handprint. The long barrel of his Colt tracked steadily; it was long range for a sidearm, but when the hammer fell, the Indian tumbled over the rump of his horse.

"That one's for you, Kaylee," Randy muttered.

Someone jostled his arm. Jerking around, he almost shot his own sergeant.

"Dismount, cowboy!" the sergeant shouted, his face inches from Randy's. "Dismount and fight on foot, you're a damn sojer now, boy!" And then he whirled his mount to race back to the head of the column.

Dazed, Randy noted that the troop had done exactly that, every fourth soldier holding the horses, just like in the repetitive drills. He holstered his sidearm, grabbed his rifle, and swung down.

"We'll be lucky to see the other side of this!" Linc

exclaimed. Dropping to his knees, he pulled his knife and tried to pry a spent shell out of his rifle.

"Here!" Randy tossed Linc his own Springfield and drew his Colt again.

"Remember, fire low," Linc yelled.

"Yeah, yeah," Randy muttered, feeding fresh rounds into his Colt. That had been the advice given in the Soldier's Handbook, the reasoning being that bullets often glanced off the bones in a man's head and upper body, but a belly wound was likely to be fatal.

The battle raged all around him. The line held position, but was overrun here and there. The air was filled with dust and powder smoke, his ears rang with the sound of gunfire and the unending shrieks of the Indians. He fired at a howling warrior, fired again and again. Images of blood and death imprinted themselves on his mind: a soldier with an arrow protruding from his chest sat staring at it blankly until a howling warrior clubbed him down; a horse with blood bubbling from a wound in its throat, an Indian with the top of his head blown off, a trooper and a savage in hand-to-hand combat. He felt a fierce sense of pride in the men fighting around him. Many of them were raw, untried recruits like himself, yet they fought bravely.

Almost as quickly as it had begun, the battle was over. The surviving Indians scattered and fled, taking as many of their dead—and stolen weapons—as they could get away with. Fearing a trap, the lieutenant declined to pursue them.

Randy collapsed on the ground beside Linc. His hands were shaking now, but they had been steady in battle.

He felt a new camaraderie with the men relaxing around him, lighting up, drinking, laughing as the tension eased. They had been raw, untried recruits just minutes ago. Now they were real soldiers. The relief at having passed the test made most of them a little giddy.

Two troopers were dead, two seriously wounded, and four more down with arrow or bullet wounds.

Randy stood up and stretched. He was soaked with sweat, but by damn, he had acquitted himself well! He felt sure he had accounted for two hostiles personally, maybe more.

The sergeant spotted Randy standing and detailed him and his sidekick to check the bodies of the Indian dead that had been left behind to make sure they were dead. Randy had checked four, one of whom he was sure he had done for, when Linc called out.

"This one's still breathin'!"

While Linc covered the prostrate savage, Randy rolled him over and felt his own stomach churn when he saw the hideous wound in the Indian's belly.

"Not for long he ain't," Randy said.

The Indian opened his eyes and held up his hand, as if to ward off Linc's finishing bullet.

Randy signaled for the Army sawbones, then knelt at the Indian's side. "Speak English, do ya?"

The Indian clutched his belly. Blood oozed through his fingers. "Me speak English good."

"Have you seen a white woman in any of the camps? One with long yellow hair and eyes the color of the sky?"

The Indian nodded.

"Where?"

"In the camp of Crazy Horse."

"Where is she now?"

The Indian shuddered convulsively as pain wracked his body.

"Where, dammit?"

"She was at the Greasy Grass. I do not know where she is now."

Randy sat back on his heels. Kaylee had been at the Little Big Horn? In the camp of Crazy Horse. Good Lord! Where was she now?

"Is she still with Crazy Horse?"

The Indian started to speak, then his eyelids fluttered, and he went suddenly limp.

"Damn you, don't you dare die on me!" Randy grabbed the Indian's shoulders and shook him vigorously. "Wake up!" He shook the Indian again. "Wake up, dammit!"

"He's unconscious, son," the Army surgeon said matter-of-factly. "Be dead soon, by the look of him."

"Don't let him die, Doc," Randy said, rising. "He's got information I need."

Chapter 23

It was the Moon of the Yellow Leaves, the month called September by the *wasichu*. Blue Hawk moved quietly along the ridge, stalking a deer. A sudden change in the wind alerted the buck to his presence and it sprang forward, leaping over a deadfall. Blue Hawk's arrow flew straight and true. The buck twisted in midair, dead before it hit the ground.

Walking back to where he'd left his horses, Blue Hawk took up the reins and made his way toward his kill. Much had happened since the fight at the Greasy Grass. Crazy Horse, He Dog, Short Bull, Black Fox, and Blue Hawk had led bands of warriors against the whites infiltrating the Black Hills. They knew such raids would draw the attention of the Army, but this was sacred ground and must be defended. Too, they needed the goods the *wasichu* carried: blankets, rolls of cloth, sacks of dried fruit, coffee, and flour.

But it was ammunition for the weapons they had acquired at the Greasy Grass that they needed most of all. Additional weapons taken in more recent raids were important also.

In their scouting they had found that there were *wasichu* tent towns springing up, populated not only by men but by women and children. It was not a good sign. When the *wasichu* brought his women, it was a sign they meant to stay.

Some Cheyenne agency Indians, out hunting because food was so scarce on the reservation, had been killed on Warbonnet Creek.

Other Cheyenne had approached some soldiers in the Big Horn Mountains. They had come as friends, but the soldiers had fired on them, killing White Antelope.

There was more bad news. Agents and treaty men were talking of buying the Black Hills, threatening to starve the Indians if they refused to sell.

Three Stars Crook had attacked forty lodges near Slim Buttes. Iron Plume, called American Horse by the *wasichu,* had been killed, along with many women and children. Crazy Horse had gone there with some of his warriors as soon as news of the attack came, but there was nothing the Lakota could do. Three Stars Crook had a thousand men at his command. Outnumbered, their ammunition all but gone, even their supply of war arrows depleted, all the Lakota could do was harass the patrols and scouts that Three Stars sent looking for them.

Blue Hawk lifted the gutted buck onto the back of his pack horse, then swung onto his pony and headed back toward camp. In spite of the bad news from the agencies, in spite of his fear that the fight at the Greasy Grass had been the beginning of the end for his people, he was happier than he had been in many months. For this short time, the people were at peace. Each morning he thanked Wakan Tanka for Kaylee, now called White Crane Flying by the Lakota. Her laughter and warmth filled his lodge, and his life.

As always, she was waiting for him when he returned. Dismounting, he tethered his horse to a picket pin and followed her into the lodge. As soon as they were inside, he pulled her into his arms and kissed her. It was a long, lingering kiss, filled with promise.

"I'm glad you're back," she said when he released her.

"Miss me, did you?"

"Maybe just a little."

"Only a little?"

She punched him on the arm, her eyes shining with laughter as she followed him outside so he could unload the packhorse. Lifting the carcass, he carried it behind their lodge and lowered it to the ground.

"Go to work, woman. I am hungry."

"Yes, my mighty hunter," she retorted, and stuck her tongue out at him.

He grinned at her, then, making sure no one was watching, he drew her close for a quick kiss. "I must go look after the horses," he said.

"All right, but hurry back. I have something to tell you."

It had become their habit to take a walk after the evening meal. Kaylee loved the Black Hills. The terrain was wild, rugged, a land of meadows and valleys, a land filled with color, from the deep green of the pines to the red of shale, clay, and sandstone. Blue Hawk had shown her the places sacred to the Lakota. Bear Butte, called Mato Paha by the Lakota, was a place where the Lakota and the Cheyenne went in search of visions. She had seen Mateo Teepee, the Devil's Tower, which rose thousands of feet above the surrounding prairie.

She gave Blue Hawk's hand a squeeze as they paused atop a ridge that looked down into a lush green meadow cut by a ribbon of blue water. The world must have looked like this on the day after creation, she mused, when the Lord rested and found it good.

"It's so pretty here," she remarked. "No wonder your people love it so." And even as she spoke the words, she wondered how long the Lakota and the Cheyenne would be able to live here, in this sacred place. It was a million acres of rich land. Though she hadn't paid much attention at the time, she recalled Shaun and Garth talking about Custer going on some sort of expedition into the Black Hills and finding gold there. The story had made the papers. Three of the Double R cowhands had quit the ranch and gone hunting for gold. One of them had returned a few months later, the sole survivor of an Indian attack. She had forgotten about that until now.

"Blue Hawk?"

He looked at her, his gaze dark, haunted.

"What is it?" she asked anxiously. "What's wrong?"

"I am reminded of something Sitting Bull said at the Greasy Grass when he called off the battle. He said he feared the victory would also be our defeat. He said the *wasichu* would be angry because we had killed Yellow Hair. Perhaps he was wise to take his people into the land of the Grandmother." He drew her into his arms. "The White Eyes are riding toward us. Tomorrow we will strike the camp and move farther north."

Kaylee said nothing, just put her arms around him and rested her head on his shoulder. Only a few days ago, Blue Hawk had told her they would spend the coming winter in the shelter of the Black Hills, but now all that was changed. She clung to him, filled with a growing sense of unease. If the soldiers caught them, there would be another fight.

"What did you wish to tell me, Kay-lee?" he asked.

She looked up at him, wondering what he would think of her news. Would it make him happy? Or would it only add to the deep sadness she saw in his eyes? She had a sudden longing for her mother. Emma would know what to do. A wave of homesickness swept over Kaylee. Never had she needed her mother's wisdom more than she did now.

"It can wait. Look!" She pointed up at the sky. "A falling star. Make a wish, quickly."

He looked at her, puzzled. "A wish?"

Smiling, she shrugged her shoulders. "It's something we do," she explained. "If you make a wish on a falling star, it's supposed to come true."

"And what did you wish for, Kay-lee?"

"If you tell, it won't come true. What would you wish for, Blue Hawk?"

He placed his hand over her belly. "Peace for our son."

"You know?"

He smiled down at her. "Kay-lee, did you think I would not see the changes within you? I know the rhythms of your body as I know my own," he said quietly, and folded her into his arms. "When will the child be born?"

"In the spring. April, I think. The Moon When the Geese Return."

He made love to her gently later that night, each kiss and caress an affirmation of his love. He stroked her breasts and she felt them swell in his hand, knew he was thinking, as she was, of the baby that would one day suckle there. He placed his hand over her belly, his fingers spreading, as if he could already feel their child moving within her womb. He ran his fingertips over her arms, down her thighs, dropped butterfly kisses on her eyelids, her nose, her lips. His kisses, for all their tenderness, still held the power to arouse her, and she writhed beneath him, her whole body tingling with need.

"Blue Hawk . . ."

He had kissed and caressed her, and now, to her dismay, he hesitated. "I do not want to hurt you."

"You won't," she murmured. "You won't." She slipped her arms around his neck, her hips lifting to receive him. Holding her close, he moved deep within

her. She closed her eyes, and let herself be carried
away on a warm tide of sensual pleasure.

By midmorning the following day, there was little
left of the village to show the Lakota had been there.
A few bones, the outlines of their campfires, were all
that they left behind. Several of the families that had
been with Crazy Horse's people broke off and went
their own way. Blue Hawk and his people stayed with
Crazy Horse.

Mounted on Dusty, Kaylee rode beside Sisoka. The
Lakota were subdued as they rode northward. Even
the children and dogs were quiet, as if they knew this
was not a happy time.

Kaylee was sorry to leave the beauty of the Paha
Sapa. During the few months they had been there, she
had learned so much, had come to feel as if she belonged to the land, to the people.

Most important, she had come to understand why
the Lakota loved the Black Hills so much. It had happened the day Blue Hawk had taken her to Bear
Butte. He had shown her the place where he had received his vision when he was a youth of sixteen win-
ters. He had taken her hand in his and they had stood
there quietly for several moments, gazing out over the
endless prairie. It had been then that she had felt it,
a sense of infinite power rising from deep in the heart
of Bear Butte, enveloping her. She had squeezed Blue
Hawk's hand; he had looked at her and nodded. She
had known then why the Lakota believed that everything had its own spirit, why they believed that the
rocks and the trees, the very earth itself, were alive.
She had felt the breath of Mato Paha in the prairie
wind that blew across her face, felt the spirit of the
mountain seep into her soul. And felt as if she had
been accepted as one of the People.

And now they were leaving it all behind.

*   *   *

The first sign of trouble appeared the following afternoon. They were crossing a shallow stream when a riderless horse came galloping up. Blue Hawk muttered an oath he had often heard on Kirkland's lips. The horse belonged to Hoka, one of the warriors who had been scouting ahead.

Moments later, the other scout came racing toward them, waving a blanket over his head.

Clucking to his horse, Blue Hawk rode up beside Crazy Horse. "There is trouble ahead."

"Tell the women to fall back and hide in the trees," Crazy Horse said. He brandished his rifle over his head. "All strong hearts, follow me!"

"Huhn! Huhn! Huhn!" The Lakota kill cry gained in strength and power as warrior after warrior rode forward to join Crazy Horse.

Blue Hawk glanced over his shoulder, seeking Kaylee. She was riding in her usual place beside Sisoka. Even from a distance he could see the worry in her eyes as she watched the warriors riding to the head of the line.

There was no time to ride back and tell her what was happening. Already the air was filling with the sound of the charge from the *wasichu* bugler; already the dust cloud from their horses could be seen.

And then the soldiers were upon them.

Cold dread exploded through Kaylee as she saw Blue Hawk and the other warriors ride off in the direction of the bugle call.

"Kuwa!" Sisoka said urgently. Come!

"Blue Hawk . . ."

Sisoka shook her head. *"Hiya! Kuwa!"* No! Come! Sisoka tugged on Kaylee's arm. *"Inankni yo!"* Hurry!

With a last glance in the direction of the disappearing warriors, Kaylee reined her horse around and followed Sisoka and the other women back the way they had come. The women rode into a stand of timber, seeking cover where they could find it. Behind them, where the warriors had gone, gunshots began to pop, first individually and then in crescendo. She saw some of the women dismount and turn their horses loose. Others continued riding until they were out of sight. The loose horses followed behind.

Kaylee wanted to ride and keep riding, but she couldn't leave Blue Hawk. She dismounted behind a thick growth of trees and brush and held tight to Dusty's reins with one hand, her other hand covering the mare's nose to keep her quiet. She waited, her heart pounding in frantic fear for Blue Hawk, for herself, for Sisoka and the other women and children. The sharp retorts of gunfire and the deeper roar of heavy Army rifle fire drifted on the wind.

She felt the ground tremble as the Lakota horse herd thundered past. Had they been spooked by the battle, she wondered, or had the warriors stampeded them to cover the tracks of the women?

It seemed she stood there for hours, her imagination painting horrible pictures of blood and death in her mind.

The sounds of battle came to an abrupt end, but the silence was somehow worse than the rattle of gunfire had been.

Kaylee swallowed hard as the minutes passed, felt her insides knot as the tension mounted. She wanted to run back and find Blue Hawk, wanted to scream with the frustration of not knowing what was happening. Several women were crouched nearby; as the silence continued, they rose and began to walk away, heading back the way they had come earlier that day.

One of the women gestured for her to follow them.

Kaylee shook her head, torn between the need to go with them and the desire to go back and search for Blue Hawk.

She was still staring after the last of the women and wondering if she should have gone with them when she heard a rustling noise in the underbrush to her right.

She went suddenly still, hardly daring to breathe as she listened. She understood then why Lakota children were not allowed to cry. The slightest whimper would alert the enemy to their presence.

Her mouth went dry as she drew the knife from the belt sheath at her back. And waited.

Chapter 24

Randy stood beside his horse, panting almost as hard as his mount. The battle had been short, frightening, and exhilarating. They had charged the redskins, driving them back. Though outnumbered and outgunned, the Indians had put up a hell of a fight. He'd never had much use for Indians, but they had earned his respect this day. He would never call one a coward again.

"Gosh almighty, that was some fight, wasn't it?"

Randy looked up into Linc's grinning face. "That it was."

"Don't know how they whipped Custer! They scattered like chickens before a fox."

"They fought until their women were out of harm's way," Randy retorted.

Linc snorted. "Well, we whipped their butts, and we'll do it again!"

"You don't know what tribe they were, do ya?"

"Sioux, I reckon."

A rush of anticipation swept through Randy. "You think maybe this bunch was at the Little Big Horn?"

Linc shrugged. "How the hell would I know?"

"See ya later," Randy said. Swinging onto his horse, he rode over to a group of Crow scouts gathered near a dead warrior. Randy pointed at the dead Indian. "What tribe?"

The scout known as Gray Bull looked up at him. "Oglala."

"Crazy Horse's band?"

Gray Bull nodded.

"Did we take any prisoners?"

"One."

"Where is he?" Randy asked.

Gray Bull shrugged.

"Thanks," Randy said. Reining his horse around, he rode over to a cluster of men. "Hey, anybody know if these are Crazy Horse's people?"

"That's what Sergeant Mills thinks. One of the scouts is with the cap'n. They're questioning some redskin now."

"Thanks, Ryker."

"What the hell difference does it make?" Fergus asked.

"It makes a difference," Randy said curtly. "Did any of you see a white woman?"

"A white woman?" Ryker exclaimed, his eyes suddenly alight. "Hell, no. Did you?"

"Crazy Horse's band has a white woman with them. I think it might be a girl who was kidnapped."

"You know this girl?" Fergus asked.

"Yeah."

"What makes you think she might be here?"

"One of the wounded redskins from that last battle told me he'd seen a white girl with Crazy Horse's people. She fit the description."

"Ya know," Fergus drawled, "I recollect I might have seen her, now that I think about it."

"Where?" Randy demanded. "When?"

"I recollect as how I saw a little light-haired gal mounted on a pretty little bay, now that you mention it."

Hope flared in Randy's heart. Dusty was a bay.

"Where, dammit?"

"Hell, I don't know. She run off when the shootin' started, 'long with all the other squaws."

Randy glanced toward the woods behind them. It was the only place where the women could have gone to hide. Was Kaylee there?

"Harris! Lincoln! Fergus! Ryker! Mullins! You're on cleanup."

Randy swore under his breath. Looking for the bodies of the dead was the worst detail he'd ever been on. The first time he'd found what was left of a former trooper, he'd gone to his knees and retched until his stomach was empty.

"That damn sergeant," Linc muttered. "This is the third time I've had this duty."

"Yeah," Ryker growled.

"It's 'cause we're the newest recruits," Fergus muttered.

Randy and Linc rode off together.

"Mills has a scalp," Linc remarked.

"A scalp!" Randy exclaimed. "Did you see it? Where'd he get it?"

Linc shrugged. "Dunno. He was showing it off to one of the other sergeants. I reckon he took it after the last battle. Whitey has a quiver he took offen a Sioux burial scaffold before a couple of his pals tore it down. He said they used the poles in their campfire that night."

Randy swallowed the bile rising in his throat. He had heard talk that some of the more seasoned troopers took scalps, but he'd never believed it. He had heard that a couple of Reno's soldiers had been caught cutting up a redskin's body after the battle of the Little Big Horn, but he hadn't believed that, either. Didn't want to believe that soldiers, men he rode with, were capable of inflicting the same kinds of mutilations as the Indians. The Sioux could be excused. They were godless savages, after all.

He looked over at Linc. "Could you . . . would you take a scalp?"

"Damn right!"

Randy stared at Linc, surprised by the vehemence in his tone.

"Hell, wouldn't you? Did you see what those damned redskins did to Corley?"

Randy nodded. George Corley had been a farm boy from Iowa. He had signed up about the same time as Linc and Randy. When they had been attacked the week before, Corley had taken to his heels and fled. They had found his body later. He'd been scalped and his privates cut off.

Randy shook the grisly memory from his mind. They didn't find any bodies, red or white, but the sporadic sound of gunfire from the other end of the battlefield told a different story. This was war, and wounded Indians were shot. Randy knew that often included women and children. Lying in his bunk at night, he had listened to some of the seasoned Indian fighters talk about battles they had been in. Some of the stories they told had made him sick to his stomach, stories of women killed, babies whose heads had been bashed against trees.

Randy veered his mount toward the trees, the image of a light-haired woman on a bay horse too big a coincidence to ignore. He dismounted near the tree line, his gaze moving over the ground. Kay's mare had a tendency to drag the toe of her right rear hoof. It left a telltale print.

He spent a quarter of an hour cutting back and forth, and then he found it, one print that looked like it could belong to Dusty. It wasn't much, but it was all he had.

Swinging into the saddle, he rode into the trees, calling her name.

Chapter 25

Kaylee heard hoofbeats and then a familiar voice calling her name. That voice, here, shocked her. She ran out from her hiding place, startling his mount.

"Randy! What are you doing here?" She stared at him as he calmed his lathered horse, stunned to see him in sweat-stained Army blue.

Dismounting, he dropped his horse's reins and rushed toward her. He grabbed her in a bear hug and held her tight. "Kaylee Marie! Are you all right? Lord, I can't believe you're here!"

"You're squishing me," she squeaked, certain that he was going to crack a rib.

He loosened his grip but didn't let her go. "Sorry, Kay, but I'm so damn glad to see you."

"I'm glad to see you, too," she said. And she was. Randy was like a breath of fresh air from home. But where was Blue Hawk? "Is . . . is the fighting over?"

"Yeah. You're safe now."

"Safe?"

Randy nodded. "The redskins are gone."

"Gone!" She twisted out of his arms, her heart pounding with fear and worry. Where was Blue Hawk? If he was alive, he would be here, looking for her.

Randy frowned at the note of panic in her voice. "Don't worry, Kay. We'll protect you."

She backed away from him. "I don't need any protection. Do you know where they went?"

"Where who went?"

"The Lakota! Where did they go?"

"You mean the Sioux? They ran." He looked at her curiously, no doubt wondering at her concern for a bunch of savages. "Beats the hell out of me, but you don't have to worry, Kaylee. They won't bother you anymore. We killed a good many of them. The redskins that survived turned tail and ran. Come on," he said, "let's go."

Feeling her fear give way to exhaustion, Kaylee did not protest when Randy lifted her onto Dusty's back and then mounted his own horse.

Taking up the reins, she followed Randy's lead, the words "we killed a good many" echoing in her mind. Was Blue Hawk dead? No, he couldn't be!

They reached the site of the Army encampment a short time later. Kaylee's gaze swept the area, anxiously searching for Blue Hawk, even though she knew her chances of finding him were slim. Whenever possible, the Lakota carried their dead and wounded away, often at the risk of their own lives. She saw several Lakota dead, left where they had fallen. Men she had seen smiling at their wives, laughing with their children. Shuddering, she looked away.

The soldiers stood or sat in small groups, talking. A doctor moved among the wounded. In the distance, she saw several covered bodies. Those would be the Army casualties. A detail was digging graves. Several wagons formed a circle on the edge of the camp. Horses stood hip-shot along a picket line; several mules were tied to the tongues of the wagons.

She reined her horse to a halt beside Randy's. He dismounted and lifted her from the saddle.

"Well, now, Harris, who's this?"

Kaylee turned to see a large red-haired man striding toward them.

"Kaylee Matthews, Sergeant."

"Pleased to make your acquaintance, Miss Matthews. How long have you been a prisoner?"

Kaylee started to reply that she hadn't been a prisoner, then paused. She glanced over at the covered bodies, thinking now might not be a good time to tell Randy and the sergeant that she was with the Indians because she wanted to be.

Randy answered for her. "Miss Matthews is from my hometown, Sergeant. She was kidnapped by the Sioux several months ago."

"Well, you're safe now, Miss Matthews. We'll be leaving for the fort in the morning. You can notify your family when we get there."

Leaving? She couldn't leave, didn't want to leave. She clasped her hands together to still their shaking. She murmured her thanks, wondering if they would let her stay behind.

"Harris, you'll be in charge of looking after Miss Matthews."

Randy nodded. "My pleasure."

With a grunt, the sergeant took his leave.

"Let's go over to the mess tent and get a cup of coffee," Randy suggested.

Coffee. It seemed a lifetime since she had tasted coffee. Memories of home flooded over her, warring with her fears for Blue Hawk's safety.

Kaylee sat down in the shade, her thoughts racing, while Randy went to get the coffee. Surely she would know if Blue Hawk was dead! Surely her own heart would have stopped beating the instant he was struck down.

She looked over at the bodies again, then shook her head. She could not—would not—believe that Blue Hawk was lying somewhere like that, dusty and still.

Randy returned from the mess tent a short while later, carrying two tin cups of coffee. He handed her one, then sat down beside her. "Careful," he warned. "It's hot."

Needing to think of something besides Blue Hawk, she asked about her mother. Randy hesitated a moment before replying, "She's not well, Kay."

"What's wrong?" she asked, alarmed. "Tell me, Randy. Is she sick? Is it serious? When did you see her last?"

"She's not sick, not exactly. I got a letter from my old man. Your ma's been failing ever since you went missing, Kay. Doc Emery says there's nothing he can do, that she's lost her will to live."

Guilt pierced Kaylee's heart. It was all her fault. She should have made Blue Hawk take her home. How could she have been so thoughtless? But then, her mother had always seemed so strong, how could she have known her disappearance would cause Emma to take to her bed? Oh, Lord, she couldn't lose her mother and Blue Hawk, too.

"I went to see her right before I enlisted. I have to tell you, she didn't look all that good then. But I'm sure she'll be all right, Kay, soon's she knows you're safe."

She could tell he was distressed at the effect his news had on her and was trying to ease the blow.

"Like the sergeant said, we'll be back at the fort in a couple of days. You can send word to your mother and let her know you're all right." He put his hand on her arm. "Don't cry, Kay, please."

But she couldn't help it. Once the tears started, she couldn't stop them. She cried for the pain she had caused her mother, cried because she didn't know if Blue Hawk was dead or alive. She wept for the Lakota who had been killed, wept for her unborn child. What if her mother and Shaun turned her away because she was carrying Blue Hawk's baby?

Randy glanced around and then, muttering, "Oh, hell," he put his arms around her and held her tight.

Kaylee rested her head on his shoulder. His arms were warm, familiar, reminding her of home. But they weren't Blue Hawk's arms. She cried until she was empty inside, and then Randy dried her eyes with his neckerchief.

"Feel better?" he asked.

"Yes," she said, sniffling, and it was both the truth and a lie. "You always said you wanted to enlist, but I never thought you'd really do it. Do you like being in the Army?"

Randy shrugged. "It's all right." His gaze moved over her. Even in buckskins, with her hair in braids, she was still the prettiest girl he'd ever seen.

That night, Kaylee stared unseeing into the darkness. It had been a long day. Randy had stayed close to her side, keeping her company at dinner, entertaining her with humorous stories of his first few weeks in the Army.

At bedtime, the lieutenant, a handsome young man with brown hair and blue eyes, had gallantly insisted that Kaylee sleep in his tent.

The cot was narrow, but more comfortable than the ground. Turning on her side, Kaylee closed her eyes. She was bone-weary, and yet sleep eluded her. She was worried about her mother's health, worried about Sisoka and the other women, but not knowing Blue Hawk's whereabouts was what kept her tossing and turning. She tried to tell herself that he was still alive, that he had managed to escape, but . . . what if he had been killed? Hot tears burned her eyes at the thought of never seeing him again. He couldn't be dead!

She wondered how long it would take to get home, how she would explain her absence to her mother and

Shaun. They thought she had been kidnapped. What would they think when they learned she had stayed with Blue Hawk because she wanted to, that she had married him of her own free will.

She placed her hands over her stomach as a new fear crossed her mind. Shaun hated Indians. What would he say, what would he *do,* when he learned she was carrying Blue Hawk's child?

The troops were on the move shortly after dawn the following day. Kaylee rode beside Randy, her eagerness to see her mother overshadowed by the thought of facing Shaun, by the ever-growing fear that Blue Hawk had been killed.

The hours passed slowly, the silence unbroken save for the jangle of bits and spurs and the creak of saddle leather. She thought of the Lakota, remembering how the women chattered and laughed when they moved camp, how the young men paraded up and down the line, showing off their horsemanship for the maidens. There was no gaiety here. The soldiers rode two by two, grim-faced and silent, no doubt remembering the dead they had left behind. With his sergeant's permission, Randy stayed close to Kaylee. She was happy to have his company.

It grew increasingly hot as the day wore on. There was no shade, no respite from the heat. They stopped at noon to eat and water the horses. Kaylee knelt beside the shallow buffalo wallow. She splashed water over her face and arms, hoping to cool her heated skin, but the water was warm and did little to ease her discomfort.

She wasn't much impressed with Army food, which seemed to consist of salt pork, hardtack, bacon, sugar, and coffee. Lunch was hardtack and black coffee.

It wasn't long before they were riding again.

It was late afternoon when they stopped for the night. Kaylee sat on a wooden stool, watching the soldiers make camp. Picket lines were set up, guards were posted. Several men hauled buckets of water up from the stream; others took sacks and went in search of buffalo chips, since there were no trees in the area.

Soon a couple of the men started a fire, and shortly after that each man in the outfit was given a cup of strong black coffee. She was amazed at how quickly the men seemed to recover their energy after a simple cup of coffee.

After mess, the men spread their blankets. The lieutenant again offered Kaylee the use of his tent, and she accepted gratefully.

Utterly weary, she slid under the thin summer blanket and closed her eyes.

They would reach the fort tomorrow. She would send word to her mother and Shaun as soon as she arrived, assuring them that she was well. The lieutenant had informed her that he would assign a detail to see her safely home.

She stared at the shadows moving over the walls of the tent. She could hear the men settling down for the night, the rattle of chains on the wagon tongues as the mules stamped their feet, the snorts of the horses.

Lying there in the dark, feeling lost and alone, she closed her eyes. "I will not cry," she whispered, but even then tears were stinging her eyes, trickling down her cheeks, squeezed from a heart that felt as though it was breaking.

And suddenly she couldn't wait to get home, to rest her head in her mother's lap and pour out all her hurt and heartache. Shaun might disown her when he discovered she was carrying Blue Hawk's baby, but her mother wouldn't care. Emma would understand. And forgive.

Kaylee woke to a gray dawn and a flurry of gunshots. Scrambling out of the cot, she pushed open the tent flap and peeked outside. Soldiers were running everywhere.

She called to one of them, "What's happening?"

"Injuns spooked the horses, ma'am!" he shouted and ran past her.

A moment later Randy came running up to her. "Stay inside!" he instructed.

"Randy, wait!"

"Can't talk now," he said. "Just stay inside!"

"Be careful," she called, but he was already gone. She jumped when the mess tent suddenly went up in flames. Had the Lakota come back to retaliate for their losses? Or was it another tribe?

"Kay-lee."

She whirled around at the sound of his voice, hardly daring to believe it could be him. "Blue Hawk!" Joy flooded her heart and soul, spilled out in a rush of tears. "Blue Hawk! Oh, Blue Hawk, I thought you were dead!"

He shook his head, then held out his hand. "Come. We must go quickly."

She didn't question him, didn't hesitate, merely put her hand in his and followed him through the slit he had cut in the back of the tent. Dusty was waiting for her. The mare whickered softly as Blue Hawk lifted Kaylee onto her back.

"You will have to ride bareback," he said, swinging onto his own horse.

Kaylee nodded. She would have run alongside the horse, barefoot, over hot coals, to be with him again. Taking up the reins, she followed Blue Hawk into the gray landscape. Long shadows fell over the land.

They held the horses to a walk until they were well away from the camp, then Blue Hawk urged his mount into a gallop.

Exhilaration flowed through Kaylee as she followed Blue Hawk across the prairie. He appeared, and all her doubts and fears took flight. She sent a fervent prayer of thanks to God for reuniting them.

They were far away from the camp before Blue Hawk reined his horse to a halt.

Kaylee pulled up beside him. "Are you all right?"

"I am fine." Dismounting, he lifted her from the saddle and drew her into his arms. "You are well?"

"I am now. What happened? Where are the others?"

"They have scattered like shadows before the sun. Crazy Horse will gather them together. Perhaps they will fight again. Perhaps they will go north, to join with Sitting Bull."

"You didn't go with them."

"How could I?" he asked quietly. "When my heart is here?"

"I missed you," she whispered. "I was afraid, so afraid." With a sigh, she rested her head against his chest.

His hand stroked her hair, his touch ever so gentle. They stood that way for several minutes before Blue Hawk spoke again. "Matoskah was killed."

"Oh, no!"

Blue Hawk nodded.

"Poor Sisoka."

"We will not think of it now. Come, let us rest. The *wasichu* will be all morning gathering their horses."

She smiled faintly as he spread two Army blankets on the ground, then offered her a drink from an Army canteen.

He looked at her and shrugged. "It is a good thing, to steal from the enemy."

In this instance she had to agree. The Indians had lost much when the Army attacked; it was only fair that they get something back.

Kaylee sat down on the blanket, watching Blue Hawk hobble the horses. She welcomed him with open arms when he came to her, and for a time they sat quietly close. Then he placed his hand on her belly.

"The little one is well?" he asked.

With a nod, she placed her hand over his.

"The boy is here, with the soldiers. His head has healed."

"What boy? Oh, you mean Randy."

"He watches you with hot eyes."

Kaylee started to laugh, then thought better of it. "We're just friends, that's all. We grew up together."

"He does not want to be your friend, Kay-lee."

"I know, but it's you I love, not Randy." She frowned. "How do you know how he looks at me?"

"I have watched you with him. I have watched him with you."

"You've been following us."

"Of course. Did you think I would leave you?"

"I didn't know what to think. I was so afraid you'd been killed."

He placed his hand over her heart. "You would have known, in here, if that were true."

She nodded, knowing it was true. "Blue Hawk?"

"What is it you wish?"

"I need to go home."

He went suddenly still. "It is your wish to leave me?"

"No! No, of course not. But Randy told me my mother is ill, that she's been sick ever since I left home. I have to go to her. You understand, don't you?"

"I will see that you get home, if that is what you wish."

Something in his tone gave her pause. "You'll come with me, won't you?"

"Will your people welcome me, Kay-lee?"

She thought of the way the Lakota had welcomed her. She wished that Shaun and her mother would be as kind to Blue Hawk, but knew it was highly unlikely. Indians had been stealing Double R cattle for months; they had killed two of the cowhands.

"No," she said regretfully, "probably not, but I won't go without you. Please, Blue Hawk, my mother needs me. She's sick. I need to help her get well. And there's something else, something very important to me. I . . ." She paused.

"Speak, Kay-lee."

"I want to be with her when the baby comes."

"Very well, Kay-lee. I will take you home."

Somehow, he would find a way.

Chapter 26

It was just the two of them again, traveling across the vast grassy plains. Blue Hawk had a rifle and a few cartridges taken from a soldier he had killed. He hunted game along the way, when his snares failed to provide or when he felt it safe to risk a gunshot. He never needed more than one shot. They ate their evening meal near whatever water they could find, letting the horses drink and graze, and then they moved on, always spending the night three or four miles away from their last rest stop, in a cold camp. Kaylee missed the comfort of a campfire, but she knew it was for their safety. Out here, the smoke from a fire could be seen for miles.

They traveled for several days. Once, they saw a column of soldiers far in the distance. Another time Blue Hawk spied a Crow hunting party riding along a ridge.

Blue Hawk said little as they journeyed toward the ranch, and though he treated her as lovingly and gently as always, she felt as though her longing to go home had created a gulf between them. It grieved her to think she had offended him by her request, yet the need to return home burned strong within her. What if her mother was dying? Already dead? How would she ever live with herself if her mother died and she was to blame?

Now, as she spread their blankets beneath a moonlit

sky, she sent a fervent prayer to heaven that she would get home before it was too late. She sat down wearily and closed her eyes, one hand resting on her belly. She seemed to tire easily these days. Her breasts were tender to the touch, and the smell of cooking meat sometimes left her feeling queasy. A baby. She was going to have Blue Hawk's baby. The thought filled her with a mixture of excitement and fear, happiness and uncertainty. Tales of labor that went on for days, of babies born dead, of mothers who died in childbirth filled her mind. She was swamped with doubts about her ability to be a good mother. What did she know, after all, about taking care of a baby?

"You are troubled, Kay-lee?"

"Yes. No."

He sat down beside her. "Will you tell me what it is that worries you?"

"Nothing," she said and burst into tears.

"Kay-lee! Tell me what is wrong."

"I don't know," she wailed. "What if I'm a terrible mother? What if the baby dies? What if I die?"

"Kay-lee . . ."

"I'm scared, so scared." She clutched his arms. "And so afraid of losing you."

"You will not lose me, *mitawicu*. What has put such a thought into your mind?"

"You've seemed so . . . so far away . . . these past few days," she said, sniffing. "I was afraid you were angry with me."

"I am not angry with you. But you must know that we cannot be together in your world, Kay-lee."

She looked at him, blinking back her tears, suddenly realizing that he thought she was choosing her world over his, her people over him.

"You're not going to stay with me when I get home, are you?"

"How can I?"

He was right. Shaun would never allow it. "I have to see my mother. You understand that, don't you?"

"I would not keep you from your family."

"You're my family, too, now." She took his hand in hers and placed it on her belly. "We're a family now."

"It pleases you?"

"Of course! I love you, Blue Hawk. You know that, don't you?" She looked up at him, her gaze searching his. "I love your people, Blue Hawk. I was happy with them, and with you, but I have to make sure my mother is all right."

Blue Hawk nodded. It was the Lakota way to look after their parents, their old ones. Among his people, the family was an extended one, with grandparents, aunts, uncles, and cousins all taking part in the rearing of children, with each member of the family concerned for all the others.

"We will reach your land tomorrow," he said. "I will see you safely there."

It wasn't safe for him, though. Yet even knowing that, she couldn't turn back. She had to see her mother, to assure herself that Emma was still alive, that she would recover. "You won't leave me?"

"No. I will stay close by."

"But where will you stay? What will you eat?"

"You forget. I am Lakota," he said, and that said it all.

It was late afternoon the following day when they splashed across the river that separated Indian territory from the land of the *wasichu*. Though Blue Hawk knew it was only his imagination, the grass seemed less green on this side of the river, the sky less blue.

He reined his horse to a halt when they were within sight of the ranch. Several corrals held horses. Chickens scratched in the dirt. He heard a calf bawling, the crow of a rooster. A single cowhand was saddling a horse near the barn.

Blue Hawk looked at Kaylee and wondered what the future held for the two of them.

"If I can get away, I'll meet you at the line shack tomorrow night," Kaylee said. "Can you find it?"

He looked at her, one brow raised in amusement.

"I forgot," she said. "You're Lakota."

Dismounting, he lifted her from her horse and drew her into his arms. She snuggled against him, her cheek resting on his chest, her hands caressing his back.

"I'll miss you," she said.

His lips brushed the top of her head. "I will be close by."

"How will I get in touch with you if I need you?"

"If you need me, I will know it."

She looked up at him, her head tilted to one side. "I guess Mato will tell you."

He nodded solemnly. "Do you doubt it?"

"No." Rising on her tiptoes, she kissed him. "Tomorrow night," she said. "Don't forget."

"Can I forget to breathe?" He lifted her onto Dusty's back and handed her the reins.

She leaned forward and kissed him again. And then, taking up the reins, she urged the mare into a lope.

"Lord A'mighty, is that you, Miss Kaylee?"

Kaylee smiled at Hobie as she reined Dusty to a halt in front of the barn. "It's me, all right. What are you doing here this time of day?"

"Horse pulled up lame. Come in for a fresh mount." His gaze took in her tunic and moccasins. "You all right?"

"I'm fine."

"You been gone all this long time, kidnapped by Injuns, and all you got to say for yourself is you're fine? Your mama's worried herself most to death about you! You get up to the house, pronto." He patted Dusty's neck. "I'll look after your horse."

Kaylee smiled at the cowboy as she handed him Dusty's reins. "Thanks, Hobie."

"Hurry now. I reckon seeing you will do your ma a world of good."

With a nod, Kaylee hurried up the path that led to the main house. She climbed the stairs to the porch, opened the door, and stepped inside. After living in the confines of a hide lodge, the parlor seemed enormous, but she spared hardly a glance for the room save to notice that there was a layer of dust on the tables, something her mother would never have stood for.

Running up the stairs, she paused on the landing. It occurred to her that she should probably clean up and change her clothes before going to see her mother, but she decided against it. She had to see her mother. Now.

Taking a deep breath, she hurried down the hall, opened the door to her mother's room, and peeked inside. The room was dark, with the drapes drawn against the sun.

Emma was asleep. She looked small and frail lying there, almost childlike, with her hair in braids. Kaylee felt a twinge of guilt when she noticed how gray her mother's hair had become. Her face was pale, lined with worry even in sleep. And she was thin, so thin.

"Oh, Mama," she whispered, "what have I done?"

"Kaylee? Kaylee, is that you?" Emma sat up, her eyes searching the room's dusky interior.

"I'm here, Mama."

Emma held out her hands. "Kaylee! Oh, Kaylee, the Lord be praised! It is you, home at last! I'm not dreaming again, am I?"

"You're not dreaming, Mama. I'm here."

Kaylee took her mother's hands in hers. They were so cold.

"Let me look at you." Her mother's voice sounded raspy, as if she hadn't used it much.

Emma took in Kaylee's disheveled hair, her sun-tanned skin, the Indian tunic and moccasins. "You look like something the dog dragged in! But, Lord, you're a sight for sore eyes! Where have you been?"

"I'm fine, Mama, honest. I've just been living with the Indians, and this is the way they dress."

Emma's eyes filled with tears. "That Indian . . . I thought . . ." She placed one hand over her heart and closed her eyes.

"Mama!" Kaylee cried anxiously. She squeezed Emma's hands. "Mama, are you all right?"

Emma opened her eyes. "I am, now that you're here. I've been so worried, so afraid."

Kaylee sat down on the edge of the bed. "I'm sorry. I didn't mean to worry you. I never thought . . . and then I saw Randy . . ."

"Randy! Randy found you? Did he bring you home? Where is he?"

Now was not the time to explain, at least not fully. "Randy found me. He told me you weren't feeling well."

"Is he all right? Rachel's been worried sick ever since he joined up."

"He's fine. You know he's always wanted to join the Army. He makes a fine-looking soldier, and his officer says he's very brave." Kaylee squeezed her mother's hand, with a silent apology to the Lakota Randy had killed to earn the lieutenant's commendation. "I need to get cleaned up. Why don't you go back to sleep for a while?"

Emma clutched her hand tightly. "You won't go away again? Promise me?"

"I promise, Mama," she said. Wondering if it was a promise she would be able to keep.

With a radiant smile, Emma lay back and closed her eyes. "Prayers do get answered," she murmured.

Kaylee sat there a moment, her heart aching for the pain she had caused her mother. She had known her mother would miss her, worry about her, but this— she shook her head. She had never expected anything like this.

Tiptoeing out of the room, Kaylee went downstairs. In the kitchen, she put some water on the stove to heat, then looked through the pantry, taking stock of the supplies, wondering as she did so who had been fixing dinner during Emma's illness. Not Shaun, surely. Perhaps Roscoe was cooking for Emma and Shaun, as well as the cowhands.

When the water was hot, she carried it upstairs and poured it in the bowl on the washstand. Tomorrow, or later tonight, she would haul the tub into the kitchen and take a real bath, but not now. She didn't want to take the chance that Shaun or one of the men might walk in on her.

When she finished bathing, she went to the armoire and opened the doors. It seemed strange to have so many dresses to choose from. She picked a simple blue muslin. Wearing a chemise, drawers, and petti-coats felt odd, almost smothering, after wearing a doe-skin tunic for so long. Her shoes felt tight.

She brushed out her hair, then tied it back with a ribbon and went downstairs.

She put on one of her mother's aprons and spent the next hour cleaning the house. She swept and dusted, washed the dishes, peeled potatoes for dinner and put them on to boil. It seemed strange to cook over a stove instead of a campfire, and all the while she wondered where Blue Hawk was and what he was doing. Had it been a mistake to ask him to stay? It was dangerous for him to be so near the ranch. What if one of the hands saw him? But how could she send him away?

*   *   *

Blue Hawk watched Kaylee until she was out of sight, and then he rode back across the river. He could not blame Kaylee for wanting to care for her mother. It was the Lakota way to care for their own, and he was proud that she felt responsible for her mother.

He glanced at the sky. It would not be dark for several hours. Nudging his horse into a lope, he rode across the prairie. Once, it had been home to thousands of buffalo. When he was young, the herds had been so big, it had taken days to ride around one. No more. The *wasichu* had come with their guns and wagons, killing *pte* and taking the hides and the tongues, leaving tons of fresh meat to rot in the sun. Other whites had come from across the Big Water, hunting the curly-haired buffalo for sport, taking only the head and leaving the rest behind. It was waste on a grand scale. The Lakota did not kill for sport, but to live. And always a part of the kill was left behind for the *wanagi*. Always, the Lakota offered a prayer of thanks to the spirit of whatever animal had been killed, thanking it for giving up its life so that the Lakota might live. When a warrior killed *pte*, nothing went to waste. Horn and hide and hair, all were used by the People. They ate his flesh and made lodge coverings and clothing from his hide, their dishes were made of his horn, glue from his hooves, thread from his hair, his paunch was used as a cooking pot, tools were made from his bones.

Blue Hawk reined his horse to a halt in the shade of a cottonwood tree. The Lakota and the buffalo had been closely linked ever since Ptesan-Wi visited the Lakota people in that long-ago time when the earth was new, a time before the People had horses. It was a time when the Seven Council Fires of the Lakota had come together.

In that long-ago time, two warriors had been sent

out to find food for the People. They had searched in vain and were about to give up when they saw a beautiful woman clad in a white buckskin dress walking toward them. She carried a bundle and a fan of sage leaves in her hand. She was the most beautiful woman the two men had ever seen. One of them, looking at her with lust in his heart, reached out to touch her. But this woman was like no other. This woman was *lila wakan*, very holy, and lightning danced out of the heavens and struck the young man, burning him until nothing but ash remained.

The woman spoke to the other young man, telling him that she had come from the buffalo nation with a message for the People, and when all were gathered together, she opened the bundle she carried and withdrew a sacred pipe. She showed it to the People, holding the stem in her right hand and the bowl in her left. Ptesan-Wi filled the pipe with *chan-shasha*, red willow-bark tobacco, then walked in a circle four times before lighting the pipe. Four was a sacred number, she said, representing the four directions and the four ages of creation. The smoke from the pipe was Tunkashila's breath, she told them. She told them many other things, and then she taught them how to pray, admonishing them that they must always offer the pipe to Wakan Tanka, to Mother Earth, to the four directions. The pipe would carry their prayers to Wakan Tanka, and now, because of the pipe, they were all related, the two-legged and the four-legged, the earth and the grass, all living things. Ptesan-Wi told them that the red pipe bowl represented the buffalo, but also the red blood of the People. The stem represented all that grew upon Mother Earth. Twelve feathers hung from the bowl. These were feathers from Wanblee Galeshka, the spotted eagle, who is Wakan Tanka's messenger. There were seven circles carved in the bowl, one for each of the seven council fires of the Lakota.

Ptesan-Wi then spoke to the women, telling them it was their sacred duty to bear children. She showed them how to make fire and taught them how to cook.

Before leaving the People, she told them that, in her, there were four ages. She told them she would not forget them, but that she would look back upon them in every age. She also told them that she was leaving a buffalo in the west, to hold back the many waters. Every year, the buffalo would lose one hair, and in every age, it would lose one leg. When the buffalo had lost all its hair, and all four legs, the waters would cover the earth again.

When she had finished teaching the People, Ptesan-Wi walked away. After going a short distance, she sat down upon the ground and when she rose again, she had become a young red buffalo calf. The red calf walked a short distance and rolled on the ground, and when it rose, it was a white buffalo. Looking back at the People, it walked further away and rolled once again, and when it rose, it was a black buffalo. The black buffalo nodded to the four directions and then disappeared.

A short time later, the buffalo came to the People, allowing themselves to be killed so that the People might live.

With a sigh, Blue Hawk stared out at the vast empty land. Only Ptesan-Wi could save the People now, he thought. Perhaps, if his people prayed hard enough, she would come again and bring back the buffalo. Perhaps, if they prayed hard enough, the *wasichu* would disappear.

With a shake of his head, he urged his horse into a gallop. Leaning low on the stallion's neck, he forgot everything but the exhilaration of racing over the prairie with the wind in his face. The past could not be changed. The future was a mystery unknown to man. But today . . . today he was still free, and tomorrow night he would hold Kaylee in his arms once again.

*   *   *

Shaun took off his hat and tossed it on the rack inside the door. He frowned, the worries of the day momentarily forgotten as his nostrils filled with the scent of fresh-baked bread. His heart skipped a beat at the thought that Emma had left her bed.

His footsteps quickened as he walked toward the kitchen. "Emma?" He came to an abrupt halt when he opened the door and saw Kaylee standing at the stove.

"Hello, Shaun."

"What the—how—when?" He noted how sun-bronzed her fair skin was. "You're back."

She nodded.

Shaun grunted softly. She was back, just like that. And seeming quite calm and self-contained about it, too. "Where the hell have you been all this time? Your mother's been worried sick."

She lowered her eyes. "I know. I'm sorry. I had no way to send word, but I've been with her since I got home, and she seems to feel a lot better now. Why don't you clean up? Dinner's ready."

"Not so fast, missy. I want to know where you've been all this time."

"With the Indians, Shaun—but I'll tell you all about it after dinner, when I tell Mama."

With a curt nod, Shaun turned on his heel and left the room. He had never been a praying man, but he muttered a fervent prayer of thanks as he climbed the stairs to Emma's room. Kaylee was back. Maybe that would put the glow back in Emma's eyes, the color in her cheeks.

They ate dinner in Emma's room, with Shaun sitting on the edge of the bed and Kaylee sitting in the rocker. The atmosphere was strained. Kaylee could feel Shaun and Emma watching her while she ate, wondering what had happened to her in her absence.

She hated to see the meal come to an end, but the time came when she couldn't avoid answering their questions any longer.

She couldn't meet Shaun's gaze as she told how she had treated Blue Hawk's wounds and then volunteered to take him back to his people in exchange for Randy's life. She told them something of life in a Lakota village, and how she had come to respect the Lakota and how kindly Blue Hawk and his people had treated her. She told them everything except the two most important things: that Blue Hawk was her husband and that she was carrying his child.

"Where is he now, this Indian?" Shaun asked.

She looked up into her stepfather's probing eyes. "I don't know."

With a grunt, Shaun stood up. "I can't believe you think so highly of a bunch of murderin' redskins that held you against your will, but that's neither here nor there. You're home now, and we can put the whole nasty business behind us." And so saying, he left the room.

"Kaylee?"

She looked at her mother, afraid of the censure she would see in Emma's eyes.

"You left something out, didn't you?"

"What do you mean?"

"You love him very much, don't you? This Indian of yours?" Emma's voice was surprisingly gentle.

"What do you . . . how did you know?"

Emma held out her hand. "You're my daughter, after all, flesh of my flesh. Of course I know."

Rising, Kaylee went to sit on the bed beside her mother.

"I'm sorry you're away from him, dear," Emma said, "but I can't be sorry you're home again, or that you're back here with your own people, where you belong."

"Oh, Mama, how can I make you understand how wonderful he is? How wonderful his people are? They aren't savages. They aren't horrible, like Shaun says. Mama, I *liked* living with the Lakota."

"Kaylee, I'm sure that much of what you say is true." Her mother patted her hand. Even in her weakened state she seemed like the Emma of old, rising to the occasion. "But it's a lot to digest in one night, along with this wonderful meal." She smiled wanly. "We can talk of it more later. For now I think we could all use some rest, don't you?"

With a nod, Kaylee bent to give her mother a quick hug before going to her own bedroom.

Closing the door, she threw herself facedown on the bed and let the tears flow. She sobbed until she was empty inside, weeping for the life she and Blue Hawk had left behind and for the uncertainty of the future.

Chapter 27

Blue Hawk awoke to clear blue skies and the touch of the sun on his face. His first thought was that he would see Kaylee before Old Father Wi rose again. He had considered spending the night in the line shack, but sleeping outside under the stars was preferable to sleeping inside the white man's square walls.

Rising, he faced the east, lifted his arms overhead, and offered his morning prayer to Wakan Tanka, thanking the Great Spirit for a new day, asking for wisdom and patience, for health and safety for his woman and unborn child.

Breakfast was the last of the beef jerky. Tomorrow he would have to go hunting, or go hungry.

Sitting in the sun, he watched the stallion graze. Later, he rode up to the line shack to make sure it was still empty. Tonight, he mused, she would be there tonight. And suddenly it was too long to wait. Swinging onto the stallion's back, he rode toward Kaylee's lodge.

Kaylee pinned another bedsheet to the clothesline, then paused to stretch her aching back and shoulders. It was only a little after three in the afternoon, and she had already prepared two meals, washed and dried the dishes, cleaned the kitchen, scoured the stove, changed the linens on all the beds in the house, and done four loads of wash. She had two loaves of bread rising; they would be ready to put in the oven by the time she finished hanging the wash. And when that was done, it would be time to start dinner.

She was reaching into the laundry basket when a sudden prickling along her nape warned her that she was no longer alone. Straightening, she glanced over her shoulder. No one was there.

"I must be imagining things," she muttered, and then squealed when a hand closed over her mouth and an arm snaked around her waist.

An arm she recognized all too well. She whirled to face him. "Blue Hawk! Are you crazy? What are you doing here?"

He brushed a kiss over her lips. "I missed you."

"And I've missed you."

He kissed her again, his lips ravishing hers while his arm drew her up close against him, letting her feel just how much he had missed her.

She moaned softly, her body pressing closer to his. "Blue Hawk . . ."

His hands slid up and down her back, then cupped her buttocks, his hips moving suggestively.

"Blue Hawk!" she exclaimed breathlessly. "You've got to get out of here. What if someone saw you?"

"No one saw me, Kaylee. I am—"

"Lakota," she said, grinning at him. "Yes, I know."

He grinned back at her, his eyes filled with mischief. How she loved him! How much she had missed him. But he had to go. Anyone could come riding up—one of the hands, Shaun, anyone.

"Blue Hawk, please go. You're in danger here."

"You will come to me tonight?"

"Yes. As soon as I can."

He kissed her again, a deep searing kiss that sent every other thought flying out of her mind. Time and place faded away, and there was only Blue Hawk's mouth on hers, the touch of his hands on her skin, the need spiraling through her. She pressed against him; he groaned low in his throat, and then gently put her away from him.

"You are right." His voice was ragged, but his eyes were filled with silent laughter. "There is danger here. And it is you."

"Me?" she asked with mock innocence.

He nodded. "Come to me quickly, *tekihila*."

"I will."

He kissed her again, and then he was gone.

She was distracted for the rest of the day, her mind racing with thoughts of the night to come. She burned the biscuits, had trouble concentrating on what was being said to her during dinner. She washed the dishes quickly and sat with her mother until Emma fell asleep. She went downstairs and bid Shaun goodnight, then went up to her room and bathed. She brushed her hair until it was a soft, shimmery mass of waves, spritzed herself with lavender-scented toilet water, put on a dark-blue shirtwaist and a divided skirt, and climbed out the window.

It was a beautiful night, cool and clear. She thought of how silently Blue Hawk moved and pretended to be him as she tiptoed across the yard.

Dusty whickered softly when she entered the barn. She quickly saddled the mare and led her outside, her excitement building at the thought of seeing Blue Hawk.

As soon as she was out of sight of the house, she swung into the saddle and urged Dusty into a gallop.

Blue Hawk melted into the darkness near the side of the line shack when he heard the sound of hoof-beats. Moments later, Kaylee came into view, her golden hair like a beacon in the night.

He was waiting for her at the front of the shack when she rode up.

She reined her horse to a halt and slid into his waiting arms. Murmuring her name, he carried her into the darkness away from the shack.

Kaylee locked her hands behind his neck. "Where are we going?"

"I do not want to make love to you in the *wasichu*'s lodge."

"Oh." She rested her head against his shoulder, content to let him take her wherever he would.

After a short walk, he lowered her to the ground. Kaylee glanced around. They were in a small glade near a stream. A blanket was spread on the grass. She looked up at him, one brow raised. "Wasn't that blanket hanging on my wash line this afternoon?"

With a shrug, he grinned at her.

Kaylee laughed softly as she sank down on the blanket, pulling him down beside her.

He gathered her into his arms. "How is your mother?"

"Better, I think. She's still in bed, but she seems stronger."

He grunted softly. "And when she has regained her strength, what then?"

"What do you mean?"

"Will you stay here, or come away with me?"

"You're my husband. My place is with you."

"You would leave here, leave your mother?"

Kaylee nodded, though she knew it would be hard to leave home knowing she might never see her mother again.

"*Mitawicu,*" he murmured. "Truly our spirits are one."

"Yes," she whispered. And looking into his eyes, she undressed, anticipation spreading through her as his heated gaze caressed her body.

He stripped away his clout and moccasins, and then they were in each other's arms and it was like the first time all over again. She ran her hands over his shoulders and chest, down his belly, teasing and tormenting him with her touch, reveling in the play of muscles beneath his skin, shivering with pleasure as his hands stroked her breasts and thighs.

And when she couldn't stand it any longer, when she was burning with a flame that only he could quench, she took him into herself, his body merging with hers, his heart beating to the rhythm of hers, his soul bound to hers, until there was no beginning and no end, only two halves now made whole, two people now made one.

It was sometime later before she could trust her voice.

"I hate to go back." Kaylee rolled onto her side, one arm draped over Blue Hawk's chest. "I want to stay here, with you."

Blue Hawk's arm tightened around her shoulders. "It is what I wish, as well."

"Soon." Her fingertips made lazy circles on his chest, gradually moving down, down. "Soon."

He gasped as her hand brushed the inside of his thigh. "If you keep doing that, I will never let you go."

"Promise?" She braced herself on her elbow and gazed down at him. "Promise you'll never let me go?"

"You are my woman, Kay-lee. Nothing, and no one, will ever take you from me."

The next week passed quickly. Kaylee rose shortly after dawn to fix breakfast for her father and prepared breakfast for herself and her mother a few hours later. She set the bread dough, made the beds, did the laundry, did the ironing, did the mending. She tended her mother's vegetable garden, fed the chickens, gathered the eggs. She dusted and polished, swept and mopped, beat the rugs, washed the dishes, filled the lamps with oil. She spent a part of each day with her mother, telling Emma about the Indians and their way of life. Sometimes she read to her mother. Emma subscribed to *Scribner's Monthly*, but when she wasn't in the mood for politics or short stories, Kaylee eagerly picked up a copy of *The Fair God*, by Lew Wallace, a historical novel set in Mexico.

Each day saw her mother growing stronger, more vibrant. Soon, Kaylee thought, soon Emma would be on her feet again. They talked privately about Blue Hawk, and her mother's determination that Kaylee somehow be happy with her chosen man seemed to infuse Emma with new strength. Kaylee was thrilled at her mother's new perspective.

Some women found housework monotonous, but not Kaylee. Every day was an adventure, because she never knew when Blue Hawk would pop up. She never heard him, but she would be feeding the chickens and suddenly he would be there, or she would be weeding the garden and he would appear beside her. His presence delighted her even as it frightened her. It was true that the cowhands left the ranch early each morning, but there was always a chance that a horse would go lame or a man would get hurt and need attention. Sometimes she had nightmares, horrible dreams in which Shaun or one of the men found Blue Hawk leaving the ranch and shot him on sight.

She'd been home almost two weeks when the Thomas sisters came to call. Charlene and Geraldine were a study in brown: brown hair, brown eyes, brown dresses, brown shoes. They looked like a pair of guinea hens as they perched on the sofa, their backs ramrod-straight.

Kaylee couldn't have been more surprised if the president of the United States had knocked at her door. She couldn't remember the last time the Thomas sisters had come to visit; of course, she never went to see them either.

Kaylee excused herself to go into the kitchen to brew a pot of tea, wondering what their visit might mean. She poured three cups of tea, put some cookies she had made that morning on a plate, pasted a smile on her face, and returned to the parlor.

"This is a pleasant surprise," she said, though she almost choked on the words.

"We came by to inquire after your mother's health," Charlene said primly. She took a sip of tea, dabbed the corner of her mouth with a napkin.

"Yes," Geraldine said. "We've been so worried about her."

"She's doing much better," Kaylee said. "I'm sure she'd love to see you both. I'll just go tell her you're here."

"No, no," Charlene said quickly. "We don't want to bother her."

Kaylee glanced from one sister to the other. They were both watching her intently. "So," she said, "how is everything at home?"

"Fine," Charlene said.

"Yes, fine," Geraldine said.

For the next fifteen minutes, they made desultory small talk and then, as if unable to help herself, Geraldine blurted, "What was it like, living with savages?"

Ah, Kaylee thought, *that's why they are here.*

"Do they eat their young?" Charlene asked.

"Did they—" A rush of color swept into Geraldine's cheeks. "You know?"

Kaylee bit back the sharp retort that rose to her lips, frowned as a flash of movement in the kitchen caught her eye. The Thomas sisters had their backs to the kitchen, but Kaylee could see it clearly from where she sat. Her eyes widened when she saw Blue Hawk standing in the doorway.

"Do tell us everything," Charlene said.

"Who told you they eat their young?" Kaylee asked.

"Everyone knows that," Geraldine said.

In the kitchen Blue Hawk swallowed and licked his lips.

"Well," Kaylee said, smothering a grin, "I never saw them eat their young, but there were a lot of bones lying around. You know, little bones."

"Oh, my." Charlene gasped, one hand going to her heart. "That's awful!"

"What do the Indians look like?" Geraldine asked. "Do they really run around naked, with feathers in their hair?"

Kaylee swallowed a giggle as Blue Hawk puffed out his chest and began to strut back and forth. "Oh, they're ugly," she said. "Really ugly. Especially the men."

Blue Hawk came to an abrupt halt, a wounded expression on his face.

"It must have been awful for you," Charlene said.

"Yes, awful," Geraldine agreed. "Maybe it would help if you talked about it."

Kaylee nodded, as though considering it. They wanted to hear something wild, she thought, something risqué, something shocking. And who could blame them? They lived such dull, boring lives. Charlene was a schoolteacher, and Geraldine stayed home to look after their invalid father.

"Do tell," Charlene urged. She clenched her hands and leaned forward. "It will do you good, I'm sure."

"Well." Kaylee glanced into the kitchen. Blue Hawk was watching her, a big grin on his face. "It was awful, just awful. They eat dog meat and they cook it in the stomachs of wild animals . . ."

Geraldine lifted a hanky to her mouth. Charlene's face paled.

"Yes," Kaylee said, warming to her subject. "And they wear deerskins, when they wear clothes at all. And do you know how they make their dresses? Let me tell you. They take a hide and stretch it on the ground, and then they scrape all the hair off with a flesher made of bone, and when all the hair has been scraped away, they soften the hide by rubbing it with a mixture of bear fat and buffalo brains."

In the kitchen Blue Hawk was doubled over with silent laughter.

In the parlor Charlene and Geraldine looked as if they were about to be sick.

"I think we'd better go," Charlene said.

"Yes, I think so," her sister agreed.

"I'm so sorry," Kaylee said. "I've so much more to tell you. You must come again."

With a faint nod, Charlene stood up. She put her arm around her sister's waist, and they staggered toward the front door.

Kaylee saw them out, then went into the kitchen. "You!" she said. "What are you doing here?"

He shrugged. "Do I need a reason to want to see my woman?"

"Of course not, but—"

Taking her in his arms, he kissed away her fears, and because he seemed to come and go like the wind, she convinced herself there was no need to worry.

That conviction lasted until the morning she woke to find him stretched out beside her on the bed.

She bolted upright. "What are you doing here?" she exclaimed. She glanced at the window, at the faint golden light creeping under the curtains.

He lifted one brow. "Are you going to ask me that every time you see me?" His hand slid up her arm and gently drew her back down. "How do you sleep on such a soft bed?"

"Very well," she retorted. "Blue Hawk, you have to go. Now! I can't believe you came here again."

"I missed you." His hand stroked her cheek, glided slowly down her neck, to settle softly over her breast. "I miss waking up with you beside me."

"I miss you, too, but this is madness. You can't stay here!"

"Such a large house," he mused, unperturbed by her concern. "I have never seen a lodge this big."

"You went exploring?"

He nodded. "I did not see it all last time I was here."

"What if my stepfather had seen you?"

Blue Hawk looked at her, his expression amused, as if the mere idea that he could not elude a white man was ludicrous.

"I know, I know, you're Lakota," Kaylee said, her voice tinged with irritation. "But floorboards creak even for Lakota. Especially big ones."

"You worry too much," he said with an indulgent smile.

"Maybe," she replied, poking him in the chest with her finger. "But you don't worry enough."

Blue Hawk glanced at the window. "I must go soon."

"You must go now."

He leaned forward and brushed a kiss across her shoulder. "After I risked my life to get here, would you send me away with no reward?"

The man was incorrigible, she thought, but she couldn't help grinning at him. "What kind of reward did you have in mind?"

"Whatever you would like to give. But I would remind you that generosity is a virtue much prized by my people."

"Well," she said, caught up in the game, "I suppose I could spare a kiss."

"One kiss?" He looked offended. "Is that all my life is worth to you? One kiss?"

"You said there was no danger."

"Only because I did not wish to worry you. A very large *wasichu* came very close to my hiding place when I rode up."

"Oh, that's Roscoe," Kaylee said. "He cooks for the cowhands."

Blue Hawk grunted derisively. "He looks like he eats most of the food himself."

Kaylee laughed softly. Roscoe was only an inch or two taller than she was, and as round as he was tall.

Blue Hawk released a long, aggrieved sigh. "Very well, if one kiss is all you can spare."

She should have known better than to kiss him, because one kiss invariably led to another, and another, and soon her nightgown joined his clout on the floor, and her hands were eagerly exploring him, as if it had been months instead of one night since she had last touched him. She reveled in the feel of his skin, the way his muscles rippled at her touch, the way his breathing quickened as her fingertips slid across his belly, the husky timbre of his voice when he whispered her name.

All fears, all worries, all thoughts of any moment save the one at hand fled as he rose over her. She clutched at his shoulders, her hips lifting to receive him, a soft moan rising in her throat as he possessed her.

He smiled faintly as he covered her mouth with his, loving the way she came alive in his arms, the way she responded to his slightest touch. He kissed her, and kissed her again, caught up in her warmth, in the sleepy scent of her skin as their bodies joined in the age-old rhythm. His hands tunneled into her hair and he kissed her again, felt her body convulse. Her heat surrounded him, carrying him to completion.

Sated, they rested in each other's arms.

"You'd better go," she said, her voice filled with regret.

"You will come to me tonight?"

Kaylee nodded. "I may be a little late, but—" She froze, the rest of the sentence forgotten as someone knocked on the door.

"Kaylee? Are you ill?"

She looked at Blue Hawk, her eyes wide "It's my stepfather!"

"Answer him."

"I—I'm fine. I overslept. I'll be down directly."

"Hurry it up. We lost another hundred head or so last night, and I want to get after them as soon as possible."

"Yes, sir, I will." She waited until she heard Shaun walk away, then she scrambled out of bed and pointed her finger at Blue Hawk. "This is all your fault."

He sat up, his skin looking very dark against the sun-bleached white linens. "Are you sorry to see me here, *mitawicu*?"

"Of course not. I'm never sorry to see you, but what if it had been my mother at the door? She might not have knocked, you know."

Looking unconcerned, he rose and pulled on his clout and moccasins. "I have every right to be here, Kay-lee. I am your husband."

"I didn't mean it like that. Don't be angry."

"I am not angry." He drew her into his arms and kissed her, his hand sliding up and down her bare back. "Only impatient for us to live together as husband and wife again."

"Me, too."

He gazed into her eyes for a long moment, then vanished out the window, as quick and quiet as a shadow running before a storm.

*   *   *

It was an easy task, sneaking out of Kaylee's lodge. When he was again across the river, Blue Hawk found a secluded spot and took the time to bathe, wishing Kaylee was there with him. Later, he sat in a patch of sunlight while his horse grazed. He had no need for food, having helped himself to some meat and bread he had found in Kaylee's house earlier. He had never been in a white man's house before, had not known the big lodge was broken up into many sections. He had seen the place where her mother slept, and the place where her stepfather slept, and thought it odd that the *wasichu* did not sleep with his woman, but the whites were a strange people, content to live summer and winter in the same place.

Having little to do while he waited for nightfall and Kaylee, he rode across the prairie, letting the big stallion stretch out in a full gallop. He put everything out of his mind, exhilarated by the wind in his face and the power of the horse beneath him.

It was when he reined the stallion to a halt on the rim of a box canyon that he saw the cattle penned below.

Dismounting, Blue Hawk tethered his horse to a clump of brush well out of sight, then snaked forward and peered over the edge of the canyon wall. Three cowhands were huddled around a fire, keeping watch.

He grunted softly. The cattle wore the Double R brand; the horses of the cowboys were unbranded. He knew enough about *wasichu* customs to find this unusual. Looking closer, he realized they were Indian ponies wearing saddles and bridles.

He melted into the brush and continued his scout. Deeper in the canyon, he spotted a picket line of horses along a small stream. These horses, he noted, were branded with the G Slash J. Why would the cowhands leave their own horses and ride untrained Indian ponies to work cattle?

His eyes narrowed thoughtfully. The *wasichu* who had shot him and stolen the Lakota horses had ridden a flashy blood bay with a G Slash J brand.

Curious, he settled down to watch.

Chapter 28

Kaylee was washing the dishes from the noonday meal when she heard the rattle of wheels in the yard. Glancing out the kitchen window, she was surprised to see Randy drive up in his family's buckboard. She wiped her hands on a towel, and hurried out to meet him.

He was still sitting in the buckboard when she reached it. He looked thinner, older, than the last time she had seen him. His shirt and jeans hung on him as if he was wearing another man's clothing.

"Randy! What a surprise! I'm so glad to see you."

"I'm a little surprised to see you, too."

"Let's go inside," she suggested. "Roscoe found some lemons in town yesterday, and I just made a pitcher of lemonade."

She started for the porch, then stopped when she realized he wasn't with her.

She glanced over her shoulder, her eyes widening when she saw him lift a pair of crutches from under the wagon seat.

"What happened?" she asked. "Are you all right?"

"Damned redskin, that's what happened!"

He climbed slowly down from the wagon, settled the crutches under his arms, and hobbled across the yard and up the porch stairs. Kaylee held the door open for him, then followed him into the parlor.

"Would you like to sit in here or in the kitchen?"

"In here." He sat down in one of the easy chairs,

dropped the crutches on the floor, and propped his right leg up on the hassock.

With a nod, Kaylee went into the kitchen and poured two glasses of lemonade. She put them on a tray, along with a couple of slices of pound cake and two napkins, then carried it into the parlor.

She sat down on the chair across from Randy's, the tray between them. "Tell me what happened."

"We ran into a pack of Cheyenne dog soldiers while we were out looking for you. I got cut off from the others. One of the red bas—Sorry, Kay. One of the Injuns shot my horse out from under me. My horse went down hard, and I got caught underneath it."

Kaylee glanced at the crutches. "But you'll be all right? Once your leg heals, you'll be all right?"

Randy shook his head, his expression bitter. "My leg was crushed under the saddle. If I'm lucky, I'll be able to walk with just a cane in a month or so."

Kaylee blinked back her tears. "I'm so sorry," she said, knowing the words were inadequate. "So sorry."

Randy shrugged, as if it didn't matter. "Just bad luck. What happened, Kay? Where'd you go? How'd you find your way back home?"

How, indeed, she thought.

"Randy, is that you?"

Kaylee glanced over her shoulder to see her mother standing at the top of the staircase. It was the prettiest sight she had ever seen. "Mama! You're out of bed!"

Emma smiled. "I heard voices." She put her hand on the banister and started down the stairs.

"Wait!" Kaylee jumped to her feet and ran up the steps. "Let me help you."

"Thank you, dear. I am feeling a little wobbly."

Kaylee slid her arm around her mother's waist, and they made their way down the stairs together.

Emma sat on the sofa, Kaylee beside her.

Emma smiled at Randy. "It's so good to see you," she said warmly

"Afternoon, Mrs. Randall," Randy said. "You're looking a lot better than when I saw you last."

"And you're looking worse." Emma patted Randy's knee. "Doctors have been wrong before, you know," she said encouragingly.

"Yes, ma'am." He looked at Kaylee. "How'd you get back home?"

"Blue Hawk brought me."

"Blue Hawk? Who's Blue Hawk? One of our Crow scouts?"

"No, he's Lakota. The wounded man you helped me with, remember?"

"I'm not likely to forget that redskin, not after he brained me and stole my horse. Where is he now?"

The exact same question Shaun had asked, and, she was sure, for the very same reason. "I don't know." It was only a partial lie, she thought. She really didn't know exactly where Blue Hawk was. He could be at the line shack, or out riding, or hunting.

"The only thing that matters is that she's home again, where she belongs," Emma said.

"Yes, ma'am," Randy agreed.

The next hour passed pleasantly. Kaylee made another pitcher of lemonade, encouraged her mother to have a piece of cake. Every time Randy or Emma mentioned Blue Hawk or the Indians, Kaylee answered as quickly and briefly as possible and then changed the subject.

"Well," Randy said, setting his glass on the table, "I'd better be heading back."

"I'm glad you came by," Kaylee said.

"So am I," Emma said. "Come again soon, Randy. And bring your mother with you."

"I will." He leaned forward to get his crutches.

"Here, let me get those for you," Kaylee said. She

handed him his crutches, then walked him out to the buckboard.

"He's still here, isn't he? That redskin?" Randy shook his head when she didn't answer. "He still got my gelding?"

"He didn't steal your horse, Randy, I let him take it so I could get him home to his people," she said.

"Oh, you did, huh? Weren't yours to give away."

"I had to protect you!"

"That what you call protection? Leaving me out cold while you ride off with some Injun?"

"Blue Hawk is a good man."

Randy looked at her speculatively for a long moment and then smacked his hand on the side of the buckboard. "I don't believe it! You're sweet on that damn redskin! Does Shaun know? Stupid question. Of course he doesn't! If he did, he'd lock you in your room and throw away the key. Dammit, Kaylee, are you out of your mind?"

"Randy, for goodness' sakes, calm down!"

"Calm down! How the hell can I calm down?" He grabbed her arm and pulled her up against him. "I love you, Kaylee Marie. I've loved you as long as I can remember."

"Randy, don't—"

"Kay." Drawing her closer, he kissed her.

Kaylee squirmed in his embrace, and when he refused to release her, she put her hands on his chest and gave him a push. Already off-balance, he stumbled backward and his shoulder hit the corner of the buckboard. His face twisted in pain as his full weight came down on his crushed leg.

With a cry, Kaylee made a grab for his arm, but he waved her off.

"I don't need your help," he said gruffly.

"Randy, please—"

"Please what?" he asked, his voice bitter.

"I can't help how I feel."

He snorted softly. "Did you give yourself to him, Kaylee?"

"You have no right to ask me that."

"Maybe not, but I'm askin'. Did you spread your legs for that dirty buck? Did you let that filthy Injun crawl all over you?"

She slapped him. Hard. "I think you'd better go."

"I'm goin', all right." He shook his head. His eyes, which had always been filled with affection when he looked at her, were narrowed with disgust. "To think I wanted to marry you. White squaw."

The venom in his words chilled her heart.

She looked up at him, at the red mark her hand had left on his cheek. Randy had been her best friend, her only friend. He was a part of her childhood, of her growing-up years. But that was over now.

She blinked back her tears as he turned his back to her, tossed his crutches into the buckboard, then pulled himself up onto the seat.

He gave her one last withering look, then took up the reins and clucked to the team.

With tears trickling down her cheeks, she watched until he was out of sight. She started to go into the house, then turned and headed toward the pond behind the barn. She was in no condition to face her mother or to explain her tears.

She was splashing water on her face when Blue Hawk appeared beside her. One look at him, and she knew he had heard every word. The words "dirty buck" and "filthy Injun" rang out in her mind.

Blue Hawk held out his arms, and she went into them gladly. "Why did he say those things?" she sobbed. "I thought he was my friend."

"You cannot blame him," Blue Hawk said quietly. "He is a man, jealous because you have given your heart to another. No doubt it hurts his pride, to know you chose a filthy Indian over him."

"Don't say that! I don't think of you that way, and you know it."

"But he does." His hand stroked her hair. "And so will most of the people you know."

"I don't care!"

He wiped a tear from her cheek with his finger and held it up, his meaning all too clear.

"Randy's different. We grew up together. I thought he'd be my friend no matter what. I wouldn't stop being his friend, no matter what he did." She sniffed back her tears. "What are you doing here, anyway?"

"I am never far away from you, *mitawicu*. Even when distance separates us."

With a sigh, she rested her head on his shoulder. It didn't matter if everyone she knew ostracized her, so long as Blue Hawk loved her.

Shaun was visibly pleased and surprised when he came home that evening and found Emma sitting downstairs. Kaylee had brushed her mother's hair, then gathered it at her nape with a white ribbon. Emma had insisted on getting dressed and when her own clothes proved too large because she had lost so much weight, she donned a dress of Kaylee's, a dark-green cotton with a collar of white lace.

Kaylee had never seen any open sign of affection between Shaun and her mother, so she was completely taken aback when Shaun crossed the floor, knelt at Emma's feet, put his head in her lap, and wrapped his arms around her waist.

Emma stroked his hair, her expression serene.

"I'll go check on dinner," Kaylee said, and hurried out of the room.

Later that night, after Emma had gone to bed and the house was quiet, Kaylee went into the parlor to read until she could sneak out of the house and into Blue Hawk's arms. She picked up an old copy of *Godey's Lady's Book* and settled down on the sofa. She thumbed through the pages. It was an interesting publication, filled with pictures of dresses and bonnets, patterns and instructions for sewing and crocheting, fiction and poetry, recipes for cakes, pickles, and pudding.

She was in the middle of a story called "From May to November" by Miss Mary Durfee when Shaun entered the room.

He looked tired, she thought. His collar was open and his hair was mussed, as if he'd run his hands through it. He walked to the window and looked out, his hands clasped behind his back, and then he turned around to face her.

"I want to thank you," he said, his voice gruff. "I don't know what would have happened if you hadn't come home."

Kaylee blinked up at him, not knowing what to say. In all the years she had known Shaun, she had never heard him thank anyone for anything.

Shaun shifted his weight from one foot to the other, his discomfort obvious in every line of his body. "I know we've never been fond of each other, you and I, and I'm sorry for that. I—I hope you'll forgive me for not being a better father to you. I love your mother more than anything in my life, and you—" A dull red flush crept up his neck. "Every time I looked at you, it reminded me that she had loved somebody else first."

Kaylee stared at him in stunned silence.

Shaun cleared his throat. "Anyway, I just wanted to thank you for coming home, and—" He blew out a deep breath, and she saw him clench his hands. "And ask you to forgive me."

Tears burned Kaylee's eyes as she put her book

aside. Rising, she went to Shaun, stood on her tiptoes and kissed his cheek. "Don't worry," she said, her own voice thick and unsteady. "Between us, we'll get her well again."

Shaun nodded, and she saw there were tears in his eyes as well.

Kaylee stood there long after he left the room, her mind replaying everything he had said. She had misjudged him, she thought, and she felt a deep sense of regret for the years they had wasted, the heartache the two of them had caused Emma. There was no way to heal the mistakes of the past. She placed her hand on her stomach, wondering how the coming of her child would affect their future as a family. Would it be the link that brought them closer together or the wedge that drove them apart?

Chapter 29

Kaylee gazed up at the night sky, the stars twinkling like tiny jewels on a bed of dark velvet. Life was so perfect when she was in Blue Hawk's arms. If only she could stay locked in his embrace and never leave. A shooting star plummeted toward the earth, and she closed her eyes and made a wish.

Please, she thought, *please let the people I love learn to love each other.*

"You are very quiet," Blue Hawk remarked.

"I'm sorry."

The nights were turning cold, and they were lying on a heavy quilt she had brought from the house. The blanket Blue Hawk had taken from the clothesline was spread over them. It was very cozy, lying there with her head pillowed on his shoulder.

"Something troubles you?" he asked.

"No." She laughed softly. "Yes."

"Which is it?"

"My mother got out of bed today. She came downstairs and ate dinner in the dining room."

"That troubles you?"

"No. But she's been doing so much better the last few days. I'm just afraid of what might happen if I leave again." She regretted the words as soon as she said them, but there was no calling them back. She felt Blue Hawk's arm tense beneath her, knew he was thinking she had decided she wanted to stay here with her mother, instead of going with him.

"Go on," he said.

"I know it's a lot to ask, but—but I want to stay here, at least until the baby is born. If Shaun will let me. And if it's all right with you."

"We will stay, if that is your wish. You are my home now. My people are dead or scattered. Sitting Bull has gone to Canada. And Crazy Horse—who knows where Crazy Horse is tonight?"

He sounded so forlorn, it broke her heart. Putting her arms around him, she held him tightly. "I've been waiting for the right time to tell my mother and Shaun about the baby, but who knows when that will be, what with all the trouble at the ranch. Of course, if I wait long enough, I won't have to say anything."

"What trouble?"

"Indians have stolen another hundred head of our cattle."

"Indians?"

"That's what Shaun says."

Blue Hawk sat up. "Indians did not steal his cattle."

"The thieves rode barefoot ponies, Blue Hawk. Shaun's men may not be Lakota, but they can read sign."

"White men can ride ponies stolen from Lakota," he said grimly. "Your cattle are in a canyon across the river. Guarded by *wasichu* riders with unshod ponies."

Kaylee sat up. "You've seen them?"

He nodded. "Some white men are holding them there."

"White men took our cattle!" She sank back. "Rustlers? Are you sure they're our cattle?"

"They wear the same brand as your mare. But there is more to tell."

"More?"

"The horses of the *wasichu* wear the same brand

as those of the men who left me for dead and stole my ponies."

"You've got to tell Shaun!"

Blue Hawk shook his head. "He would shoot me before I could say the words."

"You're probably right," she said ruefully. "You're sure the cattle are still there?"

"Yes."

Kaylee stood up and reached for her undergarments. "I've got to tell Shaun before the rustlers have a chance to move the herd."

He didn't argue. It would be good for her stepfather to know that it was *wasichu* and not Indians who were stealing his cattle.

Blue Hawk rode back to the ranch with her. They parted near the barn. Dismounting, he took Kaylee in his arms and kissed her.

"I hate telling you good night like this," she said.

"You could end it," he replied. "Say the word, and we will leave this place."

"Shaun is my family too, Blue Hawk. I must tell him about his enemies."

He nodded. "It is good. The cattle will not be moved without my knowing it."

"Be careful out there."

He gave her that look, the one that silently chided her for worrying, then took up his horse's reins.

"I love you, my husband," she said simply.

"I love you, my wife."

She watched him swing effortlessly onto the back of his horse, watched him ride away until he was out of sight. Then, she took a deep breath, and went in to talk to Shaun.

"Who told you this?" Shaun leaned forward, his gaze fixed on Kaylee's face.

They were sitting in the parlor. Shaun and Emma sat side by side on the sofa. Kaylee sat in the easy chair, facing them, feeling as though she was on trial. "A friend."

"A friend? Does this friend have a name?"

Kaylee glanced over at her mother, then met Shaun's gaze once more. "Blue Hawk."

"Blue Hawk? Who the hell is that?"

Kaylee clenched her hands at her sides. She had to tell him sooner or later, she thought. It might as well be now. "He's the Indian who brought me home. The one I helped when he was wounded."

"What?" Shaun bolted to his feet, the veins standing out in his neck. "I thought the cavalry brought you home!"

Emma caught his hand in hers and pulled him back down on the sofa. "Shaun, calm down. Let's hear what she has to say."

"Calm down!" he roared. "Don't you realize what she's saying? If she talked to that damned redskin, that means he's here! Here! And if he's here, who knows how many other redskins are prowling around."

"There aren't any other Indians here," Kaylee said. "Just Blue Hawk."

"And why the hell is he hanging around?"

"I would think the answer to that is obvious," Emma said quietly.

Shaun frowned at his wife. "What the hell does that mean?"

"Ask Kaylee."

Shaun glanced from one woman to the other. "What's going on here?"

"Tell him, Kay."

"Yes, tell me," Shaun demanded. "And start from the beginning."

"I found Blue Hawk across the river. He was

wounded, and Randy and I took him to that abandoned line shack. I treated his wounds as best I could—"

"Yes, yes, I know all about that. And about you taking him back to his tribe and all the rest of it. But I thought the cavalry rescued you and brought you home. Now you say this redskin did that. That he's still around. What I want to know is what the hell he's doing here now . . ." Shaun's voice trailed off and he looked at Kaylee speculatively. "Go on."

"He's been staying nearby," Kaylee said. "He saw some cowboys in a box canyon, holding cattle there, cattle wearing the Double R brand. But the cowboys had their saddles on unshod ponies and their own horses out of sight on a picket line. The brands on their horses were the same as on the horses of the men who shot him and stole his ponies just before I found him."

"Oh, my," Emma murmured.

"I still don't understand why he brought you home," Shaun said.

"There was a battle between Blue Hawk's band and Randy's troop of cavalry. Randy found me and took me into the Army camp, but Blue Hawk came the next morning and stampeded their horses and got me back. I told Blue Hawk what Randy had said about Mama being sick and asked him to bring me home."

"And he did, just like that?"

"And he did," she affirmed. "Just like that."

Shaun's eyes narrowed. "Why would a redskin do that? There's more, isn't there? What aren't you telling me?"

"Blue Hawk is my husband."

Silence fell over the room.

Shaun's expression was murderous. "Husband?" His voice was hoarse with disbelief. "How? When? Who would marry a white woman to an Indian?"

"We were married according to Lakota custom."

Shaun made a sound of disgust. "Heathen customs. That doesn't carry any weight here."

"It does with Blue Hawk, and with me," Kaylee said.

"She's in love with him, Shaun," Emma said softly, almost pleadingly.

"In love!" Shaun's face was almost purple. "You knew? You knew about this, too?"

"Not until she came home," Emma said quietly.

"Blue Hawk is my husband," Kaylee said again. She met Shaun's furious gaze stubbornly. "And we're going to have a baby."

"A baby!" Shaun was on his feet again.

"A baby." Emma's gaze ran over Kaylee. "How far along are you?"

"About four months, I think."

"A baby." A slow smile spread over Emma's face. "Our grandchild, Shaun. Think about it."

Shaun paced the floor in long, angry strides. He seemed to be having a hard time finding his voice. "A half-breed brat," he grated finally. He glared at Emma. "What the hell are you so happy about? She's carrying some redskin's brat. Dammit, think what people will say. And what about Garth? He's not gonna want to marry her now, not when she's been ruined by some dirty—"

Emma stood up, her hands fisted on her hips. "You watch your language, Shaun Randall! Kaylee is carrying my grandchild! *Our* grandchild. And don't you forget it."

Shaun dropped down on the sofa, like a puppet whose strings had been cut.

Emma sat down beside him, suddenly pale. She reached for Kaylee's hand. "Are you feeling all right?"

"I'm fine, Mama. Are *you* all right?"

Her mother smiled serenely. "Yes, love, I am perfectly fine. And Shaun will be too. You'll see."

Shaun just shook his head, a bewildered bull at bay. "Dammit, what about Garth?"

"Shaun, I was never going to marry Garth Jackson," Kaylee said firmly.

"Well, I doubt if even Randy would have you now."

Kaylee felt a sharp pang of regret as she recalled the last time she had seen Randy. "He's made that quite clear." Then, squaring her shoulders, she said, "And it doesn't matter. Not now. I'm already married. To Blue Hawk."

He snorted, somewhat weakly. "Married to an Injun. Don't that peel the paint off the barn. Where is he, this Blue Hawk?"

"Nearby."

Shaun glanced at Emma. "I'm going out and have a look around. Why don't you go on up to bed?"

"You're going out now?" Emma said.

"Yeah. I need some fresh air and thinking time."

Kaylee frowned. Had she made a mistake in telling Shaun that Blue Hawk was nearby? Was Shaun going out to look for him?

"I don't think that's a good idea, Shaun," Emma remarked quietly.

Kaylee couldn't remember ever hearing her mother question Shaun's decisions in the past. "You're not going looking for Blue Hawk, are you? You wouldn't hurt him?"

"What kind of man do you think I am?" Shaun asked brusquely. "I've got no love for Injuns, that's for damn sure, but I wouldn't hurt a man who thought enough of you to bring you home. It probably saved your mother's life." He ran a hand through his hair. "And then there's this business about the cattle. Rustlers, pretending to be Injuns! Don't that beat all? I've got a lot of thinking to do!"

Emma laid her hand on her husband's arm. "Shaun—"

He blew out a breath. "I'm just going out to look around some. Don't worry."

"I have to worry," Emma said with a sad smile. "It's what I'm good at."

Rising, Shaun drew Emma into his arms and kissed her lightly. "I'll be back soon. Wait up for me, okay?"

Kaylee stared at her mother and Shaun. She couldn't remember ever seeing them kiss before.

Emma's cheeks were pink as she watched her husband leave the room. She grinned self-consciously at Kaylee as she sat down.

"I told you he'd come around," Emma said. "He'll be fine. He just needs a little time to get used to the whole idea. It sure helps that your Blue Hawk found out who's stealing the cattle."

Kaylee went to her mother and hugged her impulsively. She smiled, remembering the shooting star she had wished upon before Blue Hawk made his surprising revelation about the stolen cattle.

Maybe wishes did come true.

"So," Emma said, "tell me all about him, this Indian of yours."

After leaving Kaylee, Blue Hawk rode back to the canyon to check on the cattle. They were still there, their guards bedded down around a dying campfire. He reined his horse around and rode across the plains. Splashing back across the river, he made a wide circle around Kaylee's home, then rode up into the hills beyond the ranch house. He rode for several miles, letting the stallion find its own way, until he came to a small valley watered by a slow-moving stream. It was a beautiful place, peaceful and untouched, reminding him of one of the valleys located in the Paha Sapa.

Sitting there, staring out over the moonlit landscape,

he wondered if he would ever see the Black Hills again. He thought of his parents, long dead, of his grandmother, of Matoskah and Sisoka, of Crazy Horse and Sitting Bull. He wondered if it had been a mistake to bring Kaylee home, wondered if he should have taken her and gone to the land of the Red Coats with Sitting Bull. Wondered what the future held for his people, his child. It was with sadness that he realized that his son or daughter would not grow up as he had. The *wasichu* were here to stay, and the world would never be the same again. They had brought diseases for which the Indians had no resistance, raped Mother Earth, killed off the buffalo, polluted the rivers and streams in their search for yellow iron. They had broken treaty after treaty as their greed for Indian land grew, until the Lakota and the Cheyenne, the Arapaho and the Pawnee and the Crow, had been pushed off the land of their ancestors and forced onto reservations.

He rubbed a hand over his jaw, remembering an old story his grandmother had told him, something about Iktome, the Trickster, going to visit the Lakota in ages long gone, to warn them of the coming of Hu-hanska-ska, the White Spider Man, who would come to them from across the great water to steal the four directions. Iktome warned them that the White Spider Man would steal the animals, the grass, and the trees, and that he would give the Lakota a new life, a new religion. "You must say 'Hiya!' to him, say no! to everything he asks for. The White Spider Man will bring sickness and hatred; he will make a great black hoop around the world. He shall be called Washi-manu, one who steals all, or *wasichu*, the fat-taker, because he will take all that is good. Wherever he walks, he will leave a track of lies. He is not wise, this White Spider Man," Iktome said, "but he is clever, and if you are not careful, he will steal all that you have—your land, your religion, your life."

After many years, the Lakota forgot about the coming of the White Spider Man, and then, one day, a black cloud covered the land of the Lakota, and the People saw a strange creature walking out of the blackness. He wore a strange-looking black hat and black clothing. His skin and hair were pale, and his eyes were blue. He had hair on his face. He spoke to the People, but they could not understand him. He carried a cross in one hand and a firestick in the other. And then the People recognized him. He was the White Spider Man. *Wasichu* had come.

Blue Hawk sighed. Nothing was ever all bad, he mused, for the *wasichu* had brought Kaylee into his life.

Swinging onto his horse, he rode back toward the canyon.

Chapter 30

Shaun debated the wisdom of riding out alone as he saddled his horse, then shook his head. Chances were, he was riding out on a wild goose chase, and if that was the case, he'd just as soon do it alone. If he saw anything suspicious, he would ride back and get reinforcements. Anyway, a man alone was probably better for a scouting mission.

He thought about what Kaylee had said earlier as he rode out of the yard. She was in love with a damned savage, and the Indian was hiding out somewhere nearby.

Feeling suddenly uneasy, Shaun looked out over the countryside. What if this was some kind of trap? What if Kaylee and this Injun— He swore under his breath, ashamed of himself for what he was thinking.

An hour later, he was lying on his belly on the rim of the canyon. The cattle were down there, just as Kaylee had said. At least three or four hundred head, maybe more. It was hard to tell in the dark. A few head were bunched near a campfire. Lifting his binoculars, he studied the cattle closest to the fire. One of the steers wore a Double R brand. He grunted softly. There were a couple of other brands, too: Jackson's G Slash J, Ernie Milford's Rocking M, Zeke Price's Circle P.

There was only one man riding nighthawk, walking his mount lazily back and forth across the mouth of the canyon. He saw two men standing near the fire, drinking coffee. Probably getting ready to relieve the nighthawk. He thought he saw two more forms rolled into blankets some distance away from the fire, but he couldn't be sure.

The nighthawk moved out of sight for a while. When he came back, he was leading a horse. Shaun read the brand through the binoculars: G Slash J. One of the men by the fire swung a stock saddle over the horse's back. At this distance it was hard to tell for certain, but he was pretty sure the two men near the fire had been with Jackson when they went in search of Kaylee.

Shaun grunted. When he got his men together, he'd have to send word over to the G Slash J and let Garth know that some of his men were doing a little night riding on their own time.

"Hell, I've seen all I need to," he muttered. He was about to back away from the rim when another rider rode into the firelight down in the canyon.

A rider mounted on a big gray thoroughbred.

"Garth." He swore softly. "Don't tell me you're mixed up in this."

He was still trying to convince himself it wasn't what it looked like when a harsh voice spoke from behind him. "Get those hands up, nice and slow, and keep 'em where I can see 'em."

Shaun rolled over, then sat up, his arms raised. He recognized the man who had him covered. "Sweeney! What the hell's going on here?"

"I was just about to ask you that very thing, Randall." Sweeney made a gesture with his gun. "Toss me your pistol, nice and easy, then get up."

Shaun drew his Colt and tossed it at Sweeney's feet. Then he stood, his arms raised over his head. "Now what?"

Sweeney bent down and picked up Shaun's weapon,

never taking his eyes off the other man. "Get on your horse."

Shaun hesitated a moment, weighing his chances of jumping Sweeney and making a break for it. Slim and none, he thought. Bob Sweeney was a big man, with a thick neck and powerful arms. But even if he'd been short and skinny, the gun in his hand made him a giant.

Sweeney eased back the hammer of his Colt. "Don't even think about it, Randall. Mount up."

Garth Jackson couldn't hide his surprise when Shaun rode into the canyon, followed by Bob Sweeney. "What the hell—?"

"Found him spying on us, up there," Sweeney said, jerking a thumb toward the canyon rim. "What do you want me to do with him?"

"For now, just tie him up."

Sweeney dismounted. Grabbing Shaun by the arm, he jerked him off the back of his horse. One of the other G Slash J hands tossed Sweeney a strip of rawhide, and he tied Shaun's hands behind his back, then pushed him down to the ground.

Shaun glared up at him, then at Jackson. "It's been you all along, hasn't it?" He shook his head. "I can't believe it. Dammit, why?"

Garth shrugged. "Why do you think?"

Shaun snorted. "You don't need the money! You've got the biggest spread in the territory."

"Hell, yes! And I aim to keep it that way. But it takes money to keep the place up. A hell of a lot of money."

"So you're stealing from your neighbors and blaming the Indians."

" 'Bout time those damned savages were good for something, don't you think?" Jackson said with a laugh. "Keep an eye on him, Bob. We'll be moving the cattle late tonight."

"Right, boss."

With a last look at Shaun, Jackson went to join the two men by the fire.

"He said you were moving the cattle tonight," Shaun said. "Moving them where?"

Sweeney hunkered down on his heels. "I don't reckon you need to know that." A slow smile spread over his face, but didn't reach his eyes. "And after tonight, it won't matter to you any more than it matters to him."

Shaun followed Sweeney's gaze, felt his stomach knot when he saw a body lying a short distance away. The clothing, as familiar to him as his own, belonged to Tom Grady, one of the Double R cowhands. It was the only way to identify the body, though—the head was a bloody mess. Shaun felt his gorge rise. Grady had been scalped. Dried blood caked his head, looking black in the firelight.

Shaun looked back at Sweeney. "Why the hell did you kill the kid?"

"Caught him snoopin' around earlier."

"So you killed him? And scalped him?"

Sweeney shrugged. "He shouldn't 'a come poking his nose in where it don't belong," he said, rising. "And neither should you."

And with that, he turned and walked away.

Shaun swore softly. Why the hell had he come out here alone? He worked his hands back and forth, trying to loosen the rope. He had to get out of here, and damned quick!

He could see Jackson's men saddling their horses, getting ready to move the herd. Move it where? He frowned. Mexico? He didn't think so. More likely to Canada, he mused. It was closer. And Canada was a ready market, needing beef for the railroad workers who were laying track across the country.

Shaun shifted his weight on the hard ground. Damn,

but time passed slow when a man was waiting for something unpleasant. Or when he was just downright piss-in-his-pants scared. He told himself that Jackson wouldn't kill him. Hell, they'd been friends for almost twenty years. But he couldn't forget the way Jackson had gunned down that Indian kid, or the look in his eyes when he did it. Couldn't ignore Tom Grady's body lying only a few feet away either.

Fear was a hard lump in his belly, the taste of bile in the back of his throat as he continued to work his hands back and forth, trying to loosen his bonds, but Bob Sweeney had done a helluva good job, and the rawhide wouldn't give at all.

And time was running out. Jackson's men were rounding up the cattle. A thick layer of dust rose in the air, punctuated by the sound of bawling cattle and the shouts of the cowhands as they drove the herd toward the canyon entrance.

Shaun's mouth went dry when he saw Jackson and Sweeney walking toward him. Heart pounding, he gained his feet. If he was gonna take a bullet in the back, he'd by damn take it standing up.

"I'm sorry you had to find out about this," Jackson said.

"I'm sorry you turned out to be no better than a damned thief."

Jackson shrugged. "I'll wait for you at the entrance, Bob. Don't be long." With a last glance at Shaun, Jackson turned and started walking toward his horse

Sweeney drew his gun. "No sense drawing this out."

"You're right about that," Shaun said, and lowering his head, he charged Sweeney.

Sweeney's gun went off on impact. Shaun grunted as the bullet slammed into his left side. Thrown off balance, Sweeney stumbled backward and went down hard. Unable to catch himself, Shaun hit the dirt beside him, felt lights explode inside his head as Sweeney brought the butt of his gun down on the back of his skull. Dazed, Shaun rolled onto his side.

Scrambling to his knees, Sweeney lifted his gun and aimed it at Shaun's chest.

Shaun blinked up at him. "Go ahead, you bastard," he said, gasping for breath. "Do it." He took a deep breath and closed his eyes, his heart thundering in his chest. Not now, he thought. Dammit, not now! Not when he and Emma were reaching out to each other again.

The bullet he expected didn't come. He heard a thud, and the ground beside him shook slightly. Opening his eyes, he saw Sweeney lying beside him, his hands clutched around an arrow protruding from his chest.

Shaun's vision blurred as an apparition rose up out of the dust several yards away. A nearly naked savage, his bronze skin gleaming in the firelight.

At least I'll be unconscious when they scalp me, he thought ruefully, and sank into a black sea of oblivion.

Blue Hawk slung his bow over his shoulder, then walked toward Kaylee's stepfather. He paused to retrieve his arrow from the man he had shot. He jerked the arrow out of the man's chest, knew a moment of satisfaction when the *wasichu* cried out and then went limp. For a moment he considered taking the man's scalp, then shrugged. There was no honor in taking the scalp of a coward.

Blue Hawk knelt beside Kaylee's stepfather. The man was still breathing. Blood oozed from the wound in his side. He groaned as Blue Hawk pressed a handful of dirt over the wound to stop the bleeding.

Rising, Blue Hawk went to get the horse that had been left behind for the man called Sweeney. After untying Shaun's hands, Blue Hawk placed him facedown across the saddle, then secured his hands to the stirrups to keep him from sliding off the horse's back. Taking up the reins, he led the horse toward the entrance to the canyon.

In the distance, he could see the dust churned up by the herd. It took only a few minutes to walk to where he had left his own horse. Vaulting onto the back of his pony, Blue Hawk turned north, toward Kaylee's lodge.

Kaylee had been unable to sleep, waiting for Shaun to return. She sat up in bed at the sound of hoofbeats. Two horses, she realized, moving slow. Seized by a sudden foreboding, she grabbed her robe and ran down the stairs and out of the house.

"Oh, no," she whispered. "Shaun!" She turned on Blue Hawk "What happened?"

"He has been shot."

"Shot! Is he still alive? Shot? By who? Oh, Blue Hawk, not by you?"

"Not by me. We will talk of it later. He is badly hurt."

Blue Hawk lifted Shaun from the back of his horse and carried him up the steps to the porch. Kaylee ran ahead to open the door.

"Where shall I put him?"

"Follow me," she said, and hurried up the stairs. She opened the door to Shaun's room, pulled down the covers on the bed, lit the lamp.

Blue Hawk lowered Shaun to the mattress. Blood still leaked from the edges of the wound.

"I need to heat some water," Kaylee said. "Will you stay with him while I'm gone?"

Blue Hawk nodded. He waited until Kaylee left the room, then removed the *wasichu*'s boots and foot coverings and tossed them aside. He took the man's shirt, belt, and pants off, shook his head as he removed the long red shirt he wore underneath his other shirt. No wonder the *wasichu* were always so irritable, he mused. Not only did they live in the same place summer and winter, they wore too much clothing. He glanced around the room, amazed again at the size of the *wasichu*'s lodges.

Kaylee returned a few minutes later, carrying a tray. She set it on the table beside the bed, frowned when she saw the dirt packed over the wound. She looked up at Blue Hawk, a question in her eyes.

"To stop the bleeding," he said.

"Oh." There was a time when she would have questioned such methods, but no more. Since living with the Indians, she had learned there was a lot she didn't know.

Soaking a cloth in warm water, she gently rinsed the dirt from the wound.

"The bullet is still there," Blue Hawk said.

"It is?"

He nodded.

"I'd better get Mama," Kaylee said. "She's better at this sort of thing than I am."

Leaving the room, Kaylee hurried down the hall and knocked softly on her mother's door. "Mama? Mama."

"Come in, dear."

Kaylee opened the door and stepped into the room. She could see her mother sitting up in bed.

"What time is it, Kay? I thought Shaun would be back by now. Kay?"

"He's back, Mama, but he's hurt—"

Emma was out of bed before Kaylee finished speaking. "What's happened? What's wrong?"

"He's been shot. Blue Hawk brought him home."

"Shot! Merciful heavens. Where is he? How did it happen?"

"He's in his room. I'm not sure what happened."

Emma slipped on her robe and hurried toward the door that connected her room with her husband's.

Kaylee followed her mother into Shaun's room.

Emma paused, her eyes widening in recognition when she saw Blue Hawk standing beside the bed. "You're looking much better than the last time I saw you," she said somewhat distractedly. "Thank you for bringing my husband home."

Blue Hawk nodded, unable to hide his surprise. Among his people, a woman did not look at or converse with her father-in-law; a man did not look at or speak to his mother-in-law. When a man's mother-in-law came to visit, he left the lodge and politely stayed away until she went back to her own lodge. Apparently it was not so among the *wasichu*.

Emma quickly overcame her surprise at seeing him there and went straight to her husband's side, giving him her full attention. Lifting the cloth Kaylee had placed over the wound, she examined the injury, which was raw and red and oozing blood.

"Kaylee, go downstairs and bring me a thin-bladed knife. Boil it first. Then get my sewing kit. Oh, and bring a bottle of whiskey. The one Shaun keeps for special occasions. And some sulfur. And some more clean cloths."

"Yes, Mama," Kaylee replied, and hurried out of the room.

"Mr. Hawk, I'll need your help."

Blue Hawk nodded.

Emma smiled her thanks, then brushed a lock of sweat-dampened hair from her husband's brow.

At her touch, Shaun's eyelids fluttered open and he stared up at her. "Emma? Emma—is that you?"

"Yes, I'm here." She pushed him back when he tried to rise. "You're hurt, Shaun. Lie still."

"Thought I was a goner for sure. Jackson—"

Emma frowned. "Garth? What about him?"

Kaylee bustled back into the room. "Here, Mama, I think I've got everything."

"Emma—listen," Shaun whispered hoarsely. "It's important. Damn important."

"Later, Shaun," Emma said gently. "You're bleeding all over my good sheets."

Kaylee yawned as she gathered up the soiled linens and other supplies and carried them down the stairs. Blue Hawk followed her. Emma was going to spend the night in Shaun's room. There were a lot of unanswered questions, but they could wait until tomorrow. Shaun was home and resting as comfortably as possible. Emma had managed to remove the bullet and stop the bleeding, and he was sleeping now. Emma was pretty sure he was in no immediate danger. For now, that was all that mattered. She was too tired to think straight.

It had been a long night. Emma had poured whiskey into Shaun until he was past feeling, then Kaylee had held the lamp while Emma probed for the bullet lodged in Shaun's side. Emma had asked Blue Hawk to hold Shaun down, even though Shaun had argued against it. As it turned out, it was a good thing Blue Hawk was there. The whiskey had numbed some of the pain, but the bullet had been buried deep. As Emma had probed and twisted delicately with the knife, Shaun had come half off the bed. Blue Hawk had needed all his strength to hold the injured man still.

For all that it had been a long night, it had also been one of revelation as Kaylee realized that Emma truly loved her husband. She had watched her mother tending Shaun's wound, noticed the gentleness in her touch, the worry in her eyes, the tenderness in her voice when she spoke to him, reassuring him. She had once accused her mother of marrying for security, not love, but she knew now that she had been mistaken. Emma loved Shaun and, she realized, with some surprise, Shaun loved Emma. How had she missed seeing it before? Had she purposely ignored the little signs, the touches, the veiled glances? Or was it just that she saw more now that she was in love herself? How often in a day did Blue Hawk find an excuse to touch her hand, her arm, her shoulder? How many times, when they found themselves alone, did they share a hurried embrace, a quick kiss? How many times did she look up to find him watching her, his dark eyes filled with love and desire?

Kaylee lit the lamp in the kitchen, filled a pail with cold water, and dropped the soiled sheets in it.

She turned to find Blue Hawk standing in the doorway, watching her. His presence seemed to fill the kitchen. "You'll spend the night here, with me, won't you?"

"If you wish me to."

"I do. Why don't you sit down? I'm going to make Mama a cup of tea. Do you want some?"

With a nod, Blue Hawk pulled out a chair and sat down. He looked uncomfortable in a chair. He watched with interest as Kaylee moved about the kitchen, filling a kettle with water, stoking the fire, putting the kettle on to heat. She pulled a tray and three cups from a shelf and set them on the table.

"Do you take milk or sugar?" she asked, and then smiled self-consciously, certain that no one had ever asked him that question before.

He grinned back at her, then drew her down in his lap. She went willingly, her arms twining around his neck, her eyelids fluttering down as his mouth sought hers. His hand moved slowly up and down her back, then slid around to cup her breast. She sighed with pleasure, her heart racing as she thought of spending the night with him. She didn't feel sleepy anymore.

He deepened the kiss, his arm tightening around her, his desire evident in the tremor in his arms, the quickening of his breath.

She drew away reluctantly when the water began to boil. She kissed him on the cheek, then went to make the tea. When it was ready, she poured three cups, added sugar to all three, a bit of milk to one. "I'll just take this up to Mama."

Blue Hawk sipped the hot beverage while Kaylee was upstairs. It tasted different from the willow-bark tea Kaylee had given him before, different from the tea his grandmother had given him when he was a child and had an upset stomach. The thought filled him with sadness, reminding him anew that, save for Kaylee, all those he had loved were gone. So much killing, so much violence. And it was not yet over. Kaylee had almost lost her second father tonight.

Rising, he went outside.

Kaylee found him there a few minutes later. Coming up behind him, she slid her arms around his waist and pressed her cheek against his back. She sensed the tension in him immediately. "What is it?" she asked quietly. "What's wrong?"

He shook his head.

"Tell me," she said. "Maybe I can help."

"No one can help."

She heard the sorrow in his voice and knew, in that instant, what he was feeling, thinking. "I love you," she murmured. "We'll be your home, Hawk, your son and I, for as long as we live."

He turned in her arms and hugged her tight, his chin resting on the top of her head. A long, shuddering sigh went through him.

"Blue Hawk?"

When he didn't answer, she took him by the hand and led him into the house, up the stairs, into her bedroom. She lit the lamp, gave him a gentle push to make him sit down on the bed. She removed his moccasins and his clout, then removed her robe and her gown and sat down beside him.

"I love you, Hawk. Please don't shut me out."

His arm curled around her waist, and he buried his head in the cleft of her breasts. "Hold me, Kay-lee," he said, his voice hoarse. "Just hold me."

She put her arms around him and held him tight, rocking him as a mother might rock a child. "It'll be all right," she crooned. "You'll see. Everything will be all right."

Yet she was beset by doubts even as she spoke the words. They had no money, no home, no place to live if Shaun refused to let them stay on the ranch. Sitting Bull had taken his people to Canada. The Lakota had scattered. And as much as she had loved living with the Indian people, she didn't want to have to worry about being attacked by soldiers while she was pregnant, and she didn't want to spend the winter hiding out in the mountains, wondering if there would be enough to eat. Even as those thoughts crossed her mind, she was plagued with a sense of guilt and shame. Blue Hawk had lost so much. If he told her he wanted to go back to his people, how could she refuse?

"It will be all right," she murmured again, and prayed to God that it would be so.

Chapter 31

Jackson swore a vile oath. "What do you mean, Sweeney's dead?"

"I mean he is dead, *jefe*." Jorge Batista shrugged. "I can say it no plainer than that. Looked to me like an arrow got him. Hard to say for sure. Whoever shot him took the arrow."

Jackson frowned. "An arrow?" They'd heard a gunshot and assumed that Sweeney had plugged Randall. When Sweeney hadn't shown up, Jackson had sent Batista back to check on him. "What about Randall?"

"He is gone."

Jackson swore again. It didn't make sense. What was an Indian doing in the canyon? And why would an Indian kill one white man and not the other? The best he could hope for was that the Indian had killed Randall. But with no body, he had to plan for the worst and assume that Randall had made it back home. Dammit!

"All right, you go on with the herd. I'll go back to the ranch and see what I can find out."

"*Si, jefe.*"

Jackson kneed his big gray into a lope. He couldn't believe all this bad luck at once. He'd been having things his own way on the range for too long. Everybody assumed the worst about the Indians, so they didn't give much thought to rustlers. Throwing a wide loop had been lucrative from the start, with relatively low risk. Since his night riders all had prices on their heads in other parts of the country, their silence was assured.

Setting it up in the beginning had been a piece of cake. Easy to leave a few false clues—an arrow here, a feather there, some unshod-pony tracks—and lay the blame on the Indians.

But maybe it was time to quit. Maybe having two men that he knew stumble onto the canyon within a day of each other was a warning. Killing the Double R cowhand had been easy enough. There'd been no choice, really—Grady knew him on sight. But he had hesitated over Randall's death, and now that hesitation had cost him. Might cost him the whole operation, Jackson thought angrily, and if Randall had managed to make it back home, might very well cost him his life.

Jackson urged his horse into a gallop. It was time to lay low for a while. The last herd was on its way to Canada. He had paid off his gambling debts, squared his overdue account with the bank. All he had to do now was hightail it home. If there was no sign of Randall, well and good. If Randall was still alive—

He shook his head ruefully. Like it or not, he would do what had to be done.

Chapter 32

Emma woke with a start, wondering what had roused her. And then she heard it again, a low groan that quickly brought the events of the previous night rushing back to her.

Rising from the chair she'd been dozing in, she hurried to Shaun's bedside. He was tossing restlessly, and sweat beaded his brow.

"Jackson!" he exclaimed. "What the hell—"

She leaned forward, frowning as his words slurred and became incoherent. He was sweating out some of the whiskey. The bedclothes smelled like a distillery. His hand was knotted in the bedding, his knuckles white.

Emma shook his shoulder gently. "Shaun? Shaun, wake up."

His eyelids flew open and he stared up at her, his eyes wild.

"Shaun, it's all right. You're home."

"Emma—Emma, listen—"

"I'm here."

"Garth—" He licked his lips. "Garth's the one."

"Shh. Rest now."

"No—no time—Garth—Gotta get the sheriff."

"Later," she said. "Rest now."

He shook his head. "Listen to me! He killed Grady."

"You were dreaming, Shaun." She brushed a lock of hair from his brow. "Garth hasn't killed anyone. Go back to sleep now."

"No! Dammit—" He grabbed her hand. "Listen to me!" He took a deep, calming breath. "Jackson's the one stealing our cattle. I saw him. He killed Grady. Scalped him to make it look like Injuns did it. He was gonna kill me." He frowned. "How did I get here?"

"Blue Hawk brought you home."

He grunted softly. So the apparition he'd seen had been real. "Emma, Grady's body is in that small box canyon across the river. Send Quint for the sheriff. Murder's been done."

Emma studied her husband and realized that even though he was feverish, he was rational. "I'll take care of it, Shaun. Don't worry. Anything else?"

"I reckon not."

She bent down and kissed his cheek. "You get some rest now, hear?"

Shaun squeezed her hand. "Be careful, Emma. Don't go anywhere alone, you or Kaylee. And keep the men close to home. Where's that redsk—where's Blue Hawk?"

"Downstairs with Kay."

Shaun grunted. "Tell him to stick close."

Kaylee shook her head. "Garth Jackson a rustler and a murderer? I don't believe it."

"I don't want to believe it, either," Emma said. She took her shawl from the hall tree and draped it around her shoulders. "Noah is taking me to see Grady's mother. If we leave now, I should be able to catch her before she leaves for church. Oh, and I already sent Quint after the sheriff. And I told Roscoe to keep the rest of the men nearby until the sheriff gets here."

Emma looked at Blue Hawk. For all his natural physical grace, he still looked ill at ease while sitting in a chair. "Shaun said you should stay close."

Blue Hawk nodded. He had no intention of leaving

Kaylee, or her mother, as long as the *wasichu* Jackson was alive. He knew the man's treachery all too well.

"Keep an eye on Shaun, dear. I'll be back as soon as I can."

"Mama, do you feel well enough for this?"

"I'm fine, dear."

"You haven't even had breakfast yet."

"I'll eat when I get home." Emma hugged Kaylee, then left the house.

Kaylee sat down on the sofa, her thoughts troubled. "I just don't understand it," she said. "Garth Jackson has everything anyone could want. Why would he steal our cattle?" She shook her head. "I just can't believe he killed Grady, that he was going to kill Shaun. And yet . . ."

"Something else troubles you?" Blue Hawk asked.

"I never liked him. I never trusted him."

"My woman has the wisdom of Wanblee Galehska."

"I don't know about that."

"You must always listen to what your heart tells you, *mitawicu*."

"How about what my stomach tells me?" she asked. "It's been a long busy time since supper last night. Are you hungry?"

He nodded. "I will go bathe while you eat."

"Where do you wash?"

"In the creek behind the barn."

Kaylee shook her head. "That's silly. I'll heat some water while I cook breakfast. It's time you had a hot bath."

She filled several large pots with water, put them on the back of the stove to heat, and prepared breakfast. She watched with pleasure and amusement as Blue Hawk wolfed down six hotcakes, four eggs, and four pieces of bacon, along with two cups of coffee heavily sweetened with sugar. Their troubles seemed far away just then.

"I guess we finally found something from the *wasi-chu* that you can appreciate," she remarked as he ate the last piece of bacon.

He looked at her across the table, one brow raised. "I like you," he reminded her with a wry grin.

"I'd better take this plate up to Shaun before you eat his breakfast, too," she said with a laugh.

When she returned to the kitchen, the water was hot. She carried the big old wooden tub into the kitchen and emptied the pots into it, then added some cool water until the temperature was just right.

Blue Hawk eyed the tub and the steam rising from it with suspicion.

"Go on, get in," Kaylee urged. "It won't bite you."

He still looked skeptical.

Kaylee checked to be sure the curtains were closed and the back door was locked. The hot water was too tempting to pass up.

"Well, if you're not going to use it, I will." Undressing, she wound her hair into a knot, then picked up the soap and stepped into the tub. She sat down, sighing with pleasure as the hot water closed over her.

Blue Hawk watched her for a moment, then stripped off his clout and moccasins and stepped into the tub behind her. Water sloshed over the sides.

"What are you doing?" Kaylee exclaimed. "There's not enough room in here for both of us."

His arms slid around her waist and he leaned forward, nuzzling her shoulder. "We will make room."

It was a tight squeeze, but very cozy, especially when she turned to face him. When he would have kissed her, she shook her head. "Oh, no," she said. "We're here to bathe."

He looked at her, momentarily taken aback, until she began to wash him. His body responded instantly to the touch of her hand dragging the soap across his skin. She washed his neck, his shoulders, his arms, his chest, his belly, and his legs. He watched her through heavy-lidded eyes, every nerve humming with desire.

"So," she asked, a smile playing over her lips, "how do you like the *wasichu* way of washing?"

"Very much," he replied, his voice thick with need. "But you have not washed all of me."

"I was saving the best for last."

With a growl, he caught her hand in his.

"I thought you said I wasn't finished."

"I think we will finish together." Taking the soap from her hand, he washed her until her need was as great as his, and then he lifted her from the tub and carried her, naked and dripping, up the stairs to her bedroom and closed the door.

The water in the tub was cold and it was time for lunch by the time Kaylee got back to the kitchen. She had given Blue Hawk a pair of Shaun's pants and one of his shirts to wear. At first he had refused, but when she had reminded him with a grin that it was wise to dress as the enemy did when in the enemy camp, he had seen the wisdom of it and agreed. He had refused the long underwear, though, preferring to wear nothing at all beneath the trousers, and he insisted on keeping his moccasins. She had offered to trim his hair, but he had refused, and she hadn't argued. A lot of the men wore their hair long.

He looked quite handsome, she mused as she warmed up a pot of beef stew. The blue shirt complemented his dark skin and eyes. His hair fell shiny black and clean well past his shoulders. She felt a flush sweep into her cheeks when he gazed at her, lingering on her breasts. She knew he was thinking, as she was, of what had happened earlier.

She had never known that physical love between a man and a woman could be so wonderful, so beautiful. Her mother had been reticent on the subject, saying only that a woman should save herself for her husband and try to please him in the marriage bed. She thought of Shaun and Emma and wondered why it was so difficult to imagine them making love.

Emma came home looking as though she was carrying the weight of the world on her shoulders. Shaun was asleep, and Kaylee insisted that her mother sit down and rest while she fixed her a long-delayed meal.

Emma let out a sigh as she removed her shawl and draped it over the back of her chair. She smiled her thanks as Kaylee placed a cup of hot tea in front of her.

"Poor Clarice," Emma remarked. "Tom was her only son, you know, and all he ever wanted to do was work cattle. I stayed with her while she got dressed, and then we went to church to say a prayer for him."

Kaylee set a bowl of stew in front of Emma. "I can make you some bacon and eggs if you'd rather have that."

"This is fine, dear. Nothing I could say would comfort Clarice." Emma took a few bites of stew. "I need to look in on Shaun. He's been all right?"

"Yes, Mama."

Emma nodded. "Where's Mr. Hawk?"

"I'm not sure." Kaylee smiled a sad smile. "He said he needed to get out of the house for a while."

"He's like a wild bird, Kay. I don't think he'll ever be happy living in a cage."

"I know."

Emma was finishing up her meal when Quint knocked at the back door.

"Drum's out of town," Quint said, removing his hat. "He won't be back until day after tomorrow, and his deputy quit. I left a message in his office telling him we need to see him as soon as he gets back. I'd of been here sooner, but it took me a while to track down Drum's whereabouts. I saw one of Jackson's men in town, but no sign of Jackson."

"Thank you, Quint," Emma said.

"How's the boss man?" he asked anxiously.

"Resting," Kaylee said.

"Is there anything else I can do?" he asked.

"Yes," Emma said decisively. "Round up half the hands and have them go up to that box canyon and get Grady's body. If the sheriff isn't coming, it's not right to leave him for the vermin. His mother's bad enough off as it is."

"Yes, ma'am. We'll get right on it."

"And Quint? Be careful. And make sure everyone takes a rifle."

"Yes, ma'am!" He replaced his wide-brimmed hat, then shuffled from one foot to the other. "There's just one other thing . . . Some of the men were wondering . . . ah," he cleared his throat. "Is that Injun gonna be stayin' on here?"

"Yes, he is," Kaylee said sharply. "If the men have a problem with that, tell them they can collect their wages. Is that clear?"

"Yes, ma'am, it surely is. When things start changing, they really get to going, don't they?" He turned and left, spurs jingling.

"That's just what I told Noah," Emma said approvingly.

"What did you tell Noah?" asked a masculine voice.

Emma gasped, almost spilling her tea. "Mr. Hawk, you gave me quite a start."

"He's Lakota, Mama." Kaylee smiled. "You never hear him arrive." She sobered as she turned to face Blue Hawk. "Some of the hands may be a little uneasy about—"

"Having a painted savage so close to home," Blue Hawk finished for her.

"Yes, but they'll get used to it, or they can leave."

"And if they all leave," he asked quietly, "what then?"

"We'll worry about that when it happens," Emma said.

"That's right," Kaylee said. "Where have you been?"

He shrugged. "Nowhere. Just riding. Looking around."

"Is everything all right?"

"The boy's body is protected," Blue Hawk told Emma. Entering the room, he sank cross-legged onto the floor. "I returned to the canyon. The *wasichu* and their stolen cattle are all gone. It is not right to leave a brave man where he fell. So I gave him Lakota burial."

Emma's eyes brimmed with tears. "That was so thoughtful, Mr. Hawk. But the men will have to bring him back for a proper Christian funeral. I hope you understand that? For his family's sake?"

"It is good for a man to be mourned in keeping with his custom," he said. "Your husband is awake."

Emma cocked her head to listen. "I believe you're right." She put her teacup aside. "I'd better go see how he is."

Kaylee put her mother's dishes in the sink, gave the table a cursory wipe, and then went into the parlor. Blue Hawk rose effortlessly and followed her. She sat on the sofa and patted the cushion. "Come sit beside me."

He did so reluctantly, not caring for its softness, afraid it would make him soft. The white man seemed to have a weakness for soft things—soft beds, soft chairs, soft clothing. He looked at Kaylee. She was soft on the outside but had great strength on the inside. She had endured much to be with him. Could he do less?

"You're not very happy here, are you?" she asked.

"Do you read my thoughts, *mitawicu*?"

"No, only the look on your face. Do you want to leave here?"

Blue Hawk shook his head. As much as he wished to be among his own people, worry for Kaylee and their child outweighed his yearning for home. It would be winter soon. He knew Kaylee was nervous about the birth of their child. It was her first pregnancy, and it was natural for her to want her mother close by. It was the same for Lakota women, and he would not deny her the comfort her mother could offer.

He drew her into the circle of his arms, his fingers splayed over her softly rounded belly. His child rested there. It was a solemn, sobering thought. What would life be like for his child? The Lakota way of life was almost gone. The Army would hunt Crazy Horse and his people relentlessly, killing them or forcing them onto reservations. He did not want his child to grow up on the reservation, never to be free, forced to accept the white man's charity. He had heard that Indian children were often taken from their parents and sent away to schools where they were forced to learn the white man's language and were whipped for speaking their native tongue. Their hair was cut, and they were dressed in *wasichu* clothing. They were taught the white man's religion and forbidden to practice their own. What way was that for a Lakota to live? He glanced around the room. The parlor, it was called. Perhaps it would be better for their child to grow up here.

And then he heard Shaun's voice, bellowing for Emma, and he wondered if staying here would be wise. Kaylee had told him of her stepfather's hatred for Indians. Would Shaun Randall's hatred extend to his own grandchild? Children were prized among the Lakota. Not only did parents, grandparents, brothers, sisters, aunts, uncles and cousins contribute to the rearing of a child, but the rest of the village was involved as well. Was it so among the *wasichu*? Or would Kaylee's stepfather turn his back on the child because of its mixed blood?

Shaun was a horrible patient. One day in bed had him complaining about everything. He complained about the broth Kaylee prepared, and then the soup Emma prepared, declaring that he was a man, not a child, and he wanted something he could sink his teeth into. His grumblings and groanings could be heard throughout the house. At the end of her patience, Emma threatened to have Blue Hawk tie Shaun to the bed if he tried to get up one more time, and that, finally, brought peace to the household.

Kaylee and Blue Hawk looked at each other, suppressing their smiles, when Emma entered the parlor that afternoon, a harried expression on her face. "That man is going to drive me insane. If he isn't complaining about the food, he's insisting he's well enough to get out of bed. That gunshot wound's not twenty-four hours old! He's lucky to be alive. Doesn't he know that?"

Kaylee could no longer suppress her smile. "Blue Hawk's the same way, Mama."

Emma laughed.

Blue Hawk scowled at Kaylee.

"Well," Emma said, "I give up. If the man wants steak, I'll give him steak."

"I made potato salad and beans," Kaylee said. "Do you think he's strong enough to get out of bed? We could make a picnic in the yard. It's such a nice day."

"What is a pic-nic?" Blue Hawk asked.

"It's when you spread a blanket on the ground and eat outside."

Blue Hawk grunted softly. His people had been having picnics all their lives without knowing it.

"That's a good idea, dear. I'll ask Shaun." Emma glanced around. "Do you need help with anything?"

"No, Mama."

"All right." Emma drew a deep breath. "I expect we'll be down directly."

They made their picnic in the shade of the big old tree that grew alongside the house. Kaylee carried the plates and glasses outside, and after she and Emma got Shaun propped up on a comfortable mound of bedding, Kaylee went back inside to cook the steaks. Emma stayed outside with Shaun.

Blue Hawk kept Kaylee company in the kitchen. "Do you think this is a good idea?" he asked, glancing out the window.

"You two will have to talk sometime."

"I do not think your stepfather and I will have much to say to each other."

"Well, he owes you a thank-you, if nothing else. You saved his life, after all."

Blue Hawk grunted softly. He didn't think Shaun Randall would enjoy being reminded of that fact. Knowing how Shaun felt about Indians, he had avoided the man since bringing him home, which hadn't been too difficult since Shaun was bedridden.

"Well, the steaks are done," Kaylee announced. "If you want to eat, they're being served out there. You ready?"

With a nod, he followed her outside.

Shaun's scowl was firmly in place when he saw Blue Hawk trailing after Kaylee. He said something to Emma, who laid her hand on his arm. It didn't take much to figure out that Shaun had protested his presence and Emma was trying to calm him.

"Everything looks wonderful," Emma said as Kaylee sat down. "Doesn't it, Shaun?"

"Yeah, wonderful," her husband muttered.

Blue Hawk sank down across from Shaun, and the two men eyed each other warily while the women served the food. Emma hovered over Shaun, watching each bite he took, looking as though she would like to feed him herself.

"Emma," Shaun said at last, "enough is enough."

A blush rose in her cheeks. "I'm sorry," she said with a self-conscious smile. "I've just been so worried about you. So afraid."

"Well," Shaun replied gruffly, "now you know how I felt the last couple of months."

A long look passed between them.

The color in Emma's cheeks burned brighter. "Well," she said, her hands fluttering over the napkin in her lap. "More lemonade, anyone?"

Kaylee laughed softly, and the spell was broken.

Shaun fixed his gaze on Blue Hawk. "You saved my life. I reckon I owe you a debt."

"No. You are related to Kaylee and as such, you are related to me. There is no debt to repay."

"Well," Shaun said gruffly, "I'm obliged to you just the same."

It wasn't much, Kaylee mused, looking from one man to the other, but it was a start.

Chapter 33

He moved through the shadows, his gaze fixed on his destination. It would be over soon. He didn't think of what he was about to do, only the necessity for it. A means to a vital end.

As soon as he reached the ranch, he had sent Batista into town to see what he could learn. Batista had returned with the troublesome news that Randall had survived. He had overheard one of the Double R hands asking after the sheriff's whereabouts, saying that Randall was badly hurt and they needed Drum out at the Double R right quick.

He moved into the barn, opened the stall doors, and freed the horses, leading them outside as quietly as possible to avoid rousing any light-sleeping cowpuncher over in the bunkhouse. It had to look like a midnight raid, after all. Retrieving the bow and quiver he'd left by the door, he fired the cloth wrapped around the tip of an arrow and launched it into the loft of the barn. The straw ignited instantly, and he moved hurriedly toward the house. The flickering light and the acrid smell of smoke would rouse someone, surely. He upended the can of kerosene he'd left by the porch on his way to the barn, lit a match, and tossed it into the kerosene. That done, he fired the tip of another arrow and shot it through the open parlor window, then launched a third through the kitchen window. He waited to make sure the last arrow found fuel for the hungry flame, then dropped the bow and quiver where they were sure to be found and ran for his horse, tethered out of sight a short way from the house.

He was reaching for the reins when a dark shape moved across his field of vision.

"What the hell?" he exclaimed. Drawing his gun, he peered into the shadows, but there was nothing to see. "Who is it?" he demanded. "Who's there?"

Silence was his only answer.

A shiver of apprehension crawled up his spine even as he told himself it was only his imagination. And then he saw it again, a shadowy shape that rose up tall, and menacing, like an angry bear.

And then the shadow materialized into the shape of a tall, dark-skinned man clad in a clout and moccasins.

"I have come for the guns you owe me, *wasichu*."

Fear wrapped a cold, clammy hand around Garth Jackson's innards as he stared at the apparition before him, his eyes widening in disbelief. "You!"

His finger was curling around the trigger when the arrow found him.

Blue Hawk stood over his enemy, his heart pounding, a cry of exultation rising in his throat. Head thrown back, he raised his arms. Mato's voice echoed in the back of his mind. *Follow the woman. She holds the answer.* Mato had been right, he mused. He had followed Kaylee home, and she had led him to the *wasichu* traitor.

"*Hecheto aloe,*" he murmured. It is finished.

He opened his eyes as the scent of smoke was carried to him on the night wind. Turning in the direction of the ranch, he saw the glow of flames lighting the night sky. The barn and the ranch house were burning.

Racing toward the bunkhouse, he burst into the room and roused the men, then hurried outside.

After dousing himself in the horse trough, he ran for the house. The parlor and the kitchen were in flames. Crying Kaylee's name, he raced up the stairs.

She was sleeping soundly, one hand tucked under her cheek. "Kaylee!" He shook her shoulder. "Kaylee!"

She woke slowly. "What is it?" she asked sleepily, and then her eyes widened. "I smell smoke!"

"The house is on fire. We must get your mother and Shaun and get out." He gave her a little push. "Hurry!"

Kaylee scrambled out of bed. Barefoot and clad only in her nightgown, she ran down the hall and rushed into Shaun's room. "Mama! Shaun! Wake up!"

"Kaylee," Emma murmured. "Is something . . ." She bolted upright and shook Shaun's shoulder. "Shaun! Shaun! Wake up. Wake up! The house is on fire!"

"Hurry, Mama!"

"I can't wake him up!" Emma cried. "He was in pain, and I gave him something to help him sleep."

"Go," Blue Hawk said. "I will bring him."

"I can't leave him," Emma said. "I won't."

"Mama, come on!" Kaylee grabbed her mother by the arm and practically dragged her out of the room. "Blue Hawk, hurry!"

Shaun Randall was a big man. Blue Hawk had carried him up those stairs to this room. He could take him down again. Sucking in a deep breath, he slung Randall over his shoulder. Grabbing a blanket off the bed, he draped it over Randall's head and bare back and then, staggering a little under the man's dead weight, he left the room and headed for the stairs.

A wall of flames danced across the bottom of the staircase, licking at the banister, creeping up the steps.

Blue Hawk took a deep breath, then, holding tight to Randall, he ran down the stairs, through the flames, across the parlor floor. Smoke stung his eyes, blurring his vision. Flames licked at his skin; heat penetrated the soles of his moccasins. A piece of the blanket covering Randall's back caught fire. Ignoring the pain, Blue Hawk smothered it with his hand.

At last he reached the front door. Air exploded from his lungs as he burst through the doorway onto the porch. Without pausing, he ran down the stairs and across the yard until he was well away from the house, and then he lowered Randall to the ground, stood there, drawing in great gulps of fresh air.

The barn was engulfed in flames.

The yard was filled with men. They formed a long line, passing full buckets to the three men who were throwing water on the flames in a vain attempt to put out the fire.

And even as he watched, the ranch foreman called the battle off. "It's no use, men," Noah hollered. "We're just wasting water."

Emma and Kaylee hurried toward Blue Hawk.

"Are you all right?" Kaylee asked anxiously. She ran her hands over his face, his arms, gasped when he flinched. "Oh, your poor arms," she wailed.

Emma hovered over Shaun, making sure the wound in his side had not reopened, trying to rouse him. Tears ran down her cheeks and dripped on his face.

"I am all right, Kay-lee," Blue Hawk said.

"You could have died in there! And you're not all right. Your arms and legs are burned, and . . . what's wrong with your hand?" She picked up his left hand. His palm was badly blistered. She looked up at him, her eyes filled with tears. "Does it hurt dreadfully?"

"A little," he admitted.

"Shaun! Oh, Shaun." The sound of Emma's sobs drew Blue Hawk's attention and he glanced over Kaylee's shoulder. Shaun was struggling to sit up. He looked dazed and disoriented, his face pale.

"What the hell's goin' on?" he exclaimed.

"The house," Emma said. "Oh, Shaun, our lovely house is gone."

"Don't fret, Em," Shaun said. "Won't . . . take long . . . to rebuild." He took a deep breath. "How'd it—start?"

"I don't know," Kaylee replied. "All I know is we would have all burned to death if it wasn't for Blue Hawk."

"Hey!" Hobie ran into the yard. "I just found Garth Jackson's body! He's dead, killed by Injuns!"

Several of the men turned to look at Blue Hawk. "There's only one Injun 'round here," Quint said.

One of the other men stepped forward and held up a bow and an empty quiver. "I found this near the barn."

The cowhands had begun to gather around Blue Hawk, their expressions increasingly hostile. Garth Jackson had been a neighbor, a frequent visitor at the Double R. A white man. But their boss's next comment stopped them cold.

Shaun rose to his feet, with Emma's help. "Hold on, men," he said. "I've known Garth Jackson for twenty years. I never would have guessed he was capable of anything like this. But I'm telling you, he was rustling our cattle. Putting it off on Injuns to avoid suspicion. When Grady spotted the setup, Jackson had him killed and scalped. And when I went up there, he had me shot, too. This here Injun saved my life."

Noah stepped forward. "The barn and the house was set on fire with flaming arrows. That's Injun work." He jerked a thumb in Blue Hawk's direction. "And this is the only Injun here 'bouts."

Shaun looked at Blue Hawk. "Did you kill Jackson?"

Blue Hawk nodded. "He was a thief and a liar."

"And you killed him for that!" Kaylee exclaimed.

"He is the man who shot me and left me for dead."

"Well, by damn, we've got that in common, then," Shaun muttered, " 'cept he had somebody else shoot me. And he killed Grady, and who knows how many others?"

Kaylee moved closer to Blue Hawk, as if she could somehow protect him from the anger humming all around them.

"You heard him—he admitted he killed Jackson!" Quint declared. "I say we string him up here and now, damn murderin' savage!"

"That murdering savage came into a burning house and hauled me out," Shaun said. "Hell, those flaming arrows were probably just more of Garth Jackson's trying to put everything off on Injuns."

"So you say," Quint said stubbornly.

"So I say? You're damn right," Shaun said, his voice rising. "And I'm the damn boss around here. Blue Hawk saved my sorry hide twice, and no one's stringing him up. Next man even thinks about it can draw his wages. Is that clear?"

An uneasy silence fell over the crowd. Shaun waited until he was certain no one would challenge him, then he began issuing orders.

"Hobie, you and Tyler go see if you can track down our horses. Jack, take a couple of men and make sure all the fires are out. Quint, go get Jackson's body and put it in the spring house. Noah, ride into town and round up some men who are handy with a hammer and nails, and tell Henderson to stop whatever he's working on and be here first thing in the morning. We need to get this house rebuilt before winter sets in. Hal, set up some extra cots in the bunkhouse. We'll be needin' a place to sleep tonight. Roscoe," he added wearily, "I could use a cup of coffee."

The men went to do as they were told, all but Noah. "What about him?" Noah asked, jerking his chin in Blue Hawk's direction.

"I'll look after him," Shaun said. "He's not going anywhere."

The next few hours were busy ones. Kaylee treated Blue Hawk's burns, weeping softly as she bandaged his forearms and his right hand. Roscoe put on a pot of coffee and fixed a big breakfast. Shaun caught a little shut-eye, exhausted from his efforts and his already weakened condition. Emma and Kaylee began the dreary task of sorting through the wreckage of the house looking for anything they could salvage. Several hands were doing the same in the barn, dragging saddles out that were burned almost beyond recognition. Shortly before noon, Hobie and Tyler rode in, herding the horses they had rounded up.

And then the sheriff arrived.

Chapter 34

Sheriff Matthew Drum was a tall, angular, no-nonsense man with a shock of wheat-blond hair and ice-blue eyes. The star pinned to his black leather vest glinted in the early-afternoon sunlight as he swung out of the saddle, settled his gunbelt around his hips, and strode across the ranch yard, taking in the still smoldering remains of the barn and ranch house. Shaun had insisted on being carried to the bunkhouse porch to oversee cleanup operations. A group of his men were gathered around him.

Drum tipped his hat to Emma and Kaylee. "Ladies." He fixed Shaun with a steely gaze. "Shaun, what the hell's going on here?"

"Nothing you're gonna believe," Shaun replied. "How the hell are ya, Matt?"

"Hell of a lot better than you, by the look of it." Drum's gaze rested on Blue Hawk for a long moment, then dismissed him. It wasn't entirely unheard of to find Indians working on a ranch now and then. Most of them were good with horses. He turned his attention back to Shaun.

"It's a long story," Shaun said.

"I've got all day," Drum replied.

Shaun took a deep breath. "You know I've been losing cattle, like all the other ranchers around here."

Drum glanced at Blue Hawk and nodded. "Injun thievin', yeah. Hard to stop."

"Yeah, well, turns out it's not Injuns," Shaun said. "You're not gonna believe this. Hell, I don't hardly believe it myself, but, dammit, I saw it with my own two eyes. Matt, Garth Jackson was behind all that rustling."

"Garth!" Drum removed his hat and ran a hand through his hair. "Why the devil would he be rustling? He's got more land and cattle than anyone else hereabouts."

Shaun shrugged. "I guess he had his reasons. All I know is, he murdered Tom Grady when Grady stumbled onto his operation, and he damn near killed me. If it wasn't for Blue Hawk here, I'd be dead." Shaun waved a hand at the rubble of the barn and his house. "He set those fires last night. Trying again to kill me, I reckon, before I could talk to you."

Drum's eyes narrowed as he looked at what was left of the house. "You're saying Jackson did this?"

Shaun nodded.

Drum shook his head. "You're right, Shaun, I can't believe it. Dammit, I don't believe it. I've known Garth Jackson for near fifteen years." He jammed his hat back on his head. "I'm going over there now and get this whole mess straightened out."

Shaun and Blue Hawk exchanged glances.

"What is it?" Drum asked. "What aren't you telling me?"

"Jackson's dead," Shaun said. "His body's in the spring house."

Drum rested his hand on the butt of his pistol. "You kill him?"

"No, but I wish to hell I'd had the chance. Dirty coward! Afraid to face me head-on. Burned the house down instead. Would have killed my womenfolk, too, if it hadn't been for Blue Hawk here."

Drum looked at Blue Hawk again. "Exactly who is this Injun, and what's he doing here?"

"You're not gonna believe this, either," Shaun replied with a wry grin, "but he's my son-in-law. And if it wasn't for him, we'd all be dead."

Drum stared at Kaylee, a look of disbelief in his eyes. "You're married to that buck?"

Kaylee lifted her chin defiantly. "Yes."

At this bit of news there was a stirring among the ranch hands who had drifted over to hear what the sheriff had to say. Until now her marriage had been a secret. Some of them had been having trouble with the Indian being around the ranch at all.

Drum grunted as he focused his attention on Shaun once again. "So who killed Jackson?"

Emma gripped Shaun's arm when he started to speak. Kaylee glanced nervously from Shaun to Emma to Blue Hawk.

"Well," Shaun said, "it's like this—"

"I killed him," Blue Hawk interrupted.

The sheriff's gun appeared in his hand like magic.

"What the hell are you doing?" Shaun exclaimed. "Put that damn gun away and go after my cattle. Jackson's men are on their way to Canada with cattle they've stolen from me and the other ranchers hereabouts. They don't have much of a head start, and I reckon they'll be moving slow so's they don't walk too much weight off 'em. Shouldn't be too hard to catch up with 'em."

"I'm not worried about your cattle," Drum retorted.

"You sure you don't wanna rethink that?" Shaun said hotly. "Election time ain't all that far off."

"Lookahere, one of this town's leading citizens has just been killed, and—"

"Leading *thieves*, you mean," Shaun snorted. "And a murderer too. I told you he killed Grady. Some of my men brought the boy's body back this morning."

Drum shook his head like a baffled range steer. "There's too many unanswered questions right here."

He pulled a pair of handcuffs out of his back pocket. "Turn around, Injun," he said, "and put your hands behind your back."

Kaylee's eyes widened in disbelief.

Blue Hawk took a step backward, his whole body tensed, poised for flight. He looked at Kaylee, who was staring at him, and at Emma, who was clinging to Shaun's arm.

"Dammit, Matt, be reasonable," Shaun said. "You go after Jackson's men and my cattle and you'll find the answers you're looking for. I'll vouch for Blue Hawk. He'll be here if you need him."

Drum shook his head. "I can't do that, and you know it. Any vouching you do will be in a court of law, under oath. I got Jackson's body right here, and this Injun just admitted to killing him. I have to lock him up."

"No!" Kaylee cried. "You can't!"

"I'm sorry, Miss Kay, but the law's the law."

"Last I knew, cattle rustling, murder, and burning a man's house down over his head were all against the law, too," Shaun said bitterly.

"I ain't got no deputy right now, Shaun. I'll have to get back to town and deputize a couple men to go look for that herd. Iffen any of your boys want to volunteer, that's fine by me. In the meantime, I'm taking Jackson's killer in."

Blue Hawk took another step backward.

"Hold it right there!" Drum said brusquely.

"You can't take him in," Shaun said. "Dammit, you know he'll never get a fair trial in this town."

"Don't tell me how to do my job," Drum retorted. "He'll get a fair trial, just like everybody else." He tossed the cuffs to the cowhand nearest him. "Hal, put those on him."

Shaun's expression was grim. "You're making a big mistake, Matt."

Drum shrugged. "I've made 'em before."

Shaun's gaze settled on Blue Hawk. "Don't worry," he said. "I'll get you out of this."

Blue Hawk shook his head and took another step backward. "I will not wear those. I will not be locked up."

"Listen," Shaun said, "I know this looks bad, and you have no reason to trust anything I say, but—"

When Hal reached for him, Blue Hawk made a break for it. A wild cry echoed over his shoulder as he spun around and raced for the sheriff's horse.

Drum's Colt came up swiftly, tracking his flight.

Kaylee cried, "No!" and threw herself in front of the lawman.

Blue Hawk grabbed the reins and vaulted into the saddle. The horse reared and came down running.

Emma screamed.

Drum swore. Pushing Kaylee out of the way, he fired two quick shots, cussed again as both missed their target. Before he could fire a third time, Blue Hawk was into the trees and gone from sight. Drum methodically punched the empties out of his cylinder, replaced them from his cartridge belt and reholstered his gun.

"Well, I guess that proves he's guilty as hell," the sheriff muttered. He looked over at Shaun. "I'll need the loan of a horse to get back to town so I can round up a posse."

"He didn't run because he's guilty," Kaylee said angrily. "He ran because you were going to lock him up."

Drum snorted. "Innocent men don't run."

Kaylee's eyes blazed with anger. "Whatever Blue Hawk did, he did to protect his family. My family!"

Drum grunted, his glance darting back and forth between Kaylee and Shaun. "I still need that horse."

"Help yourself," Shaun muttered.

"Obliged."

Kaylee watched Drum walk toward the corral. "What are we going to do now?" she asked when he was out of earshot.

"In a minute, dear," Emma said. She turned to face the men. "You aren't getting paid to stand around. There's plenty of work to be done. Get to it! Hal, would you please bring Mr. Randall a glass of water?"

Shaun grinned at Emma. "Didn't realize I'd married such a bossy woman. Make it coffee instead, Hal."

The men dispersed to do Emma's bidding. Moments later, Drum rode out on the horse he'd caught up.

"We have to go after Blue Hawk," Kaylee said anxiously. She glanced in the direction Drum had gone. "We have to find him before anyone else does."

Emma nodded. "Yes, of course. Do you know where he might go?"

"The old line shack," Kaylee said. "I think he'll go there and wait for me."

"He shouldn't have run," Shaun remarked. "Matt's right. It makes him look guilty as hell."

"So what are we going to do about it?" Emma asked.

"I'll think of something," Shaun said. "Don't worry."

"I know you will," Emma replied, patting his arm. "I'm not worried."

She smiled at Hal's approach. Taking no chances, he had brought Shaun both coffee and a glass of water.

"Thank you," Emma said. She took the glass and the cup from his hands. "Would you tell Roscoe he'd better go into town and stock up on supplies? He'll be cooking for all of us for the next little while. Oh, and ask him to—oh, never mind, I'll go into town with him." She put the glass on the rail and handed the cup to Shaun.

"Yes, ma'am. How soon will you be wanting to go?"

"Within the hour."

Hal nodded. "Yes, ma'am."

"Is there anything you want from town, Kay, besides a change of clothes and underwear?"

Kaylee glanced at the ruins of the house. Everything she had owned was gone. "Whatever you think I need, Mama. In the meantime, I can borrow some jeans and a shirt from one of the men."

"All right, dear. And try not to worry. We'll get this sorted out somehow."

Blue Hawk rode for the line shack. He took the long way around, crossing the river several times, laying several false trails.

It was near dusk when he reached his destination. Dismounting, he unsaddled the sheriff's horse. It was a nice animal, with large nostrils to drink the wind. Grabbing a handful of grass, he rubbed the horse down, then tethered it behind the shack.

He wondered if the sheriff was hunting him even now. Wondered how soon Kaylee would come to him.

He knew it had been foolish to run, but he could not, would not, allow the *wasichu* to lock him up. He had heard too many tales of Indians who had been taken prisoner by the whites, locked up in their iron houses, and hanged, or sent to reservations far from home.

He had thought to stay with Kaylee, at her lodge, but that would not be possible now.

He would hide out from the *wasichu* until the baby was born, and then . . . he gazed into the distance, his heart aching for the lush hills and valleys of home. Would he ever see the Paha Sapa again? If the pull of home became too great, would Kaylee go with him? He did not doubt her love, yet she would soon have a little one to think of, and he knew in his heart that his child would have a better life with Kaylee's people than with the Lakota. His people had no future, nothing to look forward to except life on the reservation, which was no life at all for a warrior.

Feeling suddenly restless, he walked away from the shack, and then he began to run. He ran mile after mile, losing himself in the joy of the moment. He ran until his lungs were on fire, until his legs ached and each breath was an effort.

Slowing, he began to walk back toward the shack. Worrying over the future had never solved anything. He would take each day as it came.

"Blue Hawk?" Kaylee opened the door to the shack and peered inside. Where was he? The sheriff's horse was tethered out back, but there was no sign of Blue Hawk.

Where could he have gone?

She dropped the basket and the blankets she was carrying on the floor. The basket didn't hold much, just a canteen of water, a box of matches, half a loaf of bread, a hunk of cheese, and some dried apples.

She was pacing back and forth in front of the shack, growing more worried every minute, when she felt his presence. She peered into the distance. It was too dark to see anything, yet she knew he was nearby. Moments later, she saw him running toward her.

With a glad cry, she raced to meet him. "Where were you?"

"Waiting for you." His body was damp with sweat.

He reached for her, but she glanced at his bandaged arms and shook her head. "How do you feel? Do your arms hurt very much?"

"I am all right, *mitawicu*."

"You'd say that if you were bleeding to death," she muttered.

"My arms ache, Kay-lee, but only when I am not holding you."

With a sigh, she leaned against him, her head resting

on his chest, as his arms enfolded her. She closed her eyes, and for a moment nothing else mattered. The house would be rebuilt. Shaun would buy more cattle. Drum would realize Blue Hawk was innocent.

"Everything will be all right," she murmured. If she said it, if she believed it, maybe it would be true. "You'll see."

He made a low sound of disbelief. He had no hope for the future. He could not live here; he could not ask Kaylee to hide out in the hills with him. But for now she was in his arms, where she belonged.

"You shouldn't have run away," she said, her voice muffled against his chest.

"I will not let them lock me up, Kay-lee."

"I understand how you feel, truly I do, but it makes it look as if what you did was wrong, don't you see?"

He tilted her chin up so he could look into her eyes. "I do not believe the *wasichu* will believe anything I say. Do you?"

"No, I guess not. But what are we going to do now?"

"You will stay with your mother until the child is born, and then we will decide."

"Where are you going to stay?"

"I will find a place."

"No. I want you with me."

"I will see you every day."

"If you can't live at the ranch, then I'll move out here, with you."

"No, *mitawicu*, we must think of the little one. It will be winter soon."

"It's going to be winter for you, too," she retorted. "Oh, I brought you something to eat, and some water."

His hand slid up the back of her neck and tunneled into her hair. "Do not worry about me—"

"I know, I know, you're Lakota. But you're not

invincible. You don't have a rifle, or even your bow. And I'm not going to stay in the bunkhouse with Mama and Shaun while you're out here, alone and unarmed. That's all there is to it!"

He smiled down at her tenderly. "Shall I find us another cave?"

"Whatever you find is all right with me, so long as we are together."

They spent the night in the shack. She knew it was not a place Blue Hawk cared for, but it provided shelter from the cold. He built a fire in the fireplace, then dragged the mattresses off the cots and spread them on the floor in front of the hearth. Wrapped in the blankets Kaylee had brought, they sat in front of the fire and watched the flames.

Kaylee talked softly, spinning dreams of a future where their troubles would be behind them, hoping she could convince him that it would come true.

Chapter 35

The dreams of the previous night died in the face of reality the following morning. Blue Hawk woke to find himself staring down the barrel of a rifle held in Matthew Drum's capable hands.

"Don't even twitch," Drum warned.

Kaylee stirred at the sound of the sheriff's voice. Her eyelids fluttered open. She gasped and drew the blanket up to her chin when she saw Drum standing over them.

"Miss Kay, move away from him."

"I will not."

"Kay-lee, do as he says."

"No." She glared up at the sheriff. "Why aren't you out catching the rustlers?"

"I've got a job to do," Drum replied curtly. "And I'd be obliged if you'd do as you're told and let me get on with it."

"Blue Hawk didn't do anything wrong! You heard what Shaun said. We'd all have burned to death if it wasn't for Blue Hawk."

Drum nodded. "Be that as it may, I don't have any proof that Jackson tried to kill your father, or that he started that fire. The only evidence I've got is a bow and a quiver and this here Injun who admits he killed Jackson."

"The bow and quiver are not mine," Blue Hawk said flatly. "They are Crow, not Lakota."

Drum shook his head. "This isn't getting us any-where. I'm taking you in, dead or alive. It's up to you."

"I will not be locked up in the white man's iron house."

"Blue Hawk!" Kaylee clutched his shoulder, afraid he would try to run again, afraid Drum would kill him. Afraid that was what Blue Hawk wanted. She took his hand and put it on her stomach beneath the blan-kets. "Think of our child. Please don't leave us. I'll come to the jail and stay with you. Please, *higna*."

The sheriff made a sound of disgust, but she didn't care. She saw the change in Blue Hawk's face, knew he would do as she asked, for the sake of their child.

He sat up slowly, his arms raised over his head. "I will go with you."

Without lowering the rifle, Drum stooped and tossed Blue Hawk's clout at him. "I've got your knife, Injun. So roll on out of there and get dressed. No reason to be shy. I don't guess any of us will see anything to make us faint."

The jail was located at the end of the town, sand-wiched between the offices of the newspaper and the telegraph. Blue Hawk was aware of the curious stares of the people on the street as they rode by.

It was with a sense of doom that he entered the building. He had no faith in the lawman's promise of protection or a fair trial. He was an Indian who had killed a white man, and the penalty for that was al-ways death.

The cells were located in a separate room—four of them, two on each side of a narrow corridor. All were empty. The sheriff opened the door to the last cell on the right.

Blue Hawk took a deep breath, offered a silent prayer for strength and courage to Wakan Tanka, and stepped inside. The cell was small and square, hemmed in on three sides by thick iron bars. The back wall was made of stone. A small barred window was set high in the back wall. There was a narrow cot topped by a faded brown blanket.

He flinched when the cell door closed behind him.

The sheriff locked the door, then told him to turn around so he could remove the handcuffs that had chafed his burned wrists. He was flexing them gingerly when he heard light footsteps and then Kaylee's voice.

"Blue Hawk?"

He turned around. The sheriff had left her at the shack to get dressed. She had told him she was going to the ranch to tell Shaun and Emma what had happened. Dusty had made good time.

She came forward quickly and folded her hands around the bars.

"It will be all right," she said earnestly. "You'll see."

He nodded.

She held out her hand. "You've got to believe me."

He took her hand in his. It was soft and small. His gaze moved over her face and came to rest on the slight swell of her belly. Would he live long enough to see her cradling their child at her breast?

Kaylee glanced over her shoulder at the sheriff. "Could we have a few minutes alone?"

Drum nodded.

"Thank you." Her stomach growled loudly.

Blue Hawk squeezed Kaylee's hand. "You cannot stay here."

"No, you can't," Drum agreed. "I gotta lock up so I can go get some breakfast. My stomach thinks my throat's been cut."

Her hand tightened on Blue Hawk's. "You'll see he gets something to eat, too?"

"I don't make it a habit to starve my prisoners," Drum said gruffly. "Come along now."

"I won't be gone long," she promised. Standing on tiptoe, she leaned forward.

Knowing what she wanted, Blue Hawk bent down and kissed her. She slid her arms through the bars and held him as tight as she could.

"I'll be back soon," she promised.

He watched her walk away, wondering, as he did so, if he would ever hold her in his arms again.

Kaylee managed to hold back her tears until she got out of the sheriff's office, and then the dam burst. Until Drum had found them, she had hoped they would have a life together, had imagined them living near her mother and Shaun. But now—she dabbed at her eyes, conscious of the curious stares of passersby. Shaun was right. Blue Hawk would never get a fair trial in this town. Never.

There was just too much bad blood between her people and the Indians. Distrust had hardened into hatred, along with the belief that Indians were nothing but trouble and should be confined on reservations or exterminated.

Sniffing back her tears, Kaylee entered the dry goods store, relieved to see that there were only a few women inside. Everything seemed so normal in the shop, it almost brought tears to her eyes again. In the past, she had enjoyed perusing the aisles, looking at the new gadgets that Mr. Hardesty imported from Boston and New York City, browsing through the latest catalogs, contemplating material for a new dress. But not today. She picked out a simple cotton day dress, a change of underwear, a pair of stockings, a set of combs for her hair. She found a red shirt she thought Blue Hawk would like and a pair of trousers. She didn't bother with underwear or shoes, both of which she knew he would refuse to wear.

"Miss Kaylee!" Mr. Hardesty exclaimed when she

approached the counter. "I heard you were back home. I'm glad to see you got away from those red devils. We were mighty worried about you, the wife and I."

Kaylee smiled faintly. "I'm sorry you were worried, but as you can see, I'm fine."

"Yes, ma'am, I see that you are, and I'm damn glad—er, darn glad of it. They didn't hurt you none then, them redskins?"

"No." She pushed the clothes on the counter toward him, hoping he would take the hint. He did.

"Do you want me to put these on Shaun's account?"

"Yes, please."

Mr. Hardesty pulled out his account book and began writing down the prices of the items she had bought. He frowned when he came to the shirt and trousers. "Are these yours?" he asked.

"We had a fire at the ranch," she said.

"Oh, my word, that's right! Your mother was here yesterday with old Roscoe, rounding up supplies. Trouble does seem to come in bunches. I hope it's over for you and yours now."

She smiled weakly.

"You sure these trousers are the right size?"

"Yes," Kaylee said, "I'm sure."

"Big man," he said.

"Yes." She knew what he was thinking. The pants weren't Shaun's size and he was wondering what man she was buying them for. She saw no need to enlighten him.

Hardesty grunted softly as he totaled her purchases and wrote the amount down on a slip of paper. He wrapped them in brown paper, tied them with string, gave her the receipt, and bid her a good day.

She could only imagine what he would have said if she told him the shirt and trousers were for Blue Hawk, didn't even want to think what the townspeople would say when they found out she was married to an Indian, carrying his child.

On the way back to the jail, Kaylee stopped at the confectioner's.

"Kaylee! Land o'goshen, child, I thought we'd lost you for good." Martha Higgins smiled broadly as she emerged from behind the counter and hugged Kaylee to her bosom. "Child, it's so good to see you again! We heard about your ordeal. It must have been dreadful, just dreadful."

Kaylee accepted the older woman's embrace. Martha Higgins was a kindly woman with white hair and twinkling blue eyes. She'd never had children of her own, and consequently she mothered the whole town.

Martha gave her a final hug, pinched her cheek, and let her go. "I was so glad to hear you were safely home. And now this fire business! I saw your dear mother yesterday, and she seemed much stronger. I'm not surprised, now you're back."

Martha took her place behind the counter once more. "Now, what can I do for you this fine day?"

"I'd like some licorice, please. And some peppermints. And some taffy."

Martha put Kaylee's selections in small individual sacks, then put them all in a larger bag.

"You be sure and tell your ma hello for me," Martha said. "I'll just add this to Shaun's account. He sure does have a sweet tooth, that man, yes, indeed." She pulled out her account book and added Kaylee's purchases, and then she picked up another bag and put in half a dozen pieces of divinity. "Give this to your ma for me, and tell her I'll be out to see her just as soon as I can."

"Thank you, Mrs. Higgins. That's very kind of you."

"Pshaw, it's nothing," Martha said. "I know how much your ma loves my divinity. Just don't tell Mr. Higgins."

Smiling faintly, Kaylee left the candy store. Lyle Higgins was the biggest penny-pincher in town and everyone knew it.

She sobered again as she neared the sheriff's office. It grieved her to think of Blue Hawk behind bars. He wasn't accustomed to small places or to being confined. He was like the wild stallion Shaun had caught when she was twelve. Every hand on the place had tried to break the animal to ride, but to no avail, and in the end, Shaun had turned him loose.

She prayed that Blue Hawk would be as lucky.

He paced the cell floor, back and forth, back and forth, restless as a trapped mountain lion. Three long strides carried him from one end of his prison to the other. He paused now and then to look out the window. He looked past the town, his gaze focused on the sky. Late last night he had asked Kaylee what a trial was. He had listened carefully to her explanation, heard the fear in her voice when she told him that twelve white men would decide if he was innocent or guilty of killing Garth Jackson. He had asked her why a trial was necessary. He had killed Jackson, had admitted as much. She had replied that according to the law, he was innocent until proven guilty.

"Even if I had not killed him, do you think any white man would find me innocent?" he had asked.

There had been no need for her to reply. They had both known the answer.

Gazing up at the sky, he lifted his arms and prayed to Wakan Tanka, praying for health and safety for Kaylee and his unborn babe, for strength to endure, for the courage to die well in front of his enemies.

He turned at the sound of the cellblock door opening, felt his spirits lift when he saw Kaylee walking toward him. She had changed her clothes and brushed her hair, and she looked as lovely as a summer morning.

"Told you I'd be back," she said with a smile. "Here, I brought you a change of clothes. Did Drum get you something to eat?"

"Yes." He looked at the parcel in her hand and shook his head. "I am Lakota," he said. "I will not wear the white man's clothes now."

"Well, they didn't have any clouts at the store, so you're stuck with what they did have."

He shrugged with resignation. "Wearing *wasichu* clothing will not hide what I am." He ran his knuckles lightly over her cheek. "You should go home and rest."

"Are you trying to get rid of me?"

His hand curled around her nape to draw her closer. "No, *mitawicu*. I am only thinking of the small one you carry."

"Everything will be all right." How many times had she repeated those words to him? To herself? "Here." She reached into her skirt pocket and handed him a small bag. "I brought you something else."

He took it from her and peered inside.

"It's candy," she said. "You eat it."

He took one, looked at it a moment, then popped it into his mouth. A faint smile curved his lips as the peppermint dissolved on his tongue. *"Lila waste."*

"I thought you'd like it."

"Pilamaya, Kay-lee."

Drum entered the cellblock a few minutes later, a short double-barreled shotgun cradled in the crook of his arm. "You might want to head on home, Miss Kay," he said. "There's trouble brewing outside."

"What kind of trouble?" she asked.

"Seems word of Jackson's death has gotten around. There's a bunch of angry men gathering. I've deputized a few more men, but it's liable to get ugly. There's talk of a lynching."

"I'm not leaving."

Hopelessness settled over Blue Hawk, weighing him down. "Kay-lee, do as he says. You must not put your life in danger."

She looked at him a moment, then nodded. "I think you're right." She kissed him quickly, then turned and ran out of the room.

A great heaviness settled over him as the door closed behind her.

As the day wore on, the crowd outside grew larger, louder, uglier. Blue Hawk paced the floor, trying to shut out the sound of their voices, angry drunken voices demanding justice, hollering for vengeance. For a hanging.

He tried to pray, but he couldn't concentrate, couldn't think of anything but a rope around his neck, strangling him while a crowd of angry white men looked on.

At least Kaylee would not be there to see it.

Chapter 36

The hours passed with agonizing slowness, and yet it seemed as if night came all too quickly. The mob, which had been increasing in size all afternoon, grew louder and bolder under the cover of darkness.

Blue Hawk whirled around at the sound of the door opening, breathed a sigh of relief when he saw that it was just one of the deputies. The lawman placed a chair near the first cell, then closed and locked the door between the jail and the cellblock. He glanced at Blue Hawk, then sat down, his rifle across his knees.

A clock chimed the hour.

A dog howled.

There was a gunshot outside, close by, the deep boom of a shotgun, followed by the sheriff's voice. "You men go on home before somebody gets hurt!"

"The only one who's gonna get hurt is that murderin' redskin!" someone shouted.

"Bring him out, Drum," another man called, "and let's get it over with!"

"They'll be no lynching," Drum said. "Now go on home and sleep it off, all of you!"

There was another gunshot, followed by several shouts, and the sound of a scuffle. Then with a loud crash the mob broke down the door to the sheriff's office.

The deputy stood up and jacked a round into the breech of his rifle.

Blue Hawk gripped the bars nervously, his heart pounding.

Fists hammered on the cellblock door. "Open up, Crenshaw! We know you're in there!"

"Where's Drum?"

"Out of the way for now. And you'd best open that door unless you want some of what he got!"

The pounding on the door resumed. "Open up, dammit! That Injun killed Jackson, and he's gonna pay for it!"

Crenshaw glanced over his shoulder, his eyes wide and scared.

"Dammit, Crenshaw, you're gonna regret it if you don't open this door right quick!"

"Hang on," Crenshaw said, fumbling for the key. "I'm not getting myself kilt to protect no Injun."

"Now you're being smart," said the first man through the door. "Stand aside."

The deputy pulled a big brass key out of his pocket and moved purposefully toward Blue Hawk's cell. A dozen heavily armed men followed him.

Blue Hawk took a step backward, murmured, "Wakan Tanka, give me courage," as the door to his cell swung open and four men stepped inside.

One of them carried a piece of rope in his hands. "Turn around, Injun."

Knowing it was futile to resist, Blue Hawk backed away, his gaze darting from man to man, seeking a weakness, a way to escape, but there was none.

Two of the men lunged at him. He struck out at them, twisting, ducking, but to no avail. A third man came up behind him and brought the butt of a rifle down on the back of his head, driving him to his knees. Moments later, his hands were bound and he was herded out of the jail and down the street to where a noose swung gently in the breeze.

Two men lifted him onto the back of a horse, a

third dropped the noose around his neck. Feeling groggy, his head throbbing, Blue Hawk stared down at the men around him. They had fallen silent when the noose was dropped in place.

"Go on, Eb," someone hollered. "Let's get it done."

The arrival of half a dozen mounted men drew everyone's attention. The rider in the lead reined his horse to a halt. "What the hell's going on here?"

Blue Hawk recognized the harsh voice of Shaun Randall. Even in his dazed state he was impressed that the older man had found the strength to ride so far so soon after being wounded.

"We're having a little necktie party, Shaun," one of the men replied cheerfully. "Come join us."

"Turn that man loose," Randall commanded. "He's innocent."

"Like hell! He killed Jackson, and he's gonna pay for it."

"Is that you, Price? I've got those cattle you lost last week. Yours, too, Milford."

"That ain't got nothing to do with why we're here tonight," somebody shouted. "We got this redskin dead to rights."

A burly man broke through the crowd and planted himself in front of Shaun's horse. "What are you talking about?" he demanded. "Those cows were rustled by Injuns. Everybody knows that."

"Those cattle were stolen by Garth Jackson," Shaun said loudly. "Listen to me, all of you! All that beef we been losing was the work of Jackson and his night riders. Where the hell is Drum?"

"The sheriff's sleeping a little," somebody said, and there was a general laugh.

"Well, get him up!" Shaun demanded. "He deputized some of my men, and they caught up with the last stolen herd. They're on the way back with the cattle, some prisoners—and some bodies, too. And

there ain't an Injun among them! Lenny, get up here
and tell 'em."

A weary-looking rider edged his horse forward.
"We caught 'em all right, and they put up a hell of a
fight, too. Jackson's men, every one of 'em."

For the moment, everyone seemed to have forgotten Blue Hawk. He worked his burned wrists back
and forth slowly, painfully, trying to extricate them.
While the *wasichu* talked perhaps he could—

"Take the rope off that man's neck. Now," Shaun
Randall said.

Blue Hawk felt the crowd's attention swing back
to him.

"Even if all you say is true, when did you turn redskin lover?" somebody yelled from the back of the
crowd.

"You damn fool!" Shaun thundered. "That redskin
is the one who tumbled to Jackson's scheme and
found out where he was holding our cattle, and lived
to tell about it. Tom Grady wasn't so lucky. Jackson
had him killed and scalped to look like Injuns did it."

A murmur of disbelief rolled through the crowd.
Grady had been well known and well liked.

"None of this ain't proved," a tall man said.

"Maybe not," Shaun said. "But this much is proved:
the first man that makes a move to spook that horse
takes a bullet from me. That man is my son-in-law,
and I look after what's mine!"

This time there was a shocked silence. Blue Hawk
waited, his impassivity concealing his roiling emotions.
Shaun Randall was a warrior! It was good to have
saved the life of such a brave man. Even if the price
was his own life. He knew that his life was still poised
in some delicate balance he did not understand, but
he also knew Kaylee's stepfather was now on his side.

After a lengthy silence, a kind of sigh of released
tension drifted through the crowd. The tall man, his

expression somewhat sheepish, removed the noose from Blue Hawk's neck and untied his hands.

Weak with relief, Blue Hawk slid off the back of the horse.

And then Kaylee was beside him, laughing and crying as she ran her hands over him, assuring herself that he was all right.

"You came back," he said, still stunned by the turn of events.

"Of course I came back! The only reason I left was to get Shaun. You saved his life—twice—and I knew he wouldn't let this happen if we could only get here!"

Several of the men who had been ready to hang him only moments earlier gathered around Blue Hawk.

"Hope there's no hard feelings," Milford said. He stuck out his hand. "Reckon I owe you a debt of gratitude."

Somewhat dazed, Blue Hawk shook the man's hand.

"Guess we all jumped to the wrong conclusion," another man muttered.

"Damn glad Randall showed up when he did," said another.

"Hell, we'd better go wake up Drum and turn Crenshaw loose," Milford remarked.

"You sure that's a good idea?" one of the men asked. "Drum's going to have a powerful bad headache when he comes to, and he's like to arrest all of us for what we've done."

"Yeah, and you'd all deserve it," Randall said, riding up behind them. "Since it was my son-in-law you were gonna hang, maybe Drum'll listen if I put in a word. I got a house that needs rebuilding before winter sets in. Make better use of your time than sitting in jail waiting for a circuit judge to come through. Milford, Price, my men are driving the cattle to my ranch. They should be there sometime after noon tomorrow."

"Obliged to you, Randall," Price said. "And to you, too," he added, nodding at Blue Hawk.

"We'll be out at your place tomorrow to start building that house," Milford said. "All of us."

With a nod, Shaun looked at Kaylee, who was clinging to Blue Hawk's arm as if she would never let him go. "You two ready to head on home?"

Kaylee looked up at Blue Hawk and smiled. "Yes," she said. "Home."

Epilogue

Kaylee bent over her son's cradle, her heart swelling with love as she gazed down at her second child, now a month old. Nothing in her life had prepared her for motherhood. She had never known she could love so fiercely, so protectively, but from the moment her mother had placed her daughter in her arms, Kay had understood why mothers were willing to sacrifice their lives for their children, had understood, at last, the depths of her own mother's love and concern. And now she had two fine, healthy children with tawny skin and raven-black hair.

Much had happened in the last two years. The Double R had been rebuilt even bigger and better than before. Apparently thinking he would live forever, Garth Jackson had left no will and no heirs. The G Slash J ranch and livestock had been put up for auction shortly after his death. To her surprise, Shaun had bought the place. There had been no end of surprises in those first few weeks after Jackson's death.

The second came when Shaun gave Kaylee and Blue Hawk the deed to Jackson's ranch. As a belated wedding gift, he had said gruffly.

The third had come soon after, when Emma announced that she was going to have a baby. Kaylee had worried the whole nine months. Shaun had been a nervous wreck. But Emma had been delivered of a healthy seven-pound baby girl.

It had not been easy for Blue Hawk, learning to live among the whites he had once considered his enemies. There were times when she saw the sadness in his eyes, his longing for home, but never more so than last year when they heard that Crazy Horse had been killed in Nebraska, at Fort Robinson. Blue Hawk had left the ranch the day they heard the news. He had returned two days later, his arms and chest bearing the wounds of his grief.

Gradually, he had grown more at ease among her people, and the townsfolk had grown more at ease around him. Roy Milford and Bill Price had had a hand in that. Both men had been grateful to get their cattle back and quite vocal in letting people know that Blue Hawk had been responsible.

She glanced up, smiling as Blue Hawk entered the nursery carrying their daughter, Emmalee, on his shoulders. As always, just the mere sight of him made her heart skip a beat.

"The little one sleeps?" he asked.

"Yes, finally." Kaylee looked at her daughter. "And it's time you were in bed, too, miss."

"Not tired," Emmalee said, yawning.

"Yes, you are."

Blue Hawk lifted Emmalee down from his shoulders and placed her in Kaylee's arms. Though there was much he missed of his old life, he was happier than he had ever been. He had a son and a daughter and a wife he loved more with every passing day. He lived as a white man now, but he had not forgotten his people. He had hired several young Lakota men to work on the ranch. Last year they had driven part of their herd to the Lakota reservation so that the people might have meat through the winter. They would do so again this year, and every year.

Follow the woman, his spirit guide had said. *She holds the answers.* Mato had spoken truly, for Kaylee was the answer to his every dream, his every prayer.

Dear Reader,

Sometimes a book practically writes itself. This wasn't one of them! I might never have finished *Lakota Love Song* if it wasn't for three talented authors who gave me their support when my Muse decided to take a vacation.

Christine Feehan encouraged me (sometimes several times a day) when I was ready to throw in the towel and take up another line of work.

Spirit Walker shared his knowledge of Indians and the Old West with me and came up with some terrific ideas that made my Muse so jealous she went back to work.

William Burkett edited the final draft before I bundled it up and sent it to New York.

Thanks bunches, you guys. I couldn't have done it without you.

My thanks, also, to Mitch Dearmond for letting me use his property.

Last but not least, I'd like to thank my readers. You guys are the best! Thanks for all letters and e-mails and gifts you've sent over the years. They mean a lot to me.

Madeline

www.geocities.com/Madelin_Baker/News.html